THE
NIGHT
GATE

Also by Peter May

PETER MAY

THE NIGHT GATE

riverrun

First published in Great Britain in 2021 by

riverrun

an imprint of
Quercus Editions Ltd
Carmelite House
50 Victoria Embankment
London EC4Y 0DZ

An Hachette UK company

A CIP catalogue record for this book is available
from the British Library.

HB ISBN 978 1 78429 504 2
TPB ISBN 978 1 78429 505 9
EBOOK ISBN 978 1 78429 506 6

This book is a work of fiction. Names, characters,
businesses, organisations, places and events are
either the product of the author's imagination
or used fictitiously. Any resemblance to
actual persons, living or dead, events or
locales is entirely coincidental.

10 9 8 7 6 5 4 3 2 1

Typeset by CC Book Production
Printed and bound in Great Britain by Clays Ltd, Elcograf S.p.A.

MIX
Paper from
responsible sources
FSC® C104740
FSC
www.fsc.org

Papers used by riverrun are from well-managed forests and other responsible sources.

This book is dedicated to the memory of Maud Taillard

'Art is the lie that enables us to realise the truth.'

Pablo Picasso

PROLOGUE

Emile Narcisse is pleased by his appearance. Vanity has always been a weakness. Where, perhaps, others see him as just another old man, he still perceives himself as the young Emile whose smile won hearts, whose blue-eyed looks turned heads. And after all, sixty-five is not so old. Vintage. Like a good wine, some men just get better with age. Were he not so focused on his reflection in the mirror as he adjusts his tie and straightens his collar, he might have been able to look beyond it and see the certainty of death that lies in wait. But pride and greed blind him to his fate.

He has chosen a room at the back of the hotel with a view of the river. Or, rather, its black slow-moving backwater broken only by the reflection of trees on the sliver of island beyond. On the far side of the island the River Dordogne, swollen by recent rains, makes a stately but more rapid progress towards the Atlantic two hundred and fifty kilometres to the west. But it is dark now, and he can see nothing beyond the glass.

He glances at his watch. Time to go. He feels a tiny, excited frisson of anticipation. But also doubt. Is it really possible that fate could have sent such good fortune his way? It is hard to believe. And, yet, here he is.

Floorboards creak softly beneath his shoes as he descends lightly to reception. The hotel is quiet, the tourist season a distant memory. A notice on the counter reminds customers that the hotel will be closed in just a few weeks for a full month. The annual congés. *It will reopen in December in time for Christmas and* la nouvelle année, *if indeed Covid will allow for a celebration of either.*

Narcisse glances through double French windows that open into the restaurant. Empty tables beneath cold yellow light, the chill October night pressing darkly against windows all along the far side. Not yet seven-thirty. Too early for the French to dine. But on his return he expects to eat, and crack open a celebratory bottle of Bordeaux. A car passes in the street outside. He drops his key on the counter, pleased that there is no one around requiring him to wear his mask. He fingers it in his pocket, glad to keep it there. He detests the damn thing, stuffy and claustrophobic. Yet, he knows, it is a significant barrier against the virus. And at his age he cannot afford to take any risks.

He does not see the man sitting in the bar, face obscured by a local newspaper, a half-drunk beer on the table in front of him. But as Narcisse steps out into the frosted air, the solitary drinker lowers his paper, rising to cross quickly to a door that leads to the terrace. From here he watches the art dealer make his way towards the palisade, breath billowing in the street lights. Anger burgeons in this man's breast, a seething rage close to boiling point. The duplicitous peacock has no idea that Bauer is even here. Bauer knows he is not expected for another thirty minutes. But he knows, too, that beyond the gate opposite, a path will lead him through a garden straight to the top of the hill, where another gate will provide direct access to the terrace at the side of her house.

Narcisse turns left at the post office, before he reaches the palisade.

Above it, the château cuts a shadow against the starlit sky, and Narcisse shivers, pulling his collar closer to his neck. Medieval shuttered stone dwellings crowd him on either side, reducing the sky to a ribbon of black overhead. The icy air is almost heady with the sweet-smoke smell of autumn oak, the cold of it burning his nostrils.

Where the road opens out left and right, the gate to the small park at the top of the hill lies open. Some work in progress near the war monument has been taped off, and Narcisse sees the thin strip of plastic catch light from the street lamps as it flutters gently in the cold air that snakes through these fifteenth-century streets. But before he reaches the park he turns off to climb the long flight of stone steps to the house that overlooks it. A small covered landing at the door lies in shadow. He pauses and takes a deep breath before slipping on his mask, as if to hide his identity. This is the moment of truth, perhaps the moment to which his entire career has led him. The window shutters to the left of the door stand open, but only darkness lies beyond. There is not a light to be seen anywhere in the house, and Narcisse experiences his first sense of apprehension. He lifts the cast-iron knocker and sharply raps it twice against the wood. Inside he hears the echo of it smothered by the dark. Apprehension gives way to irritation as he knocks again, louder this time. Irritation burgeoning to anger, and then frustration. Is it all just some elaborate hoax? He tries the door handle and to his surprise feels it yield to his hand. The door swings into darkness.

'Hello?' His voice seems strangely disconnected from his body.

There is no reply. He steps into the doorway and reaches around the wall, searching for a light switch with his fingers. He finds it. But it brings no light to this world. He curses softly behind his mask and calls again.

'Hello?'

Still nothing. He takes another step forward. He knows that he is in the kitchen because he was here earlier. A door at the far end, beyond a long table, leads to a short hallway, and then the grand salon. But he can see almost nothing, his eyes made blind by the streets lights he has just left behind. The house feels cold and empty, and his anger becomes incandescent, as if that might light the way ahead. He takes less cautious steps further into the kitchen, his fingertips finding the tabletop to guide him. Shapes are starting to take form around him now.

A sound that whispers like the smooth passage of silk on silk startles him. Movement in the darkness ahead morphs into silhouette. Momentary light catches polished steel, before he feels the razor-like tip of it slash across his neck. There is no real pain, just an oddly invasive sensation of burning, and suddenly he cannot breathe. His hands fly to his neck, warm blood coursing between cold fingers. He presses both palms against the wound as if somehow they might keep the blood from spilling out of him. He hears it gurgling in his severed windpipe. Just moments earlier he had been consumed by anger. Now he understands that he is going to die, but somehow cannot accept it. It is simply not possible. Consciousness rapidly ebbs to darkness and he drops to his knees. The last thing he sees, before falling face-first to the floor, is his killer. Caught in a fleeting moment of moonlight. And he simply cannot believe it.

CHAPTER ONE

SOUTH-WEST FRANCE, OCTOBER 2020

A notice pinned to the door warned that the maternity unit was open only from 7 a.m. until 8.30 p.m., and Enzo wondered what happened if a woman's waters broke in the middle of the night. Or were all births scheduled to fit into working hours these days?

He held the door open for Sophie who stepped out carefully, her left arm linked through Dominique's right. They all removed their masks, and watched their breath billow in the cold afternoon air that blew up the Rue Wilson from the River Lot and the historic Valentré bridge that spanned it.

Sophie was radiant and just six weeks from full term. Her check-up had gone well, and she had gazed in wonder at the ultrasound images of her baby boy. But she was thirty-five now, and with two miscarriages behind her, and a pandemic still sweeping the country, it was impossible to be too careful.

Enzo walked behind his daughter and the woman who had been such a large part of his life these past nine years and felt a wave of emotion wash over him. They were just like mother and daughter, even though Sophie's birth mother, Pascale, had died giving birth to her all those years ago. He found himself fighting an internal conflict between happiness and regret. But only briefly. How could he be anything but happy for them both?

He listened to their excited chatter in the late autumn chill and felt a twinge of sadness for Dominique. They had both known from the start that she could not have children, and she had claimed to have come to terms with it. But he had seen that look in her eyes when glimpsing a baby in a pram, or a heavily pregnant woman, and knew that the absence of children would always mean there was something missing in her life.

In a way she had lived through Sophie's pregnancy vicariously, and Enzo knew that she anticipated the imminent birth with the same unbridled joy of any grandmother. She had, too, been the only mother that Laurent had ever known beyond the first few months of his life. The child that he and Charlotte had made together. And even after all these years, Enzo could not shake off the image of Charlotte standing over the father of her son in the rain, a gun in her hand. Preparing to kill him.

They passed plasticised posters tied to rusted railings, and on the other side of the street the spreading branches of a *pin parasol* cast its shadow over the facade of the Banque de France. At the post office they took a right, and turned down towards the Place Gambetta.

'Can't wait till this is all over,' he heard Sophie say, 'and I can have a drink again!' He grinned. Like father, like daughter.

In five minutes they were crossing the Boulevard Léon Gambetta opposite the Théatre de Cahors, to stroll down the Rue Georges Clemenceau to the little tree-lined square in front of La Halle. The trees were almost naked now, drifts of brittle, brown leaves blowing along the gutters. Tables and chairs still stood on the pavement outside La Lamparo pizzeria, peopled by a few hardy customers huddled in coats, to smoke or avoid wearing masks.

A familiar figure stood outside the door to Enzo's apartment. She was in uniform, her brown hair neatly pinned beneath her hat. She had put on a little weight, but was still an attractive woman. Enzo had not seen her for some years, and his first thought was that something bad had happened. But her smile when she saw them allayed his misgivings. His instinct was to kiss her on each cheek, but he forced himself to leave a socially distanced two metres between them.

'Hello, Hélène,' he said, a little awkwardly. It must have been fifteen years since their nearly relationship.

'Enzo!' She beamed at him. 'You've aged.'

He didn't dare return the compliment.

Sophie said, 'My dad's always been old. Ever since I've known him.'

'Ancient,' Dominique chipped in.

Enzo spread his arms in despair. 'My life is full of women who do nothing but abuse me.'

Hélène examined him more closely and frowned. 'What happened to your hair?'

'It's still there,' he said, reaching back to grasp his ponytail and run it through his hand, as if for reassurance.

'A little thinner, perhaps. But that's not what I meant. Your white stripe. It's gone!'

Enzo pulled a face. The white stripe in dark hair running back from one side of his forehead had been a distinguishing feature for most of his life. A physical manifestation of a condition known as Waardenburg syndrome, which had also gifted him one brown eye and one blue, but left him otherwise unaffected. At school it had earned him the nickname *Magpie*. 'It's still there, too,' he said. 'You just can't see it any more for all the grey.'

'Shame.' Hélène stifled a smile. 'Now you're just plain old Enzo Macleod. Nothing to distinguish you from any other Enzo Macleod.'

'Except for the ponytail,' Sophie said, 'and the donkey jacket, and the cargoes.'

'And the hippy canvas shoulder bag.' Dominique gave it an affectionate tug.

And Sophie added, 'He still looks like an exile from the sixties.'

Hélène seemed to notice her bump for the first time. 'Looks like you and Bertrand have been busy.'

Sophie's pleasure showed in her smile. 'Due next month.'

'Well, congratulations.'

8

PETER MAY

'Are you coming up?' Enzo said.

But Hélène shook her head. 'I won't invade the Enzo bubble.' It's what the government was calling allowed family groupings to prevent spread of the Coronavirus. 'I just came to pass on a message.'

'See you upstairs, then,' Sophie said, and she and Dominique pushed open the door of the brick tenement to release a breath of warm, damp air into the late October afternoon.

When they were alone, Enzo said, 'So who's trying to get a message to me?'

'An old friend.'

'Who?'

'Professor Magali Blanc.'

'The forensic archaeologist? Why didn't she get in touch herself?'

'Lost your contact details it seems. She's based in Paris these days, and her request for help in finding you landed on my desk.'

Enzo frowned. 'What would she want with me? It's years since I worked with her.'

'She appears to be engaged on a rather interesting unsolved murder, not far from home. *Your* home, that is.'

Enzo let his eyes wander towards La Halle and the little bistro that had opened on the terrace. He and Dominique quite often caught lunch there. In the square beyond, in the shadow of the twin-domed cathedral, he still took coffee every morning at the Café Le Forum. Life in south-west France, in this 2000-year-old Roman town contained by a loop of the river, flowed by as gently as the Lot itself. No stress. And he was enjoying it. He sighed. 'I'm retired from all that these days, Hélène. Five years since I packed in my position at Paul Sabatier.'

'I thought cold cases were your speciality.' There was mischief in this.

He narrowed his eyes. 'Only when I get conned into it by accepting a bet after too many glasses of wine.' He had solved all seven murders in journalist Roger Raffin's book on French cold cases, but still lost his bet with Hélène and the préfet on a technicality.

'I wouldn't have thought that a man with your forensic talents would ever lose his appetite for the challenge.'

Enzo smiled wryly. 'You're a wind-up merchant, Hélène, you know that?'

'Is that a technical term, or one of your quaint Scottish witticisms?'

He glared at her. 'What's the case?'

A smile divided her face, ear to ear. 'I knew it.'

'Hélène!' The warning was clear in her growled name.

'It's an old one, Enzo.'

'If Magali's looking at it, it must be a *very* old one.'

'Seventy-five years or more.'

He frowned. 'That would make it Second World War. A lot of people died then. What makes anyone think it was a murder?'

'The remains of a ranking officer of the Luftwaffe with a

bullet hole in his skull, shallow-buried in a tiny medieval village on the banks of the River Dordogne, wouldn't exactly fit a conventional wartime scenario.'

'They're not likely to catch whoever did it now.' He was interested, in spite of himself.

'I don't think that's the object of the exercise. Isn't it the job of archaeologists to unravel the mysteries of history? I think she just wants you to cast a professional eye over the grave, if one could call it that. She's been unable to visit the site herself.'

'Where is it?'

'The village is called Carennac. It's in the north of the Département. Not much more than an hour away.'

The grey cast in the cold southern sky had been dispelled by the dark. Enzo came through from the kitchen to find Laurent sprawled in his father's armchair by the light of a standard lamp at the window, idly picking out chords on his father's guitar. He stopped in the doorway for a moment, gazing with unadorned affection at his son, who was oblivious to his presence.

He was a gangly kid, tall for an eleven-year-old, puppy fat shed during a recent sprouting. He took his hair from his mother, dark and falling across his forehead in luxuriant curls. He showed no signs of having inherited his father's Waardenburg. Alexis, Enzo's grandson by his Scottish daughter, Kirsty, had hearing issues, the faulty gene having skipped a generation. And although tests on Sophie's unborn child had proved negative, it was still a niggling worry.

Laurent's long fingers spidered across the fretboard of the guitar. He was showing real promise. Enzo approached silently from behind and suddenly lifted the guitar away.

'Hey!' Laurent protested.

Enzo arranged his fingers on the frets. 'Try the A minor 7th diminished,' he said. 'It follows beautifully from the B.' And he demonstrated by stroking his thumb across the strings.

Laurent sat up and looked at the shape of Enzo's fingers, then snatched the guitar back. 'Let me try it.' He found the chord almost instantly, then slid down to it from the B. 'Cool,' he said.

'It is,' Enzo said and took the guitar away again.

Laurent reprised his objection. 'Hey!'

'You've got homework to do.'

'Aw, Da-ad.' And Enzo heard his own Scottish drawl in his son's plea. They always spoke English together, and Laurent had quickly acquired his father's accent. Like Sophie. But also like Sophie, he was truly French, culturally and linguistically.

'Come on, Lo-Lo, I'll give you hand with your maths.' Dominique swept in from the hall and sat down at the table, placing both hands flat on its surface. She was well practised now at home-schooling. 'Where's your bag?'

'In my room.'

'Go get it, then.'

'Aw, Mama, do I have to?'

She canted her head and raised one eyebrow, which was enough to force him out of his chair to slope off to his bedroom, hands pushed deep into his pockets.

Sophie, in coat and scarf, passed him in the doorway and went to the French windows that overlooked the square. She pressed her nose to the glass. 'Bertrand's late. I'll expire from heat if he's any longer.' She turned back into the room. 'So what are you going to do, Papa? Are you going to go and take a look at that burial site?'

Dominique cast an enquiring look in his direction. 'Are you?'

He slumped into the chair that Laurent had vacated and strummed a chord on the guitar. 'I don't really feel like travelling far from Cahors during this bloody pandemic.'

'You'll be alright if you wear a mask,' Sophie said.

'It's alright for you, Soph. You're not in a high-risk age group.'

'I'll go with you, then,' Dominique said. 'We'll go in the car. I'll drive. We don't have to mix with anyone.'

'What about Laurent?' The schools had been closed again after a spike in cases.

'Bertrand and me can look after him,' Sophie said. And they all turned at the sound of a whooping noise in the doorway.

A grinning Laurent, satchel hanging from one hand, punched the air with the other. 'Yesss! Bertrand is ace at *Resident Evil*.'

Enzo glanced at the discarded PlayStation controller and thought that maybe escape from the house for a few hours might not be such a bad idea after all.

CHAPTER TWO

The old lady sits in her favourite rocker. To her listener it seems unyieldingly hard, softened for her fragile frame only by the thinnest of cushions at her back. Her hair, silver grey, has lost neither its lustre nor its abundance, but is pulled back into the severest of buns. The smooth, shiny-thin skin of her face is flushed from the heat of the fire, embers glowing in the blackened hearth of this vast cheminée that so dominates the end wall of the salon.

Her voice, like her frame, is slight, and he finds himself realising that at seventy-five she is really only ten years older than he. Will the next ten years reduce him as it has her?

But still, there is a clarity in her voice, confident and unwavering as she begins the story she has heard many times, and no doubt repeated as often for hushed gatherings of silent confidantes. Thought-through, honed and polished to a professional patina.

He crosses his legs in his comfortable armchair and folds his hands in his lap, mirroring the storyteller, inclining his head very slightly to one side as she relates her tale.

*

His name was Paul Lange. A man who never took life too seriously. I suppose he would have been in his forties. Forty-two or forty-three, perhaps, and so must have been born just after the turn of the century. I am sure that he had never expected, in his wildest dreams, to find himself in a peasant cottage in the north of France in the early hours of June 25th, 1940, on the day the Armistice took effect. But there he was, listening to Adolf Hitler's account of negotiations in the Compiègne Wagon. And only there, apparently, because of his friendship with Hitler's favourite architect, Albert Speer.

A group of them, adoring artists and architects, gathered around the Führer as he expressed his pleasure at reversing the humiliation of the Treaty of Versailles, forced upon Germany after its defeat in the Great War. Hitler explained how he had taken the very railway carriage in which that treaty had been signed from a museum, and had it placed on the very same stretch of line in the Compiègne Forest, where he then forced the French to accept defeat and sign an armistice that would cut France in two.

Herr Hitler was very pleased with himself.

Lange was impressed. He had fought briefly in the last war, then lived through the years of degradation and spiralling inflation imposed on the German state by the victors. Dark, troubled years, swept aside now by victory over the French in just six short weeks. Honour restored. But it was after one in the morning, and Lange was desperate for a cigarette as were, he was sure, many of the others. No one would smoke in the presence of the Führer, a former smoker himself who had issued strict non-smoking instructions to uniformed police, SA and SS soldiers when seen in public, even when off duty. There was nothing worse, Lange thought, than a reformed smoker. Perhaps he would be able to slip out later for a quiet smoke in the garden.

But not yet. It was almost 1.35 a.m. Hitler ordered the windows thrown open and a rush of warm humid air filled the house. In the distance, above a chorus of frogs and insects, they heard the rumble of thunder. A summer storm somewhere beyond the next valley, lightning crackling in an ominous sky. And then they all heard it. Clear and true, resonating in the night air. The bugle call that heralded the end of the fighting.

Drinks were filled, glasses raised, and some of the party slipped off for that cigarette that Lange so craved. But Hitler caught his arm, dark blue eyes shining with the dew of victory. 'A moment, please, Paul. I may call you that?'

Lange was astonished that Hitler even knew his given name. 'Of course, Mein Führer.'

Hitler steered him towards the drinks cabinet and refilled both their glasses. Scotch for Lange, sparkling water for himself. 'In a couple of days,' he said, 'I'm going to take a little tour of Paris. No gloating, no triumphal procession down the Champs Elysées. Just a tiny group of us. A very private tour. You know the city well, I'm told.'

Lange was both surprised and a little disquieted that the German leader had been discussing him with others. 'Yes, I've been many times.' He glanced up to see Speer watching them, listening intently. 'No reputable art dealer could call himself a professional if he weren't familiar with the galleries and sale rooms of the world's capital of art.'

'Good, good. So many places to go, so much to see, but so little time. The Arc de Triomphe, the Eiffel Tower, the Tomb of the Unknown Soldier, and of course Napoléon's tomb at Les Invalides. Where would you recommend I begin?'

Lange drew a deep breath. This seemed like an onerous responsibility. 'I would start with the Opéra, sir. It's one of the most beautiful buildings to be found anywhere in the world.'

Hitler grinned, and Lange saw why this apparently insignificant little man had inspired such loyalty and following. A charisma finding extraordinary expression in a smile that seemed only for you, eyes that held you unwavering in their gaze. It made you feel special somehow. 'Good man. That's exactly the start I would have chosen myself. And, of course, we'll finish with a visit to the Louvre. It's been a lifelong ambition to become personally acquainted with the *Mona Lisa*. Whatever one might think of the Italians, da Vinci was undoubtedly one of the greatest artists in human history.'

Lange felt a knot of dread anticipation tighten in his stomach and he flicked a quick glance in Speer's direction. He could see his own foreboding mirrored in the tightness around his friend's mouth. Clearly no one had told the Führer.

*

It was three days later, on June 28th, that Hitler's little entourage landed at the tiny airfield of Le Bourget, north-east of Paris, at 5.30 in the morning. Lange and the others had been provided with field-grey army uniforms to lend this disparate group of artists and architects and sculptors a military air.

Awaiting them on the tarmac were three black sedans, including Hitler's specially built Mercedes-Benz Tourenwagen with its three rows of seats and fold-down roof. Hitler sat up front beside his driver, SS Officer Erich Kempka, while Lange sat on the jump seats with Speer and a sculptor called Breker. Hitler's adjutants perched in the back.

Lange gazed in wonder at the bleak, deserted suburbs of this fallen city as the little procession drove through the drab early morning light. Soon, more familiar Parisian landmarks began to grow up around them and Lange found it oddly depressing to think of it having fallen under German control. It was such an irrepressibly French city. German utilitarianism could only take the shine off it, the joy out of its joie de vivre.

Kempka took them straight to the Palais Garnier in the Place de l'Opéra, in the ninth arrondissement, where a colonel of the German Occupation Authority awaited them at the entrance. Lange knew Charles Garnier's great neo-baroque building well, and took delight in Hitler's pleasure at the great stairway with its excessive ornamentation, the resplendent foyer, the elegantly gilded parterre. Before they left, Hitler caught Lange's elbow and whispered, 'Splendid choice, Paul.'

Afterward, they drove past the Madeleine, down the Champs

Elysées and on to the Trocadero, before Hitler ordered a stop at the Eiffel Tower to have photographs taken. At Napoléon's tomb he stood, head bowed, in solemn contemplation for several minutes. One dictator's reverence for another.

Finally, they arrived at the Louvre, with its vast Place du Carrousel, and twin galleries linking the original palace with the Tuileries. Lange and Speer had not spoken since that night at the peasant cottage, and they shared now a silent tension as Hitler strode off across the Cour Napoléon demanding to know where he could see the *Mona Lisa*, or *La Joconde* as the French called her. The colonel from the Occupation Authority struggled to keep up with him, head tilted down to one side, speaking in hushed and rapid tones. Lange and the rest followed behind apprehensively.

Suddenly Hitler stopped, his eyes darkening with fury. 'Why was I not told?' he shouted. And he turned towards his little coterie of artists. 'Who knew?'

'Knew what, Mein Führer?' Lange thought Speer's disingenuousness was horribly transparent.

'The bloody French have emptied the entire museum. Ten months ago! Shipped every last piece of art off to châteaux in the Loire. In the Free French Zone. *La Joconde* among them.'

Lange watched the spittle of Hitler's anger gather at the corners of his mouth. He said, 'I imagine, sir, that they moved the art out of Paris to protect it from possible bombing. Who could have guessed that we would defeat them in six weeks with barely a fight?'

But Hitler was not to be mollified. His anger seethed in a long, dangerous silence, before he turned and marched back through his band of artists, dividing them like the Red Sea, shadows cast long across the cobbles as the sun rose above the skyline. 'This tour is over! We will not be back to this accursed city.' The royal *we*, it seemed.

And he never did return.

The old lady is silent for a long time, then, before turning to her listener. 'Could you put a couple of logs on the fire, please? I feel the temperature falling.'

'Of course.' Her listener eases himself out of his armchair to take three fresh logs from the basket and throw them on to the embers. Red sparks fly up against the black, tarred stone, and the new logs crackle and spit and issue smoke into the upper reaches of the chimney.

When he sits down again, she watches the logs until the first flames lick up around them, and, satisfied that they have caught, settles back to continue her story.

It was a week later, after their return to Germany, that Lange received an unexpected summons to a meeting with Hitler at the Führer's mountain residence, the Berghof, in the Obersalzberg of the Bavarian Alps.

He made the journey by rail from Berlin, arriving in the early afternoon at Berchtesgaden, where Hitler's Tourenwagen was waiting for him. If Erich Kempka remembered him, he gave no sign of it, taking Lange's overnight bag to place it in the boot before setting off on the relatively short drive up into the pine-clad foothills of the Hoher Göll mountain that straddles the border between Bavaria and the Austrian state of Salzburg.

It was hot, the summer mountain air alive with flying things, and Lange removed his hat and jacket to roll up his shirtsleeves, and enjoy the soft wind in his face. The road was narrow, and Kempka had to employ all his driving skills to manoeuvre the big Tourenwagen around the bends in it as they climbed higher and higher. On his right, Lange saw the tree-covered slopes fall away to the valley below, tiny conurbations like clusters of toy houses following its contours towards a misted horizon. The land seemed to rise up all around them in both soft and jagged peaks.

Ever since receiving his *invitation* to the Berghof – a private messenger had arrived at his door with an envelope bearing a seal of the state, a handwritten note from the Führer within – Lange had experienced a gradual tightening of the muscles of his stomach. Increasing in severity now to a vice-like cramp. You wouldn't have known it to look at him, but his mouth was desert-dry and his heart rate almost off the scale. He had no idea what Herr Hitler could possibly want with him, but he feared the worst. Especially after the debacle at the Louvre.

Why had nobody warned the Führer in advance? No doubt the evacuation of the Louvre would have been well documented by German intelligence in advance of the invasion of Western Europe, but perhaps it was judged that Hitler had more pressing matters on his mind. The invasion of Poland, the declaration of war by Great Britain, the sabre-rattling of the Russians. Art seemed like such a low priority. And yet the Nazis placed so much store by it, trading in the international marketplace to augment their private collections, as if its civilising influence could somehow mitigate their inherent barbarity.

Finally, they turned off on to an even narrower private road and pulled in at a stone gatehouse beneath a shallow, tiled roof where a uniformed guard checked their papers. Hitler's chalet perched proud on the rise above them, and Kempka only just made the hairpin before the final climb to the foot of the steps leading up to Hitler's front door.

Lange slipped his jacket back on, donned his hat and ran quickly up the stone steps to a flagged terrace where Hitler stood waiting to greet him. Each raised his palm in the Nazi salute before Hitler extended his hand to shake Lange's. 'Glad you could make it, Paul. Welcome to my little retreat.'

Lange glanced up at the impressive building, with its terraces and balconies, and thought it anything but little. And acceptance of Hitler's invitation to visit was not, he knew, a matter in which he'd had any choice. 'It's my pleasure, sir.'

Despite the temperature, Hitler was wearing a brown suit with a stiffly pressed white shirt and a blue tie. His complexion was ruddy, and his mood a great deal more convivial than when they had last met. 'Come in, come in,' he said, and led Lange into the cool of the house. The walls of the entrance hall were hung with paintings, some of which Lange recognised

PETER MAY

with surprise. Portraits of Hindenburg, and Frederick the Great, and Bismarck. A Canaletto reproduction. There were numerous family portraits. 'My niece,' Hitler said. And pointing to another, 'My mother.' This, a muddy painting illuminated only by a pale, sombre face and a white ruff. Either her hair was cut short, or pulled back from her face and tied behind her head. But Lange was struck by the family resemblance.

They moved then into the great hall. An enormous salon on two levels, with an elaborate wooden ceiling. Next to the fireplace hung a vast canvas of a naked reclining woman, a tiny cupid figure with a quiver of arrows about to release one at the recumbent beauty. Hitler waved a proud arm towards the painting. 'Recognise it?'

'Of course, sir.' Lange wondered if this were some kind of test. '*Venus and Amor* by Paris Bordone. A wonderful piece of Venetian Renaissance painting.'

'Bravo. You know your stuff, then.'

Lange inclined his head modestly, resisting the temptation to point out that the history of art had been his major at Frankfurt.

'I have a personal preference for classical Greek and Roman art myself, Paul. It's uncontaminated by the Jews, you see. Unlike the degenerate modern filth they are producing now. I find the impressionists distasteful in the extreme, and the so-called heroes of modern art, like that dreadful Spaniard, Picasso, are simply symbolic of the decline in Western society.'

Lange turned the brim of his hat slowly around in his hands, holding it at his chest, not quite trusting himself to speak.

23

Before the war, like many of his contemporaries, he had traded extensively in modern art. Now the sale of confiscated modern works on the international market was seen as a way of raising funds for the war effort.

'Come.' Hitler took his arm and led him out on to a wide stone terrace. From here it felt like you stood at the very top of the world, with extravagant views out across the Bavarian Alps. Only a scrappy handful of clouds gathered around some of the peaks, puffs of white in an otherwise unbroken blue. The further summits were lost in a heat haze that shimmered off into the distance.

Hitler perched on the wall, one leg raised, the other still planted on the terrace, and eyed Lange speculatively, for what felt like an uncomfortably long time. 'Ever been to Austria?'

'To Vienna, yes.'

'I grew up in Linz. A beautiful city.'

Lange nodded, though he had never been.

'The secret of success in this life, Paul, is to know your limitations, and play to your strengths. It has been a matter of eternal regret to me that I was not blessed with the talent as a painter that I would have wished for.'

Lange smiled in regretful empathy. 'You and I both, sir.'

Hitler raised an eyebrow in surprise. 'You painted?'

'Very badly.'

Hitler smiled in return. 'Then perhaps I was a little better than you. But not good enough. Not for me, anyway. And so I devoted myself to politics and the service of my country.'

Lange nodded. 'At which you have succeeded rather well.' He had heard that Hitler enjoyed praise. But there was a fine line between complimentary and patronising. Hitler's smile suggested that he knew just how successful he had been, and did not need to be told.

'The love of art is never far from my thoughts. It's in my soul, you see. The quintessential expression of the finest human qualities, of aesthetics and sensibility, the human experience, the very human condition. Everything that separates us from the animals.' He turned then to gaze out across the alpine peaks. 'I have a dream, Paul. A dream of creating the world's most fabulous museum. An eighth wonder of the world, where people will make pilgrimage to pay homage to the very best art of which Man is capable.' He dragged his eyes away from his distant dream and fixed them once again on Lange, as if to make the dream concrete. 'I'm going to build it in Linz. It will be my lasting legacy. The heritage of Nazism in its purest form.' He paused. 'Does that excite you?'

'Very much, sir.'

Hitler beamed. 'Good.' He slipped off the wall. 'But what kind of host am I that hasn't even offered you a drink? Give me a moment to fetch my hat and stick and we'll walk down to the Mooslahnerkopf for some tea.'

It took them twenty minutes, following the winding path down through the trees, to reach the tea room. Hitler wore a soft brown hat and walked briskly, swinging his walking stick and speaking of how he had once considered the total destruction of Paris. Lange was appalled, but nodded with raised eyebrow to suggest only surprise. 'Having seen it for myself, however, I didn't feel as if I could carry it through,' he said.

Lange risked a comment. 'I would have been disappointed if you had.'

Hitler glanced at him sharply. 'Would you?'

'I have come to know Paris well over the years, sir. There is much to be admired in its history and its architecture.'

'Indeed.' Though the Führer seemed less than convinced.

The Mooslahnerkopf was Hitler's favourite tea room. It was built into the hillside, nestling among the pines, an unimposing rectangular building attached to a conical tower punctuated by windows all around its circumference. But they didn't enter immediately to drink tea together in its cool interior. Instead Hitler led them out on to a grassy, horseshoe-shaped promontory where he waved Lange to a seat on a wooden bench that looked out over the view below. Lange laid his hat on the bench beside him and loosened his tie at the collar. The walk down through the heat of the afternoon had brought him out in a sweat. Hitler, by contrast, seemed perfectly cool. He leaned on the wooden rail that delineated the outer curve of the horseshoe and studied Lange thoughtfully. With his eagle's nest on the hill above, his tea room a few paces away, and a view of breathtaking scope behind him, Hitler seemed like a man entirely in his element. Very nearly godlike. You could almost believe there was nothing he could not achieve.

'You're wondering why you're here, aren't you?'

Lange's smile belied the turmoil behind it. 'It had crossed my mind.'

'I want the *Mona Lisa*,' he said.

Lange felt his skin prickle with shock. He held his breath.

'Not for myself, you understand. For the museum in Linz. It should be its centrepiece. Its crowning glory. Where else should the greatest painting on earth reside?'

Lange took the question to be rhetorical and did not respond.

'And I want you to procure it.'

Lange felt a trickle of sweat run down the back of his neck.

'For the German state.' Hitler's gaze swung away again towards the magnificence of the view below. 'We cannot be seen, of course, to have stolen it. There would be international outrage.' And he turned cold blue eyes back on Lange. 'The painting should simply disappear. In the confusion of war, that shouldn't be too difficult. But it will require stealth, and know-how, and above all, patience. You will have to await your moment, Paul. Choose it carefully. It may take a year, two, who knows? But its disappearance must not be linked in any way to the Reich. Then, at some future date, it will' – he shrugged – 'turn up in some sales room somewhere in occupied territory, and we shall confiscate it to put on display at Linz for safekeeping.'

A long silence fell between them. It was clear to Lange that this was not a request, but it was not obvious to him how he should respond. Finally, he nodded his head slowly and said, 'Of course, sir.'

'Good.' Hitler pushed himself away from the fence, his dream banished for the moment to make way for practicalities. 'You will be drafted into the Wehrmacht on a temporary commission. The rank of Hauptmann should suffice. You will be attached to the Kunstshutz. I take it you know what that is?'

Lange nodded again. 'That admirable organisation for preserving enemy art in order safely to return it at the end of hostilities,' he said.

Hitler beamed, apparently impervious to Lange's straight-faced sarcasm. 'Very well defined, Paul. You will be a Kunstoffizier, drawing a salary and expenses from that organisation, as well as comfortable lodgings in Paris. And I will see that you are provided with a letter of authorisation from my office, which will procure for you anything you might need.'

The sun was already starting to sink in the sky, and their shadows lengthened across the grass.

'You have no idea how disappointed I was not to make acquaintance with the *Mona Lisa* in Paris.' The merest of pauses. 'I am trusting that I will not be disappointed a second time.'

The implication of the consequences resulting from a second disappointment hung briefly in the warm air of the alpine early evening, before Hitler broke into a smile, tapped the retaining rail with his stick and said, 'Let us take some tea.'

Lange stood up to follow his Führer, and knew that his life had just changed irrevocably.

CHAPTER THREE

She sits for a long time staring into space, lost in thoughts and memories that he suspects she will not share with him, before suddenly she turns as if just remembering that he is there. 'Would you like a cup of tea, monsieur?' And without waiting for his response, eases herself stiffly out of her chair. 'You won't mind if I do?'

Her listener smiles. 'Not at all.' He would prefer a coffee, but doesn't want to put her to any trouble.

She is back in her seat a few minutes later, reaching down to lay her mug on the hearth. 'Too hot to drink just yet. But it'll not get cold there.' Bony hands clutch the ends of the chair arms. 'Now, where was I? Ah, yes. London. July 1940.' And she resumes her story.

Georgette was a feisty young thing. Well, not so young, I suppose. Although twenty-eight is a very distant memory to me now. And you, too, I daresay. How can I describe her? Not tall, not short. A skinny girl with not much in the way of hips. A bit of a tomboy, I suppose. She liked to wear her hair cut short, which was not very fashionable for the time. Thick, dark, abundant hair. Knee-length pleated skirts and flat shoes, and a worn old leather satchel that she habitually slung from right shoulder to left hip. Wiry. Strong, of body and spirit. You would think twice about picking a fight with her.

She had been stranded in London for several weeks, frustrated and distracted by the news from France. Defeat at the hands of the Germans, an armistice that tore France in two, handing the lesser part of it over to Pétain's collaborationist régime to administer under orders from the Third Reich. The Free French Zone, they called it. But there was not much free about it.

It was one of those sticky summer days in the English capital when the humidity hangs thick in the air, the sun almost obscured by haze in a nearly colourless sky. She was sitting at a table in the bay window of her mother's Kensington home, sunlight slanting through the glass, holding suspended the sparkling motes of dust that hung in the still air. She had tried appealing to the more influential of her mother's friends to find some kind of work for her in London to help in the war effort. Without success. And she was in the process of writing a letter to a certain General Charles de Gaulle. An old friend of her father from the diplomatic corps had told her at her mother's funeral that de Gaulle had created a Free French Force based right here in London. He had, apparently, made some sort of appeal via the BBC to his fellow countrymen to resist the Nazi occupation. But she had missed it as, it seems, had most of her compatriots. She was only now writing to him as a last resort.

She had barely made a start on it when she was interrupted by the ringing of the front doorbell. Irritated, she padded barefoot across the parquet in the hall and opened the door to a uniformed telegram boy.

'Telegram, ma'am,' he said and thrust an envelope at her. 'Sign for it here.' He held out a lined pad for her signature and was gone, leaving Georgette to wonder who on earth might be sending her a telegram.

She carried it back to her seat at the table in the window and tore it open as she sat down. Only to gasp in astonishment.

Please attend meeting with General Charles de Gaulle at 11h tomorrow STOP 4 Carlton Gardens SW1 STOP

What was this? A response to her letter, even before she had written it? Was he a mind-reader? And this didn't seem so much like an invitation as an instruction. In spite of the fact that she had been in the process of writing to him in search of a job, she felt herself bristle.

She knew nothing at all about this man. And yet he, it seemed, knew all about her – or, at least, exactly where to find her. Dark eyebrows furrowed over warm brown eyes.

The air was clearer the next day. A cooling breeze blew softly along Pall Mall, caressing Georgette's bare legs. Legs that had seen precious little sun this year and were unusually white. Her face, too, which habitually tanned to a golden brown in summer, was pale and colourless. The spattering of freckles across her nose, a genetic inheritance of her mother, seemed all the more prominent. But she was pretty, and in spite of her pallor drew looks wherever she went.

At Waterloo Place she turned down to the left, her corn-blue skirt billowing in the breeze, and then right on to Carlton House Terrace. This was a leafy street, dappling sunshine on the pavement and the elegant frontage of the classical white-stoned Royal Society.

In Carlton Gardens, two French soldiers stood guard at either side of a wall built in front of the porticoed entrance to number four. She fished her telegram out of her satchel and showed it to one of them. He smiled and waved her inside, calling *bonne journée* at her back, and it felt good to hear French again.

Inside, everyone spoke French, and Georgette was glad to be speaking it again, too. A middle-aged woman in a dark business suit led her up shiny stairs to the first floor, where a door in the corridor to their right stood open. The chatter of a typewriter came muted from within. The woman knocked twice and ushered Georgette into the room. A younger woman sat behind a Royal typewriter that stood on a desk littered with paperwork. Her scrutiny of Georgette lingered a little longer than perhaps even she had expected, surprised possibly by what she saw – a girlish, short-haired young woman wearing a dark blue summer cardigan over an open-necked white blouse, a brown leather satchel pressing her skirt to her thigh. She waved a hand towards a chair. "He'll be with you when he's free." As if, Georgette thought with a prickle of annoyance, that it was she who had asked for an audience with him.

Still, she found herself fidgeting in nervous anticipation, aware of the secretary's frequently stolen glances, before finally she met the woman's eye, silently daring her to keep staring. It was no contest. The secretary's eyes fluttered back towards her keyboard. On such tiny triumphs was Georgette's life built these days. Of course, she had no idea what lay ahead.

She was startled as the door suddenly flew open, and an enormous man stood framed in the doorway. He had to stoop to avoid the lintel. He wore a dark uniform, leather-belted at the waist, a grey shirt and darker tie whose colour was impossible to identify. His dark brown hair was slicked back and shining, parted severely on the left. His long face was dominated by an even longer nose above a neatly trimmed moustache. The severity of his expression was mellowed by a peculiar warmth in the orange-flecked brown eyes that he turned on Georgette. She stood hastily.

'Mademoiselle Pignal?'

She nodded, barely able to take her eyes off the size of his ears. At the Beaux-Arts in Bordeaux, she had been taught in portrait class that the top of the ear should be level with the eyebrows, the lobe with the bottom of the nose. De Gaulle's ears broke all the rules, even for a man with such a long nose.

He jerked his head towards his inner sanctum. '*Entrez.*'

She followed him into a large office with tall windows that overlooked the street below. Sunshine lay in narrow strips across a desk that suggested it had only just survived a hurricane. The place reeked of cigarette smoke, and blue ribbons of it still hung in the sunlight.

He dropped into a captain's chair that creaked as it swivelled, and a shard of sunshine cast the shadow of his nose across one side of his face. A large map of France hung on the wall behind him. A telephone stood on a small table to one side. He nodded towards the chair opposite and she sat down, perching on the very edge of it.

He gazed at her appraisingly as he prised a cigarette pack from a breast pocket, and tapped out the last but one. He lit it with an engraved American brass lighter. 'Do you have any idea why you're here?'

'Should I?'

'I would hope not. But it's hard to know these days who you can trust.' He tipped forward to sift through the chaos in front of him to extract a buff-coloured folder. He flipped it open and lifted the top sheet of several.

She inclined her head towards the folder. 'Is that my file?'

'It is.'

'I'm surprised there's that much in it.'

He looked at her very steadily. 'So am I.' His eyes dropped again to the sheet that he held between fingers that were also occupied by his cigarette. He read, 'Marie Georgette Pignal. Born August 1912. British mother, French father, Georges Pignal, who served in the diplomatic service. Raised in Bordeaux, but fluent in English as well as French.'

Georgette sighed her exasperation. 'Did you really ask me here to tell me things about myself that I already know?'

'No, mademoiselle. I asked you here to gauge what lies unwritten between the lines.' And he returned, undeterred, to the sheet in his hand. 'It seems you achieved a remarkable score in your Baccalaureate. Forty-two out of forty-five.'

'Does that surprise you?'

'On the evidence of what I have seen so far, yes. But I have learned never to judge a book by its binding.' He continued reading. 'You graduated from the Ecole Supérieure des Beaux-Arts in Bordeaux, and' – he paused to raise a sympathetic eyebrow – 'your father passed away just weeks before you topped the competitive exam for the Ecole Nationale Supérieure des Beaux-Arts in Paris. No doubt he would have been very proud of you.'

Georgette kept her lips pressed firmly together, biting the lower lip hard inside her mouth. The death of her father had blighted her adolescence, and the scar it had left was still painful to the touch. But she was determined to give nothing away to this cold fish opposite. Though something in his knowing assessment told her that she was doing a poor job of it.

He took the sheet in his other hand, freeing his right to take a long pull on his cigarette. 'After graduation in Paris you spent two years at the Ecole du Louvre.' He looked up. 'What did you study there?'

'Is that not in my file?'

'I'm asking you, mademoiselle.'

'The history of art.'

'But you cut your studies short.'

'I volunteered to help pack the works of art being evacuated from the Louvre in August last year. Then rather than go back to school, I volunteered for the Armée de Terre.'

'And why did you do that?'

'There was a war coming. I wanted to defend my country against a German invasion.'

He made a sound that might have been a chuckle, though she could detect no sign of amusement. 'All on your own?'

She smiled sardonically. 'Well, I might have had to, General, since the Under-Secretary of State for National Defence ran off to London when the Germans came within shooting distance.'

If there had been even the merest hint of amusement in his face it was immediately banished and he visibly bristled. 'Pétain was set on capitulation.' His voice had developed a bark. 'An armistice. Collaboration. If I hadn't fled, he'd have had me arrested for opposing him.'

Now she smiled, sensing a shift in the balance of power between them. 'I know.' She nodded towards the hand which held his cigarette. 'And I know that you wear your wedding ring on your right hand because you almost lost your left to a wound during the last war.'

De Gaulle glanced self-consciously at the ring.

'Since you seemed to know who I was, I took the liberty of informing myself about you on the way here. The cuttings libraries of Fleet Street are a gold mine of information, and entirely free to the public.'

He took another long, thoughtful draw on his cigarette, and as he exhaled, asked through the smoke, 'So why was it *you* left the country?'

'I'm sure you know that, too, General. I was given compassionate leave to attend my mother's funeral here in London. Then came the invasion.' She sighed, still deeply frustrated at the thought. 'And I was stranded.'

'You and I both.' De Gaulle eased himself out of his chair and wandered to the window, still smoking, but gazing down now into the leafy square below. 'And do you still want to serve your country?'

'Of course.' Indignation was evident in her voice.

He turned back towards her. 'Let's take some air, shall we?'

Traffic in The Mall was light, its red-coloured tarmac more apparent somehow in the absence of vehicles. Sunlight caught all the curves and angles of the distant Buckingham Palace in sharp relief as they walked east to west with Admiralty Arch behind them. The sun had risen high by now above the foliage of St James's Park to the south and Green Park to the north. The trees that lined their route dispersed the light in ever-changing shapes on the pavement ahead of them.

Georgette felt tiny beside this man, barely reaching his shoulder, and she was much more intimidated by his size and presence out here than she had been seated across the desk from him. He seemed even taller with his kepi pulled down on his forehead, its brim casting a deep shadow across his face. They had been walking for some time, in what for her was an uncomfortable silence, before he spoke.

When finally he did, she was caught entirely off guard. 'What do you know about the *Mona Lisa*?'

It took a moment to process her surprise. 'I helped pack *La Joconde* for her journey to the Loire.'

'To Château Chambord, I understand.'

'That's right. It was thought that everything would be more secure moved out of Paris. Safe from bombs, and out of reach of the Germans.'

De Gaulle grunted. 'Nothing in France is out of reach of the Germans.' He paused to light another cigarette, and she waited patiently for him until they carried on their way. Her curiosity was now aroused. 'So you helped pack the actual painting?'

'I did. In a custom-built poplar case cushioned with red velvet, which was then crated up. All the crates were coded using one, two, or three coloured dots to denote their contents. Yellow for very valuable pieces, green for major works, and red for world treasures. The *Mona Lisa*'s crate was stamped with three red dots, the highest possible rating. And was the only one in the red category to get that.'

'I assume, since you studied the history of art at the Ecole du Louvre, you know all about its provenance?'

'I know every last thing about *La Joconde*, General.'

'Tell me.' He kept his eyes ahead of him as he sucked on his cigarette, but Georgette reckoned that those big ears of his would miss nothing.

'*Mona Lisa* is a portrait of the wife of an Italian nobleman, Francesco del Giocondo. Some experts believe the version that hangs in the Louvre was not the first that da Vinci painted of her. Others have speculated that it was really a feminised self-portrait.'

De Gaulle faltered mid-stride. He looked down at her. 'Really?'

She grinned. 'Highly unlikely, I think. There is so much smoke around this painting it's amazing we ever get a clear view of it.'

He sighed and resumed his pace.

Georgette said, 'What we know for certain is that *La Joconde* was painted in oils by Leonardo da Vinci on a panel of poplar wood, 77 by 53 centimetres, sometime around the year 1503, just sixteen years before he died. In 1515, da Vinci accepted the patronage of the French king, François Premier, and travelled to France on a donkey, carrying with him numerous sketch-books and unfinished artworks, as well as the *Mona Lisa* herself. Some believe that it, too, was unfinished, and not completed until the artist was safely installed in France. The journey took about three months. Over the centuries the painting has been in the possession of not only François Premier, but Louis XIV and Napoléon Bonaparte, who reportedly slept with her in his bedroom.' She grinned up at the general. 'Well, not in the biblical sense.'

Not even the hint of a smile cracked his face. In fact, he almost seemed not to have been listening. Then suddenly he stopped and turned, and she found herself craning her neck to look up at him. '*La Joconde* belongs to France. Painted by an Italian, yes, but owing her very existence and survival to the republic.'

His vehemence surprised her.

'And now the Germans want her.'

She frowned. 'They do?'

He glanced each way along the pavement before speaking again. 'More specifically, Hitler. He wants it as the centrepiece of a super museum he plans to build in his home town of Linz in Austria.'

'How can you possibly know that?'

'British intelligence have sources in Berlin. They report that Hitler has commissioned an art expert to procure it by fair means or foul.'

Georgette was shocked. 'He can't! The world would be incensed.'

'Which is why they won't just take it. But nothing is more certain than that they will find a way. And we can't let that happen. La France is the custodian of the most famous painting in the world, mademoiselle. We have kept her safe for centuries, through wars and natural disasters. And now we have to keep her safe from the Nazis.'

He crushed his cigarette beneath a shiny shoe and raised his face towards the heavens.

'God knows, I have enough to do simply trying to save my country from destruction. Which is why I am passing the baton of responsibility for *La Joconde* to you.'

Georgette's eyebrows shot up in astonishment. 'Me?'

'Beyond today I can devote no more time or thought to this. But I want it to be your raison d'être. The one thing you can do for your country that no one else can. Go back to France and keep her safe. Guard her with your life. I am in touch with Jacques Jaujard, the director at the Louvre. He will ensure a place for you as an assistant curator wherever it is that the *Mona Lisa* might end up.' He placed a hand on her shoulder, and she felt a strange sense of destiny in his touch. He looked at her earnestly. 'Mademoiselle, we are fighting the Hun not just for France, but for civilisation. This might be a small act of defiance in a world at war, but it does have a greater meaning.' He took his hand away again. 'What kind of training did they give you when you joined the army?'

The confusion of thoughts and fears that tumbled through her mind almost robbed her of the power of speech. She shook her head and pulled a face. 'Basic fitness and weapons handling. But they were never going to let a woman with a rifle anywhere near the front line. They taught me to drive and told me I would be assigned to the catering corps.'

He nodded gravely. 'In that case I'll ask the British to find you a place on an SOE training course.'

'SOE?'

'Special Operations Executive. A newly formed British

41

organisation for training operatives to be dropped into France to conduct sabotage and surveillance behind enemy lines.' He cast a sceptical eye over her. 'You're going to have to learn how to handle yourself.' For the first time she saw the hint of a smile in those enigmatic eyes. 'And how to fall out of an aeroplane at ten thousand feet.'

CHAPTER FOUR

It was a cold, crisp, clear day when Dominique parked Enzo's Citröen on the castine of the palisade, the sheer walls of Carennac's sixteenth-century château rising up behind them, lingering mist from the river below evaporating in the sunlight.

Near-naked trees cast spindly shadows on white gravel littered with leaves that crunched underfoot as they stepped out of the car. Enzo clutched the Michelin guide that he had been studying on the journey up from Cahors. On the drive into the village from the main road they had passed a couple of hotels, one of which was closed up for the season, and a small store that also served coffee. But the place was deserted.

Dominique looked around. 'Where is everyone?'

Enzo said, 'According to the guide, the out-of-season population is little more than 400. But that probably takes in the farms and outlying houses around here as well. They get hundreds of thousands of visitors in the summer, though.'

'Why? What's here?'

'Apart from the château, an eleventh-century church and cloisters, and a twelfth-century tympanum.'

'What's that? Some kind of drum?'

'An architectural feature of some kind,' Enzo said, flicking through the pages. 'And there's a tower down by the water where Fénelon is said to have written his famous *Telemachus*.'

Dominique screwed up her face. 'Never heard of it.'

Enzo grinned. 'No, neither have I.'

'Can't be that famous, then. Which way?'

'Not sure. Let's head to the end of the palisade.'

Dominique slipped her arm through his and pulled him close as they walked through the morning sunshine to where the road turned sharply to the left. Branching to the right it crossed a long bridge that spanned a dry riverbed leading down to the Dordogne. On the corner, an arch led to a steeply cobbled street that climbed along the side of the Eglise Saint-Pierre. A flight of wide stone steps led to an elaborately carved entrance, an assemblage of stone figures above a cluster of columns leading into the church itself. Enzo could almost feel the breath of centuries exhaling from its dark interior.

A small bistro on the opposite corner was shut, as was the tourist shop next to it. A staircase leading down to a terraced restaurant below was roped off. And Enzo felt a little of the sadness of the abandonment described in Francis Cabrel's evocative song, 'Hors Saison'. Out of Season.

Tall buildings with criss-crossing half timbers loomed over them as they followed a narrow street into the heart of the village. Shadows cast themselves deep across the tarmac, and the scent of woodsmoke filled the air. Evidently the diminished population of this chaotic jumble of stone houses built over centuries around the church were all indoors, huddled around hearths or wood-burning stoves.

At a curve of the street a small woman suddenly appeared, a split-cane shopping basket crooked over her arm. Grey-streaked dark hair was pulled back beneath a pale headscarf, her face deeply lined and still tanned from the long-departed summer sun.

Enzo asked if she could direct them to the park and she gave a mute flick of her head towards a street that climbed steeply away to their left, cantilevered houses pressing in close on either side to shut out the sun.

In a phone call with Magali the previous evening, Enzo had established that the Second World War remains had been found in a tiny park at the heart of the village. A recent storm had brought down a tree. Its roots, torn from the earth, had lifted a tangle of bones and leather and other remains with them.

At the top of the street the road opened out, branching up to their right and down to their left. Straight ahead stood a tiny patch of raised greenery delineated by gnarled old trees beyond iron railings and a handful of steps. A raised cross stood sentinel by the gate.

But their focus was drawn immediately away from the little park by the lights of several police vehicles, and the flashing orange of an ambulance. Uniformed gendarmes gathered on a covered landing at the top of steps leading to a house that overlooked the park. The door to the house stood open, and in the autumn silence of the village they could hear a hubbub of voices coming from within.

Dominique was instantly curious. 'What's going on here?'

But Enzo didn't want to know. 'None of our business.' And he took her hand and led her up the steps to the park. To their left three benches stood among several ancient trees amidst the drifts of brittle autumn leaves brought down prematurely by the storm. To their right a small war memorial was set among a collection of boulders, and flanked by four trees. Nineteen souls had been taken from this village by the Great War. Only one by its successor. And yet, someone else had died here. Someone quite alien, a long way from home. At the far side of the park stood an old chapel, now an exhibition space closed up for the season. To the right of it, almost against the back wall of the park, lay the skeleton of the fallen tree. The area of ground which had been torn up by its roots to reveal the long hidden grave had been taped off, and a canvas cover erected over it to protect the earth from rain.

'A lime tree,' Enzo said. 'Looks like it's been dead for some time.'

He fished out his phone and took several photographs to establish the setting, before moving in to take more detailed shots of the broken ground. He crouched down to brush aside fallen leaves, and picked up a curved piece of discoloured and broken terracotta. There were several more pieces of varying sizes lying in among the disturbed earth.

Dominique crouched beside him. 'Mean anything?'

'Probably pieces of an old clay drainage pipe.' He moved to the outer area of the grass torn up by the roots and crouched again. With delicate fingers he uncovered the remains of the pipe itself, leading away beyond the chapel, about two feet beneath the surface, the merest hint of a depression in the grass. 'Yes, here it is.' It was choked solid with earth. He glanced back along the area of disturbance to where the broken root system projected from the ground. It had brought up the bones and broken the old pipe at the same time.

Enzo stood up and took several more photographs.

Dominique slipped her arm through his again. 'So what are you divining, Holmes?'

'Elementary, my dear Watson,' Enzo said. 'The body was buried below the pipe.'

'You mean they dug beneath it to hide the corpse?'

Enzo shook his head. 'No. The pipe was laid after the body had been buried. My guess would be that the trench for laying the pipe had already been dug, and the killers of our unfortunate victim took advantage of it to hide the body. After all, if they'd dug a fresh grave here, it would have been apparent to everyone.'

Dominique nodded. 'So they dug down just below the level of the existing trench and covered it over, knowing that the drainage pipe would be laid on top of it then buried beneath fresh earth. And no one would be any the wiser.'

'The pipe was probably laid by a *cantonnier*, working for the mairie,' Enzo said. 'So in theory, all you would have to do is go back through municipal records to find a date for when the work was done, and you'd have a reasonably accurate approximation of when he was murdered. Certainly to within a day or two.'

Dominique grinned. 'Which is not at all bad after seventy-odd years.'

'Monsieur Macleod?' The voice rang out in the cold air and startled them. They turned to see a gendarme hurrying across the grass in their direction. He was a young man. Mid thirties, Enzo thought. Thinning mousy-brown hair was cut to a stubble in an attempt to disguise encroaching baldness. He was very nearly as tall as Enzo, and wore a short, dark blue fleece with a distinctive white stripe across chest and arms above a black leather gun belt hung with keys. He clutched his cap in his hands, and Enzo noted the three bars on his epaulette denoting the rank of capitaine. A pale blue mask dangled from one ear.

For a moment, Enzo thought he was actually going to shake his hand, but the gendarme stopped short, as if suddenly remembering himself. He was beaming like a star-struck schoolkid. 'Monsieur Macleod, it's an absolute pleasure.' He glanced towards Dominique and somehow managed to dismiss her with the briefest of acknowledgements before turning his gaze back on Enzo. 'I recognised you from my cuttings collection. Followed every one of your cases and kept my own album. Outstanding, monsieur, just outstanding.'

Enzo shuffled uncomfortably at this sudden and effusive out-pouring of admiration and flicked a look towards Dominique. He saw a tiny smile playing about her lips. 'That's not what the police thought at the time,' he said.

The gendarme was oblivious. 'I'd shake your hand, but of course I can't. I should introduce myself. I'm Capitaine Michel Arnaud. Based at Vayrac, just across the river.' His pale blue eyes positively shone.

To avoid further embarrassment, Enzo nodded towards the collection of police vehicles and officers at the house adjoining the park. 'What's going on here?' And he avoided Dominique's look. After all, hadn't he just told her it was none of their business?

Arnaud half glanced back towards the house. 'A murder. Not very cold though. Happened just last night.'

'Domestic?' Enzo asked, although he had no real interest.

'Oh, no. Not at all. The very opposite, actually. It's quite puzzling, and very bloody.' His face lit up with sudden inspiration. 'Why don't I walk you through it? I'd really appreciate your expert opinion.'

Enzo shook his head. 'I don't think so, capitaine. I've retired from all that sort of thing.'

'Oh, go on, Enzo. It would do you no harm to keep your hand in.'

Enzo turned a look on Dominique that might have killed a lesser mortal.

'What are you doing here anyway?' Arnaud asked suddenly.

Enzo inclined his head towards the fallen tree. 'A colleague in Paris, a forensic archaeologist, asked me to take a look at this spot where it seems they found some Second World War remains.'

'Ah, yes,' Arnaud said. 'The skeleton in the roots. The tree came down in a storm about a week ago. And the bones were hopelessly tangled in the root system. I think the tree was planted sometime after the body was buried, but it had been dead for a while. Some kind of fungus. Should have been removed. Our concern was establishing how old the remains were, given the bullet hole in the skull. But it quickly became apparent that it was historical. We were instructed to collect every last piece and send it to Paris. Not the most pleasant of jobs.'

'Indeed.'

A commotion on the steps of the house caused them to turn in time to see two men carrying a body bag on a stretcher down to the waiting ambulance.

'That's them removing the body now. Finally. It took an age for the pathologist to get here, and forensics are pretty much done. Let me show you the crime scene.' He held an arm out to guide him towards the steps, but raised a hand to stop Dominique. 'Perhaps your daughter should stay out here.'

Enzo's face darkened. 'My wife,' he said.

'Oh.' Arnaud blushed to the roots of his vanishing hair.

'And she won't be fazed by a bloody crime scene, capitaine. Dominique was a gendarme herself for many years.'

Realisation bloomed suddenly in Arnaud's recollection. 'Dominique Chazal,' he said. 'You were the investigating officer in the murder of Marc Fraysse, the Michelin-starred chef.'

Dominique inclined her head in acknowledgement.

'My sincerest apologies, madame. I had no idea.' He fought to recover himself. 'All the better, then, to have an additional pair of expert eyes on my crime scene.' He pushed awkwardly past them to lead the way. 'Come.'

Enzo glared at Dominique as they followed in his wake.

Arnaud barked a command, and the officers hanging about at the top of the steps quickly dispersed. Enzo and Dominique and the capitaine climbed up to the small covered terrace at the door, avoiding areas which had been taped off around several partial bloody footprints. A knotted old vine snaked its way up to the roof above them, shrivelled grapes still clinging to its leafless branches. The remains of autumn-withered geraniums spilled from plant pots along the top of the wall. They had a fine view from here of the uprooted tree, and Enzo paused to take another photograph. Arnaud attached his mask to his other ear, and Enzo and Dominique donned theirs. Impossible to socially distance here. Or inside the house.

'Let me explain before we go in,' he said.

Enzo sighed inwardly. This was not how he had envisaged his day. 'Please do.'

Arnaud took out a notebook to consult. 'The house belongs to a seventy-five-year-old spinster called Anny Lavigne. She was born in this house, and has lived here all her life. She inherited the property when her mother died twenty years ago, a lady then in her eighties.' Without consulting his notes he added, 'Anny took a degree in English at the Université de Toulouse Capitole, and taught it at the collège in Saint-Céré for much of her working life.'

'Saint-Céré?' Dominique asked.

Arnaud seemed mildly irritated by the interruption. 'It's a town about twenty minutes upriver.' He closed his notebook now. 'She and her mother travelled a lot when they were both younger. But Anny's been retired for over ten years now. She's a well-known village character. Organises concerts in the church every year during the local music festival, carrying on the work of her mother who brought the Heidelberg Chamber Orchestra to the festival for many years. She had a younger half-sister who died in her forties, leaving a teenage daughter, Elodie, who married young and now has a teenage son of her own. Elodie's an amateur opera singer and used to give impromptu concerts here at her aunt's house. They would draw quite a crowd. Mostly wealthy Parisians who came down to stay in their *maisons secondaires* during the summer.'

There was a dreamy quality in his smiling eyes.

'She sings very well,' he said. 'I attended a number of the concerts myself.' And then, catching himself, he cast his gaze towards the houses crowding in around them. 'Carennac was in a dilapidated state for many years – half-ruined, you might say. It's only the money of wealthy inheritors that has restored it to its present condition. Largely through the good auspices of *Les Amis de Carennac*.'

Enzo ran his eyes over Anny Lavigne's house. 'It looks like there's been money spent on this place, too.'

Arnaud nodded. 'Over many years, I think. Originally the habitable part of the house would all have been on this level. Over time they've built bedrooms in the attic, and a garage in the cellar.'

'And there's no land with it?' Dominique said.

'No, madame. But there is a decent-sized terrace on the far side of the house for sitting out in the summer, though not much privacy since it gives directly on to the park. But I suppose the park itself must seem a little like a private garden. There's hardly ever anyone in it.'

'I take it,' Enzo said, 'that since you are speaking of her in the present tense, that Anny is not the victim.'

'No, no. Only in the sense that the murder took place in her house, and she discovered the body. Until we are finished with the crime scene, Anny is staying at the only hotel still open, the Fenelon. Ironically the same hotel where both the victim and the prime suspect were staying.'

Enzo cocked an eyebrow in surprise. 'You have a prime suspect already?'

But Arnaud seemed less than happy. 'Unfortunately, we haven't the first idea where he is. Nor do we have any notion of why he might have done it. Equally odd, he appears to be entirely unknown to Anny. Although the victim himself had called on her earlier in the day.'

'And he is?'

'An art dealer from Paris. Emile Narcisse. Well known apparently, though not to me.'

Enzo shrugged. 'Nor me.' He glanced at Dominique, but she shook her head. 'And your suspect?'

'A young German in his twenties. From Berlin. His name is Hans Bauer. You might ask what either of them was doing in Anny's house.' He shook his head. 'We don't know. Although they were both staying at the Fenelon, they were never seen there together. Narcisse was observed leaving the hotel on his own just before 7.30 last night. The only tenuous connection that we can find between them is art. Bauer is the director of a small private art gallery in the German capital. Though friends of Narcisse say he had never been to Germany. And as far as we know, this is Bauer's first visit to France.'

Enzo said, 'Where was Anny on the night of the murder?'

'Dining at a friend's house in Vayrac. A few minutes' walk, in fact, from the gendarmerie. The friend came to pick her up, then drove her home afterwards. Which is when she discovered the body in her kitchen.'

Dominique said, 'What makes Bauer the prime suspect?'

Arnaud scratched his head. 'He checked out of his hotel room last night before the body was discovered, in spite of having reserved a table in the restaurant for dinner. Because no one actually saw him leave or enter the hotel during the course of the evening, it's impossible to establish where he was at the time of the murder. But after he'd gone, the proprietor went to check on his room and found traces of blood everywhere, including the shower. The lab in Saint-Céré has already established that it was Narcisse's blood.'

Enzo whistled softly. 'Well, that's fairly compelling. How was Narcisse murdered?'

'His throat was cut, severing arteries and the windpipe.'

'A lot of blood, then,' Enzo said.

Arnaud nodded grimly. 'Skid marks where it had pooled on the floor, footprints leading to the door, and bloody handprints on the door itself. And out here, as you can see. It would appear that Bauer lost his footing in the blood and fell. He must have been covered in it.'

Enzo said, 'That was careless. How do you know it was Bauer who fell in the blood?'

'They were his bloody fingerprints on the door, Monsieur Macleod.'

'How did you establish that?' Dominique asked.

'Bauer has a criminal record in Germany. Assault. A fairly minor incident, apparently, when he was a teenager. But they have his fingerprints on file. We ran a check on AFIS.'

Enzo was impressed. 'You *have* moved quickly.'

Arnaud allowed himself to bask in the glow of Enzo's praise for only a moment before his face clouded again. 'Not fast enough, though. Bauer has just vanished into thin air. He came down from Paris by train to Brive-la-Gaillarde yesterday, then took a local train to a station in a small town not far from here called Biars-sur-Cère. From there he took a taxi to Carennac. If he got away by train, how did he get to the station without calling a taxi? It would take more than two hours on foot, and there are no trains at that time of night anyway.'

'Perhaps he stole a car,' Dominique suggested.

'We've had no reports of any stolen vehicles, madame. And we're quite isolated here. There's really nowhere he could get to on foot. Certainly not without being seen.' He waved a hand towards the open door. 'Shall we go in?'

The house was shaped like the mirror of an L, and the kitchen occupied much of the lower leg. It was dominated by a long wooden table with sufficient chairs around it to seat ten. A rack suspended from the ceiling above it was hung with pots and pans and ropes of dried garlic. Beneath windows on the left were a sink and cooker and a long work surface. Enzo noted a modern knife block standing beside the gas rings with slots to take six knives of various sizes. One of the slots was empty. There were jars of herbs and spices, a tall container for bread, a rack with half a dozen bottles of wine. Beyond the table, a door led to a short hallway, and Enzo could see the bottom step of a staircase leading up to the attic rooms. Beyond that, fragments of coloured light were sprinkled by stained-glass windows across a large salon which seemed to occupy the main leg of the L. A door stood open in the far wall, leading to the terrace outside.

The blood pool and spatters were taped off, the table pushed against the wall to create enough space to squeeze by. It was a mess. The killer had clearly slithered in the blood, losing his footing and falling in it before scrambling to reach the door. The position of the body was self-evident by the absence of blood where it had lain on the floor. Like some macabre shadow cast by death.

Blood had clearly gouted from the severed arteries, projecting spatter trails across the floorboards.

Dominique sidled past the blood and went through to the hall and the salon beyond. Arnaud glanced anxiously at Enzo. 'What do you think?'

Enzo said, 'The body was lying face down?'

Arnaud nodded.

'Well, from the position of the body, and the direction of the blood spatter, it seems reasonably clear that whoever killed him approached from the front, probably extending an arm to slash him across the neck with a very sharp blade. He would have got blood on himself, for certain. But why wouldn't he have left by the side entrance at the other side of the house, rather than try to get past the man he'd just killed and tread through the blood that was all over the floor?'

'Panicked, probably,' Arnaud said, 'and he wouldn't have been able to see the blood anyway.'

'Why not?'

'Because the house was in darkness. Someone had thrown the switch on the fuse box.'

Enzo nodded. 'Well, that would explain why Narcisse never

saw the blade coming.' He crouched down stiffly and cast his gaze more closely over the blood patterns and skid marks. 'May I take some photographs, so that I can look at these in more detail later?'

'Of course.' Arnaud seemed only too happy. 'We don't get too many murders around here, monsieur. It's not exactly my speciality.'

Enzo took out his phone and rattled off as many as a dozen photos, then straightened up with difficulty, steadying himself on the table. He smiled ruefully. 'The joys of getting older.' He slipped a hand into his pocket to pull out a pair of latex gloves. 'Always carry a pair with me these days to avoid touching things in public places.' He snapped them on with practised ease. 'Mind if I take a look at the knife block?'

'Go ahead. We figure the missing knife is probably the murder weapon. But there's no sign of it.'

Enzo picked his way carefully to the worktop. 'In my experience, French kitchen knives are notoriously blunt.' He slipped one of the knives out of its block, feeling a certain resistance as he did so. He breathed his surprise. 'But not these ones. This is a self-sharpening block. A knife gets sharpened every time it is put in or taken out.' He examined the blade. 'Lethal. Wouldn't have taken much effort at all to cut open a throat with a knife this sharp.'

Dominique's voice called through from the far end of the house. 'If you're finished in there, you should come through and see this.'

Enzo raised eyebrows in Arnaud's direction, seeking permission, and the capitaine nodded. He peeled off his gloves as
he walked through the hall and into Anny's salon. It was vast,
its size somehow emphasised by the insignificance of a grand
piano in the far corner. Windows on three sides were glazed
by stained glass in dazzling patterns that filled the room with
a kaleidoscope of multicoloured light. Alcoves with concealed
lighting displayed exotic artefacts: a carved African doll, pieces
of antique pottery, a shield, wooden figurines fashioned after
the thirteenth-century Lewis chessmen. Stone walls were hung
with original art, exotic Moroccan and Chinese rugs strewn
across ancient flags. The room was divided in several ways by
arrangements of chairs and tables and metal-studded wooden
trunks. Colourfully embroidered cushions littered the floor in
front of a huge, blackened *cheminée*.

Arnaud smiled at Enzo's reaction. 'It's kind of like a living
museum,' he said, 'a room to display all the artefacts and
mementos that Anny and her mother brought back from their
travels. This is where her niece used to entertain the Parisians
in the summer.'

Enzo glanced at him curiously. He had that far-off look
again. The Scotsman's eyes flickered towards the gendarme's
left hand and he saw that there was no ring on the wedding
finger. So he was quite possibly single. Never married, perhaps,
or divorced. 'You were a regular attendee, then?'

Arnaud's eyes smiled behind his mask. 'Oh, yes. Anny and
my mother were friends from way back, we were always

59

invited.' His smile was replaced by a sudden look of frowned concentration. 'Monsieur Macleod, I've just had a thought.'

Enzo had a bad feeling already about Michel Arnaud's sudden thought.

'Would you, perhaps, consider consulting on this murder for us?' He saw the refusal rising in Enzo's chest and raised a hand to pre-empt it. 'We really do have very little experience in this kind of thing, and it would be an absolute privilege, monsieur – an honour – to benefit from your insight.'

The refusal hovered now on Enzo's lips, but this time it was Dominique who forestalled it. 'You should, Enzo. You've been complaining about having nothing to do these days.'

He protested. 'I have not!'

She ignored him. 'And it would get you out from under my feet. Particularly with Laurent at home all the time just now.' She grinned, stretching her mask wide. 'Go on, you know you want to.'

It seemed to Enzo that further denial would be futile. He sighed deeply and cast reluctant eyes in Arnaud's direction. In spite of everything, his interest was aroused, although he wouldn't want to admit it. 'I suppose I could take a look at it. Just a look, mind. Nothing more.'

As they walked together down the street towards the post office, Enzo glowered at Dominique. 'Thank you,' he growled under his breath.

She beamed. 'My pleasure.'

They arrived at the foot of the hill and turned left towards the palisade, completing a small circuit of the lower half of the village, which seemed now much bigger than they had initially imagined.

Enzo said, 'Arnaud and Anny's niece . . .' He searched for her name.

Dominique provided it. 'Elodie.'

'Yes, Elodie. They must be around the same age. He said she had a teenage son.'

'So she's married and he's not. If the lack of a ring is anything to go by.'

He glanced at her, surprised. 'You noticed.'

'He clearly has a thing for her.'

'Unrequited love.'

'Or not.'

This time he raised one eyebrow. 'Hadn't thought of that.'

She slipped her arm through his. 'That's because you're not a woman, Enzo.'

'Thank God!'

CHAPTER FIVE

The old lady has been silent for a long time, and he has been reluctant to prompt her in case somehow the spell of her story is broken and she draws a line under the telling of it.

'Shall I make myself a coffee?' he asks at length.

She looks up suddenly. 'I can do that.' She places her hands on the arms of her chair to raise herself to her feet. But he gets quickly to his.

'No, no, I'm sure I can find everything for myself.' He was quite familiar now with her kitchen. 'Can I make you tea while I'm at it?'

She shakes her head, sinking back in her rocker, clearly happy to let him get his coffee for himself. And he notices that she has barely drunk the tea she had made herself earlier. It would be stone cold by now, despite its proximity to the fire. The logs he threw on earlier have reduced themselves to embers, and are radiating a heat that he imagines must be burning her legs. He remembers how his grandmother's legs had become mottled from sitting too close to the fire. Corned-beef legs, she had called them. 'Shall I add another log?'

'Please.'

When he returns with his coffee the wood is well alight and she has not moved a muscle. As he settles once again in his chair she swings her head slowly in his direction. 'Have you ever been to the Isle of Lewis, monsieur? It's in the Outer Hebrides of Scotland.'

'I know of it, but I have never been.'

'A brutal place, by all accounts. It is first in line to welcome the gales that have gathered their strength across five thousand kilometres of Atlantic Ocean. A windbreak for the mainland beyond.'

He wonders where on earth this can be leading, but forces himself to contain his impatience as he waits for her to resume her story. Which, at length, she does . . .

Poor Georgette was as sick as a dog during her six-hour ferry crossing from Mallaig to the Isle of Lewis. It was the furthest north, and west, she had ever been, and she was not enjoying it. The rail journey from London to Fort William the previous day had been long and tedious. Poor weather had denied her any sight of the magnificent views afforded by the west coast-line of the Highlands of Scotland. The remainder of the journey from Fort William to Mallaig had passed almost entirely in cloud, mist descending from the heavens, and she spent an uncomfortable night in a basic lodging house in the town.

The blackout was still in force when the ferry left at first light, cleaving a difficult passage around the Isle of Skye and across a stormy Minch. In spite of the rain and the sea spray she had spent most of the journey on deck, her coat flapping furiously around her legs, back to the wind as she retched into the brine.

The wind died a little as they sailed, finally, into the lee of the island's east coast, and the fishing port of Stornoway emerged from the mist. Headlands to north and south took dark shape before vanishing into the featureless bog of the hinterland beyond. And it was with shaking legs that Georgette stumbled down the gangplank on to the dock and felt the world still moving. Even though the concrete beneath her feet was sunk in solid bedrock.

Sea-weary fellow passengers pushed past her, greeted by loved ones, friends or family, and were quickly swallowed by the smirr that drifted across the town like a mist. She heard idling engines rev, then accelerate into the gloom of the day, and it seemed that only a few minutes had passed before she was left standing on her own, a wet and forlorn figure clutching a sodden cardboard suitcase. The road that ran off around the southern flank of the town was lined by houses and shops that seemed painted on gauze, insubstantial, almost transparent, and she watched for the lights of the vehicle she had been told would pick her up.

It was nearly fifteen minutes before finally she heard the distant rumble of a heavy motor, then saw the lights of a canvas-covered military truck taking shape as it rumbled on to the quay. A cheery, ruddy-faced young soldier flung open the passenger door and leaned out an arm to give her a hand up.

'You look a bit wet, love,' he said.

'So would you if you'd stood for six hours on the deck of a ferry emptying your stomach into a storm, then waited twenty minutes in the rain for your lift.' She hauled herself up into the passenger seat and hefted her suitcase into her lap. She glared at the driver. 'You're late.'

His grin widened. 'Feisty one, aren't you? They can be a bit rough, them crossings. Never know when the ferry's going to arrive.'

He crunched into first gear, manoeuvred his truck through a three-point turn, and pulled out on to the road, turning hard left and over the narrow spit of land dividing inner and outer harbours. The inner harbour was packed with trawlers and small fishing vessels sitting cheek by jowl on a high tide and towering over the quayside. Beyond water that reflected a pewtery sky, a hill rose darkly into darker trees, and the lights of a forbidding-looking building emerged from the shadow of the hillside, fighting to penetrate the murk.

The driver lowered his head to look up at it. 'Lews Castle,' he said. 'That's where you're staying.'

'Is that where you're stationed?'

'No, we're at the RAF base out towards Point.' And he flicked his head vaguely to the west. Then he snuck a glance in her direction. 'I thought you was French. They said you was. And here's me practising my *parlez-vous anglais*.'

'Sorry to disappoint.'

He grinned. 'Not disappointed at all, love. Whatever nationality you is.'

And in spite of herself she blushed. 'So what's at the castle?' she said quickly to cover her embarrassment.

'They got wounded soldiers convalescing in one wing of it.

65

Some of them off the beaches at Dunkirk. Nurses live in, apparently. Some RAF brass based up there, too, and a training school of some kind. Though they don't tell us nothing about that.'

They rumbled through the deserted town, following the curve of the inner harbour, past feebly lit shop windows below a skyline broken by church spires. 'Where is everybody?' Georgette asked.

Her driver said, 'Would you go out on a day like this if you didn't have to?' He half turned and responded to her glare with a wink. 'Mind you, I been here three months and the weather don't ever get much better than this.'

They left the inner harbour behind them then before turning left, and climbing a narrow road through trees that delivered them eventually to the back of the castle. The driver brought his truck to a shuddering halt and he leaned on his horn for a good three seconds.

'That's you, love.' He reached past her to push open the passenger door. 'See you around.'

Not if I see you first, Georgette thought.

As he accelerated noisily away, a young soldier who clearly didn't relish being out in the rain emerged from a back door. Yellow electric light fell feebly from ground-floor windows to be snuffed out by even feebler daylight.

'Miss Pig Nall?' he called.

'*Peenyaall,*' she corrected him phonetically.

'You follow me, miss.' And he turned abruptly back inside. No formalities, not even an offer to carry her case.

She sighed and hurried after him, through vast kitchens, where white-aproned staff flitted from steaming pot to steaming pot, appetising smells issuing forth to fill the air with delicious condensation that ran down the windows. Georgette's stomach growled. It had been empty for a long time now but was not, she feared, destined to be satisfied any time soon.

She followed the soldier out into a long hallway that ran the length of the building. She dripped rainwater on to its shiny floor and hurried through elaborately corniced arch-ways, trying to keep up. He turned on to a broad staircase that took them then through several floors to a labyrinthine attic. At the end of a narrow corridor he stopped and opened a door into a tiny room with a sloping ceiling and small dormer window. 'This is yours. Toilet's at the other end of the hall. Briefing downstairs in fifteen minutes.'

'Wait a minute, I'm soaked to the skin. I need to wash and get changed. I can't possibly do it in fifteen minutes.'

He was unmoved. 'Fifteen minutes, miss.' And he brushed past her to head back along the way they had come.

She turned to gaze with sinking heart into the room that was to be hers for who knew how long. Drab, colourless, utili-tarian furniture. Cold green linoleum, and a wallpaper whose pattern was so faded and dull it was barely a memory. Her window looked out across a flat roof to crenellations beyond, the inner harbour almost lost in the mist a long way below. She threw her suitcase on to the bed and sat down beside it, hands clutched miserably in her lap. Rusted springs groaned beneath a lumpy mattress and she wondered what the hell she was doing here.

The same private who had taken her to her room showed Georgette into a small salon off the main ballroom which, he told her, was now being used as a dining room. Their evening meal would be served at five.

The salon was arranged with half a dozen chairs grouped around a blackboard on a tripod, two windows along one side giving out on to a view of the town below. Four young women, seated around a burly non-commissioned officer standing at the blackboard, turned curious heads in her direction as the door opened. The women gazed at her with unglazed interest. As the door closed behind her again, the NCO cocked his head to one side, a sarcastic smile playing around pale lips. 'The late Miss Pig Nall, I take it.' His sarcasm was very nearly lost in an almost unintelligible Geordie accent.

'Pignal,' she corrected him. 'And if I hadn't been left standing in the rain for half an hour I wouldn't have been late.' Which elicited some stifled giggles from the others.

The NCO silenced them with a look and folded his arms. 'Is that so? And I suppose you just had to change, and repair your make-up?'

'I'm here now,' she said sullenly.

'Yes, you are. Though God knows why.' He cast his gaze over the other women. 'These young ladies all know why they're here. And so do I. But I haven't the first fucking idea who you are, or why you're at my castle. Perhaps you'd like to enlighten us, *mam'selle*. If your English is up to it, that is.'

Georgette felt her hackles rise. 'I think you'll find . . .' She looked pointedly at the three stripes on the arm of his khaki green pullover, assessing him as a man in his forties who had long ago achieved a certain rank and never surpassed it. 'Sergeant, is it?'

'Connolley,' he growled.

'Well, I think, Sergeant Connolley, you'll find that I speak English a great deal better than you do. And as to why I'm at *your* castle, if your superiors haven't enlightened you, then I'm not about to. Information above your pay grade, I imagine.'

There was an almost collective intake of breath in the room.

The sergeant was fuming. But he kept a lid on it. He would get his revenge in his own good time. 'Well, Pig Nall,' he said, 'we'll just have to train you up for any eventuality, won't we? Which means you're going to have to work twice as hard as anyone else.' He smiled ominously. 'That'll be fun.' He paused. 'Sit down.'

Georgette, flushed with anger and humiliation in equal measure, dropped herself into an empty seat, and felt the eyes of the other women upon her. Sergeant Connolley turned towards the blackboard and began to scrawl on it with a piece of chalk.

'You are all, at some point, going to be dropped behind enemy lines, or in the case of the frog among us, *home*. And primarily we'll be working on fitness. But I'll also be making you familiar with this little beauty.' He turned around and they saw that he had written *Westland Lysander* on the board. 'She's a single-engined light aircraft capable of short take-off and landing in moonlit conditions. There is a ladder attached to the fuselage below the cockpit behind the pilot. You're going to learn to get down that ladder faster than you ever thought possible. Speed is the key. The plane simply can't remain on the ground for more than a few minutes. You have to get off *fast*.'

Georgette frowned. 'I thought I was to be parachuted into France.'

Connolley's face folded itself into a genuine smile. 'You? Parachute? Who told you that?'

And Georgette realised de Gaulle had been having his little joke with her. But in spite of having made a fool of herself, she was really rather relieved.

The polished wooden floor of the one-time ballroom was crammed with tables filled with men in uniform, nurses, soldiers with arms in slings and legs in plaster, a man with a horribly burned face that drew everyone's eye. Not out of curiosity, but out of fear. Sometimes, in war, a fate worse than death awaits.

Georgette and the other women in her group sat around a table by one of the tall rain-streaked windows that flooded the room with light. The sky had cleared a little, and although now early evening, the sun was still high in the late summer sky, sprinkling broken light across the hillside and the town and inner harbour below. A spectacular panorama stretched away to the Minch beyond, where burnished patches of sunlight scalded the surface of the sea.

But none of the women was looking at the view. It was the first time they had been alone together, away from the watchful eye of Sergeant Connolley. They were excited to get to know their fellow travellers on this demanding road. Eager to forge friendships and share of themselves in the hope of dispelling inner fears and finding the courage in comradeship they would need to face an uncertain future.

'Are you really French?' one of them asked Georgette.

'Half and half. But I grew up in France.' She shook everyone's hand around the table. 'Georgette. But my English friends just call me George.'

It turned out that all the girls spoke French and were anxious to try it out on Georgette. So introductions were made in her native language. It gave the women an instant and conspiratorial sense of sisterhood. No one else would know what they were saying.

Alice was a pretty girl with blond curls and a Home Counties accent that seemed both alien and intimidating to the others. She told them that she came from London, and that her father held a rank high up in the Admiralty. Though exactly what she couldn't say. Georgette thought she was possibly twenty-two or twenty-three, and was impressed by her accent when she spoke French.

Joan was a middle-class girl from Manchester who looked to be barely out of her teens. Her straight dark hair was cut in a fringe above a plain face. But she had an attractive smile and an infectious laugh that endeared her to everyone. A plain-speaking Mancunian whose grasp of pejorative French slang had Georgette in fits of laughter. 'Real bastard that sergeant,' she said. 'Bet he's only like that in front of us women cos he's got such a tiny tadger.'

'How would you know?' Georgette twinkled. She was warming to the company.

'Tiny feet, George. Didn't you notice? It's a sure sign.' They all laughed and felt a release of tension.

Another of the women, a striking girl with shoulder-length black hair and cobalt blue eyes, raised both of her hands. 'He'll love me then,' she said. 'My brother says men *adore* women with small hands.' Her ruddy-complexioned face broke into a broad grin. 'For obvious reasons.'

This time the laughter at their table brought looks from around the room, and they instantly drew closer and lowered their voices.

'I'm Mairi,' said the girl with the small hands speaking English now, and Georgette was struggling to place her accent. 'I live just up the road at Ness, the north end of the island. And I love the way that God-almighty Sergeant Connolley seems to think that this is *his* castle, when it's *my* bloody island.'

They stifled their laughter to avoid further frowns from the other tables.

72

Georgette understood the origins of the accent now and said, 'Are you a Gaelic speaker?'

'Didn't speak English till I went to school, George.'

'So you live here?' There was an element of incredulity in Joan's voice.

'Born and bred,' Mairi said. 'Grew up in Ness. Then my parents sent me to school here in Stornoway. The Nicolson Institute. The worst years of my life. Living away from home in digs.' A look of unhappy recollection was replaced by a smile. 'Didn't stop me being school dux, though.'

The others frowned. 'What's that?' Alice asked.

'Only the smartest girl in the school.' Mairi grinned. 'Amazing how easy it is to fool folk.'

Then they all found themselves turning their heads towards the only member of their group who had not yet introduced herself. She blushed.

'Rebecca,' she said. She was older than the others, by a good ten years, and there was a weariness in her face.

'Where you from, Becky?' Joan asked.

'Abergavenny.' And her face broke into a rare smile when she saw their bewilderment. 'It's a couple of hours from Cardiff, at the foot of the Black Mountains.'

'Oh, *Welsh*,' Alice said. 'I was wondering about that accent.' She glanced at Rebecca's left hand. 'I see you took your wedding ring off.' There was the faintest band of white around the root of her third finger. 'Was that to increase your chances with the sergeant?'

The others laughed, but Rebecca's face grew even paler, and her eyes dipped towards her hands clasped on the table in front of her. She spoke very quietly. 'I took it off because my husband is dead.' A cringing hush fell on the table. 'He went to France with the British Expeditionary Force in September last year.' She paused momentarily to bite her lip. 'One of the first killed in the Battle of France three months ago.'

The wind had dropped along the sheltered east coast the next morning, but the rain fell steadily, and the women were quickly soaked as they assembled at the rear of the castle, wearing only khaki T-shirts and canvas shorts, waiting for Sergeant Connolley to appear. Cumbersome leather running shoes quickly absorbed the wet and grew heavy as the girls grew impatient.

'Where is he?' Joan growled.

'Leaving us out here on purpose, I bet,' Mairi said. They had all taken to jogging on the spot to keep warm.

At length they heard the sound of a vehicle engine, a steady throbbing in the rain, before a canvas-covered jeep emerged from the trees on a muddy track. It drew up beside them and the sergeant jumped out. He was wearing a rain cape with the hood pulled up. It was running with water, so he had been out in the rain himself.

'Morning, ladies.' He reached into the jeep and started pulling out army rucksacks to drop on the rain-sodden ground. 'Put these on.'

Alice was the first to lift one. 'God, it's heavy,' she gasped.

'You're breaking my heart, love.' Connolley's voice came muffled from inside the jeep.

Rebecca heaved hers on to her back and pulled a face. 'What's in them?'

'Rocks,' Connolley said, turning to face them. 'To simulate the kind of load you'll be expected to carry in the field.' And he grinned as he took in their expressions. 'You train to be fit. To survive in any conditions. It's what'll keep you alive.' He looked up at the leaden sky that poured its relentless tears on the poor souls below. 'I've marked out a course around the grounds with flags and arrows. It's maybe three miles in total.' He smiled at their groans. 'There's a whole network of tracks through the woods, but they've not been well maintained, so watch out for potholes. A puddle could be an inch deep, or six. So don't go breaking any ankles.'

He walked around the jeep as they all pulled the rucksacks on to unwilling backs and felt the weight of them dragging at their shoulders.

'Start over there.' He pointed towards a break in the trees, beyond which the woods seemed very dark. 'Follow the arrows. I expect to see you back here in well under an hour.'

Georgette said, 'Not coming with us?'

'No.' That sarcastic smile again. 'Scared you'll miss me?'

She shook her head. 'Just wondered if maybe you weren't up to it.'

His smile vanished. 'We'll see who's not up to it,' he said.

*

The smell of damp, rotting vegetation filled the air, along with the stertorous breathing of the girls, as they pounded off into the woods, straps chaffing at soft skin through wet cotton. They agreed quickly among themselves to pace each other and not run too fast, moving together in a close single line along narrow paths, taking turns at leading the pack and then falling to the back.

It was hard going, and Georgette found herself reciting fragments of a poem in her head from a book her mother had given her for her thirteenth birthday. She couldn't recall it exactly and improvised a couple of lines that kept repeating, like a mantra carrying her through the pain.

> *The woods are dark,*
> *My promise to keep.*
> *So far to go before I sleep.*

Georgette's promise – a promise she could share with no one – was to keep the *Mona Lisa* safe. And she wondered when, if ever, that promise might be fulfilled and she could sleep without fear of failure.

She tried not to think about it, focusing instead on the rain as it fell on her face, the beat of her feet on soft, wet ground, the inordinately loud rasping of her own breath, the cawing of rooks somewhere far above them in the canopy.

Then a cry of pain broke through her concentration, and she almost collided with Mairi directly in front of her as the group came to a muddy halt. Alice was on the ground at the head of the pack, half covered in mud, tears streaming down her face as she clutched her ankle. 'Fuck, fuck, fuck!' she whispered, and they were all shocked to hear the language of the barracks room escape such cultured lips.

'Is it broken?' Rebecca asked.

But Alice shook her head. 'Don't think so. Just went over on it. So stupid!'

Georgette stepped forward to help her to her feet. She knew she was fitter than the others. 'Can't be much further to go,' she said, checking her watch. 'You girls go on, I'll help Alice back to the castle.'

The girls exchanged glances, reluctant to leave Alice and Georgette behind. But Georgette waved them on. 'Go,' she said. 'Don't give that sarcastic bastard any excuses to come down harder on us than he already has.'

When the girls had gone, and the pounding of their feet in the wet had receded to a muffled reverberation among the trees, Alice wiped the tears from her face and turned it towards Georgette. 'I'm sorry, George. I really am.'

'Hey,' Georgette said, 'if we can't look after one another, who else will?' She slung Alice's rucksack over her left shoulder and supported Alice with her right arm as they set off through the woods at a painfully slow pace.

They arrived back at the castle a good twenty minutes after the others. The girls were crowded together for warmth and shelter in the doorway to the kitchens, their rucksacks in a pile on the ground beside the jeep. Connolley sat behind the wheel with the engine idling, smoking a cigarette.

The girls rushed forward to help Georgette and Alice as soon as they emerged from the woods, but Connolley was quickly out of the jeep. 'Stay where you are!' he barked, and stood with his hands on his hips until the two stragglers arrived at the vehicle. Georgette released Alice's rucksack on to the pile, but Connolley stopped her from removing her own. 'Just keep that on your back, Pig Nall. Seems you make a habit of being late for everything.'

'She was helping me,' Alice said.

But Connolley ignored her protests. 'I bloody well told you to be careful, didn't I?' He hissed breath through clenched teeth and shook his head. 'You'd better go see the doc and get that strapped up.' He jerked his thumb towards the castle, and Rebecca stepped forward to help her to the door.

There was a long stand-off, then, in the rain, Connolley gazing at Georgette with ominous reflection, and she wondered when he was finally going to let her remove this aching weight from her back. He scratched his chin.

'Since I have no idea what I'm training you for, we're going to have to make sure you're doubly fit.' He tilted his head towards the start of the circuit. 'Do it again.'

There was an audible gasp from the others. 'That's not fair,' Joan protested.

Connolley turned his head dangerously in her direction.

'You want to join her?' When his question was greeted by silence, the sarcasm returned to his smile. 'Didn't think so.'

Georgette said, 'Why don't you? Scared I might beat you?'

He laughed. 'Darling, I could do two circuits in the time it would take you to do one.'

'Let's put that to the test, then.'

As if someone had flicked a switch, he suddenly became serious. 'Okay.' He pulled off his rain cape and the pullover beneath it, stripping down to a white singlet and camouflaged military trousers. 'Gimme your rucksack.'

Georgette freed herself of it with relief. There was just a chance she could avoid complete humiliation if she wasn't burdened with the extra weight. He took it from her, laid it on the ground to open it and start filling it with more stones from one of the others. 'What are you doing?'

He turned his rain-streaked face towards her. 'Evening things up, Pig Nall. I'm a good deal heavier than you. We wouldn't want you to have an unfair advantage now, would we?'

Georgette stood in the rain staring at him with hatred in her heart, and wanted to scream. She risked a glance at the others and saw the horror on their faces. But she said nothing.

When Connolley had finished loading her rucksack with more stones she took it without a word and slung it on to her shoulders. She felt the weight of it pulling her backwards and had to lean forward to maintain her balance. Still she held her peace, and kept her eyes fixed on Connolley's. For a moment she thought he was almost disconcerted by her defiance, but then he smiled and said simply, 'And we're off.' He jogged past her and headed for the trees.

Georgette gritted her teeth and started after him. She could see the muscles of his back through the wet of his singlet, and the easy lope of his strong stride. And she was pretty sure he could run six miles faster than she could run three with this weight on her back. But she was determined not to show weakness. She would finish the course, no matter what. That would be a victory in itself, albeit pyrrhic.

He very quickly disappeared from view, and she heard him crashing off through the woods, the sound of him becoming more and more distant, until finally she could hear nothing but her own breath and the sound of the rain, her feet splashing through mud, and a murder of crows laughing hysterically somewhere high above.

She found a rhythm and rediscovered her mantra of the first time round. *My promise to keep, my promise to keep, so far to go before I sleep, before I sleep.* It stopped her thinking about the pain, inducing a numbness both physical and spiritual that consumed her consciousness.

She had no sense of passing time, was barely aware that the rain had stopped. Somewhere high above the trees, a rising wind was tearing gaping holes in the clouds, and a determined sun fought to make itself seen in fleeting glimpses. Light caught droplets hanging from leaves and branches, like fairy lights in the forest, and the occasional ray of sunlight fell between trunks as a fine mist rose from the forest floor to hang suspended in bright golden shafts.

Now she could see the dark, towering shape of the castle through the trees ahead, and like the long-distance runner on seeing the finish line, almost stumbled and fell. She was nearly there. And suddenly Connolley drifted past her, long, comfortable strides, still light of foot. She hadn't even heard him coming. 'My second time round,' he called back at her. 'We can do it again tomorrow, if you like.'

The mood around the table at lunch was sombre, a sad little oasis of silence in the midst of the vocal animation that filled the dining room. Alice's foot had been strapped up by a medic, and she would be unable to take part in training for some days. She kept glancing guiltily at Georgette, burdened by the thought that somehow what had happened was all her fault.

For her part, Georgette was keeping her thoughts to herself, a simmering silence that masked the anger that burned inside her. Connolley was sitting at a table of other NCOs on the far side of the room, and each time his voice was raised in laughter there was an exchange of resentful looks among the girls. Was he relating the story of how he had managed to humiliate the insolent Frenchie and prove his athletic prowess, all at the same time? Whatever the conversation, Connolley and his friends were enjoying it.

Finally Joan said, 'It's just not fair.'

There was a murmur of agreement around the table, but no

one could think of anything else to say. They were all washed and changed now, in military fatigues and army boots, faces scrubbed clean and shiny red from the cold of the rain and the heat of their anger.

A dapper man in his fifties approached the table, dressed casually in army-green pullover and slacks. His thinning grey air was oiled back over a narrow skull, and a neatly clipped silver moustache seemed attached to the underside of his nose. Georgette saw two stars beneath a crown on his epaulettes.

'Hello, girls,' he said cheerfully. 'I'm Colonel Smith. More or less in charge of this operation. Welcome to sunny Stornoway.' He paused, allowing time for them to laugh, and when none of them did, pressed hurriedly on. 'I'm glad to see you've bedded in. We run a tight ship here, and you're all going to benefit from the training you'll get from Sergeant Connolley. A good man, one of the best.' He glanced out of the window. 'I see things have brightened up a little for this afternoon. Makes a change, eh?'

He could hardly have been unaware of the mood around the table, but if he was, he chose to ignore it.

'Well.' He thrust his hands in his pockets. 'My office is right upstairs. Any problems, you just come and let me know. Enjoy the rest of your stay.'

And with that he was off, quite probably relieved to escape the atmosphere among the newly arrived trainees. Rebecca leaned across the table to Georgette and said in French, 'Why didn't you say anything, George?'

Mairi put her hand over Georgette's. 'You should have said something. If you don't, I will.'

But Georgette just shook her head. 'I fight my own battles,' she said.

Sunlight washed across the gentle slope of the lawn as it fell away towards the trees below, and the footpath that followed the line of the inner harbour.

The girls were assembled on a flat stretch of grass immediately in front of the castle, still in army fatigues, hair pinned beneath green berets pulled down on scowling faces. On Sergeant Connolley's command they had been standing to attention for close on five minutes, feeling the wind freshening around them. He had gone back into the castle and left them standing stiffly in line, and they were aware of curious faces watching from the other side of the glass behind them.

Glancing to her right, Georgette saw, adjoining the castle, a length of white-painted greenhouse and wondered if they grew their own food here. Her body ached from this morning's exertions. All she wanted was to flop on to her bed and sleep. This was far worse than anything the Armée de Terre had put her through in France, but the air she breathed was so pure it was almost intoxicating. Late August, and there was already a chill in the air. Although it was lighter for longer this far north, there was a watery weakness about the sun, and a pallor about the people who lived here. In the bay beyond Stornoway, she saw the water grow choppy as the wind got up, and the sun reflected in coruscating diamonds all the way out into the Minch.

'At ease!' Connolley's bellow carried to them on the breeze and he strode out on to the lawn in front of them. 'We're going to start learning some basic self-defence. A few simple moves that might one day save your lives.' He chuckled. 'After all, no man expects a girl to be able to upend him. Which gives you an advantage in the element of surprise.' He placed his hands on his hips and surveyed them speculatively. 'I'm going to need a volunteer.'

When no one stepped forward, he laughed and pointed at Georgette.

'Pig Nall, you're it.'

Georgette was aware of the others glancing in her direction. They all had a sense of what was coming. And she wondered how much more of this she could take. She drew a deep breath. 'Sir!' She had no idea where she found the strength in her voice. She took one step forward.

He waved his hand to bring her closer and she moved warily out on to the grass. He addressed the others. 'Things to remember. First off, stance and balance. Stand in a crouch, dominant leg behind the other.' He demonstrated. 'Keep your elbows at a little less than ninety degrees and always keep your hands in front of your face. Keep your stomach tense, because you never know when you're going to be hit. You can predict when an opponent is going to strike by keeping your eyes on his chest. Keep his shoulders and hips in peripheral view.' He straightened up. 'Do not bunch your fists. That'll make your whole arm tense, and you slower to react. Clench your jaw and keep your chin low. That'll minimise any damage to your mouth and teeth. When you're moving you need to be aware of constantly keeping your balance. And that means taking short steps, never crossing your feet, and maintaining a low centre of gravity.'

He turned towards Georgette and grinned.

'Got that?'

She stared sullenly back at him.

'Good. Let's see how you do.' He immediately adopted the crouching position, open hands raised in front of his face. Georgette did the same, and they began a slow-motion dance that took them one around the other. She stared her hatred into his face, and for a moment thought she might have unsettled him. 'Look at my chest, not my eyes,' he bawled. And as she lowered her eyes he moved in so quickly she had no time to react. One hand grabbed her tunic at the neck, the other slipped behind to grab her at the waist. He turned side-on and she found herself swivelling over his hip before crashing to the ground, landing on her back, every last drop of air expelled from her lungs. The full weight of him seemed to drop on top of her, and she saw his grinning face leering into hers, hot breath bursting in her face. If she'd had the strength, she'd have spat in it.

Then he was up and on to his feet again, and addressing the watching girls. 'Divide yourselves into pairs, and I'll show you just how I did that so you can try it on each other.'

Georgette was still on the ground trying to catch her breath. He leaned down, offering a hand to pull her to her feet. But she rolled away from him and regained her feet for herself, standing tense and ready for him to come again.

'Stand easy, Pig Nall. We're going to do this in half time.'

He stepped in to grab her collar again with his left hand.

'The secret is to turn side-on as you step in, presenting your hip for your opponent to roll over. You give them a helping hand by grabbing on to anything at their back. If they have a belt all the better.' He slipped his right arm around her to grab on to the pleats of her tunic. And suddenly she was pivoting over his hip again and crashing to the grass. This time he stayed on his feet and held out a hand to help her up. Again she refused it. He shook his head and smiled. 'You don't learn easy, do you, Pig Nall?'

She scrambled to her feet and stood gasping, fighting back tears of sheer frustration. Beyond him, she saw several of the NCOs who'd been sitting at his lunch table watching from inside, clearly enjoying her humiliation.

It was more than anger she felt. More than frustration. More than humiliation. But she could no more find a word for it than a voice to express it. All she could do was close her eyes, grit her teeth, and turn to face him once again.

She buried her face deep in the pillow to smother her sobs. Humiliation at the hands of Sergeant Connolley was bad enough, but she didn't want the other girls to know just how much he'd got to her. She had no idea how long she'd lain crying in the dark. But the moon had risen in a clearing sky, and was now casting half of her room into deep shadow.

Their evening meal had been conducted in silence, and Georgette had retired to her room almost immediately afterwards. She felt bruised and broken and couldn't face the company of her fellow trainees. If she could, she would have made the night last forever, to avoid the indignities that almost certainly awaited her tomorrow. Staying awake might make it appear to last longer, but lack of sleep would also drain her of the physical and mental reserves she was going to need. Swollen eyes were already growing heavy, and she knew it was only a matter of time before she drifted away.

A soft knocking at the door startled her, and seemed absurdly loud in the muffled silence of the castle. She sat up and quickly wiped the tears from her wet face, then crossed to the door and whispered, 'Who is it?'

'Mairi,' came the tiny whispered response from the other side. 'Let me in, George.'

Georgette sighed and unlocked the door. Mairi slipped quickly into the room. Like Georgette she wore plain flannel pyjamas, and her bare feet slapped softly on the linoleum. Georgette kept her back to the window to hide her face as Mairi sat on the bed. The islander supported herself with a hand on the pillow and must have felt the dampness there. For she immediately withdrew it and peered through the moonlight at her new French friend. It was clear she knew that

87

Georgette had been crying, but she said nothing. She patted the bed on her left. 'Come and sit beside me.'

Reluctantly Georgette dropped on to the bed next to her and crossed her arms. The warmth she felt emanating from Mairi made her realise just how cold she'd become. Mairi must have felt it, too, for she moved a little closer.

She said, 'My brother has a word for people like Connolley. It's an English word. Begins with a C. We don't have words like that in Gaelic. We have far too much respect for a woman's private parts.'

In spite of everything, Georgette found herself smiling.

'Listen, it turns out we've got this coming weekend off, so we were thinking we might go to Uig Beach on Saturday.'

'Where's that?'

'Uig's down in the south-west corner of the island. When the tide's out, the sands just stretch for miles. We're going to fly kites if it's dry, and have lunch at my granny's.'

Georgette felt her tears of earlier receding. 'Who's *we*?'

'All of us.' Mairi's face was shining in the moonlight. 'My brother's home on leave just now, and he's managed to get access to a jeep. So we're all going to squeeze in and drive down together. You'll like Alasdair. He's fun. And a good-looking boy. Spent his entire teen years fighting off the girls.' She grinned. 'Not very hard, mind you.' She lowered her voice to little more than a breath. 'He's attached to some kind of special forces unit that's being trained to operate behind enemy lines. So he's not someone to mess with.'

Georgette raised a self-mocking eyebrow in the dark. 'As if I would *mess* with anyone,' she said.

The only thing that got Georgette through the next few days was the thought of that outing to Uig on Saturday. Like release from a prison sentence, albeit temporary. Conditional parole awarded for good behaviour.

She tried hard to be on her very best behaviour. But if she brought out the worst in Sergeant Connolley, he did exactly the same for her, and they ended up barely acknowledging each other. The days passed in an endless cycle of running through the castle grounds with weighted rucksacks, and throwing each other to the ground on the lawn in front of the castle. Connolley continued using Georgette as his demonstrator. She offered no resistance to his moves and that helped her each time to break her fall.

They'd had two evening sessions indoors when he took them on a pictorial tour of the Westland Lysander that would fly each of them to France at different times. A light, single-engined aircraft that was deemed too fast for artillery spotting, and too slow and cumbersome to avoid fighters, but perfect for clandestine short take-off and landing.

None of the girls had ever flown before. 'How safe is it?' Joan had asked.

Connolley just smiled. 'Put it this way, love: there were 175 of them deployed over France and Belgium in the spring; only 57 of them made it back.' Which had filled none of them with confidence, and left each contemplating her own mortality in the dark of their attic rooms that night.

Georgette woke up on the Saturday morning to find her room filled with the reflected glow of sunlight that seemed to paint the entire island gold. The sky was cloudless, and she was not sure she had ever seen such a deep, clear blue. It reflected in the gentle swell of the Minch, transforming slate grey to crystal cerulean. And her spirits soared.

The girls chattered excitedly around the breakfast table before heading off on the narrow road towards the town to meet Alasdair on the way up. They were halfway down the hill when he rounded the bend in his green and grey camouflaged jeep and screeched to a halt. He jumped out and gave Mairi a big bear hug, before spinning her round once to then plant her on her feet again and gaze with unabashed love at his little sister.

'Alasdair, meet the gang,' she said, and made all the introductions.

Alasdair shook each of their hands solemnly, until he came to Georgette and Mairi told him that she was French. He turned to his sister. 'How do you say *ciamar a tha thu* in French?'

But Georgette pre-empted Mairi's response. '*Comment allez-vous*,' she said. 'Or if you want to be less formal, simply *ça va*.'

'You speak Gaelic?' he said in Gaelic.

Mairi laughed. 'No! I've been teaching them some basic phrases.'

Alasdair turned towards Georgette again. He had Mairi's

cobalt blue eyes but unlike her, a shock of unruly fair hair. The army had clearly tried to tame it with a razor, but it was growing back in extravagant curls. His smile was irresistible. 'So how does a gentleman greet a lady in France? I should really know in case I end up there.'

Georgette contained her smile. 'With a kiss on each cheek, of course.'

'Well, then, I'd better start practising.' And he leaned forward to kiss her once on each cheek. She smelled his aftershave, and felt the smoothness of his skin. He was probably three or four years younger than her, but she was aware of the first butterflies fluttering in her tummy.

She said, 'In some places it's three.'

'Oh,' he said, and kissed her a third time. She heard the other girls giggling.

'And in other places, four.'

'Enough!' Mairi glared at her. 'Time we were off.'

Alasdair leapt back into the jeep, jerked his head towards Georgette and patted the seat beside him. 'In we get, ladies. It'll be a tight squeeze.'

Georgette got next to Alasdair before Mairi could insinuate herself between them. It was clear that she was very possessive when it came to her big brother. The other three shoehorned themselves into the back. A quick three-point turn and they were off, shrieking in delight at the sunshine in their faces and the wind in their hair.

They were quickly out of the town, and heading south down

the east coast on a single-track road towards a place called Leurbost. Endless acres of featureless peat bog stretched away on either side of them, broken only by tiny scraps of water, miniature lochans reflecting the blue of the sky. Sheep that grazed among the purple heather wandered with unerring regularity on to the road.

Alasdair drove, it seemed to Georgette, far too fast, but she found it exhilarating and leaned in close to him.

At Leurbost they turned off on to what seemed an even narrower stretch of road that took them through the village of Achmore, a collection of houses that looked as if they had been threaded on a string and stretched out along a mile of single track. To their left the land dipped away across a shimmering plain that was as much water as land. On the far side of it a line of dark mountains pushed up into a clear sky.

'That's Uig down there,' Mairi shouted above the roar of the wind. 'And the Isle of Harris beyond that.'

Georgette felt that the others probably shared her sense of intrepid adventure in a strange land. Her first impressions of the island had not been particularly auspicious. But this was magical. She wanted to shout out, to release all of the pent-up anger and frustration of the last week. And restrained herself only with difficulty.

At a place with an unpronounceably long name comprising strings of consecutive consonants, they turned south again. And now the Atlantic Ocean lay shimmering in sunshine off to the west. The road wound endlessly among hills and lochs and inlets from the sea. And Georgette realised that in all this time they had not seen a single tree. Nor another vehicle.

At a hairpin bend in the road blue water sparkled away to their right, an abandoned croft house set in the bog above the rocks.

'Little Loch Roag,' Mairi told them. 'It's a sea loch. I suppose they'd call it a fjord in Norway.'

It seemed to stretch endlessly off to the north, before they left it behind and cut through bleak, deserted bogland to descend, at last, to a tiny fishing village and church at Miavaig, at what Mairi said was an offshoot of West Loch Roag.

Off, then, through a long, curving valley following a rock-littered riverbed, hills rising steeply on either side, until they emerged finally at the settlement known as Timsgarry. The huge, yellow-painted Uig Lodge stood proud on a rock promontory overlooking the biggest expanse of beach Georgette had ever seen. In the distance, between rocky headlands, they could see waves breaking blue and white at its extremity.

'Tide's out,' Alasdair shouted. 'Perfect for kite-flying.'

He manoeuvred his jeep around a tiny winding road that took them to the far side of the bay, and then on a sandy track through the dunes to a stretch of flat machair land above the beach. They all piled out of the vehicle and Georgette felt the power of the wind tugging at her hair and her slacks and her blouse. It was fresh in her face, but softened by the sun. She had not felt this good since leaving France.

From under the back seat Alasdair pulled out short lengths

of bamboo cane that he quickly assembled into braced kite shapes. He turned to look up at the watching girls. 'You know what a kite is?'

Georgette said quickly, 'It's a quadrilateral whose four sides can be grouped into two pairs of equal-length sides adjacent to each other.'

Everyone turned to look at her in astonishment. For a moment Alasdair seemed perplexed, then his face broke into a broad grin. 'No, I mean, do you know what it's for?'

Georgette shrugged coquettishly. 'Flying, of course.'

And they laughed now, and helped Alasdair stretch different-coloured cotton shapes across the frames of the kites, and attach long rolls of string.

Mairi said, 'We used to come kite-flying every Saturday when the weather was good, and stay over with our granny and go to the church over there on the hill.' The grey presbyterian stone of a stubborn religion stood foursquare against the wind on the far side of the bay. Closer to the shore a big white house sat among the rocks, and Georgette thought she saw headstones almost lost in the grass.

It was not easy to get the kites airborne because of the strength of the wind, but once they were up they soared, scraps of colour dipping and diving against the blue. They ran across the sands, the wind and the sea at their backs, following the erratic path of the kites, string unravelling, tugging at reddened hands, and they whooped and hollered at the sky.

The morning vanished far too quickly, and was gone almost

before they noticed. Alasdair nodded towards the far head-lands. 'Tide's turned. Time to go and eat. We might get some more flying in after lunch.'

They threw their kites into the back of the jeep and set off across the machair, tall grasses eddying like water in the wind, towards where a long, squat stone dwelling with a thatched roof sat on the rise. There was a broken-down drystone wall around it, and sheep clambered over the shambles of spilled stones searching for grasses growing tall among them. The toasty smell of peat smoke laced the air, but the smoke itself was lost in the wind and not visible where it left the house from a hole in the thatch. The thatch was weighted down with stones on ropes, and several sheep stood grazing on a line of turf that ran around the top of the exterior wall.

Joan stopped and looked at it in amazement. 'Your granny lives here?'

Alasdair laughed. 'Everyone on the island used to live in one of these. It's called a blackhouse.'

'I don't see any windows,' Alice said.

'That's because there are none.' Mairi grinned at her. 'The cows live at one end, and Granny at the other, and she still lights the place with oil lamps.'

Rebecca said, 'And do you and Alasdair live in a blackhouse?'

'No, thank God,' Alasdair said. 'Our old blackhouse is now an agricultural shed. We grew up in a whitehouse. Which is more like the kind of house you would recognise.' He looked at his granny's blackhouse. 'A few hardy folk still live in these, though.'

He ducked to enter by the only door in the side of the building, and called to his granny in Gaelic. He waved the others to follow him in.

A dark little entrance hall gave off to the cattle shed on the right, and the living quarters on the left. The place was full of choking peat smoke, and Georgette quickly found her eyes watering. Alasdair led them into what he called the fire room. It was a large, stone-flagged living room, with chunky items of old furniture lined up along each wall. A peat fire smouldered in the middle of the floor, a large blackened pot hanging above it on a chain that fell from the rafters. Sunshine slanted through the smoke-hole in the thatch, smoke from the fire hanging blue in its angled light. Beyond the fire a square wooden table was set for seven, and beyond that a door stood open in a wooden partition, affording a glimpse into what looked like it might have been a bedroom.

Granny was a tiny skelf of a woman in a dark skirt and quilted jacket. She wore a long white apron and a grey head-scarf, a bird's nest of pure white hair pulled back beneath it. She had a weathered brown face and a smile that took years off her. 'Fàilte,' she said. 'Welcome. You're just in time. The pot's as good as ready.'

Georgette glanced at the pot above the fire and wondered what on earth they were going to be served. But it smelled good. At least, what she could smell of it above the reek of the smoke.

It turned out to be lamb stew, served with potatoes. 'From

the lazy beds,' Granny told them, without explaining. They quickly got used to the smoke, and the stew tasted wonderful, and they all discovered just how hungry they were.

When they had eaten, and Granny poured them hot milky tea into big china mugs, Joan said, 'What's that place on the far side of the bay? The big white house. From the beach it looked like there was a graveyard there.'

'Baile-na-cille,' the old lady said. 'And, aye, there's a grave-yard there. Not in use any more. But they say that Coinneach Odhar was born in that house in the seventeenth century.'

Mairi frowned. 'Dark Kenneth?' This was not a story she had heard before.

'Aye, they also called him the Brahan Seer because he could see the future through the hole in an adder-stone. They say that he predicted the Battle of Culloden, and the Highland Clearances, and many things still to come.'

Alasdair grinned. 'You're making it up, Granny.'

She turned a scowl in his direction. 'I am not! He was a Mackenzie. Same as us. You can follow the line of descent right down through the centuries.'

Mairi laughed then. 'Oh, Granny, you're not telling us you can see the future, too?'

The old lady shook her head. 'No, I can't see the future, *a ghràidh*. But sometimes I can see light around people. A little like a halo. Or darkness. Like cloud or mist. The light augers well, the darkness does not.'

'You've never told us this before,' Mairi said.

'I didn't want to scare you when you were children. But ask your folks. They know.'

Alice said, 'Do you see light, or darkness, around any of us?'

Alasdair stood up. 'Not a good idea,' he said. 'If we want to get kite-flying again, we'd better get out before the tide's in.'

But no one stirred from their seats. Granny said, 'There's only one among you who has the darkness.' Her eyes flickered unmistakably towards Georgette, and Georgette felt a creeping coldness envelop her, like the mist rising from a river at dawn.

Mairi was on her feet in an instant. 'Alasdair's right,' she said, 'the tide'll be in soon. Come on, before we lose the day.'

They all tumbled out, blinking, into the afternoon sunshine, the wind, if anything stiffer now, blowing away the smoke and the old lady's words. But Georgette still felt the chill of them, and had lost her appetite for kite-flying. As the others retrieved their kites from the jeep, she said, 'I'm going for a walk. See you later.' And she set off among the dunes. The girls stopped and exchanged glances, aware of the sobering effect on Georgette of what the old lady had told them. Mairi looked at Alasdair and in a barely discernible flick of her head indicated that he should go after her.

Georgette strode through the spiky long grass, feet sinking in soft sand, hugging her arms around herself for comfort, and was not aware for the first few strides of Alasdair falling in step beside her. She looked around in surprise, and the sheer openness of his smile lifted her spirits. He said, 'Pay no attention to Granny. She's been scaring folk all her life.'

She shrugged it off unconvincingly. 'I don't believe in that stuff anyway.'

'Of course not. Why would you? None of us knows what's going to happen. Especially with the world in the state it's in now. We've all got a cloud hanging over us. It's called war.' They walked some way before he spoke again. 'When my training's over and I get deployed on some mission, I don't *expect* to come back. I hope I do. But I'm not going to be thinking about that. I'm going to be focused on getting the job done. And if I come back in one piece, they'll send me off on another. Like those brave young men dying in the skies over the south of England right now, the only reward for staying alive is getting sent out to risk being killed all over again.' He shook his head. 'In wartime, we can only live in the moment, George. But it's not a bad way to live your life at any time.'

She nodded mutely, and they walked in silence for some minutes. Beyond the dunes they could see the ocean rushing in across the wide, naked expanse of golden sand. It was no more than a foot deep, frothing and gleaming turquoise in the afternoon sun.

'What are they training you for?' she asked at length.

'No idea. And I couldn't tell you even if I knew.'

'What kind of training is it?'

'Same as you girls, I imagine, but tougher probably. Armed

and unarmed combat. How to stay alive. To kill your enemy before he can kill you.'

Suddenly she stumbled and fell in the sand, and he stooped quickly to help her to her feet.

'Silly!' She laughed and brushed the sand from her slacks, and found that he was still holding her arm. Straightening up, her face was very close to his, and she searched the depths of those blue, blue eyes in search of the soul that lay behind them. He returned her gaze, unblinking, and his intensity frightened her. Had they held the look a moment longer, she was sure they would have kissed. But she forced herself to break eye contact and turned to wade off again through the dunes. In a handful of strides he was at her side again.

There was a tension between them now that almost crackled in the wind. She was frightened to look at him.

'Are you scared?' she said finally.

'God, yes.'

She looked at him quickly and saw that he meant it. She was surprised. Big boys didn't admit to being scared. 'Me, too,' she said.

'But I'm good,' he added. 'At what I do, I mean. So the other fella should feel a lot more scared than me.'

The tide was fully in now, and in the far west there were clouds gathering along the horizon. The girls had long ago packed in the kite-flying, and they were lying on the machair in the lee of the jeep, soaking up the sun. Joan and Rebecca were smoking, watching how the wind made the ends of their cigarettes glow, and whipped the smoke from their mouths.

Georgette and Alasdair had been gone for over an hour and Mairi was becoming agitated. She kept glancing at her watch and scouring the dunes for any sight of them. 'Where are they?'

'Relax,' Alice said. 'They've probably found a sheltered spot somewhere and are having wild sex.'

The others laughed, but Mairi didn't smile. 'That's what I'm worried about.'

Joan dunted her. 'Hey. Calm down, Mairi. It's what boys and girls do.'

'He's my brother,' she said through clenched teeth.

Rebecca said, 'He's a big boy, Mairi. I'm sure it wouldn't be his first time.' But Mairi just scowled.

It was fully fifteen minutes or more before they saw the diminutive figures of Georgette and Alasdair making their way back through the dunes. They were arm in arm and laughing, and chatting away like they'd known one another all their lives.

Mairi scrambled to her feet. 'Where have you been?' She ran suspicious eyes over them both. 'You're covered in sand.'

Georgette began brushing the golden grains self-consciously from her clothes and shaking them from her hair. 'We found a sheltered spot on the far side of the headland and just lay in the sand talking.' She looked at Alasdair. 'Didn't we?'

Alasdair said, 'Didn't realise it had got so late.' He checked his watch. 'We'd better get back.'

Joan and Alice and Rebecca exchanged looks and cast envious glances at Georgette as they all piled into the jeep. But Mairi managed somehow to squeeze herself between Alasdair and Georgette in the front, scowling at her French friend as her brother swung the jeep around and accelerated along the track towards the road.

The drive back seemed to take longer than the journey there, and spirits which had so soared earlier in the day were dampened now. There was very little conversation, and each of them was aware of the cloud bank moving in from the west. What had once seemed like innocent white clouds bubbling along the horizon had darkened and assumed a portentous air, laden with the promise of rain.

Sunday blew a hoolie, as Mairi described it to the others, black clouds rolling off the moor from the west, lashing Stornoway with relentless rain that darkened the stone of the castle. By Monday morning the wind had died down, but the rain still fell in a steady, monotonous tattoo.

The girls stood in a knot at the rear of the castle. They were all soaked through and depressed to be back, even before Sergeant Connolley sent them off on their three-mile run through the woods, laden once more with weighted rucksacks. When they returned he took Georgette's rucksack and loaded it with more stones and told her to do it again.

'I did warn you we'd need to double up on your training,

Pig Nall,' he said. 'And who knows what two days off will have done to your fitness.'

Mairi and Rebecca, and Joan and Alice, glowered at him in the rain, but Georgette hefted the rucksack on to her back and set off without a word.

At lunch they sat once again in silence, a shadow having fallen somehow over their sense of togetherness. And they couldn't help but be aware of the animated conversation going on at Connolley's table on the far side of the dining room.

'I'm sick of it,' Alice said suddenly. 'This isn't what I signed up for.' She had been recruited, she'd told them, by an uncle who wasn't really an uncle, but a good friend of her father's, because of her language skills and physical fitness. She was a member of a local harriers club, and had won a steeplechase somewhere. Connolley had let her off lightly last week because of her ankle, but she was back now on full training.

'I suppose,' Joan said, 'that any of us could quit any time we wanted.'

Alice shook her head. 'I couldn't let my dad down. He'd be mortified.'

And Georgette knew that even if she wanted to, there was no way she could quit.

After lunch they assembled as usual on the lawn in front of the castle. It had stopped raining finally, but a bruised and battered sky hovered low over Stornoway and held the threat of more to come. The Minch lay brooding darkly beyond the town, the colour of polished pewter.

'Pig Nall, step out!' Connolley barked, and Georgette moved sullenly forward to join him. He turned towards the others. 'The fastest way to end an unarmed fight is to disable your opponent. Any way you can. None of you girls is likely to be able to knock anyone out. But you want to aim for your opponent's face, hit him as often and as hard as you can. That serves three purposes. First, a good head shot will stun anyone. Second, it'll put him on the defensive. Third, it'll knock him off balance. But here's the thing to remember. A skull is hard as hell, and will do as much damage to your hand as your hand can do to it. So aim for the softest spot. Anyone know what that is?'

'The nose,' Mairi said.

'Right. A good blow to the nose will bloody him and bring tears to his eyes so that he can't see you properly. So we're going to take a look at how to cut through your opponent's defences to achieve a face strike.'

He half turned towards Georgette and was completely unprepared as she leapt from his blind side on to his back, legs locking around his midriff. Her right arm crooked itself instantly around his neck, her right hand locking on to her left bicep, her left hand pressing hard against the back of his head. By pulling her elbows together she was able to bring huge lateral pressure to bear on both sides of his neck.

Caught on the turn, Connolley was off balance, and the unexpected weight of her on his back caused him to stumble and fall. Fortunately for Georgette they landed side-on, before he managed to roll on to his back, trapping her beneath him. But her legs were still firmly crossed around his middle, and no matter how he bucked and kicked, he couldn't break the lock she had on his neck.

His weight on top of her was crippling, but she knew she only had to hold on for a few seconds more. Ten at most and he would start to lose consciousness, the blood supply to his brain from the carotid arteries cut off by her chokehold.

She heard the girls screaming, uncertain whether they were cheering her on, or shouting at her to stop. She felt the fight going out of the sergeant, and knew that a black cloud was descending on him. A second or two more and he would be gone. A second or two more than that and he would be dead.

She released her hold and tried to push him away. For a moment he was like a dead weight. Then he coughed and sputtered, gasping for breath, and rolled over to pull himself to his knees, leaning forward on clenched fists. Georgette staggered to her feet, standing over him, breathing hard, exultant. 'You're right, sergeant,' she shouted at him. 'No man expects a girl to be able to upend him. And maybe that's his weakness.'

He turned a murderous face towards her. 'You damn near killed me, you fucking bitch.'

Georgette looked towards the castle and saw Connolley's fellow NCOs at one of the tall windows. They weren't laughing now. She looked back at the sergeant. 'You're fucking lucky I didn't.'

*

Beer bubbled in the necks of short brown bottles as the girls chinked the glass and tipped back their heads to suck down the cold frothing liquid. Nothing had tasted quite so good to Georgette in a very long time. They were huddled together in her attic room, the rest of the castle asleep now. Somehow Mairi had managed to smuggle in five bottles that Alasdair had acquired for them, and this was the first chance they'd had to be all together to drink them since the incident that afternoon.

Training had been abandoned for the rest of the day, and Georgette summoned to the colonel's office on the first floor. He had delivered what he imagined was a dressing-down as she stood to attention. But she'd barely heard a word. Wasn't listening. In retrospect the only things she could remember were his whining voice telling her that she was only here as a *favour for the French*, and that she was an *ungrateful little minx*. She didn't care any more. Making her run six miles a day with stones on her back and throwing her repeatedly on to wet grass in front of the castle was not going to make her any more capable of performing the task de Gaulle had set her. She was glad to have humiliated the bully Connolley in front of his peers, and in front of the girls. He had so richly deserved it.

But she had learned something, too. Something about herself that scared her more than she would admit. That she was capable of killing another human being. A few seconds longer and the sergeant would have been dead, and she knew that she had actually wanted to do it.

In the end, though, she was happy that she hadn't. To him,

the humiliation was probably worse than death, and it would live with him for the rest of his days.

'Where the hell did you learn to do that?' Joan whispered, full of admiration.

Georgette grinned and glanced at Mairi. 'Your brother,' she said.

Mairi frowned. 'Alasdair?' She was incredulous. 'When?'

'Saturday. On the beach beyond the dunes.'

Rebecca's jaw was gaping. She said, 'We thought you and he were . . . you know . . . ?'

Georgette laughed. 'I'm sure that was what Alasdair was hoping for, too. But I made him spend the whole hour teaching me that chokehold. It's called a figure-four variation, apparently. One of the things he was taught in training. We did get up close and personal. I mean, I spent half the time with my legs wrapped around him. But maybe not in quite the way he'd imagined.'

Mairi burst out laughing, to a chorus of shooshes from the others, and her hand shot to her mouth to mute her mirth. She was clearly relieved. When she got herself under control again she said, 'George, where did you learn to swear like that?'

'My mother,' Georgette said. 'She was Scottish.'

Georgette lay awake in the dark, tired and strangely fulfilled, but unable to sleep. The events of the day were going round and round in her head, and she couldn't help but speculate on what tomorrow would hold for her.

As so often happens when you think you can't sleep, it creeps up on you unawares. A banging on her door startled her awake, and she wondered how long she'd been out. It was still pitch-dark, and she blinked the grit from her eyes as the banging came again. 'Pig Nall,' a man's voice came from the other side of the door.

She slipped from the warmth of her bed, shocked by the cold linoleum beneath her feet, and opened the door. The young private who had first shown her to her room stood in the corridor. He wore a thick camouflage jacket over his fatigues, and a beret pulled down over an unsmiling face.

'Pack your bags, Pig Nall, you're leaving.'

'What? Now?'

'Now.'

It took Georgette less than ten minutes to dress and pack her few belongings in the battered old cardboard suitcase she had arrived with just a week before. There was no time for more than a splash of water on a face drawn by lack of sleep, and pale with the cold.

She hurried along the gloomy attic corridor after the private, and struggled to keep up with him on the stairs as he took them two at a time down to the ground floor.

'Where am I going?' she called breathlessly at his back.

'Ferry leaves in half an hour.'

'What?'

'You heard.'

All along the hall, night lights reflected off its polished

surface, and darkened kitchens smelled of stale cabbage. A truck was waiting for her behind the castle, its engine idling loudly in the dark, belching clouds of toxic carbon monoxide into cold night air to be whipped away by the wind.

A light shone in the cab, and the same driver who had picked her up at the quayside leaned down to give her a hand up into the passenger seat. His skin was yellow by the light of the cab, and his eyes puffy from lack of sleep. He grinned, though. 'Hello again, *mam'selle*. Been a naughty girl, I hear.'

Georgette settled her case on her knees as the private slammed the door shut behind her. 'Have I?'

'Gave some sergeant's arse a good kicking, so they say.'

She smiled palely. 'Maybe he deserved it.'

'Bet he did.' He ground into gear and swung his truck through a semi-circle and headed off between the trees on the strip of potholed tarmac that wound through them down to the town. Leaves fell like snow in his headlights. September was stating its case for an early winter.

Blackout Stornoway huddled in darkness, and moonlight made the rippled surface of the inner harbour seem almost alive. By the time they reached the outer harbour, the first light was discernible in the east, and by the time she was aboard, the whole eastern sky was ablaze. Banks of cloud close to the horizon lay in long dark baubles of blue and grey, set against a wash of red that reflected itself like fire on the water. Almost as if the island were putting on its best show to bid her farewell.

The crossing was rough, but not as bad as the outward journey, and she sat inside, squeezed into a corner trying to keep warm and catch some sleep.

It was mid-morning and fully light by the time they reached Mallaig, and she had to wait until the afternoon for the connection to Fort William. Several hours spent in the station buffet there gave her time to think about the future. Where she was going and when. No one had given her the least idea of what the next days might hold. Just onward instructions at each stop, to be followed to the letter.

Depression settled on her like dust in a still room. There was nowhere she could go to seek comfort. No one in whom she could confide, or share her fears. The impossible task that de Gaulle had set her. The dangers that awaited when finally they dropped her into occupied France. With her father, and now her mother, both dead, she was a twenty-eight-year-old orphan. There was no such place as home. No family into whose bosom she could escape. She had only herself to rely upon. She wondered if she had ever felt so small and so alone. A cork bobbing in an ocean of uncertainty, being carried along by forces over which she had absolutely no control. And it occurred to her with a stab of sadness that she would never see Mairi, or Joan, or Alice or Rebecca again. Or Alasdair. Fate had brought them together for one short week in this first year of the war and would deliver them in different ways, and different times, into uncertain futures. Who knew which, if any of them, would survive. But Georgette was the only one whose future had been seen clouded by darkness in the eyes of the old lady in the blackhouse at Uig, and she shivered with disquiet, pushing the thought to the very back of her mind.

The night train to London delivered her early into Euston Station. She thanked God that there was, at least, time for her to get back to her mother's house in South Kensington, to take a bath and change and pack fresh clothes, before being picked up early that evening and taken to some unrevealed destination.

The soldier who came to her door this time was French. But he was sullen and untalkative as he drove her out of the city and almost due south towards the coast. They frequently passed military vehicles on the road and Georgette sat beside him in the passenger seat of the black Citroën stealing occasional glances in his direction. He looked no more than twenty-three or twenty-four, stranded in a strange land, while his mother country had been occupied by a barbaric foreign invader. He could have been no happier about it than she.

'Where are we going?' she said eventually. She had seen several road signs for Chichester.

Her voice had evidently interrupted some inner dialogue, for he looked at her as if surprised to find he had a passenger. 'RAF Tangmere,' he said.

'What's there?'

'It's one of the airfields the British are using to fight off the Luftwaffe. If they can't stop the Germans in the air, it won't be long before the land invasion will come across the Channel.'

Georgette had never seriously considered the possibility of Britain falling to the Nazis. It seemed unthinkable, somehow. But neither could she imagine her precious Paris under the heel of the invader. It made her feel sick.

It was dark by the time they reached the tiny village of Tangmere, driving through its blacked-out main street, to pull up finally outside an ivy-covered cottage opposite the gates to the airfield.

'This is us,' said her driver.

'This is us where?'

'Where I've been told to drop you.' He nodded towards the cottage. 'You're expected.'

When she stepped out of the Citroën, she felt the air much softer than it had been on the Isle of Lewis, as if autumn had not yet reached the southern extremes of the British Isles. On the airfield opposite, she could see rows of planes in dark silhouette on the tarmac, the constant roar of engines as fighters came and went, the huddled shapes of hangars against a clear sky. She turned as her car drove off – her driver had not even said goodbye – and looked at this quintessentially English cottage, its ivy already turning rust red. The windows on both ground and upper floors were blacked out, and it wasn't until she knocked on the door that any light at all spilled out into the night. A young man in a leather flying jacket pulled her quickly inside to shut the door behind her. 'This way. Miss Pignal, is it?' For once someone had pronounced her name correctly.

'That's right.'

He steered her into a brightly lit sitting room. Comfortable, well-worn leather armchairs lined the walls, angled towards a large fireplace where the embers of a coal fire glowed in the hearth. Beer bottles stood along the mantelpiece, two placed on the top of a large wooden clock that was chiming as she entered. Tattered paperback and hardback books lined bookshelves along the fireplace wall. A model airplane stood on the top one, next to a framed headshot of Churchill. It was warm and welcoming here.

The young man turned and she saw him clearly for the first time. Sandy brown hair swept back from a high brow. Well-defined eyebrows and sad eyes. He reached out a hand to shake hers. 'Squadron Leader Hugh Verity,' he said. 'You can get a cup of tea in the kitchen, and change upstairs if you like. I'll be flying you later.'

This was all happening so quickly. 'Flying me where?'

'To France, of course. We'll be taking off a little after midnight. We had a full moon about three nights ago, and the forecast's good, so conditions should be perfect.'

The black-painted Lysander banked against a sky so clear Georgette felt as if she could reach out and touch the stars. She had never seen the Milky Way so well defined before, like smoke and a shower of silver sparks rising from a galaxy on fire. Moonlight had reflected itself on the dark waters of *la Manche* all the way across, and washed now over the plains of northern France which lay below in random patterns of farmers' fields and dark Loire Valley forest.

The flight had been exhilarating, but it was time now to set herself in preparation for landing. Space in the rear cockpit was tight, with the bulkiness of her coat, and barely enough room for her case. The same battered suitcase that had accompanied her all the way north to the Outer Hebrides of Scotland. There was a short ladder attached to the fuselage below her cockpit, and she knew that once they had touched down she had to get out and down it fast. She had no idea what awaited her on the ground, and as they banked again to swoop low over a freshly shorn hayfield to land, exhilaration turned to fear, and she found it almost choking her.

The landing was even bumpier than she had expected, and the Lysander seemed to bounce several times before settling its wheels to rattle over rutted ground. As it came, finally, to a stop, Verity turned, and all she saw was the palest of smiles as he said, 'Good luck.' And she was out and down the ladder, throwing her case ahead of her, and jumping the last metre. Almost before she hit the ground, she heard the squadron leader gunning the Lysander's engine and setting off to trundle it to the far end of the field where he swung it through a tight turn in preparation for taking off again.

A single dark figure emerged from the woods away to her left, and she picked up her case and hurried towards it, aware of the Lysander gathering speed behind her. She looked back momentarily as it soared off once more into the magnificence of the night sky.

She met her contact halfway towards the trees. He was a short, unshaven man in his mid-thirties, dressed in shabby country clothes and wearing a sweat-stained flat cap. He grabbed her case. 'Follow me.' And they set off as quickly as they could for the cover and safety of the woods.

It took some moments for Georgette's eyes to adjust to the sudden darkness. The man was jogging through the under-growth just ahead of her, following some kind of well-beaten animal track. They kept going until she thought her lungs would burst, before suddenly he jumped down into the bed of a dry stream and crouched among the rocks gathered along one bank. She climbed down beside him, her coat trailing among the boulders, and he put a finger to his lips.

They remained there in silence for several minutes, until their breathing had subsided. The distant drone of the Lysander's engine was gone now, and a silence so thick you could almost touch it settled on the forest.

Moonlight fell in dappled patches on the boulders all around them, and the man turned to Georgette, his face strained with tension. 'Welcome to the Free French Zone,' he said in a voice laden with sarcasm. 'Only it's not like any France you might ever have known, and it's certainly not free. I'm Lucien.'

He shook her hand, and it felt coarse and cold.

'We've not received your papers yet, so you can't go to Paris.'

'Paris? I thought the artworks had all come here, to the Loire.'

He shook his head. 'I know nothing about that. You've to go to Paris. But not yet.'

The disappointment of his words hit her hard. 'Well, what am I supposed to do?'

'We've prepared a bed for you in the attic of a farmhouse about five kilometres from here. You'll have to stay there, hidden, until your papers come.'

'How long will that be?'

'Mademoiselle, your guess is as good as mine. It could be days. It could be weeks. Even months. Who knows?'

And she felt a crushing sense of despair descend on her from the heavens.

CHAPTER SIX

Ever since lockdown had first been enforced in March, Zoom had become the universal go-to means of internet communication between friends and family. Enzo had never heard of it before, but Dominique downloaded the software, and it had rapidly developed into their daily means of communication with Kirsty in Paris and Sophie here in Cahors, at a time when no one was even allowed to leave the house. It was easy to use and you could, it seemed, have unlimited numbers of participants in a single session, their images appearing in tiles across the screen, with whoever was speaking coming automatically to the fore. Ten years ago, Enzo thought, such technology might have been considered space age. But it was now taken completely for granted. All part of what everyone was calling the *new normal*.

On this session there were just three participants. Enzo in Cahors, with Dominique looking on, and Nicole in Gaillac. Nicole had effectively been Enzo's research assistant during his investigations into the Raffin murders, his star pupil at Paul Sabatier University in Toulouse where he had established a department of forensic science. Had she ever chosen to measure it, her IQ would probably have been off the scale, and Enzo knew no one better able to winkle information out of the ether through her extraordinary manipulation of the internet. Sadly, from Enzo's perspective, she had not pursued a career in forensic science, choosing instead to marry a wine-maker she had met in Gaillac, and have what seemed like an army of children.

In fact there were only three of them. It just felt like more as they ran around behind her shrieking and throwing things. He heard Fabien's sharp admonishments in the background, the strain in his voice suggesting that paternal patience was wearing thin.

Nicole, however, appeared oblivious, chattering away at the screen without pause. It was some time since they had last spoken. He had emailed her earlier in the day, asking if she could dig up information for him on the victim and suspect in the Carennac case, then set up an evening session for them on Zoom. Now he found himself fielding a barrage of questions about Sophie and her pregnancy, Bertrand and whether or not his gym would survive the pandemic, Kirsty and Raffin and little Alexis in Paris, and of course Laurent – who was strumming Enzo's guitar loudly on the other side of the room.

'Nicole, Nicole, can we get back to the murder?' Over his shoulder he shouted at Laurent, 'Will you knock that off?' But the guitar only seemed to get louder.

'Oh, Monsieur Macleod, you're no fun. Work, work, work.

For someone who retired five years ago, you still seem obsessed by it.'

'Oh, this is brand new, Nicole,' Dominique said. 'For months he's been kicking his heels around the apartment complaining about boredom, and reminiscing about the good old days when people were trying to kill him.'

Enzo scowled at her. 'I have not!'

She laughed and told Nicole, 'At least this investigation seems unlikely to produce any attempts on his life.'

'Emile Narcisse,' Enzo said emphatically. 'What can you tell me about him?'

Nicole frowned and scanned her screen, navigating away from Zoom to her research document. 'Emile Narcisse . . .' Her eyes flickered from one side of the screen to the other. 'Born 1955, in a small industrial town called Annonay, near Lyon. Only child of an art teacher and a local *fonctionnaire*.' She refocused on Enzo. 'Did you know that Annonay was the home of the Montgolfier brothers who invented hot-air ballooning?'

'No, Nicole, I did not.' Enzo sighed. 'Emile Narcisse,' he prompted, in an attempt to get her back on track.

'Yes, yes, getting to it.' Now her head moved up and down as she scanned a document. 'Encouraged by his mother, apparently he bought his first painting at the age of fourteen. By the time he opened his private collection to public view in 2005, it comprised more than 1300 pieces. In 2008 he donated 300 paintings from his collection to the French state. Worth, at that time, somewhere in the region of 63 million euros.'

Enzo whistled softly.

'Evidently he was a man of considerable means, then,' Dominique said.

Nicole confirmed. 'His personal wealth has been estimated at more than 500 million.'

Enzo said, 'Well, there's motive straight away. Who stood to inherit?'

Nicole shook her head. 'No one. He was an only child, never married, lived alone.'

Dominique said, 'You can bet that some second cousin some-where will come crawling out of the woodwork to stake a claim.'

Nicole seemed to be flicking through more documents, her eyes darting about the screen. 'He had a gallery in New York City, and recently acquired a second Parisian gallery in the Rue des Filles du Calvaire in the Marais. Although his training was in classical art, he has traded almost exclusively for the last few years in modern contemporary, exhibiting a lot of new young American painters. He was a huge name in the world of international art, Monsieur Macleod, although you and I would never have heard of him. But he came to the attention of the general public about seven years ago, when he uncovered a haul of looted Nazi art in Switzerland.'

Dominique blew air through pursed lips. 'I remember reading about that.'

'Found in an apartment in Geneva,' Nicole said. 'It had belonged to the son of one of Hitler's art dealers, a man called Anton Weber, who had been trickle-trading them in the marketplace for years to finance a very handsome lifestyle. Narcisse had sold a number of them, unaware, he claimed, of their provenance. The discovery was made when Narcisse flew to Geneva to keep a long-standing lunch appointment with Weber. When the man failed to turn up, Narcisse went to his apartment, where he got no reply. But a smell of gas prompted him to alert the authorities. The police broke in and found him dead.'

'Suicide?'

'Apparently. But anyway, it turned out the apartment was chock-full of looted Second World War art. Much of it stolen from Jewish collectors in France by Hitler's art thieves, an organisation called ERR. Do you want to know what that stands for?' Nicole was nothing if not thorough.

'You're going to tell me anyway,' Enzo said.

'Einsatzstab Reichsleiter Rosenberg,' she said carefully. 'The Reichsleiter Rosenberg Taskforce. Alfred Rosenberg was the Nazi's chief ideologue, and he set up the ERR to appropriate cultural property from occupied countries during World War Two. In Weber's apartment there were paintings by Claude Monet, Paul Cézanne, Henri Matisse, Paul Gauguin, Edvard Munch, and lots of other star names. Worth so much they couldn't even put a figure on it. Narcisse was appointed to track down the heirs of their rightful owners, and if no heirs were found to send them to auction. Mostly they were bought by museums and art galleries, and a few private collectors.'

'With Narcisse picking up the commission, no doubt,' Enzo said.

Nicole nodded. 'Exactly. He was active in the art market right up until . . . well . . . until he was murdered. Working from his base at the Marais gallery.'

Enzo scratched his head thoughtfully. What was a man like Narcisse doing in an old lady's house in a tiny village in south-west France? He said, 'What about Hans Bauer?'

Nicole pulled a face. 'Not nearly so much online about Herr Bauer, Monsieur Macleod. Twenty-five years old. Graduate of the Universität der Künste, Berlin. That's the University of the Arts. I had to look it up. He got into a lot of trouble as a teen-ager and earned himself a conviction for assault when he was eighteen. From the newspaper cuttings I was able to find, it seems that it was only his mother's money and influence that managed to keep him out of jail. But he appears to have put his wild days behind him and is now the director of a small Berlin art gallery owned by his mother.'

A crash and a shriek drew her focus away from the screen.

'Oh God!' she said. 'What a mess!' And turned back to Enzo. 'I'm going to have to run, Monsieur Macleod. Delphine has just dropped her dinner on the floor. I think Fabien is going to kill her!'

And her screen went blank. Dominique leaned in to shut down the application and glanced at Enzo. 'So what do you think?'

He shook his head. 'No idea. But if I were to hazard a

guess – which I won't – I might think it had something to do with art.'

She grinned. 'You don't say.'

He leaned back in his seat and interlocked his fingers behind his head. 'The thing that still troubles me about the crime scene, though, is how Bauer managed to get himself covered in so much blood. I'm sure I'm missing something.' He tipped forward again. 'But we'll not get anywhere until we find out why the two of them were in that house.'

Laurent was still strumming at his father's guitar, trying to link an unlikely sequence of chords. Enzo turned and gazed at him fondly. 'Try F sharp minor 7th after the E,' he suggested.

Laurent looked at him as if he were mad. 'What?'

'Try it.'

The boy focused his concentration on making the right shape with his fingers, played his father's suggested chord once, then tried it in the sequence. His face lit up. 'That works!'

Enzo just smiled.

Dominique said, 'Will I put the fish under the grill now?'

Enzo had prepared the dish before the Zoom call. White fish fillet in lime juice and ginger with sliced white grapes. The potatoes were already boiled. 'Yes,' he said. 'Five or six minutes is all it needs. I just want to have a look at those pics I took in the house at Carennac.' And as Dominique went through to the kitchen he crossed to the table and opened up his iPad. The photographs taken with his phone had already synced and he was able to look at them more closely on the larger screen.

Again he shook his head. It made no sense. Bauer had attacked his victim face-on, slashing across his throat, probably with the missing kitchen knife. Narcisse had fallen in a pool of his own blood in the narrow passage between the table and the sink. Why would Bauer try to squeeze past, rather than make his escape through the side door behind him?

Enzo slipped half-moon reading glasses on to the end of his nose and peered more closely at the blood spatter on the floor, a frown slowly forming itself in two deep creases between his eyes.

CHAPTER SEVEN

BERLIN, GERMANY,
TEN DAYS BEFORE THE MURDER

Bauer was in his tiny office at the back of the gallery when he received the news that his mother was dead.

He replaced the phone in its cradle and tipped back in his seat, swivelling to look out of the large window that gave on to the exhibition space below. His reflection in it was pale. He thought he looked like a ghost, with his blond hair drawn back from the too white skin of his forehead. He forced himself to jump focus to the gallery beyond. White walls, white ceiling, white floor, all burned out by dilated pupils. A row of ceiling lights was angled towards the walls, and the work of an aspiring young German artist whom Bauer had discovered at the end of last year. But what should have been a startling debut exhibition had been ruined by the pandemic.

Bauer had been forced to close the gallery after the government implemented the pandemic plan of the Robert Koch Institute in March, just two days before the exhibition was

125

due to open. When restrictions were finally eased, he had only been able to reopen the gallery to view by appointment. Face coverings obligatory. But very few people had ventured in across the summer. He had promised the artist that he would keep his work on show until the end of the year. So far it had generated very little interest, and he had nothing lined up to replace it. The virus had plunged the art world into crisis and Bauer had no idea how much longer he could keep the gallery going.

He had always supposed that his mother would continue to subsidise it no matter what. Because, after all, wasn't it really her son that she was subsidising?

And now she was gone. And he probably wouldn't have to worry about money ever again.

He glanced at the laptop open on the desk in front of him, and an unfinished draft of a new website designed to raise the profile of the gallery. Maybe he would just close down and sell up. But, then, what would he do with his life?

For several minutes he sat staring at the screen, wondering why he didn't feel anything about the death of his mother. Was he really so insensitive? His eyes felt gritty, but there were no tears in them. He reached out and snapped the lid of his laptop shut and stood up. His coat and scarf hung on a coat stand by the door. He pulled them on as he ran down the stairs on long, spindly legs. The girl who welcomed visitors and took care of the gallery's administration, such as it was, looked up from her desk in surprise and seemed fleetingly guilty. She ran rapid fingers over the keyboard of her computer, and he saw her screen reflect a brighter light in her face. She'd been playing some computer game, probably, or talking to friends on social media.

'I'm going home for the rest of the day, Erika. If there are no other appointments, you might as well just close up.'

She looked pleased and smiled happily.

Outside, a cold wind blew all the way down from Boxhagener Platz. The Italian trattoria across the road, where he used to lunch almost every day, was shut. It had never reopened after the lockdown, and the tables and chairs they set out on the pavement during the summer were stacked against the front of the restaurant, dusty and forgotten.

This, he thought, was the first day of the rest of his orphan life.

Bauer's Wilhelminian-style apartment was on the third floor of a restored building on Paul-Lincke Ufer. It offered glorious views through nearly leafless trees of the canal opposite. It was not an apartment he could ever have afforded himself. His mother had bought it ten years previously as an investment and rented it out until her precious Hans had graduated from university and wanted a place of his own. Now he shared it with Lise, but he was sure that the only reason she stayed with him was financial.

His heels echoed back at him off the tiles of the building's beautifully restored entrance lobby, and all the way up the marble staircase as he climbed briskly to the third floor. He turned his key in the lock and pushed the door to the apartment open. 'Lise, I'm home.'

The sitting room was beautifully sunlit, rows of windows along the front wall divided by French doors that opened on to a terrace overlooking the street. Two sofas stood around a large wall-mounted television at one end, and Bauer kept a desk for work and his home laptop at the other. Polished floorboards were strewn with oriental rugs, and the walls were hung with startling modern works by young German and American artists. Bauer had been building his own collection since opening the gallery.

Lise was sitting at his desk, his laptop open in front of her. She looked up, startled, when he came in. He should not have been back for at least another two hours. Her face flushed. An attractive face, with slightly wide-set dark eyes and full lips. Black hair cut in a fringe hung in curtains to her shoulders to hide the bruising.

He stopped in the doorway. 'What are you doing?' He could read panic in her eyes.

'I let the battery in my iPad run down, and I needed to do a couple of internet searches.' She closed the lid of the laptop quickly and stood up. 'I didn't expect you home so soon.'

'No, you didn't, did you?' He reached the desk in three strides and lifted the laptop to crook it in his arm and throw open the lid. Fingers slid back and forth across the trackpad to launch the browser, revealing it to be open on a history of his own internet searches. He glanced up at Lise with dangerous blue eyes. He felt anger suffuse his whole body like ice-cold water surging through a sluice. 'You've been spying on me!'

She moved around the desk, keeping it between them. 'No, honestly, Hans. I was just checking my own history.'

'You have no history on this computer. Or, at least, you shouldn't.'

Her frightened rabbit eyes glanced around the room as if looking for some means of escape. The late afternoon sunshine flooding through the windows behind her cast her face in shadow. 'No, I was, honestly.'

'Don't lie to me!' His voice reverberated in the stillness of the room. 'You were fucking spying on me, weren't you?' He almost threw down his laptop and started around the desk towards her.

She moved quickly away, across exotic floor coverings that felt soft beneath her bare feet, and he broke into a run to catch her. She knew there was no escape, and lifted clenched fists to protect her face, pulling her elbows tight into her sides. He grabbed her and swung her violently across the room. She hit the wall with a sickening thud. The whiplash slammed her head back and her world filled with light and pain. As she slid to the floor she curled up in a foetal position to shield herself from his kicks, and heard herself pleading, 'Please, Hans, don't. Please. Please.'

Blinds were drawn on the last light of the day, but evening sunlight still leaked in all around their edges. Lise lay face down on the bed amidst a chaos of twisted bed sheets, her face pressed into the pillow. Her tears had long since dried up, but the occasional sob still tore itself from her chest to be muffled by duck down.

Bauer sat on the edge of the bed hanging his head in shame, hands clasped in his lap, knuckles bruised, fingers whitened by their tortured wringing. His voice was barely audible in the hushed stillness of the room. 'I'm so sorry, Lise. Honest to God, I'm so sorry. You know I didn't mean it.'

Which prompted her to roll, finally, on to her side and gaze up at him with the strangest look in her eyes. She seemed tiny and vulnerable curled up like that on the bed. In a voice even smaller, she said, 'You're always sorry, Hans. Always. You never mean it. Ever.'

He screwed up his eyes and shook his head. 'I know, I know!' He stole a glance at her. 'I don't even know why you stay with me.'

She drew a long, slow, trembling breath, summoning all of her strength and courage. 'I can't,' she said.

'Can't what?'

'Stay with you. Not any longer. I can't, Hans. I can't take it. I can't.' She had lost count of the number of times she'd said it. But this time, she swore to herself she really meant it.

'Jesus, Lise, don't leave me. It won't happen again, I promise.'

'How many times have you promised me that?'

He turned and reached out to brush the hair gently back from her face and saw the fresh bruising he had inflicted, older yellow bruising behind it, and he felt nothing but shame.

'I just don't know what comes over me,' he whispered. 'I really don't. It's like some angry red mist that just takes control. I'm not me any more. I have no way to stop it.'

She hesitated, aware that what she was about to say might stoke the flames of the anger that had prompted the attack in the first place. 'Is that why you've been doing research on the evil gene?' Which was an open admission that she *had* been spying on him.

But his shame was greater than his anger. He hung his head again. 'There's no such thing. It's a myth.'

'But you believed in it enough to search for it on the internet.'

He shrugged hopelessly. 'I just need to understand why, Lise. Why I'm like this.'

'And what did you find?'

'Nothing conclusive. Maybe some sort of genetic predisposition to violence, but' – he looked at her imploringly, as if seeking her sympathy – 'there's no one in my family that I know of with that kind of history. My dad was a mouse by all accounts. Though I barely remember him. I was only six when he died.'

'He was a lot older than your mother, wasn't he?'

'Twenty years.' He nodded. 'I know, it's a lot. She was still in her thirties when he had his second heart attack.'

'What about *his* family?'

He shrugged. 'I don't really know much about them. His mother was a gentle soul. He always had a great fondness for her. Though, of course, I never knew her. And his father died before he was even born. Happened a lot in the war, I think.'

'And your mother?'

He felt the first flush of emotion since hearing the news. Perhaps he wasn't so dead inside after all. He pressed his lips together, trying to hide it from her, but a large tear trickled down his cheek.

She frowned, stung by surprise and confusion. She had never seen Hans cry before. She sat up, concerned, in spite of everything. 'What's wrong?'

He looked away, unable to meet her eye. 'It's why I came home early,' he said. 'She passed away this afternoon.' And just saying it seemed to open the floodgates. Tears streamed down his face now. 'She'd been ill for so long, I should have been expecting it. But somehow I didn't.' He hurriedly wiped his face dry with the backs of his hands, taking a deep breath to control himself. 'I'm going to have to shut down the gallery for a while, to make arrangements for the funeral, and deal with the estate. I know she's named me as executor in her will.' He turned to gaze at her very directly and said solemnly, 'We're going to be very wealthy, Lise, you and I.'

The leaves had almost all gone from the trees in the cemetery at Mariendorf. It was little more than fifteen minutes' walk from his mother's suburban villa on Röthspitzenweg. She must have passed it many times.

A woman of strong opinions, she'd had few friends, as evinced by the handful of mourners who turned out on this bright, cold, mid-October day to bid her farewell. Bauer recognised a couple of faces, but knew none of them. Not even the pastor. His mother had not been a religious woman.

Sunshine cast the elongated shadows of semi-naked trees across the freshly dug earth as the young man in the cloth of his church muttered oft-recited banalities from the Bible for a woman he had never known.

Bauer stood apart from the others, aware once again of how little affected he was emotionally by her death. Perhaps the tears with Lise had been an aberration. Relief more than grief.

She had not accompanied him to the funeral. An excuse about a meeting at the Gorky Theatre where she worked as a make-up artist. Despite all the months of unemployment brought on by the Coronavirus, she had still been able to practise her art. On herself. After nearly two years, she had become adept at hiding the fruits of her relationship with Bauer from others.

He was glad to be on his own, though. He did not relish the idea of company going back to his mother's house after the funeral. He wanted to rake through the ashes of his past in private, wallow in his memories, cry without shame if that's what he felt like.

Although the wind was chill, there was still warmth in the sun, and he raised his face to its light, feeling it on his skin, and wondering how it was possible that the world still turned even when the woman who had borne him was gone.

Mariendorf was an upmarket suburb of south Berlin. His mother had bought a house here in the early 2000s and, stealing a playbook from the Americans, torn it down to build a large pink and white villa in its place. The house sat in extensive private grounds, and reflected echoes of the art deco period of the 1930s.

Tall narrow windows around the curve of its front wall lay long slabs of daylight across the polished floor of the huge salon beyond. Bauer wandered listlessly among the soft furnishings and lacquered Chinese cabinets with their intricate inlays of mother-of-pearl. His mother had been possessed of a passion for oriental furniture. It had always left Bauer cold.

He had spent most of his teenage years here, seething with adolescent rage, wrestling with the violent urges that had lost him so many childhood friends. Lashing out without thinking at every contradiction, every imagined slight. The gift of the apartment and the purchase of the gallery were, he was sure, his mother's way of steering him towards a safe and responsible career, and away from the violence that had led to his conviction for assault as an eighteen-year-old. A stupid fight in a bar to impress a girl who was not even interested in him. A fight that he had taken a step too far.

And it had worked. To all intents and purposes he appeared, to those who knew him, to be a serious and responsible young man carving out a career for himself in the world of modern art. His violence was private now, taking place only behind closed doors.

He shied away from thoughts of the damage he had inflicted on the girl he professed to love. He really didn't mean to harm her, and the pain of regret each time he did was almost overwhelming.

Light refracted through frosted glass in the semi open-plan kitchen, and lay in dappled patches all across the work surfaces that his mother had kept shiny clean. He opened the fridge and took out one of the bottles of beer she'd always kept for his visits, and heard the *pfft* as he removed the cap.

He drank from the neck of it as he wandered through the house from room to room. The TV room at the back, off the formal dining room. The second reception room on the east side. Walls hung with paintings that were not to his taste. She had been very traditional.

A wide, polished timber staircase curved up to a first-floor landing that ran like a gallery around the entrance hall below. He hesitated for a moment at his old bedroom door before pushing it open to revisit the unhappy Hans he had been through all his miserable adolescence. Nothing had changed, though it was some years since he had slept here. The same teenage posters on the walls. Heavy metal bands and goth idols. His own electric guitar mounted on the wall above his bed. She had bought it to indulge him, as she did with everything. He had abandoned trying to play it within a week.

On a chest of drawers sat a threadbare old teddy from his childhood. She must have found it in a cupboard or a box somewhere and put it on display to remind her of the polite little boy he had been before he grew into a monster.

There was very little of himself that he recognised in this

room. Someone he had been once, in another life that he had no desire to revisit. He closed the door very firmly on that part of him that was gone.

His mother's room, by contrast, was full of her. That familiar aromatic fragrance of roses and honey. Her silvered hair clinging to the teeth of a comb on the dresser. At some point after the bed had been made, and before she had been taken to the hospital, she'd lain down on it, leaving a perfect impression of her body in the softness of the quilt, and of her head pressed into the pillow. Bauer was almost spooked by it. As if her death was somehow a hoax, and she was still here, watching him as he voyaged through a life they had once shared.

He moved quickly into the little bureau off the bedroom where she kept all her documents, and administered her lonely existence. A deep desk drawer revealed hanging folders which he laid out one by one on the desktop. Bills, insurance policies, the original architect's plans for the house. A valuation of it that she had recently requested from a local estate agent, perhaps suspecting that she was not long for this world. A cool 1.4 million euros. He exhaled softly. He was almost certain to inherit. Even after death taxes, it would be a small fortune. Taking his apartment and the gallery into account, her property portfolio alone would make him rich. He found himself suffused with a guilty sense of pleasure.

He knew that she had inherited considerable wealth from his father, though Bauer knew precious little about how Klaus Bauer had made his money. He knew, too, that she had kept items of value – jewellery, bonds, and probably cash – in a safe behind a Rubens reproduction on the wall. Although she had gone to some lengths to conceal it from him, he also knew that she kept the combination taped to the underside of the middle desk drawer. Parents always believed that they could hide things from their children, and invariably under-estimated them.

With the Rubens resting on the floor, he heard tumblers click as he turned the combination lock on the safe, until finally the door swung open and he was struck by an odd fusty smell of age.

There was, as he had expected, a jewellery case, and a port-folio of government bonds that on the briefest flick-through seemed to offer the prospect of handsome financial rewards. But he was surprised by an old shoebox, barely intact, that he lifted down to place carefully on the desk. Written in old-fash-ioned script along one end of it was his father's name. *Klaus Bauer*. One by one, he took out the items it contained and laid them beside the box. A collection of letters, franked with dates in the thirties and forties, and still in their original envelopes, yellowed now and brittle with age, tied together with a faded pink ribbon. Half a dozen black, leather-bound notebooks. The elastic band which held them had lost its elasticity, crum-bling and breaking apart at his touch. Rolled up together were a number of official documents. Again, the elastic that held them broke, and he unrolled them to smooth open on the surface of the desk. They were birth and death certificates.

Bauer pulled up a chair to examine them more closely. Mostly these were names he did not recognise. But here was his father's birth certificate. Klaus Bauer, son of Lisbeth Bauer and . . . Bauer paused and frowned. His father's father was listed as one Karlheinz Wolff. A man whose name had not passed to his son. Klaus, it seemed, had taken his surname from his mother. Bauer shuffled through the remaining certificates, but there was no further mention anywhere of Karlheinz Wolff.

Bauer turned to the bundle of letters in their pink ribbon. But something prevented him from untying them immediately. He had the oddest sense of tinkering with destiny. Released from their broken elastic band, the notebooks lay in an untidy pile. He lifted one to flick through it and realised immediately that it was a diary of some sort. But again he was reluctant to read, as if somehow he might be about to uncover secrets best left in the dark, where they had remained for all these years in his mother's wall safe.

But when a folded sheet of aged and brittle paper dropped from between the pages of the diary he was holding, temptation finally overcame him. He lifted it, and with faintly trembling fingers gently released the folds to reveal that this, too, was a letter. Addressed to his father. Bauer's eyes dipped to the foot of the page to see that it was from his father's mother, Lisbeth.

Dearest Klaus,

All your life I have wanted to tell you the truth, but courage failed me. I feel wretched for leaving it this long, and taking the coward's way out by reaching to you from beyond my grave. Please forgive me.

You might, by now, have seen your original birth certificate. If you have, please know how sorry I am. I'm afraid the one you have always possessed was changed by me at a later date, to list your father as 'unknown'. You will see from the original that your father was a man called Karlheinz Wolff. Karlheinz was married, with a family of his own, but during the last war he and I were lovers, and I have never loved another man since. I listed him as your father, not only because he was, but because I didn't want to let him go. On his final leave, in the spring of 1944, he and I spent a wonderful week together in the Black Forest. It was rumoured then that the Allies were about to invade, and we had no idea when next we would be together. By the time I received word that he had been declared missing in action somewhere in France, I knew that I was pregnant. I hoped against hope that the news from France was wrong, but I never saw him again and swore that I would never marry another man.

Later, I regretted having put his name on your birth certificate. During the war years, Karlheinz had been in the employ of Hermann Göring, and after the war it would not have been politic to make public a connection with the head of the Luftwaffe and the creator of the Gestapo. In the post-war confusion it was a simple matter to have your birth certificate amended. I did it to protect us both.

So now you know the truth, and I can rest easy in eternity knowing that finally you are aware of your true heritage. I am leaving you his letters to me, and his diaries which he left with me on that final visit, so that you might get to know him better.

My darling, Klaus, I have loved you with all my heart, as I loved your father before you. God keep you safe.

Your loving mother,
Lisbeth

Bauer's whole hand was trembling now as he reread the letter, not once but twice. So his father had been illegitimate. A family scandal. The fruit of an adulterous liaison. And *his* father had worked for Hermann Göring. He could only imagine how anxious his grandmother would have been in the post-war years to keep that connection to herself. But Bauer felt an odd sense of providence in it, in his own connection with history. Just three degrees of separation.

He lifted one of the diaries, and ran fingertips over the cracked leather binding. The temptation was to open them immediately. To start reading. To get to know the man who had fathered his father. But he hesitated. That could wait. He wanted to find out more about him first. To place him in time and history, to have a context for the reading of his own words. Bauer's excitement was breathless. He was the grandson of Karlheinz Wolff, a trusted associate of the infamous Hermann Göring.

CHAPTER EIGHT

Sophie's pallor seemed all the more marked in contrast with the darkness of the hair that fell about her face. Her eyes seemed darker, too, and sunk in shadow. She'd had a sleepless night.

Their breath, diffused by masks, misted about their heads in the cold air as they stood on the step outside the maternity unit on this chill October morning. Enzo pulled the door open. Sophie hurried inside. Dominique was about to follow when the younger woman turned and raised a hand. 'It's okay. I'd rather be on my own.'

Dominique exchanged a quick look with Enzo. 'Are you sure?'

'If it's bad news I'd rather hear it by myself.'

'Darling, it won't be bad news,' Enzo said.

The palest of smiles didn't even reach beyond Sophie's mask. 'Bertrand will be back as soon as he's parked the car. Just be here for us when we come out. Shouldn't be any more than about thirty minutes.' And she vanished inside.

Enzo and Dominique stood in silence for nearly a minute

before Enzo looked at his watch. 'We won't have long to see the pathologist, then. Better hurry.'

They turned down the Rue Wilson towards the Valentré and turned left along the bottom end of the hospital. Neither of them wanted to talk about the cramps which had kept Sophie awake the previous night, or Bertrand's panicked call for help at 6 a.m. His face had been even more bloodless than Sophie's when he drew up outside the Lamparo, where Enzo and Dominique were waiting for them on the pavement. Almost forty now, Bertrand's visage still bore the scars of the long-discarded studs and rings which had adorned it when he first started dating Sophie – to Enzo's horror. But after a prickly start, the old stag and the young buck had won each other's respect and were now more like father and son. Enzo would have done anything for him. But he was powerless to prevent the possibility of his losing another baby, and he shied away from the very thought of it.

Dominique said, 'You're sure the pathologist won't mind me sitting in?'

Enzo shrugged distractedly. 'She's an old friend.' It was hard to concentrate on the Carennac case when his daughter was facing the prospect of a third miscarriage. But it would, at the very least, provide another focus to prevent him obsessing about it. Thirty minutes standing on the steps outside the maternity unit would have felt like a lifetime.

'This is highly irregular, Enzo.' Dr Laurence Vidal was not tall. She sat on a desk swinging her legs in this tiny office on the first floor of the main hospital block. She was already kitted up with shower cap, gown and mask for the post-mortem she would conduct in the autopsy suite in just a few minutes' time. She kept her mask in place. A handsome woman, somewhere in her forties, green eyes smiled in a strong, quizzical face. She laid aside her briefing notes and submitted Enzo to careful scrutiny. 'It's not fair,' she said. 'You just keep improving with age. Unless you're hiding something beneath that mask, you're looking even better than you did in the days when you used to chase me round the lab.'

In spite of himself, Enzo blushed and glanced self-consciously at Dominique. 'She's joking,' he said.

Dr Vidal swung an enquiring gaze towards Dominique. 'And who's this?'

'Dominique. My wife.'

The pathologist's eyebrows flew up on her forehead. 'You're kidding? You got married? When?'

Dominique said, 'As soon as I could persuade him to stop running around solving cold cases and putting himself in harm's way.'

The doctor smiled. 'Then you succeeded where the rest of us failed.' There was a twinkle in her eye.

Enzo shuffled awkwardly. 'Laurence, we don't have much time.'

'Neither do I,' she said, jumping down from the desk to lift another file from the cabinet opposite. 'I did the autopsy on Narcisse yesterday afternoon, and I'm not at all sure I should be sharing my findings with you, Enzo.'

'I *am* officially consulting on the case, Laurence. If you want to call Capitaine Arnaud . . .'

She waved a hand to cut him off. 'Yes, yes, yes, I believe you.' Though there was the merest flicker of her eyes towards Dominique.

Enzo said, 'Dominique was a gendarme for over fifteen years. She's co-consulting with me.'

Dr Vidal nodded, but looked less than convinced. Still, she opened the file in her hands. 'The victim was killed by a single, fatal cut across his neck. Whoever did it meant business, Enzo. Not just to threaten, or fight him, but to kill him. Unequivocally. My guess is that the killer was standing right in front of him. There were no cuts on the victim's hands or arms, or anywhere else. No contusions, or anything to suggest that he was in a fight or had tried to defend himself.'

'So he wasn't expecting the attack,' Enzo said.

She shook her head. 'It would appear not.' She turned a page. 'There was just one wound. And it was huge. A cut that ran across the left and front of his neck, completely transecting the left common carotid artery. That was bad enough, but the blade also got the left external and internal jugulars, and cut the left sternocleidomastoid muscle.'

Enzo turned to Dominique. 'That's the big muscle that you see running diagonally across your neck when you turn your chin to the side.' And he turned his head to demonstrate.

'Thank you for the anatomy lesson, Dr Macleod.' Wry amusement turned up the corners of the pathologist's eyes.

She returned to her notes. 'Several strap muscles were also severed, and the blade cut halfway through the bottom of the Adam's apple and the top of the windpipe. Narcisse didn't have a chance. He would have lost blood pressure to the brain very quickly and gone down. I haven't seen photographs of the crime scene, but it must have been a bloody mess.'

Enzo nodded. 'It was.'

'He wouldn't have lasted very long. Not least because of a large air embolism from the jugular injuries.' She looked up from her notes. 'Air got drawn into the veins, went straight to the heart and filled the right side of it.' She shook her head. 'It wouldn't have pumped too well after that.' Now she closed the file and dropped it on to the desktop. 'It was a devastating cut, Enzo, made with a good sharp blade, by a strong killer, or both.'

Enzo was thoughtful. 'So apart from the fact that the killer was a powerful individual, is there anything else you might be able to tell us about him?'

But Dr Vidal immediately retracted. 'I'm sorry, I shouldn't have said that. I wasn't really thinking. I can't tell you anything about the killer, actually, not even that he was a powerful person. I make deep cuts on people every day when I open them up for autopsy, and it doesn't take much force at all. I just guide the knife. As long as it is razor-sharp, the blade itself does ninety per cent of the work.'

Enzo remembered the self-sharpening knife block on the worktop in the kitchen and the missing chef's knife.

Dominique said, 'Can you say if he was right- or left-handed?'

Enzo smiled apologetically from behind his mask. 'Dominique was an excellent investigator, Laurence, but not hugely experienced in murder.'

Dominique flushed with confusion and embarrassment.

Dr Vidal waved a hand dismissively. 'Of course I can say that he was right- or left-handed. Isn't everyone?' She smiled at Dominique. 'I just can't say which.' She started pulling on latex gloves, and Enzo reached into his shoulder bag to pull out a large buff envelope.

'I've printed off some photographs I took at the crime scene, Laurence. I'd really appreciate your thoughts on the blood spatter.'

'Very quickly, then. Though I imagine your expertise on blood spatter patterns is far greater than mine.'

'Perhaps,' Enzo said. 'But you've probably seen a great deal more blood than me.'

He spread his printouts across the desktop and the pathologist leaned over to cast an eye across a bloody scene made more lurid by the colours of the inkjet.

Enzo said, 'You can see the spatter patterns on the floor left by the blood gouting under pressure from the initial cut.' He pointed to another of the prints. 'And here, where it pooled. The police think those skid marks were made by the killer slipping and falling in his panic to get out of the house.'

'That was careless of him,' the doctor said.

'Very.' Enzo shuffled through the printouts until he found

the ones he was looking for. 'I've blown these up.' He stood back. 'What do you think?'

The pathologist leaned over to examine several close-ups of tiny peripheral blood drops around the edges of the main event. Some were intact, others smeared by what must have been the killer's feet. She glanced round at Enzo. 'What am I looking for?'

He ran a finger across several of the smeared droplets. 'If you look carefully, you can see that the outer rings of these droplets are more or less intact, while their centres have been smudged, or dragged, or smeared by the feet of the killer.'

Dr Vidal gasped realisation through her mask. 'Jeez,' she said. 'Nothing gets by you, Enzo, does it?'

Dominique peered at the droplets and frowned. 'What are you guys seeing that I'm not?'

Enzo said, 'Blood dries relatively quickly. The outer edges of droplets like these would probably dry within two to three minutes. The centres would take longer.'

Dr Vidal said, 'Sometimes, during autopsy, a drop or two of blood will get spilled on the floor. If I crouch down to wipe them up a few minutes later, the first swipe will smear most of the drop away. But the dry edge remains, and will take another wipe, or even a scrub to remove it.'

Understanding dawned on Dominique. 'So the killer didn't try to make his getaway immediately.'

'Correct,' Enzo said. 'The outer droplets were already partially dried. It must have been several minutes, or more, before he tried to make his escape. So the whole notion that Bauer panicked and slipped in the blood in his hurry to get out of the house immediately after the murder makes no sense.'

'What does it mean, then?'

Enzo started gathering up his prints. 'I have no idea.'

Dr Vidal opened the door. 'I'm sure you'll keep me informed, Enzo. But right now I have a date with a corpse.'

Enzo and Dominique were hurrying back up the Rue Wilson when Sophie and Bertrand emerged from the maternity unit. They could tell immediately from the smiles of relief on the young couple's faces that their worst fears were unfounded. Sophie threw her arms around her father and buried her face in his chest.

'Papa, I was so scared.'

'What did they say?' Dominique said.

It was Bertrand who responded. 'That it was a particularly severe case of what they called Braxton-Hicks contractions. A tightening of the uterus. They weren't too worried, as long as there were no signs of blood or the waters breaking.'

Sophie said, 'They did another scan, and the baby's fine.'

Enzo didn't want to let her go. 'Thank God,' he breathed into her hair. She clung to him just as tightly as he held on to her, and he remembered all those times when she was just a little girl, and she'd had a fall, or something had upset her, and she would attach herself to him like a limpet and not want to release him. Ever.

Bertrand said, 'The car's miles away. Will you wait with Sophie while I go and get it?'

Sophie finally liberated her father. 'I can go with you.'

'You sure?' Bertrand's concern was obvious.

'I'm not an invalid,' she protested. 'Take my arm and we'll go slow.'

Enzo said, 'Dominique and I will just walk back to the apartment, then.'

He watched Bertrand and Sophie as they ambled arm in arm together to the foot of the street and turned out of sight. He sighed audibly and Dominique squeezed his arm. 'She'll be fine,' she said.

Enzo stared down the Rue Wilson towards the river and the bridge, and saw mist rising into the trees on the far side of it. 'I don't know what I'd do if anything happened to her.'

Dominique said, 'So maybe it's a good thing that you've got this Carennac case to distract you.'

He nodded absently. 'Maybe.' He sighed again and turned towards Dominique to take her in his arms. 'And I don't know what I'd do without you.'

She smiled. 'Chase young pathologists round the lab, probably.'

Which brought a sheepish grin to his face. Then the smile slowly faded. 'I'm going to head back up to Carennac this afternoon. I want to take another look at that crime scene. And I'd like to talk to the old lady. Anny Lavigne.'

'Want me to come with you? We could take Laurent with us, and I could walk him round the village.'

He shook his head. 'I want you here in case anything happens with Sophie. No matter how much she loves her dad, it's a mother she needs at a time like this.'

CHAPTER NINE

A plumbing crisis at the apartment had delayed Enzo's departure, and it was early evening by the time he drove into
Carennac. Lights burned in the Fenelon as he cruised slowly
along the village main street. Its terrace was deserted, and
through double glass doors he could see that the restaurant
was empty, too.

Mist formed yellow halos around the street lights, and rose
up from the river as he parked on the palisade. There was not
another vehicle in sight, nor a light in any of the windows
of the château, or the houses that clustered around it. Mired
in an autumn fog, the village seemed spectral in the dark,
emerging phantom-like from centuries past. But Enzo could
smell woodsmoke in the cold, damp air, so the village had not
been entirely abandoned to history.

He buttoned his coat up to the neck and briskly climbed the
narrow street opposite the post office towards Anny's house.
Medieval stone buildings rose on either side, leaving only a
sliver of sky on view above. A gibbous moon was veiled, its
light diffused by brume as he emerged into the metalled area

before the park. The gnarled, misty silhouettes of ancient trees stood stark against the night sky all along the railing above him, the stone cross at the gate casting its moon shadow long over the tarmac.

He wondered if he should have told Arnaud that he was coming in case the house had been locked up. It was a crime scene, after all. But he did not want to share his thoughts just yet with the gendarme, and in any case he need not have worried. Although a criss-cross of crime-scene tape had been stapled across the doorway, when he reached the landing at the top of the steps, the front door of Anny's house opened at the turn of its handle. He pushed it into darkness.

The house breathed softly in his face. The faint perfume of stale cooking, and body odour, and damp. And the unmistakable metallic smell of blood. Enzo ducked under the tape and stepped inside, realising immediately that this is how it would have been for Narcisse as he had entered the house just a couple of nights earlier. It was around the same time. And stepping from street lights outside into the dark was like walking blind into the unknown. Or, in the case of Narcisse, to meet his maker.

Enzo left the door open at his back and took three short steps into the kitchen before his fingers found the table on his right. Still he could see nothing, his eyes taking an age to make the adjustment. This must have been just about as far as Narcisse had come before the blade came out of the darkness to cut open his throat.

A noise somewhere in the kitchen ahead of him brought his heart pounding up into his throat and he froze on the spot. In a moment of blind panic he imagined the same blade that killed Narcisse arcing out of the night to take his life, too.

'Who's there?' His voice died in the stillness the instant it left his mouth. He was greeted by silence.

He turned quickly, stepping back towards the door, and found the light switch. Harsh yellow light flooded the kitchen and he saw, back arched, a black cat on the far end of the table, watching him with wide green eyes. Relief escaped his lips in a long breath, and he was aware of his heart hammering an erratic rhythm against his ribs. Only to be startled as the cat made a sudden and unexpected dash for the door, bills and letters and junk mail scattering in its wake.

It was gone before Enzo could turn, and he wondered if perhaps the cat had been witness to the murder. Not much use, even if it had. He stooped to pick up the bits and pieces that had fallen to the floor and saw that someone had made a clumsy attempt to wash the blood from the floorboards. And he felt a prickle of annoyance. The victim was barely cold; there had been no arrest. This was still a crime scene in an ongoing investigation. It was just as well he had taken photographs for himself.

He straightened up and saw a bloody plastic bucket and mop leaning against the far wall. Whoever had tried to erase the stains had underestimated just how stubbornly blood is absorbed into wood. In all likelihood, this physical manifestation of the murder which had taken place in the kitchen would outlast them all. An ever-present stain on the future, a reminder that here a man had died.

A man, Enzo thought, whose reason for being in this house at all remained obscure.

He stepped over the bloodstains and walked along the hall to the grand salon. Moonlight shone through all the stained glass. A dead light. The light of the night that brought illumination only in black and white. In faded fulguration and deep shadow. By its feeble luminescence, Enzo crossed the room to try the handle of the door on the far wall. It opened, allowing a wide shaft of naked moonlight to lay itself across the flagstones. Enzo broke it with his own shadow as he stepped out on to the terrace. The pavings extended to his right and broadened out into a decent-sized sitting area where chairs were tipped against a wooden table. Beyond the terrace, the old chapel and the park were washed in misted moonlight. Overhead, a Roman-tiled canopy sheltered the doorway, and to the left a stone staircase descended steeply to a narrow alleyway running between the houses, beyond the reach of street lights, and profoundly dark.

After a moment's hesitation, Enzo descended the steps to the darkness below. On his left the alley ran along the end of the house to the street beyond, where the steps Enzo had climbed to the front door only a few minutes earlier were hidden from view. He turned to his right, and using the torch app in his phone, made his way along to a sharp turn, where the path led away between gardens and houses towards the main road above the village. The abandoned Auberge du Vieux Quercy stood in silent silhouette, dominating the village below.

Immediately ahead, a small gate opened into the garden of a large house on his left. There were no lights, no signs of life in the house. Enzo tried the latch on the gate and it swung open. A stone-tiled path fell steeply away through the garden towards large double gates at the foot of the hill, some fifty metres distant. Beyond them, he could see the lights of the main street where he had driven past the Fenelon on his way into the village.

His sense of the geography of this place was sketchy, and he determined to return in daylight at some point to make himself more familiar with its layout.

He turned back towards the alley, and was startled by the eyes of the black cat from the house glowing in the light of his phone. Staring at him out of the darkness, before slinking away to be absorbed by the night. For some reason, Enzo was spooked by it, and he hurried back up the steps to re-enter the house by the side entrance, closing the door behind him and making his way rapidly through the kitchen and out again into the light of the street lamps. He turned off the house lights and closed the door.

His breath billowed about his head like smoke as he ran down the steps to the street and headed back towards the main street. At the junction of the roads he stopped, hesitating just for a moment. It was clear that Anny had not yet returned to the house, and was likely still staying at the Fenelon. He turned to his right and walked towards the light that fell from the hotel across its terrace and out on to the road.

He pulled on his face covering before pushing open one half of the glass doors and walking into the warmth of the hostelry. From a door to his right, a young man emerged to greet him from the other side of a high wooden counter. 'Table for one?' he asked, his voice muffled by his blue cotton mask.

Tempted as he was to eat, Enzo shook his head. 'I'm looking for Anny Lavigne.'

The young man nodded towards the dining room. 'Over by the window.'

In fact she was the only diner, sitting on her own at a table for two. Windows all along the far side of the dining room would, he assumed, give on to a view in daylight of the river below. But for now, only darkness lay beyond.

Enzo approached across a tiled floor and stopped a respectful two metres short of her table. She didn't see him coming, lost in some private reverie, and only looked up at the last moment. 'Mademoiselle Lavigne?' he asked.

Brown bewildered eyes looked at him uncomprehendingly. 'I'm sorry, do I know you?' she said. 'You must forgive me, my memory is not what it was.'

'No, mademoiselle, I'm sorry. It's me who should apologise for disturbing your evening meal. My name is Enzo Macleod. I'm consulting for Capitaine Arnaud on the murder that was committed in your house.'

A pained expression flitted across her face. 'Oh.' She seemed almost disappointed. 'I thought you might be someone I knew. Would you like to join me?'

'I would love to. But I have to get home tonight, and there will be food waiting for me on the table.'

'Where's home?'

'Cahors.'

She raised her eyebrows in surprise. 'That's a good hour or more away. You'll be eating late.'

He nodded. 'Also, I don't want to risk coming too close. At our age, we're both vulnerable to the virus.'

She sighed. 'Yes. I'm beginning to fear that this life we are being forced to live – masks, social distancing, friend and family bubbles – is going to see me out. And that a long and interesting life, that has taken me halfway around the world and back, will end with imprisonment in my own home.' She paused, and her frown gave way to a smile. 'At least take a seat at the next table. I'd enjoy a little company.'

Enzo pulled out a chair and sat at the far side of the next table along the window wall.

'Do you know,' she asked, 'when I'll be allowed home? I'd rather not spend my last days in the Fenelon.' And she smiled, a warm smile that twinkled in eyes that seemed now flecked with green. She ran age-spattered hands back through an abundance of silver-grey hair gathered in an untidy accumulation at the back of her head. 'It's so hard to keep up appearances without the lotions and potions and implements of destruction that one is accustomed to in one's own boudoir.'

He grinned, enjoying her self-deprecating sense of humour. 'Well, it looks like they've already made a start on cleaning up the blood.' And he stopped, realising how insensitive that was. 'I'm sorry, that must sound pretty shocking to you.'

'Monsieur Macleod, after seeing the body of that poor man lying in a pool of blood on my kitchen floor, there is very little I think that could shock me.' She paused. 'Have they managed to remove the stain from the floorboards?'

He shook his head.

'I didn't think so. Blood comes very easily out of people, but not so easily out of floors. Perhaps I'll lay a rug there.'

Enzo said, 'I think if you ask Capitaine Arnaud, they'll probably be able to let you back in sometime tomorrow.' He hesitated. 'But perhaps you'd be better giving it a little more time. I might think twice myself before moving back on my own into a house where a brutal murder has been committed.'

'Time is a commodity in short supply at my age, Monsieur Macleod. I have lived on my own ever since my mother passed. And the house is full of ghosts anyway. One more or less won't make any difference.' Again, that engaging twinkle. Then she said, 'Macleod. It's a Scottish name, is it not?'

'It is, mademoiselle.'

She threw up her hands. 'For God's sake, stop calling me *Miss*!' She used the English word. 'It makes me sound like some old spinster.' And she grinned. 'Even if I am.' She drew breath. 'Madame, or Anny will do. What's a Scotsman like you doing in France?'

'It's a long story. But I've been here for well over thirty years.'

She nodded. 'And why are you consulting on a murder?'

'Because forensic science was my speciality. Before I retired I was able to apply new science to some old cases that had been baffling the French police for years.'

'And solved them?'

He inclined his head in acknowledgement. 'Pretty much.'

'Bravo!' she said. 'So what do you want to know?'

'The capitaine told me that you'd been dining with a friend in Vayrac on the night of the murder.'

'Yes. Marie-Christine. We've known each other for years. Our mothers were friends before us.'

'She came to pick you up and then brought you home afterwards?'

'I no longer drive, Monsieur Macleod. I stopped feeling safe on the roads a number of years ago after a nasty accident. So I rely on friends now.'

'And it was when you came home that you found the body in your kitchen?'

'Yes.' Her lips paled as she pressed them together, her eyes glazed and stared off into some misted distance where she replayed the images that had greeted her that night in her own home.

'The capitaine also told me that the victim, Narcisse, had called on you earlier that same day.'

She nodded.

'You knew him?'

'Not before he knocked on my door. Knew of him, of course, as I discovered when he introduced himself.'

'What did he want?'

'He was writing a book, apparently, about Rose Valland. And he'd heard that my mother had worked with her during the war.'

'Rose Valland?' Enzo thought the name seemed familiar, but he couldn't place it.

'Rose worked at the Galerie Nationale du Jeu de Paume in Paris during the Nazi occupation, monsieur. The Nazis used it as a sorting house for all the art they were stealing from French collectors before shipping it off to Germany. Unbeknownst to them, Rose kept meticulous records of every piece that came through the gallery. Where it was sent to, and when. So that after the war, she was able to go to Germany and track it all down to restore to its rightful owners. A legend in the world of art, but little known by the public at large, alas.'

'And your mother worked with her?'

'Briefly. She later wrote a memoir of those times – never published, of course – though I don't think there was much in it that could have thrown light on the activities of Rose Valland. I told Monsieur Narcisse that I was dining out that night, but that I would look through my mother's papers in the morning, and that if he chose to return in the afternoon I would share with him anything that I had found.' She turned sad eyes on Enzo. 'It seems he returned earlier than anticipated.'

'And the German, Hans Bauer, the man police think killed him . . . ?'

She shook her head. 'I know nothing about this young man at all, Monsieur Macleod. What either of them were doing in my house is a complete mystery.' Her clear, pale skin crinkled in a frown and he thought for a moment that she was going to spill tears. 'In a way, I feel quite . . . violated by it.' And she gazed at him, a pained look in her eyes.

Enzo thought how fragile she seemed, and vulnerable, sitting on her own in this cold, empty dining room, with the bloodstains of a violent murder still fresh on the floor of the only place she had ever called home. Which made him reticent about asking his next question. But he did all the same. 'Your friend, Marie-Christine. I'd like to talk to her if I may.'

Anny seemed surprised. 'Why?'

'It's the nature of my profession, Anny. Forensics is the study of tiny details. She may have seen something that night when she came to pick you up, or on the way back. Something that hasn't even registered in her own consciousness. If you could, perhaps, let me have her address?'

'Well, of course. Though I'm not sure that she'll be able to tell you anything very much. Goes around with her eyes shut half the time, that woman.' She took out her phone to search for the address. 'I'll send you it.'

Enzo said, 'It's been an eventful week. A murder in your home, and the remains of a body unearthed in the park next door. I don't suppose you have any idea who was buried there?'

She looked up, surprised. 'Why would I? I must confess, I paid it very little attention. They say the body dates back to the forties. Whoever it was, he must have been put there before I was even born.'

Enzo's tummy was rumbling for most of the ten-minute drive across the flood plain of the Dordogne valley. Through the tiny village of Bétaille with its unique brick-built church standing proud on the hillside. And along the valley floor, following the railway line, to Vayrac. He found the Chemin Creux opposite the *quincaillerie* and drove down past an empty car park and an unfinished house with lights burning in all its windows. Someone had told him once that you didn't have to pay the habitation tax until the final skin of *crépie* had been applied to the exterior of the house. Which explained why so many new-build homes in France were lived in without their final external coating.

He parked half on the pavement beneath the feeble light of an old-fashioned street lamp, and crossed the road to climb a steep gravel path to the door of the house where Marie-Christine Bourges lived, apparently on her own.

The shutters were closed, but he could see light in the hall beyond the glass of the front door. He knocked and pulled on his face covering as he stepped back. A light came on above the door and almost blinded him, before the door itself opened and a small elderly lady in a pink dressing gown peered out from behind a mask that almost entirely covered her face.

'I can't tell you anything that I haven't already told the police,' she said, her voice muted by the mask.

Enzo was startled. 'How did you know what I was going to ask?'

'Anny called me,' she said. 'To tell me you were on your way.' She peered at him through the glare of the overhead light.

Enzo said, 'I just wanted to ask you a few questions, madame.'

'Well, you're not coming in, if that's what you think. You can stay out there and keep your distance.'

Enzo sighed and felt the first spots of rain start to fall. The moon had long since vanished behind clouds rolling in from the north-west. He would have to make this quick. 'I'm told you live on your own.'

'Widowed,' she said quickly, as if to make clear that she was not some old maid, like her friend across the valley.

'So when Anny came for dinner it was just the two of you here?'

'That's right.'

'What time did you pick her up at her house?'

'She told me to be there at 7.25.'

'That's a very specific time. Is that not a bit odd?'

Marie-Christine shook her head. 'Not for Anny, no. She watches a TV programme every night which finishes at that time. And she's not someone who likes to wait around. In fact, I was a little worried on the drive over that I might have left it late. Anny's such a stickler for punctuality. But no, I arrived at 7.25 exactly. I checked my watch.'

'So she was waiting for you?'

'Yes. Ran down the steps and jumped into the car just as I pulled up.'

'Was there anyone in the street when you picked her up?'

'I didn't see a single soul on the drive through the village, monsieur. Carennac is like a ghost town when the tourist season is over. Nor did we see anyone as we left. I drove to the top of the hill and turned on to the main road at the primary school. There was no traffic on the road there, either. In fact, I'm not sure I passed a single vehicle on the drive across the valley.'

The rain was starting to fall more heavily now. Enzo glanced up to see it streaking through the light above the door. He had to blink it out of his eyes. 'What time did you take her home?'

She frowned, thinking. 'I couldn't say exactly. It was probably a couple of hours. And it's a good thing I was driving. Anny likes a glass or two of wine.'

'So you got back to Carennac about, maybe, quarter to ten?'

'Probably about that.'

'And you dropped her off at the foot of the steps.'

'Yes. But I always watch her up the stairs and wait to see the light come on in the house before I leave. She can be a little unsteady on her feet sometimes.'

'So what happened?'

'Well, I saw her disappear into the shadows at the top of the steps. But no light came on in the house. I was about to get out of the car to see if she was alright when I heard her scream. I jumped out, then, and ran up the steps.' She paused, eyes burning with bright recollection. 'Anny was standing in the doorway. She had her phone in her hand, and by the light of it I could see a man lying on the kitchen floor. Blood everywhere. I never realised, monsieur, that blood could be so dark. It looked almost black.'

Enzo could feel the rain soaking into his jacket, rivulets of it running from his hair and down his face to drip from his chin. But his focus was still on the old lady, searching for the micro-signs that Charlotte had taught him to look for, and realising for the first time just how much facial expression is obscured by a mask. But in her eyes he saw genuine distress at the memory.

CHAPTER TEN

BERLIN, GERMANY,
ONE WEEK BEFORE THE MURDER

It was dark outside the apartment, but Bauer could see street lights reflecting on the black waters of the canal, the lights of the city beyond diffused by low-lying cloud. He turned back to his laptop which sat in a circle of lamplight on his desk. The rest of the room lay in darkness. Somewhere in the apartment he could hear Lise moving around, cupboard doors being opened and closed, drawers opening and shutting.

A cursor winked on the email that stood open on his screen. The reply from the diocesan archive in Würzburg. He had written to make an appointment to view his father's family records, and those of the man Klaus Bauer's mother had named as her son's father on the original birth certificate. Karlheinz Wolff.

An administrator had made a rendezvous for him at 9 a.m. the day after tomorrow. It was normal, it seemed, for the archive to appoint a *Mitarbeiter*, or volunteer, to help applicants navigate the labyrinthine records held by the diocese.

In this case, a woman called Greta Jung. She would meet him outside the archive building at the appointed time.

Ever efficient, the archive had provided him with her email address and asked that he scan any and all relevant documents and send them to her as PDF attachments, so that she might prepare. Several scanned documents lay on his desk, half in, half out of the circle of light. The scans themselves were selected on his virtual desktop, ready to drop into his responding email. He would fetch the remaining documents from his mother's house tomorrow and ask Lise to send them.

He clicked *Reply* to confirm the appointment and attach the first tranche of PDFs. The sent mail left a *whoosh* in its wake that moved from left speaker to right, like an audible contrail, and he navigated along the dock to select Google Maps.

The route from Berlin to Würzburg would take him via the A9 and the A71 and would be a five-hour drive. He closed the lid of his laptop and got stiffly to his feet. The only other light in the apartment came from the bedroom. He crossed the hall and pushed open the door. Lise turned, startled, from open drawers in the dresser. Folded underwear and T-shirts sat in neat piles on top of it. Had he been less distracted, he might have interpreted her nervous response to his unexpected interruption as guilt. But his mind was elsewhere.

He dropped on to the bed and said, 'I'm going to Würzburg tomorrow. I'll be staying overnight for an appointment the following morning. So I'll be gone for the best part of two days.' He paused. 'Unless you want to come with me?'

'No,' she said quickly. Then hurriedly justified her too rapid response. 'I've got a pre-production meeting at the theatre tomorrow. We're going ahead with prep in the hope that they'll let us reopen for the Christmas season.'

He nodded. Relieved, though he wouldn't have said so. This was something almost too personal, a search in the past that might shine unexpected light from history on his present. He was not sure he wanted to share whatever it might reveal.

But Lise put his thoughts into words. 'You think maybe this . . . *your* predilection for violence is inherited somehow from your paternal grandfather.'

His eyes flickered reluctantly in her direction, then quickly away again, anxious not to meet hers. 'Until I know more about him, it's impossible to say.'

'But you think it's a possibility.'

He nodded, hesitant to concede. In truth he was almost afraid to know. In some ways it would be a relief. To learn that his behaviour was conditioned by something beyond his control. But if it was, then it was in his genes, and there was nothing to be done about it.

The Bavarian city of Würzburg nestled in the valley of the River Main, capital of the administrative district of Lower Franconia. Its old town was a shambles of red roofs and spires, dominated by the Marienberg Fortress. It was drizzling as Bauer made the short walk from his hotel through the blackened trees

PETER MAY

of the Hofgarten to the archive and library of the diocese of Würzburg on Domerschulstrasse.

He had barely slept the night before, rising at 6 a.m. to pass three impatient hours in the hotel's breakfast room drinking coffee and watching twenty-four-hour TV news that repeated every fifteen minutes. But he wasn't in the least fatigued. He was buzzing from the caffeine and the anticipation. As well as his nerves.

He was early for his meeting with the *Mitarbeiter*, and paced impatiently on the pavement outside the main entrance to what was a large building of glass and steel that spilled around the corner on to Bibrastrasse. Looking up, through large windows he could see researchers sitting at desks gazing at computer screens and tapping on keyboards. Buried away on hard drives and microfiches in the depths of this building were the histories of millions of people from Central Europe and beyond, dating as far back as the 1700s. But he was really only interested in one of them, and the genetic connection that led directly to him.

'Herr Bauer?'

He turned, startled, to find himself face to face with a pretty young woman whose straight, dark, club-cut hair fell short of square shoulders, a slash of virulently red lips in a pale face. She wore a short navy-blue coat above green leggings. A yellow face mask dangled from one ear. Her smiling blue eyes were disquieting and seemed to pierce right through him. She couldn't have been much more than twenty or twenty-one. 'Yes,' he said. 'Greta Jung?'

She nodded and looped her mask over her other ear.

He felt suddenly self-conscious not to be wearing his and quickly dug it out of his pocket. 'Are we going straight in?'

She shook her head and patted an orange folder under her arm. Everything about her seemed painted in primary or secondary colours. 'No need. I did all the necessary searches yesterday, but really most of what you need to know about your grandfather can be found on the internet. I've compiled a dossier for you. Have you had breakfast?'

'No,' he lied. He liked the idea of having breakfast with this girl.

'Good. Neither have I. I'm starving. There's a café just a block away. Zweiviertel. They do great breakfasts. I can go through the file with you there.'

On the five-minute walk to Zweiviertel, she told him that she was a student at the University of Würzburg, studying computer science. Working as a *Mitarbeiter* was a part-time activity, a bit of fun that gave her the opportunity to exercise her computer skills.

In the café they sat well apart at a table below a chalkboard with a handwritten menu, and she ordered a platter of cold meats, a basket of croissants and a coffee that arrived in a tall glass revealing alternate layers of milk, coffee and whipped cream. Bauer assured her that he would be paying, and she seemed anxious to make the most of it. He told her he wasn't hungry, and ordered an espresso to top up his caffeine. He downed it in a single draft, and replaced his mask to sit and watch her while she ate hungrily and talked. Most students, he recalled, did not have the money to treat themselves to extravagant breakfasts like this.

'Karlheinz Wolff,' she told him, 'was born in Dresden in 1898. His father was an architect, his mother a watercolour artist. He had an older brother and a younger sister. The family moved to Würzburg just before the outbreak of war in 1914, and Wolff served in the army on the Western Front during the last two years of it, winning himself an Iron Cross for bravery. After the war he went to the University of Frankfurt to study art. His brother, Hildebrand, became the curator of a provincial museum in Bremen, and his parents indulged his sister's desire to paint by installing her in a small apartment in Paris and enrolling her at the Beaux-Arts.' She looked up from a slice of salami sausage that was halfway to her mouth on the tines of her fork. 'Art seems to have run in the family.' She smiled. 'All the way down the generations to you.'

He was taken aback. 'What can you possibly know about *me*?'

She shrugged. 'I did a little research on you last night. You have your own gallery in Berlin.'

He felt uncomfortable to know that he had been placed under someone else's microscope. But she gave him no time to dwell on it, popping the sausage into her mouth and opening up her orange folder on the table.

'Interesting story I came across about his sister. Erika.' She leafed through several sheets in her file. 'Here we are. It seems she was having an affair with an older man. A well-known art critic in Paris called Georges Picard. He was married and had several children.' She cocked an eyebrow at Bauer. 'Some men just can't keep it in their lederhosen, can they?'

Bauer found himself embarrassed by her directness. 'And?'

'She got pregnant by him. And when he wouldn't leave his wife and family, she killed herself.' Greta Jung clearly didn't have much sympathy. 'Very dramatic,' she said flippantly. 'Anyway, Karlheinz was incensed. This was his little sister, after all. So he and a group of friends travelled to Paris where he very nearly killed Picard. Accosted him in a bar somewhere, and from all accounts beat him to a pulp. It was said he had a terrible temper and would certainly have killed him if his friends hadn't dragged him away. They had to smuggle him out of France before he got arrested.'

Bauer felt his face stinging as if he had been slapped. In a fit of temper his grandfather had very nearly killed the man he blamed for his sister's suicide. Was this a manifestation of the same volatile temperament that had so afflicted Bauer through all of his youth, and now into his twenties? An inherited intemperance that led to violence?

'Hello? Are you still with me?'

He looked up to see Greta Jung looking at him quizzically. 'You want me to go on?'

'Yes. Please.'

She consulted her notes again. 'After he graduated from

Frankfurt his brother gave him a job at his art gallery in Bremen. And that was where he met the man who would change his life. The industrialist Guido Fischer.' She looked up. 'You've heard of him?'

He shook his head.

'No, neither had I. I had to look him up.' She drained her glass. 'Do you think I could have another coffee?'

'Of course.' Bauer signalled the waiter and placed the order. She returned to her folder.

'Fischer invented engine seals and brake pads made from some kind of woven asbestos. They were gobbled up by the army during the First World War when supplies from traditional British manufacturers not surprisingly dried up. By the end of the war he was fabulously wealthy, and being courted by whoever was in government. And, of course, when the Nazis came to power *they* realised that they were going to need him to supply the whole mighty war machine they were building in the thirties. Which, in turn, gave Fischer enormous power and influence.'

'So how did Karlheinz get to know him?'

'The Wolff brothers were organising an exhibition of contemporary modern art at Hildebrand's gallery. Guido Fischer himself was a collector, and if a man of his stature asks for a preview, he gets it. That's when Karlheinz first met him. Fischer wanted to buy several of the works on display, and Karlheinz offered to negotiate their purchase on his behalf. Given his position as brother of the curator, he was able to acquire them at below market value. Apparently Hildebrand was furious, but Fischer was delighted and Karlheinz very quickly became his unofficial art dealer. In the years that followed, the relationship between the two developed and they ended up becoming firm friends, almost like father and son.'

She looked up again and surveyed Bauer with what seemed more than a casual interest. He was glad to be wearing his mask.

She said, 'It was Fischer's patronage that bulletproofed Wolff against his Jewish heritage when the Nazis came to power.'

Bauer blinked in astonishment. 'Jewish?'

She laughed. 'Well, he had a Jewish grandmother, although the family had long ago converted to Catholicism. But that didn't matter to the Nazis. To them Judaism was in the blood, so when Hitler came to power, people like Wolff, and the rest of his family, were labelled Mischling. Effectively, mixed blood. To any other family, that might have been the kiss of death. But with a friend like Guido Fischer, Wolff's unfortunate accident of birth was swept under a carpet of convenience.' She laughed. 'How else could a Mischling go on to become a dealer in art for someone second only to Hitler in the Party.'

'Göring?'

'Yes. A man, apparently, with an insatiable appetite for art.' She smiled. 'Much of which he stole.'

Bauer was physically drained. The hours of sleeplessness the night before and the five-hour drive back to Berlin had taken their toll. But his mind was still buzzing, effervescing like a headache tablet dropped in water. During the long journey he had gone over, and over again, everything that Greta Jung had told him. Her orange folder lay on the passenger seat beside him, and he wished now that he had taken the train so that he could have read it for himself on the way back. He simply couldn't wait to get his hands on it.

He parked in his reserved space under the trees on the near bank of the canal and crossed the street to his apartment block. He was earlier than expected, and the light was only just beginning to die around him, a scattering of pink and purple clouds fading into a darkening sky. Under his arm he carried Greta Jung's orange folder, and so distracted was he by everything he had learned today, that he barely noticed the two young men loading boxes and bags into a small van at the kerbside.

He skipped past them and into the entrance hall, taking the stairs to the third floor two at a time. The apartment was oddly cold when he let himself in, as if the heating had failed to switch itself on. The only light in the entrance hall fell through a gap in the door to the bedroom, which stood slightly open.

'Lise?' he called. And when there was no reply, strode across the hall to push open the bedroom door.

Lise was stooped over an open, overfilled suitcase on the bed, trying desperately to close it. She turned frightened eyes towards him, darkened by dilated pupils, and almost jumped away from the case as if she had been burned. He stopped and stared at her in consternation.

'What are you doing?'

She ran her tongue over dry lips but made no attempt to answer. He swivelled his gaze to take in wardrobe doors that stood ajar, coat hangers rattling in the emptiness beyond. Open drawers had been stripped of their contents. All of her personal items had gone from the dresser. He turned his eyes back towards his partner of nearly two years and felt that old familiar anger rising inside him.

'You're leaving me?'

Panic was apparent in her face as she glanced at her suitcase and made a decision. To abandon it and get out. She ran for the door. But he grabbed her arm as she passed him, and swung her around violently to throw her on to the bed.

'You were just going to walk out without a word?' Anger and incredulity strangled his words. 'Leave me to come home to an empty house? After everything I've done for you?'

'All you've ever done is hurt me.' She flung her defiance back at him with words she knew would only inflame him further. She scrambled off the bed, yanked the zipper of her suitcase shut and grabbed the handle. 'I've no idea why I even stayed with you this long.' She heaved it down to the floor.

'Nothing to do with the money, I suppose.' His voice was laden with sudden sarcasm.

'It was never *your* money,' she spat back at him. 'And I never gave a shit about it anyway. I thought I loved you, though God knows why. I've just never understood how a grown man with any self-respect could live off his mother. Waiting for her to die so he could inherit.'

Fury spiked through him. 'You little bitch!' He stepped towards her, clenched fist raised ready to strike, as it had done so many times before. But strong arms grasped him and threw him back against the wall. His head struck it with a resounding crack. Two young men about his own age crowded the bedroom, tense and all wound up like coiled springs.

One of them half turned towards the girl. 'Lise, get out!'

Only then did Bauer recognise them as the young men loading the van in the street outside his apartment. 'Who the fuck are you?' he shouted. 'Get out of my apartment!'

'Lise, go!' The bellow of the young man's voice reverberated around the bedroom.

She lifted her case and hurried out of the room, barely daring to glance in Bauer's direction.

'Who the hell do you think you are?' Bauer yelled again.

The young man who had shouted at Lise to go wore a sick smile on his face as he took a step towards Bauer, fists bunched at his side. 'I'm Lise's big brother,' he said. 'As you'd know if you'd ever bothered to visit the family. She's finished with you, you fuck! And you're going to get what's coming to you.'

His friend took a step to the side as the two of them moved in on Bauer, so that he could only strike out towards one at a time.

Bauer tensed, fuelled by fury and fear in equal measure. He knew he was going to take a beating, but had no intention of going down without a fight.

As she left the apartment, Lise heard his voice raised in a blood-curdling yell, and then a commotion that suggested a level of violence that could only end in blood and tears. She blinked away tears of her own that threatened to blind her as she hauled her suitcase off down the stairs.

It was several hours before the pain in his head eased. His lower lip, sliced open by a broken front tooth, had bled profusely, long after his attackers had gone. One eye was almost closed, although he was sure he had reduced the swelling and the bruising by applying a bag of frozen vegetables straight from the freezer. His ribs ached, and hurt every time he moved, making him wonder if one or more were cracked or broken. But he suspected that the heavy boots that had kicked him repeatedly when finally he went down had inflicted most of their damage on the arms with which he had tried to protect himself.

He too had managed to administer a fair amount of damage, the evidence of which remained in the swollen and bruised knuckles of both hands.

Several paracetamol had taken the edge off most of the pain, but it was only now that it was ceasing to fill his entire conscious world and fade into the background. He sat in the dark of the front room, sipping gingerly at a glass of whisky and sparkling water. It was filled to the brim with ice cubes that numbed his lips as he drank.

His rage had finally subsided, giving way to self-pity, and

he felt the first warm tears trickle down his bruised face. The tumbler shook in his hand, and he closed his eyes to try to gather himself. Through the glass all along the front of the apartment, the light of the city spilled in to lay the elongated shapes of his windows across the floor. And only now did the full sense of his loss strike him.

Lise was gone. It was over. She would never be back, and he knew that it was entirely his fault. The regret he had always felt following violent outbursts against her haunted him now. Genuine sorrow for what he had done to her, and in the end to himself. His mother, too, was gone. No one but himself left to blame.

He moved stiffly across the room and went to the kitchen to refill his glass, and when he returned, slumped into the swivel chair behind his desk. His eyes hurt when first he turned on the desk lamp, and he screwed them tight shut to reopen slowly and accustom them gradually to the light. Earlier he had gathered together all the sheets of paper that had spilled on to the bedroom floor and returned them to Greta Jung's orange folder. It lay now in the circle of light on the desk. He pulled it towards him and opened it. Photocopies of the records she had tracked down in the vaults of the Würzburg archive, printouts of obscure web pages she had unearthed in her search for details on the history of Karlheinz Wolff. The story of his sister, Erika, and of his first encounter with the industrialist Guido Fischer. There was a Wikipedia entry on Fischer, in which Wolff was mentioned, and described as having become a dealer in art for Hermann Göring. But no explanation of how that had come about.

Just beyond his reach, and outside the pool of light on his desktop, Wolff's diaries lay in an untidy pile. Silent shadows from the past, lying in the dark, inviting him to read. He gazed at them for a very long time before finally succumbing to temptation. His chair creaked as he leaned forward to corral them into the light. He sat back, flicking through each in turn to arrange them in date order. He did not have the concentration to give them his full attention right now, but he riffled through some of the earliest entries, struck by how similar Wolff's handwriting was to his own.

It seemed that Wolff had begun these diaries sometime during his early years at university. His first entries revealed a youthful lack of self-confidence, an almost obsessive exercise in navel-gazing. A growing awareness of his shortness of temper, and a propensity for violence when he lost it. Bauer found these difficult to read. They were words he might have written to describe himself, yet penned by a man who predated him by two generations.

Wolff's fascination with his sister verged on infatuation, and was clear in all his entries about her. Unhealthily so. She was beautiful, talented, beyond reproach. He missed her passionately when she went to Paris, and described sleepless nights thinking about her. Sometimes his dreams of her verged on the erotic.

Bauer skipped the account of his trip to Paris with friends

to exact revenge on the man who had made her pregnant. It struck far too close to home. And he skimmed forward until he found what really interested him. The entry that described his first meeting with the man who was head of the German air force, the Luftwaffe. The man made Reichsmarschall by Hitler at the start of the war, giving him seniority over all other officers in Germany's armed forces. Hermann Göring. Described by Greta Jung in the café in Würzburg as an art thief.

CHAPTER ELEVEN

Bauer takes a sip of his whisky and leans forward into the light to read.

Wolff's Diary: Wednesday, August 21, 1940

Guido and I drove from Berlin to Carinhall in his fabulous Mercedes-Benz 320 Cabriolet. It is a seductive powder blue, and with the top down, and the wind in our hair, the journey took little more than an hour. It was a beautiful, sunny summer's day and Guido was in a fine mood. The Wehrmacht had swept through Western Europe. France had fallen. Göring's Luftwaffe was in the process of blowing Britain's feeble force of Spitfires out of the sky over southern Britain, and we'd begun bombing London to soften up the English for the coming invasion.

Forty-two years old and I was as nervous as my first day in the trenches. Dressed in my best suit with a stiffly pressed white shirt and blue tie, I had spent a good twenty minutes shining my shoes to the point where I could see my reflection in them. I was about to meet the second most powerful man in Europe.

Guido found my anxiety amusing. He never tires of teasing me and spent much of the drive berating me for my sense of humour, or lack thereof. Göring, he said, was genial company and looking forward to meeting me. For his part, Guido is a regular guest at the hunting lodge.

'He built it in 1934 in the Schorfheide forest as a private retreat,' Guido told me, his eyes fixed on the road ahead. 'Named it after his first wife, Carin, three years after she died. But it's been much enlarged since then, and is now an official state residence and hunting lodge.' He turned towards me, amusement in his eyes. 'All paid for by the German people, of course.'

Open countryside gradually gave way to the large area of forest north of Berlin that they call Schorfheide, and eventually we stopped at the gatehouse to the Carinhall estate to have our documents checked before being allowed any further. A long, straight road cut a swathe through the trees. I could see the hunting complex in the distance, shimmering in the heat of the day. Somewhere beyond it lay the Dölln lake, and there were birds circling lazily in the sky above the water.

'There are wings for staff, and a doctor and a dental surgery,' Guido said. 'There's a sauna and fitness room, and an indoor swimming pool. And, of course, Göring's model train set.' He laughed uproariously. 'Nearly a hundred metres of electric rails, with tunnels, bridges, and even miniature aeroplanes.

There's also a cinema, if you fancy taking in a movie while we're here.' He turned and shook his head at the look on my face, which I can only imagine was open-mouthed and foolish. I have been to Guido's house many times, but wealthy as he is, he possesses nothing on this scale. It was all far beyond anything I might ever have imagined in my wildest dreams.

We drove past all the outbuildings and into a large courtyard in front of an impressive, white-painted lodge. A wild boar stood mounted on a plinth in the middle of a square pond, testament to the building's legacy as a hunting lodge. A grand entrance was framed in stone with Party flags raised on either side. Life-sized couchant stags flanked the doorway.

We drew up alongside several other vehicles, and Guido cut the motor. He turned to me then, and warned, 'Hermann's good company, as I said. But he can also be unpredictable.' He lowered his voice as if someone might be listening. 'You'll probably remember the Beer Hall Putsch when Hitler first tried to take power in Munich. 1923. It was a disaster. A failed coup d'état. A lot of Party members were shot and killed by police, and Hitler was sentenced to five years in prison. Hermann was there, too, and was wounded in the shooting. A nasty wound that got infected. The doctors gave him morphine for the pain, and the poor guy got hooked on the stuff. All these years later he's still addicted.'

Guido stepped out of the car, but then leaned back in, lowering his voice even further. 'Morphine addiction' – he shook his head – 'leads to complications, Karlheinz. Excites the

184

nervous system, creates excessive activity in certain glands. It can lead to extreme outpourings of energy.' His voice reduced itself almost to a whisper. 'And sometimes abnormal vanity.' To my surprise he winked at me and grinned. 'Which pretty much describes *der dicke Hermann* to a T. You never know quite how you'll find him.' He straightened up and his voice returned to normal levels. 'Come on, my friend. Time to meet the Reichsmarschall.'

I think he enjoyed stoking the flames of my anxiety, making me even more nervous than I already was. And to describe our host as 'fat Hermann' just before we were to meet him was clearly and mischievously designed to unnerve me.

Inside a dark entrance hall, we were greeted by a flunky in white shirt and waistcoat. He made me think of a maître d' in a restaurant. I was asked to sign the visitors' book, which stood on a lectern just inside the door. It was huge, and heavy to open, and the pages released a fusion of scents left by a procession of visitors over many years.

'You're in exalted company now, young man,' Guido said, as I leaned over it to scrawl my name and date and signature. 'If you look back through these pages you'll see that they have borne witness to such visitors as former US President Herbert Hoover, the Duke and Duchess of Windsor, Benito Mussolini, the kings of Bulgaria, Romania and Yugoslavia.' He grinned. 'Now everyone will be able to boast that they've seen your name in here, too.'

A long, tiled hallway led us past walls mounted with classical works of art, many of which I recognised from my studies in Frankfurt. There were sculpted figures and vases raised on marble plinths, all lit by ceiling panels that diffused light from overhead to minimise shadows.

Finally we were led into the *Jagdhalle*, a vast salon with exposed beams rising into the apex of the roof. It was sixty-five-and-a-half metres long, Guido had told me on the drive down, but I'd had no concept of how big that was until I walked into that great hall. A huge fireplace at the far end occupied most of the wall. Rugs laid on polished floors stretched between groupings of soft furnishings, discreetly patterned three- and five-piece suites gathered around large tables, a long dining table in front of the fire. Electric chandeliers hung from the cross-beams all along the length of the hall. Punctuating the outer wall, antlers were mounted above each arched window, and on the wall facing, formal chairs and long wooden tables stood beneath regal tapestries and priceless paintings.

Göring was lounging on a settee at the far end of the hall reading a newspaper. I could see that he was dressed in the white cotton summer tunic worn in many of the photographs I'd seen of him. A big, corpulent man with a full, round face and dyed black hair oiled back from a broad forehead.

Guido leaned in and whispered, 'He keeps lions here, you know. So make sure you don't get on the wrong side of him.'

Göring saw us coming, put his newspaper to one side and stood up to greet us. It seemed to take an age traversing the length of this *Jagdhalle*, to reach him. As we approached I saw his Iron Cross attached at the neck of his tunic, and the famed Blue Max dangling on a piece of leather from his collar. He had a florid complexion that spoke to me of too much good living and dangerously high blood pressure. He shook my hand vigorously, fat fingers adorned with ostentatious gold and silver rings.

I felt quite small in his presence, but bathed in the warmth of his bonhomie and gently smiling blue eyes. 'Herr Wolff,' he said. 'I am pleased to meet you at last. Guido has told me so much about you.'

'All of it good, I hope, sir.'

He grinned at Guido. 'Herr Fischer is nothing if not discreet . . .' He turned back to me. 'May I call you Karlheinz?'

I have to confess to being quite taken aback. Though even had I wanted to, I was in no position to decline. And why would I? 'Of course,' I said.

He took me by the arm, then, and led me a little way down the hall to show me a painting that took pride of place on the window-facing wall. It stood almost two metres high, and was a depiction of a handsome woman in hunting gear set against a clear blue sky. She wore a high, turned-up collar, and a falcon perched on her left arm, wings outspread. 'What do you think?' he said.

'Magnificent.'

He glanced at me. 'You know it?'

'*The Falconer*, by Hans Makart,' I told him. Guido had provided me with a list of Göring's most prized works. Homework for my visit. 'A gift a couple of years ago from Herr Hitler, I believe. On the occasion of your forty-fifth birthday.'

Göring turned a knowing look in Guido's direction. 'Well briefed, Guido.' His smile faded slowly. 'Would you leave us now, please?'

If anything, I think Guido was even more startled than I. I could see him choke back his surprise. 'Of course, Reichsmarschall,' he said, and they seemed suddenly on more formal terms. He nodded to me, and turned to walk back along the length of the great hall before finally vanishing through the door at the far end.

Göring turned. 'Come join me in a coffee.' The waistcoated flunky who had shown us in was still hovering at a discreet distance. Göring waved a careless arm in his direction. 'Fresh coffee for my guest, Daniel.' And he steered me back to where the impression of his ample behind remained pressed into the settee. He flopped into it again. 'Take a seat.' And I sat, uncomfortably, in an armchair opposite, wishing to God that Guido was still there.

He seemed distracted. Searching about his person, and then the settee around him, for something that remained elusive. I sat in silence and felt as if he'd forgotten that I was even there.

The coffee arrived on a tray that Daniel placed on the table between us. He poured two cups black, bowed and left. Göring emerged from his distraction to brandish a hand towards the cream jug. 'Help yourself,' he said.

I poured a tiny drop of cream into my coffee and took a

sip. It was as good a coffee, I think, as I have ever tasted. But Göring showed no interest in his. Instead he had turned his disconcerting gaze fixedly on me. 'Are you a lover of the modern, Karlheinz?' I frowned my lack of understanding and he clarified. 'Art.'

'It is mostly what I have dealt in, sir.'

'That's not what I asked.'

I panicked a little, then, wondering what would be the correct response, before deciding that honesty might be the best policy. 'Some of it, yes. I am a great admirer of the impressionists, less so of artists in the mould of Picasso or Dali.'

'You are aware that Herr Hitler believes all modern art is degenerate, a symptom of the decay of Western civilisation.'

'I have read that, sir.'

'We have accumulated vast quantities of the stuff, Karlheinz. Confiscated it. Much of it from Jewish collectors. The Führer would have it destroyed. But this work has an inherent financial value on the international market and Herr Hitler has been persuaded that its sale will boost the war coffers. I would like you to trade in this marketplace on behalf of the Reich.'

I was stunned. Why me? Yes, I'd been trading in art for Guido Fischer, but this was an entirely different level of responsibility. I had no idea what to say.

Göring smiled, as if he could read what was going through my mind. 'At least, that shall be your cover.'

'My cover?'

'This war will extend the borders of the German state across

all of Europe, Karlheinz. A redistribution of power. And wealth.'
He paused pointedly. 'And art. Our Führer has an admirable
plan to build what everyone is calling a super museum at Linz
in Austria. The world's best art will hang on its walls.' His
pause again presaged the unexpected. 'He wants da Vinci's
Mona Lisa to be the centrepiece of that collection.'

I'm sure my astonishment was apparent in my expression,
for it caused him to smile.

'You know a certain dealer in art called Paul Lange, I
understand.'

Even the mention of his name was enough to summon dark
clouds of remembered anger. I'm sure he must have seen the
shadow of it cross my face. 'Yes, sir. We studied art together
at Frankfurt.'

'Herr Hitler has attached Lange to the Kunstschutz in Paris
and asked him to secure the *Mona Lisa* for his Führermuseum.
By fair means or foul.'

My astonishment was greater than my reticence. 'Lange?'

'Yes, Lange.'

I said, 'But surely, we know exactly where the *Mona Lisa* is.
Why not just seize it?'

The Reichsmarschall smiled at my naivety. 'Because,
Karlheinz, there would be the most almighty international
uproar. We would leave ourselves open to accusations of
the looting of national treasures.' He chuckled. 'We must
be careful. Either we will go down in history as the world's
greatest statesmen, or its worst villains. So the acquisition of

this work has to be achieved with subtlety, diplomacy, and preferably in the shadows.'

He fell silent for a long time, gazing at me, or rather through me. At least, that's how it felt. And I found it hard to believe that I was sitting here, in the lion's den so to speak, being taken into the confidence of the lion himself. Me, a Mischling. A lover of modern art. Everything that was anathema to the Nazis. And I very much feared for where this all was going.

'I want it,' he said simply.

I frowned. 'Want what, sir?'

'The *Mona Lisa*. I want it for my collection. Even if no one ever knows it. Even if no one ever sees it. It will be mine, to gaze upon whenever *I* choose. And *I* will know, when no one else does, where the missing *Mona Lisa* resides.' Another pause before the coup de grâce. 'I want you to get it for me before Lange acquires it for Hitler.' His smile was filled with warmth, but his words chilled me to the bone. 'It'll be our secret, Karlheinz. Just you and me.' And I understood in that moment just how fatally dangerous it could be to share such a secret with such a man.

But now that he had taken me into his confidence, there was no way out. He had committed me, whether I wanted it or not. There was no possibility to refuse.

He said, 'You will, of course, accept my invitation to become an officer in the Luftwaffe. It will pay your wages, and open whatever doors you need. You will be attached to the ERR in Paris. You are familiar with this organisation?'

I was well aware that the raison d'être of the ERR was to confiscate art and artefacts, manuscripts and books in occupied territories. Procurement under cover of protection. 'Yes, sir.'

'Ultimately, they are answerable to me. So you will carry that authority. You know Paris, I believe.'

'I do. It *is* the world capital of art.'

'Good. ERR will arrange office and living accommodation for you there.' He shifted himself to the edge of the settee and leaned towards me. 'I'm putting a great deal of trust in you, Karlheinz. Guido speaks most highly of your discretion, and I'm going to have to ask you to exercise that in relation to Guido himself. No one, and I mean *no one* must know about this.' He reached for a small bell that sat on the table and rang it vigorously.

Almost immediately Daniel appeared from a door in the fireplace wall carrying a brown paper parcel. He laid the neatly folded package on the coffee table and retreated. Göring pushed it towards me.

'A gift,' he said, and smiled. 'Go on, open it.'

It was with great trepidation that I unpacked the parcel to reveal a black leather flying jacket with a short, elasticated waist, large lapels and a collar that could be turned up for warmth. I gazed on it with astonishment, to Göring's apparent amusement.

'Usually it is only pilots who get to wear these,' he said. 'But since it is my gift to you, you can wear it with pride. I understand that you were awarded the Iron Cross for bravery during the last war.'

'I was.'

'Then you can pin it with honour to the left breast of this jacket, and let no man doubt your courage.' As he spoke he absently fingered the elaborate gold and blue of the Pour le Mérite, best known as the Blue Max, that dangled from his collar. And, in spite of myself, I felt a frisson of excitement. I was no longer to be a bystander in this war of wars. I had a reason to be a part of it, and a precious function to fulfil.

Bauer shares his grandfather's excitement, and with shaking fingers flicks through the pages of the diary to the night before Wolff's departure for Paris.

Monday, September 16, 1940

I lay tonight with Lisbeth, in her apartment that overlooks the river. We left the drapes undrawn, and the same moonlight that reflected on the dark surface of the River Main also flooded her bedroom. I said my farewells to my wife and children this morning, and they believe me to be on my way to Paris already.

I am sitting at Lisbeth's desk in the window that looks out on the river as I write this, and she lies sleeping among the warm folds of the sheets that wrapped themselves around us in the frenzy of our lovemaking. I love her with a great intensity, and never once have I felt those same base urges that have caused me to raise my hands to Kersten. They say that your partner can bring out the best in you. But they can also bring out the worst. I am happy to escape the worst that Kersten brings out in me, but sad to be leaving my Lisbeth. I feel that I owe her my honesty. The truth. But I simply cannot break the bond of silence that has been forced upon me by Herr Göring.

On the drive back from Carinhall to Berlin last month, it was all I could do to fend off Guido's questions. He knew perfectly well there was more to Göring's request that I trade confiscated modern art in the international marketplace on behalf of the Reich. And when it became clear to him that I was not going to share it with him, he fell silent and has been cool with me ever since.

However, I am consumed by excitement now. For tomorrow I will fly to Paris. I have been there many times since they had to drag me off that vile piece of excrement who made Erika pregnant. But always incognito. And never have I dared go near him again. Now it is different. Now it is I, and not the French authorities, who hold sway. I have often heard the aphorism that revenge is a dish best served cold, but never understood it. Until now.

The very next entry is made at the end of Wolff's first day in the French capital. Bauer has long since forgotten the pain and humiliation of his beating, devouring with his eyes now the pages of his grandfather's journal.

Tuesday, September 17, 1940

What I found most extraordinary upon my arrival in Paris this morning was the sense of normalcy. If one can say that German soldiers standing on street corners in the French capital, and swastikas hanging from every other building, is normal. I think what I sensed was a lack of the tension I had most certainly expected. The streets were full of traffic, and pedestrians, all going about their daily lives as usual. Or so it seemed.

What I did perceive, perhaps, was a nervous excitement simmering just below the surface. A certain febrile quality to the atmosphere in this City of Light. But superficially at least, you would never have guessed we were at war, and that Paris was a city under occupation.

I strode along the crowded pavement of the Boulevard Haussmann, aware of drawing eyes that were reluctant to show too much interest. I cut, I think, a more dashing and exotic figure than those bored-looking soldiers in their field-grey uniforms and utilitarian helmets. As Göring had foreseen, I wore my Iron Cross pinned to the left breast of my leather flying jacket with the fiercest of pride. An embroidered Luftwaffe eagle was pinned to my right, the pips on my epaulettes denoting the rank of Hauptmann. I had not yet become accustomed to the baggy thigh britches tucked into my black leather boots, but I walked, I suppose, with a confidence verging on arrogance. France had fallen with barely a fight, and we were in the ascendancy. I was returning to Paris with a certain sense of entitlement.

I caught a glimpse of myself in the window of the Hôtel Commodore as I approached its entrance at the junction with the Rue Laffitte. With the peak of my Luftwaffe cap pulled down over my forehead, and my pistol in its leather holster, I thought I looked quite formidable. Not someone to pick a fight with lightly.

I very nearly walked smack into Bruno Lohse as I turned under the canopy at the entrance to the hotel. The Commodore had been commandeered by the ERR as its Paris headquarters. I imagined that as well as office accommodation, the hotel would also provide living quarters for many of the staff, and I wondered if I would be one of them.

I knew Lohse of old. Before the war he had traded art in many of the same markets as I, and although he was only number two to Baron Kurt von Behr here at the ERR in Paris, with the rank of SS-Hauptsturmführer and the blessing of Göring himself, he was effectively the Reich's art looter in the French capital.

But he was not in uniform today. He wore a light grey double-breasted suit, the collar of his white shirt turned up above a dark blue cravat. A matching fedora sat at a jaunty angle on neatly cut dark hair. He is a good thirteen years my junior, but comports himself like a man who considers his superiority to be apparent.

He recognised me immediately, of course. And would have

known that I was here on Göring's business. Though not being privy to exactly what that business was must have put his nose considerably out of joint. We blocked the doorway for a moment as he ran his eyes from my head to my feet and back again. 'Didn't know you'd got your wings, Wolff. I suppose you're here to take up your sinecure?' He pushed open the door and I followed him in, across the lobby and into a circular lounge beneath a stunning stained-glass cupola that shed wonderful filaments of light across a scattering of tables and chairs where officers sat in groups of two and three drinking coffee.

I hurried to keep up. 'I'm assuming I'll be allocated office space, Bruno.'

He stopped suddenly, turning abruptly, and I almost bumped into him. He lowered his voice. 'You will be a part of this organisation in name only, Wolff. And don't expect any favours from me. I have enough on my plate without having to pander to some freeloader.'

'I'll pass on your sentiments to the Reichsmarschall, shall I?'

He glared at me, and I could see latent fury bubbling up behind his black eyes. But he had no opportunity to vent it, for we were interrupted then by a laconic voice that I knew only too well.

'Well, well, I've clearly stumbled upon the place to be in high Paris society, these days. All the top people are here.'

Lohse and I turned to see Paul Lange smiling sarcastically. I was surprised to see him in army uniform. He carried his cap in his hands and looked tanned and well, and his smile suggested the confidence of a man who operated with the explicit blessing of the Führer. The very sight of him made me want to lash out. But I forced myself to return his smile. 'Hello, Paul,' I said. 'Here on holiday, are you?'

'Yes, what *are* you doing here?' Lohse growled.

Lange turned a withering look on him. 'I had a meeting with your boss, Hauptsturmführer.' And then his smile turned patronising. 'I suppose the number two doesn't always know what's going on at the top.'

I had to restrain the urge to laugh out loud. Whatever I felt personally about Lange, I knew him to be a man of far superior intellect to Lohse, and I enjoyed the latter's humiliation. Then he turned his sarcasm on me.

'Come to join up with the looters, have you, Karlheinz? The den of thieves here at the Commodore?'

'A marriage of convenience,' I told him, aware of how infuriating this conversation must be to Lohse.

'Yes, I'd heard you were into extramarital arrangements these days,' Lange said, and I felt my face colour. 'I'm with the good guys, the Kunstschutz, over at the Majestic across town. Perhaps it's just as well we're not going to be working out of the same building.'

Lohse glanced between us. 'I didn't realise you two knew each other.'

I said, 'We were at university together at Frankfurt.' And found it hard to keep the animosity out of my voice. Lohse did not miss it.

'Well,' he said, 'I have better things to do with my time than spar with two alumni from a second-rate university.' He turned to me. 'Report to personnel for office and living accommodation.' He nodded curtly, and with a click of his heels, strode away across the lounge.

Which left Lange and I on our own beneath the splendour of the Commodore's cupola. He pulled on his cap and said, 'I'm surprised that a Mischling like you should find himself working for the Party.'

In spite of myself, I glanced around in case anyone had heard him. I lowered my voice. 'I'm not a Party member.'

'I'd have been surprised if you were.'

'And you?'

'Of course. One does what one has to in order to survive, these days.' He hesitated only briefly, and the strangest smile flickered across his face. 'I heard a rumour that Herr Göring is very anxious to get his hands on what the French call *La Joconde.*'

'Did you?' I was shocked, but determined to give nothing away.

'I did. And I imagine that Herr Hitler would be less than pleased if somehow it went missing. It's no secret that he would like to see it hanging at Linz.'

I was unblinking in meeting his gaze. 'Unless, of course, it happened to go *missing* into the hands of someone in *his* employ.'

And there it was. All set out. Our shared objective for

different ends, and different masters. And Göring's assertion that the quest to acquire the *Mona Lisa* would be a secret only between him and me seemed like a distant and very hollow echo.

Lange just smiled. 'Well, since the Louvre keep moving her around the Free French Zone, I imagine it could be some time before she might turn her smile upon a new master.'

CHAPTER TWELVE

Bauer sat back in his chair, removing his eyes from the painful concentration of light that his desk lamp threw upon the diaries. All the various pains he felt seemed fused into one general ache. Bruised and battered, and enormously fatigued, the escape offered by sleep was seductive. But, still, his excitement at what he had just read banished any thoughts of calling it a night.

He leaned forward again, and selected the final diary, effectively fast-forwarding through four years of war. The entries now were much briefer, and felt hurried. Wolff's careful, considered handwriting had become slapdash and erratic. There was the sense of uncertainty, of a turn in the tide of events. The final entry pre-dated the D-Day invasion in June, and was an abrupt end to his journal. Bauer imagined that this was when he had returned to Germany on leave and left the diaries in the safekeeping of his lover, Bauer's grandmother, Lisbeth.

But before then, by the spring of 1944, it seemed he had tracked down the *Mona Lisa* to a château in south-west France, where it appeared to be in the safekeeping of a young woman called Georgette Pignal. In an increasingly irregular hand, Wolff wrote that he had heard that this woman had been specifically tasked by de Gaulle with keeping the painting safe, and out of the hands of the Nazis. He also suspected that she was somehow in league with his nemesis, Lange. Why he believed this was not clear, but Bauer imagined that the answer must lie in earlier entries.

Although it seemed that she was living a short distance from the château itself, in a village called Carennac, Wolff reported that she was spending her nights at the château.

That his grandfather's journal ended here, so abruptly and without conclusion, was infuriating. Bauer felt frustration welling up from deep inside him. But there was nothing, and no one, for him to lash out at, no focus for the venting of his vexation. He dropped the diary on to the desktop and wakened his laptop with a sweep of his fingers on the trackpad. He opened his browser and brought up a Google search page. His bruised fingers had stiffened up, and it was only with difficulty that he typed *Carennac* into the search window.

His screen immediately filled with links to tourist sites describing the village as the epitome of provincial France in the Dordogne valley, with its medieval stone houses and Romanesque church. Several sites referred to it as one of the most beautiful villages in France. Images revealed steeply pitched red-tiled roofs with towers and turrets rising over honeyed stone. The Wikipedia entry listed its permanent population as 408.

Bauer sighed. This seemed like a waste of time. He was about to give up when a link to an article in a local newspaper well down the page caught his eye. The newspaper was *La Dépêche du Midi*, and the article which had appeared on an inside page just three days earlier, was headlined '*MACABRE DÉCOUVERTE SOUS UN ARBRE MORT: UN CADAVRE DATANT DE LA DERNIÈRE GUERRE*'. Bauer selected and copied it, and entered it into Google Translate. *MACABRE DISCOVERY UNDER A DEAD TREE: A CORPSE FROM THE LAST WAR*, appeared in the translation window. Which excited his interest sufficiently for him to have the entire article translated.

A dead tree, brought down during a storm in the village of Carennac, has revealed the remains of a body buried in a park sometime during the last war.

Metal and leather artefacts recovered with the bones have led experts to believe that this was the corpse of a German air force officer. A bullet hole in the cranium appears to have been the cause of death.

All the remains, from what seems to have been a hastily dug and shallow grave, have been collected and sent to Paris for analysis by a forensic archaeologist.

Three brief paragraphs that sent all the hairs rising on the back of Bauer's neck, and his mind doing circuits around the room. The pounding of his heart actually felt painful. Was it possible that these were the remains of Karlheinz Wolff? A

German air force officer, they thought. *Missing in action*, was how Lisbeth had reported the last words she'd had of her lover in France. Bauer knew from his diaries that he had been there. Had someone shot him in the head and then buried him in haste? Just a stone's throw away from the château where the *Mona Lisa* was being kept. But who, and why?

Bauer held his face in his hands and breathed deeply for several long minutes. But it was what he read next, about the occupant of the house adjoining the park, that had him reaching for the first of the diaries. His fatigue banished. Pain retreating to the very edge of consciousness. He would refill his glass. Again. And again. However many times it took to see him through the reading of his grandfather's diaries from first page to last.

CHAPTER THIRTEEN

He asks if she would like more wood on the fire. She has remained close to it, and the embers are undoubtedly still warming her. But he feels the temperature falling.

She looks up, surprised. 'Are you cold, monsieur?' she asks.

'A little.' Perhaps it is because the sun is lost now in autumn cloud, and the warmth it shed earlier through glass has dissipated.

'By all means,' she says, and he rises stiffly to lift a couple of logs from the basket and arrange them carefully on the glowing braises, unsure whether they will catch. 'Use the bellows,' she counsels.

The bellows lean against a blackened side wall and he lifts them to direct air at the embers, watching how with each puff they glow, and then spark, raising the first smoke from the fresh logs. Satisfied now that the fire will take, he returns to his seat. Hunger is a distraction, but it is not long before he is once more absorbed in her story . . .

Georgette was almost demented after three months in the attic of her safe house in the Loire. A ramshackle old farmhouse whose roof leaked on her when it rained, and chilled her when the autumn wind blew. The risk of going out without papers was increased by the possibility of collaborators informing the authorities.

She had read until her eyes watered, and evolved a daily exercise régime to keep herself fit. Mostly it was the farmer's wife who had brought her food, but sometimes it was the farmer himself. A ruddy-faced man with eyes that undressed her. He would engage her in uncomfortable conversation, staying much longer than required, a strange, lascivious smile never far from his lips. The latent threat of something more sinister in his intent was ever-present.

Physical fitness was easy to maintain; mental acuity was not. Hope gave way to depression. Depression to despair. And she found herself, latterly, crying herself to sleep at night, burying her face in the pillow.

It wasn't until Lucien climbed up into the attic one bright winter morning that hope flooded like light back into her life. She remembered very well the man who had led her through the woods in the dark the night that Hugh Verity flew her to France, and when he grinned and brandished her papers she burst into tears.

Before the week was out, she was on a train heading for Paris, briefed on her cover story. She was an assistant curator heading for the capital to take up a post at the Musée du Jeu de Paume. It was safer that she retained her real identity. After all, her background and training made her an ideal fit for the job. Her absence from Paris was explained by an illness and lengthy rehabilitation at the home of some friends of her late parents. It was prudent always to stick as close as possible to the truth.

She found it dispiriting, sitting in that crowded railway carriage, watching her country spool by beyond the window. A country she could no longer call her own. A birthright stolen by the invasion and suppressed by the occupation. All the more poignant because nothing on the other side of the glass appeared to have changed. France looked as it always had. Her France. Her people. Except that there were few of them in evidence in the towns and villages they passed through, and even fewer vehicles on the road. And as they transited from so-called Free France into the occupied zone, it was Germans she saw. Men in long winter coats over grey uniforms, rifles slung across their shoulders, helmets pulled down on pale, alien faces. It filled her with both sadness and anger.

The station at Montparnasse was filled with commuters, and as she stepped into the street outside, she was astonished to see her beloved Paris in full, unfettered flow, almost as if nothing had happened. People crowded the cafés and brasseries, queued at bus stops, filled the sidewalks. Only the military-green vehicles of the occupying army, and the vacant stares of helmeted soldiers gazing from the back of canvas-covered troop carriers, provided a reminder, if one was necessary, that all was not as normal.

'Papers!' A harsh voice drew her head around, and she found herself confronted by two surly soldiers who stared at her with both suspicion and resentment. The suspicion she understood. The resentment surprised her. But, then, what kind of posting must it be for young men sent to enforce an occupation where they were universally despised by the population? Being resented would breed resentment, which in turn was dangerous. It would be hard to empathise with those who hated you, and you would surely end up hating them back.

Georgette placed her little cardboard suitcase at her feet and fumbled in her bag for her travel and identity documents. She thrust them at the outstretched hand. The soldier who had asked for them studied her papers carefully. The other never took his eyes off her. She was unnerved. Did he suspect her of something, or was he just indulging in some male fantasy? Either way, she felt vulnerable. Physically and mentally. His colleague returned her papers and they moved off without a word.

Only then was she aware of her increased heart rate, and a trembling in her legs. No, there was nothing normal about any of this, despite appearances to the contrary. This was not her Paris, not her France. It was a counterfeit country, an elaborate illusion to lull her into a false sense of security. And she knew she could not lower her guard for even one moment.

It took her nearly forty minutes to walk from the Gare Montparnasse to the Rue de Rivoli, past bakeries and pastry shops, butchers and wine merchants, all doing brisk business in this ersatz Paris. She felt like a ghost, or perhaps the only real person in a city of ghosts. But none of it seemed real, and by the time she reached the Tuileries gardens, and saw the street lined with giant swastikas hanging from poles set at forty-five-degree angles all along its length, she knew she had left her old world behind and stepped into the middle of a nightmare.

The Jeu de Paume was situated in a corner of the Tuileries, next to the Place de la Concorde, about a fifteen-minute walk from the Louvre. It was extended from the original *orangerie* in the nineteenth century as a sports hall for the pursuit of the game that gave it its name. Jeu de Paume. Or Real Tennis. It had tall arched windows along each side of its considerable length, designed to cast light on the game of kings. But by the early twentieth century it had become an art gallery, which it remained until the Germans rolled into the city in June 1940.

When Georgette arrived, the main hall was full of paintings leaning at all angles, arranged in makeshift racks, rows of sculptures in marble and bronze lined up between them. There was nothing on display here. It more resembled a giant warehouse than an art gallery, and Georgette picked her way through the chaos, avoiding German soldiers carrying works of art in and out, to and from a group of lorries parked outside.

She found a civilian, a harassed-looking young woman whom she was relieved to find spoke French. She caught her arm. 'I'm looking for Rose Valland,' she said.

The girl looked at her suspiciously. 'And who should I say is looking for her?'

'My name's Georgette Pignal. I'm expected.'

Not by this girl, evidently. For she simply shrugged her

indifference and told Georgette to wait, before vanishing among the stacks of paintings. It was fully ten minutes before Rose Valland appeared, looking stressed and distracted.

Rose was in her early forties, a small woman with mousy brown hair cut short and dragged back from a round face. Dark overalls provided protection for a patterned blouse and tweed skirt, and she wore a silk scarf tied loosely at her neck. She peered disapprovingly at Georgette through round spectacles little bigger than her eyes.

'I was expecting someone older,' she said.

'So was I,' Georgette replied. It did not go down well.

'Follow me.' Rose marched off among the collected art-works, heels clicking on parquet flooring. 'Too much light for paintings in the main hall,' she called back over her shoulder as Georgette struggled to keep up. 'Ideal for sculptures and other exhibits. We display our paintings in the smaller galleries upstairs.' And she started off up a marble staircase.

Two German army officers wearing swastika armbands passed them on the way down.

Rose nodded politely. 'Good afternoon, gentlemen,' she said. 'Brighter today, but still cold.'

'Freezing, madame,' one of them replied, rubbing his hands together for warmth. 'We should see about trying to get better heating in here.'

Both nodded at Georgette. The one who had spoken to Rose raised one eyebrow, denoting apparent interest, and smiled. He said, 'Afternoon, mademoiselle.'

Georgette could not bring herself to meet his eye, and hurried past them without a word. Both men stopped and looked after her. She kept her head down until she reached the top of the stairs where she found Rose waiting for her, lips pulled together and white with anger. Fingers like steel grasped her upper arm and steered her away from the staircase. Rose brought her face close to Georgette's and in a tight little whisper she said, 'When you encounter Germans in this building, you smile and say hello, and make polite conversation, regardless of what you feel. Is that understood?'

Georgette felt like a naughty schoolgirl being dressed down by a disapproving teacher.

'In here.' Rose opened the door to a small office off the main gallery, waited until Georgette had entered, then shut it behind her. She turned towards the new arrival. 'My gallery has been requisitioned by the Germans,' she said. 'It is no longer a place for the appreciation of art. It is where they store their stolen goods. Some of the most beautiful works of art anywhere in the world, confiscated from their rightful owners – mostly Jews – and reduced to a commodity. Filed and catalogued to be shipped back to the motherland and hung in the homes of huns desperate to convince the rest of the world that they are really very civilised people.'

She stopped to draw breath, and Georgette was almost shocked by her intensity.

'The rightful owners of these works have either fled abroad, or been arrested and sent to work camps in Germany. My staff and myself are here only on sufferance, as managers of this traffic in contraband. But while all the fruits of their theft come and go, they are not the only ones who are making an inventory. We have kept our own records of every piece they have brought in, and every piece which has left, and where it was sent. And one day, God willing, we will know exactly where to find it when the Nazis have been ground into the dust. And I will make it my life's work to get it all back.'

Passion blazed in her dark eyes.

'And I will not have you or anyone else put that at risk. Is that clear?'

Georgette nodded, chastened, and not a little overawed. At least, she thought, she wouldn't be here for long, and would not have to endure the disapproval of the formidable Miss Valland outside of working hours.

Rose walked around her desk and gazed from the window down into the Rue de Rivoli. The German administrative authority had taken over almost the entire street, as well as several of the blocks around it. At length she turned. Light reflecting on her glasses hid her eyes from Georgette. 'It has been impossible to find you accommodation at such short notice.' She sighed. 'So, for the moment you are going to have to stay at my apartment.' It was clear that she was unhappy with the arrangement.

She rounded the desk, suddenly businesslike.

'Now, I can't afford to waste any more time. We are setting up an exhibition in one of the upstairs rooms for a VIP visitor tomorrow.' Her lips curled with distaste. 'Hermann Göring himself.'

Rose Valland's apartment was at number four Rue de Navarre in the fifth arrondissement, in an orange-brick apartment block built ten years earlier in the art deco style. A small flat with long, narrow rooms and high, corniced ceilings. Georgette was relieved to find that there was a spare bedroom off the hall at the back of the building. But she would have to share a bathroom with Rose, and take her turn to cook for herself in the tiny kitchen.

Georgette put her suitcase on the bed and sat down beside it. She cast miserable eyes around her new sleeping quarters. Warmer and drier, perhaps, than where she had spent the last three months, but no less a prison. God only knew how long she was going to have to tread water here in Paris before finally they would send her off in the footsteps of *La Joconde*. She stood up and walked to the window to look out at lights that twinkled dully in the darkness of the back courts. Depression fell over her like a shroud shaken free of its folds, black and all-enveloping.

There was a sharp knock at the door. It opened before she had a chance to respond, and she turned to see Rose standing in the doorway. The older woman had shed her overalls now and changed her patterned blouse for a white one. She had a cigarette in her mouth, and leaned against the door jamb as she tipped her head forward to light it. She blew a jet of blue smoke through thin lips.

She said, 'I rise at 6.30 every morning and will expect the bathroom to be free. I will also expect to find it spotless. When you use the kitchen you will clean the cooker and the work surfaces after you. You may use the sitting room when I am not at home, but otherwise I expect you to remain in your bedroom. There is a phone on the hall table. If you make any calls you will be required to pay for them. I will take ten per cent of your wages as a contribution towards heating and electricity. Oh, and no smoking in the bedroom.' She blew another jet of smoke into the room where it gathered briefly before dispersing in the light of the overhead lamp.

'I don't smoke,' Georgette said testily.

'So much the better.'

Georgette stared at her very directly. 'You do know why I'm here?'

'In my apartment?'

'In France.'

Rose demonstrated her disapproval with a theatrical sigh. 'Yes, I know why you're here,' she said.

'Well, I wish I did. The *Mona Lisa* is in a château somewhere in the Loire, where I have just spent most of the last three miserable months in a freezing cold attic.'

'You are a little behind the times, my dear. *La Joconde*, along with most of the other tableaux, has moved several times since then. She currently resides in the south-west, in a museum in Montauban.'

'So why wasn't I sent there?'

'Because in this France we now inhabit, nothing is ever that simple. Arranging the appropriate papers, getting official permissions. It all takes time. And these are things which are entirely out of our hands.'

Georgette's frustration came close to boiling over. 'Well, what kind of time are we talking about?'

Rose pushed herself away from the door jamb. 'My dear, that is in the lap of the gods, or should I say the Germans. Not that I would ever be likely to confuse the two.' She drew on her cigarette. 'Right now, it's impossible to say when you might be allowed to travel.' She tipped her head back to blow smoke at the ceiling. 'If ever.'

Georgette was in the grand gallery the following morning when Göring arrived. She had been assigned to the care of the girl she had met on her arrival the day before. Lucie. Several years her junior. A student before the occupation, she told Georgette. But classes had been cancelled and she had been lucky to find work here, moving and cataloguing artworks as they arrived, before carrying them down to the basement where they would await shipment to Germany.

Göring stepped out of a large, black, touring Mercedes at the door, two adjutants at his back. Another two vehicles in the entourage drew in behind it, and officers in army and air force uniforms gathered in his wake. 'What's he here for?' Georgette whispered to Lucie.

'To choose artworks for his personal collection. He's been

two or three times already. We are instructed exactly what to put on display for him, and he always views the exhibits in person before making his decision.'

Georgette looked on with a certain sense of awe. Göring was second only in rank to Hitler himself. But he was not at all what she would have expected. A big man, overweight, wearing a long, dark military coat and wide-brimmed black fedora, he walked awkwardly with the use of a stick. His round face was flushed pink, and cold eyes surveyed everything around him with proprietorial indifference.

'Who is everyone else?'

Lucie shrugged. 'Who knows. People from the Kunstschutz and ERR. Usually different faces each time.' She nodded towards the back of the entourage as it passed, heading for the stairs. 'The one with the flying jacket, he's been before. A real cold fish. Wolff, I've heard them call him.'

Georgette ran eyes of appraisal over him. Tall and holding himself very erect. He stood out from the others, with his black leather jacket and blue jodhpurs tucked into knee-high black leather boots. Perhaps he sensed her eyes on him, for he cast her a glance as he passed, a chilling lack of warmth in pale blue eyes.

The party climbed the stairs and disappeared from view, and Lucie asked Georgette to give her a hand carrying a particularly large canvas down to the basement.

They spent most of the next forty minutes or more re-stacking labelled canvasses near the foot of the basement stairs in preparation for departure tomorrow. The *tableaux* were to travel by rail to Berlin.

'Oh,' Lucie said suddenly. 'I forgot, those have to go upstairs.' She pointed to a small pile of framed miniature paintings on the long sorting table. 'Could you take them up? First floor. They've to go to the gallery at the far end.'

'Sure.' Georgette was happy to have an excuse to go upstairs, curious about Göring and his party, and what the head of the Luftwaffe's taste in art might be. She arranged the miniatures in her arms and climbed the stairs from the basement to the ground floor, then began the ascent to the first.

Ahead of her she heard voices and footsteps, and looked up to see Göring at the head of his entourage coming down the steps towards her. He seemed in a good mood, laughing at some private joke. And it appeared that when Göring laughed everyone else was expected to laugh with him. Unless the joke really was that funny.

There was very little room on the staircase for the Göring party to pass, and Georgette stepped to one side, trying to make herself small. But her elbow caught on the handrail, and the half dozen miniatures she carried tipped out of her arms to tumble noisily all over the steps. The group came to a halt. Flustered and panicking, Georgette muttered apologies and started trying to gather up the fallen paintings.

Göring glowered at her, and supporting himself on his stick, moved to one side to squeeze past.

'Sorry,' she muttered again, as the rest of them tried to avoid her on their way down.

'You silly little bitch!' a voice hissed at her. She looked up to see that it was the officer in the flying jacket. She was still crouched down to retrieve the miniatures and he glared at her. 'Do you not know who that is? You need to take a damned sight more care, do you hear?' His French was heavily accented.

'Lay off her, Wolff, it was an accident.' More French, but less of an accent. An officer in army greys crouched down beside her so that their faces were on a level. He had luminous green eyes flecked with orange, and sandy, fair hair swept back from a broad brow. His smile revealed perfectly white teeth. Twelve, maybe fourteen years older than her, but still a good-looking man. And the warmth in his hazel eyes was almost radiant. 'Here, let me give you a hand.' And he started picking up some of the miniatures to pile up in her arms. Georgette flushed with embarrassment.

'You're a fool, Lange, if you think you can curry favour with these people by being nice to them.' Wolff had resorted to German now. Georgette's grasp of the language was limited, but she did not miss the rancour in it. Wolff turned on his heel and hurried after the rest of the group.

Lange stood up with Georgette and smiled at her mortification. 'I don't think I've seen you here before. Are you new?'

She nodded, hardly able to meet his eyes. 'I started yesterday. Assistant curator.'

His eyebrows shot up in surprise. 'And does the assistant curator have a name?'

'Pignal. Mademoiselle Pignal.'

There was a sardonic quality to his smile now. 'And does Mademoiselle Pignal have a first name?'

Her mouth was so dry that she had difficulty unsticking her tongue from the roof of her mouth. 'Georgette.'

'Well, Georgette Pignal, I very much hope that I'll see you next time I'm here.' He nodded and touched the brim of his cap, and hurried down the stairs to catch up with the entourage.

Georgette gathered herself together, breathing hard to try to slow her heart rate, and hurried on up to the top of the steps. She very nearly bumped into Rose, dressed again in her long, dark overalls. She stood, a shadow against the light, glaring down at Georgette with arms folded across her chest. Her voice was low and controlled, but laden with suppressed fury. 'What did I tell you yesterday, you stupid girl? Do you have any idea who that was asking for your name?'

Georgette shook her head.

'That was Paul Lange. He spent a lot of time in Paris before the war buying and selling art and is rumoured to be a personal friend of Hitler.' She drew a long, slow breath, still trembling with anger. 'Do you speak German?'

'I understand it.'

'Well, don't let them know that. It makes them careless in your company. But in any event, you do *not* draw attention to yourself. I don't know how long it's going to take you to learn this, but unless discussing inconsequentialities like the weather we have to be invisible, mademoiselle. Like servants waiting table for their wealthy masters. We see and hear nothing, and are neither seen nor heard. Get that through your thick skull.' And she turned and marched off towards her office.

CHAPTER FOURTEEN

Enzo had never enjoyed Paris in autumn or winter. Like London it was cold and damp and grey, and traffic pollution hung over the city in a sulphurous pall. Less so since lockdown. For several months in the spring, Paris had been an abandoned city. People working from home if they could, or simply staying away from their place of work and living on government subsidies. Traffic had reduced to a trickle and levels of pollution plummeted. Although a degree of normality had returned with the lifting of stringent restrictions over the summer, a second wave of the virus had once more curtailed daily life.

Just three-quarters of an hour north-west of the city itself, traffic on the Boulevard de l'Hautil, in the new town of Cergy-Pontoise, was light as Enzo headed past the Commissariat de police de Cergy, before turning into the car park of the IRCGN at number five.

He had driven up from the south-west the day before, and stayed overnight in Paris at a pied-à-terre belonging to friends in the Rue Guénégaud in the sixth arrondissement. It was some years since he had last seen Magali, and he was looking forward to renewing their acquaintance. They had met when he first established the department of forensic science at Paul Sabatier University in Toulouse, and she had visited as a guest lecturer. There had been an instant attraction. But, then, she had been married. And he had broken a home once, causing pain to people he loved. So had no intention of doing it again.

The IRCGN, or Institute de Recherche Criminelle Gendarmerie Nationale, was a state-of-the-art forensic science centre, providing services for gendarmeries throughout France. It comprised laboratories in four departments over 20,000 square metres. The wearing of masks was obligatory within the facility, and Enzo slipped his on before getting his security pass at reception and being directed towards the Human Identification Department, and the office of Magali Blanc on the first floor.

It was a tiny office with a view of a staff car park at the rear, and a leaden sky above. Even masked by her face-covering, Enzo could tell that she remained a good-looking woman, and that warm penetrating look in her eyes still gave him butterflies. Frustratingly, they were constrained from a more intimate greeting by the two-metre rule, and stood looking at each other across her desk.

'How have you been?' she asked.

Enzo grinned. 'Retired.'

'Yes, I heard.'

'Careless of you to lose my contact details.'

He saw her mask stretched by a smile. 'Just putting

temptation out of my way. I hear you finally settled down. Got yourself married.'

'Only because you weren't available, Magali.'

She laughed. 'You haven't changed, anyway.'

He shrugged. 'Just got older.' He retrieved a pair of latex gloves from his pocket and pulled them on before fishing a large buff envelope from his shoulder bag. He held it out for her. 'Untouched by human hand in more than twenty-four hours. Quite safe for you to handle.'

She opened it and pulled out half a dozen colour prints. The photographs Enzo had taken at the site of the fallen tree in Carennac. She looked up, surprised. 'I got the jpegs. You didn't come all the way to Paris just to give me these, did you?'

He made a moue with his lips that she couldn't see. 'I've got a date for you as well.'

She frowned. 'A date?'

'It was clear to me that whoever killed your unfortunate gentleman took advantage of a trench already dug in the park for a drainage pipe. A freshly dug grave would otherwise surely have excited interest.'

'So they buried him in the trench before the pipe got laid.'

'And records at the mairie show that work on laying drainage pipes in the park took place between June 5th and June 9th, 1944.'

'Right around D-Day.'

Enzo nodded. 'If we assume that work was completed on June 9th, that's probably when they laid the pipe and filled in the trench. If work began on June 5th, that'll be when they started digging it. By hand. So it'll have taken a day or two, presupposing the *cantonnier* was working on his own.'

'Which means that our man was probably buried on the 7th or the 8th.' She shook her head in admiration. 'That's quite a piece of detective work, Enzo. Would you like to see the remains?'

'Very much.'

She led him through to her adjoining laboratory where two long tables were covered with large sheets of newsprint. The remains found under the dead tree in Carennac were carefully laid out on both, beneath the glare of bright overhead lamps.

What was left of the skeleton was roughly assembled on the table that stood in the centre of the room. Various other artefacts recovered from the site were set out on the second table which was pushed against the window-facing wall. Many of the bones were broken. Others were simply missing. They were reddish-brown in hue, having absorbed the pigment of the soil.

Magali walked around the table. 'It's a little like trying to do a jigsaw puzzle without all the pieces. Over time the roots of the tree must have insinuated their way through the skeletal remains, breaking many of the bones.' She looked at him. 'I'm assuming that there was no tree there at the time of the burial.'

'As far as I could tell, the remains pre-date the tree. But the tree was just as dead as our cadaver. Although it had probably enjoyed many years of growth, inflicting damage on the bones before it died.'

'What killed the tree?'

'Some kind of fungal disease, by the look of it. It was a tilia.

Better known to you and me as a lime tree. And it had been dead for some time.'

'A bit like our man from the Luftwaffe.'

Enzo tipped his head in curiosity. 'Yes ... about that. Enlighten me. How can you tell?'

She crossed to the other table, and Enzo looked in detail for the first time at the odd collection of bits and pieces that the gendarmes had recovered from the grave. A rusted cigarette tin. The remains of a brass Zippo lighter. A corroded Iron Cross in poor condition. The remnants of a black leather jacket, and boots. Shrunken, faded and cracked. Cotton thread holding seams had disintegrated, and so they had mostly come apart. Magali snapped on latex gloves and very carefully turned over what was left of the jacket. 'The fabric of his clothes – cotton and wool – will have biodegraded years ago. Leather lasts much longer. And we were lucky that a fold in the jacket preserved this almost intact.'

With delicate fingers she unfolded a flap of leather to reveal the remains of a Luftwaffe eagle patch with swastika.

'Insignia of the German air force. These things were embroidered with aluminium thread, and this one would have lasted for many more decades. Like all the other metal bits and pieces recovered.' She fingered them as she spoke, almost lovingly. 'A zip fastening for the jacket, and a couple of pocket zips. Two longer zips that probably belong with the boots. We also have the remnants of a leather belt and holster. No gun, of course. Whoever killed him would have taken that.'

Using a pair of tweezers, she lifted one of a number of small, deformed metal shapes that seemed as if they might once have been round.

'Aluminium again. Epaulette buttons, and what look like they might have been four pips denoting rank. In this case, Hauptmann. Or captain, as we would say. Assuming we got them all.'

Enzo shook his head in admiration. 'It's amazing what survives us.' He looked at Magali. 'And what you can tell from what remains. That's an amazing piece of work.'

She flushed with pleasure at his compliment, but brushed it aside. 'It's my job, Enzo. It's what I do.'

'What about the guy himself? What do you know about him?'

She turned back to the table with the skeletal remains and lifted what was left of the skull. 'What appears to have been a single bullet has shattered much of the cranium. A wound like that would have killed him instantly.' With gentle reverence, she laid the Hauptmann's skull back on the newsprint and lifted the left femur. 'Fortunately this was still intact. The right femur was broken in several places and missing pieces. But from the length of this one I used an established regression formula to calculate height. He would have been around one metre eighty-two.' She smiled at Enzo from behind her mask. 'Or, as you would probably understand it better, about six feet. Tall for the time, but shorter than you.'

She moved then up to the hips and the pelvic area.

'The pubic bones present a narrow sub-pubic angle with a narrow sciatic notch, and from what we can see of the remains of the cranium he had well-developed brow ridges. Take all that into account, throw in the external occipital protuberance and the mastoids, and I would stake my reputation on this being a male. Even without the external artefacts.'

Enzo laughed. 'Not a female drag artist, then, disguising herself as the enemy?'

Magali canted her head in mock disapproval. 'I think you can take that as a given, Enzo.'

'Ethnicity?'

She removed a pen from the breast pocket of her white lab coat and poked it gently around the skull. 'High and narrow nasal root, narrow nasal aperture, nasal spine, laterally-placed cheekbones and a well-developed jaw. Almost certainly white European.'

'Age?'

'Judging by the pubic bones and the cranial suture closure, I would say somewhere around his mid-forties.'

'Sheer genius.' Enzo expressed his admiration. 'It almost makes me wish I was back in the business.' He waved his hand towards the window. 'This whole complex . . . there was nothing like it when I was working in forensics back in Scotland.'

She nodded. 'It's an amazing place to work. You know, they now have a mobile DNA analysis laboratory. They call it LabADN, and they can come up with someone's DNA profile in under four hours – *at* the crime scene.'

Enzo scratched his head thoughtfully then nodded towards the table. 'What about this fella's DNA?'

Magali laughed. 'I haven't looked at it.'

'Why not?'

'Because I'm not going to find it on any database, Enzo. As you very well know, it was nearly five decades after the Hauptmann's death before DNA fingerprinting was even developed.'

'DNA transcends time, Magali. I've lost count of the number of cases I've been able to resolve with familial matching.'

'Now, that's what I call a long shot. That the DNA of some descendant is languishing in a European database somewhere?'

Enzo shrugged. 'My whole life has been based on long shots.' He tipped his head towards the table. 'You can get a sample from ground bone?'

'I could.'

'Might be worth a try, Magali. Wouldn't it be nice to put a name to him?'

'It would be a bloody miracle.' Her smile faded as she gazed at him. 'You miss this, don't you?'

Enzo was reluctant to admit it, but in the end relented. 'I suppose I do.'

'And what do you do? All day every day?'

'I get older, Magali. A day at a time. When you're working you never stop to think about it. Time passes, and one day you look at yourself in the mirror and realise that ten years have gone by. And then twenty, and then thirty. And you only begin to notice it when everything starts hurting as you climb out of bed in the morning.' He ran a hand back through greying hair. 'When you're retired, you look at yourself in the mirror every morning and start counting off the days.' He averted his gaze from what looked like sympathy in her eyes.

'That doesn't sound like much fun.'

He laughed it off. 'I have other distractions. Like trying to keep up with the needs of a woman twenty years my junior.'

'Now that *does* sound like fun.'

They both laughed.

He said, 'And I have the joy of watching my son as he grows up.' He paused. 'And then an unexpected little murder that I have you to thank for.'

Her eyes opened wide in surprise. 'Not our Hauptmann, surely?'

'No. But going to Carennac to take your photographs, I managed to get myself embroiled in a murder committed in the house right next door.'

'Embroiled?'

'They asked me to consult on it.'

Laughter lines creased around her eyes. 'Well, maybe that'll stop you looking in the mirror every morning.' She peeled off her gloves. 'But what a coincidence!'

Enzo scratched his head. 'Maybe.'

She looked at him blankly. 'You don't think there's some connection, do you?'

'Probably not,' he conceded. 'But I do hate coincidences.'

CHAPTER FIFTEEN

The Rue des Filles du Calvaire was a long straight street of three- and four-storey apartment blocks above clothes shops and bookstores and a proliferation of art galleries.

There was little or no traffic in the street and, unusually, many of the parking slots along each side lay empty. Most of the clothes shops were shut. Helios. Danyberd. Some of the bookstores were open for business, and a number of the galleries were open by appointment.

Galerie Narcisse had lights in its window, and a large poster advertising an exhibition of the work of Canadian photographer Alix Cléo Roubaud. Enzo ignored the notice which read BY APPOINTMENT ONLY, and rang the bell. He saw a young woman approaching from the other side of the glass and pulled his mask up over his mouth and nose. She hurriedly produced one of her own before opening the door.

'Can I help you? It's viewing by appointment.'

Enzo said, 'I'm sure Ms Roubaud's photographs are excellent, but I'm here to talk to someone about the murder of Emile Narcisse.'

She looked him up and down and frowned. 'You don't look like the police.'

'I'm not. But I'm consulting on the case.'

She looked at him uncertainly. 'Wait there.' Then she hesitated. 'What's your name?'

'Enzo Macleod.'

Again, she frowned, then shut the door and hurried off into the interior of the gallery. Enzo stood shuffling impatiently on the pavement, feeling the cold and watching his breath condense around him, feeling it form droplets on the inside of his mask.

Finally the young woman returned and opened the door. 'Follow me.'

He had trouble keeping up with her as she hurried ahead to maintain a two-metre distance. Dark black-and-white images hung in frames from aluminium rails. A woman whose face was blurred by movement, hair absorbed by her shadow on the wall. A man and woman kissing against the backdrop of a brick wall, her hands on the back of his head and on his shoulder, all that could be seen of her.

'Ms Roubaud must be disappointed to be exhibiting her work during a pandemic,' he said.

'Ms Roubaud is dead,' the young woman said, and stopped at the foot of a narrow spiral staircase leading up to a mezzanine level. A man stood at a large window looking down at them. 'Upstairs,' she said. 'Monsieur Moreau was an assistant to Monsieur Narcisse.' And she stepped back to give Enzo access to the stairs.

At the top of the steps, a corridor ran off to the left, doors opening from it right and left. To Enzo's right, a door opened into the office from which the man at the window had watched him climb the stairs. The whole place was deceptively large.

The man turned from the window as Enzo appeared in his doorway and Enzo saw him clearly for the first time. A tall, willowy young man, hair cropped close on either side of his head, leaving a slick of thick black that swept back across his crown. He wore a black mask, a dark suit and white shirt, but no tie. 'Stop there, please,' he said, raising a hand to make it clear that he did not wish Enzo to enter the office. 'I'd be obliged if you'd keep your distance. I'm HIV-positive, so wary of catching Covid. What can I do for you?'

'I assume you have already spoken to the police?'

'Actually, no. Several officers arrived the day after the murder to search his office. They took away a number of items, including his laptop. They did speak to other members of staff, but I wasn't here that day.'

'Were you and Narcisse close?'

'He was my mentor, monsieur.'

'So you know why he was in Carennac.'

His face coloured slightly. 'No, I don't.'

'He didn't tell you?'

A curt shake of the head. 'No.'

Enzo raised an eyebrow. 'Is that not unusual?'

'He was my professional mentor, monsieur. We had very little personal contact outside of work.'

'So you think he went to Carennac on personal business? Otherwise he would have told you?'

Moreau seemed uncomfortable. 'Probably.'

'I assume you knew he was writing a biography of Rose Valland?'

Now he frowned, deep creases that furrowed an otherwise unlined forehead. 'I don't believe he was doing any such thing.'

'You'd have known if he was?'

'Of course. But in any case, it's not something he would ever have considered. Rose Valland? I don't think so.'

His reaction was so categorical that Enzo was inclined to believe him. He said, 'What do you know about the circumstances surrounding the murder?'

'Very little, other than what I have read in the press and heard on the grapevine.'

'You know that there is a suspect, then?'

'Yes, but they haven't released details of who that is.'

'Would it surprise you to learn that it was a young German gallery director called Hans Bauer?'

This time, the colour rose high on Moreau's face, and for the first time his cool composure deserted him. 'Bauer?' he said incredulously.

Enzo was taken aback. 'You know him?'

'Well, yes. He was here just a few days ago. He had an appointment with Monsieur Narcisse.'

Enzo felt his own cheeks burning now. 'About what?'

'I have no idea. Monsieur Narcisse didn't say. But Bauer

didn't stay long. Ten minutes at the most, and he left in a temper, the most foul of moods. A very unpleasant individual.'

'When was this exactly?'

Moreau rounded his desk to open a large appointments diary. He flicked through the pages then ran a long, thin, nicotine-stained finger down the entries. 'A week ago to the day. At 3 p.m. Monsieur Narcisse himself made the entry, so he must have arranged it by telephone.'

'Or email.'

Moreau shook his head. 'He never embraced the technology, Monsieur Macleod.'

'So what happened to put Bauer in such a bad mood?'

'I really couldn't say. Monsieur Narcisse was in his office for an hour or so after he left. Most of that time on the telephone.' He nodded towards an intercom phone on his desk. 'I could see his extension light on. Later he came and asked me if I would arrange return rail tickets for him to Brive-la-Gaillarde, and reserve him a room at a hotel in the village of Carennac. But I have to say, I never associated the trip with his rendezvous with Bauer.'

'So it was you who booked him into the Fenelon.'

'Yes. It was the only hotel open out of season.'

'And he didn't tell you the purpose of his visit?'

'No, he didn't.' And there was a defensive quality in his tone that told Enzo that perhaps Moreau had resented his mentor's secrecy. He had not connected Narcisse's hastily arranged trip with the visit from Bauer. But Enzo now realised it had everything to do with it.

If only he knew what they had talked about.

It had begun to rain, and light from all the apartments around the courtyard reflected yellow in its dark cobbles. The chestnut tree at the far side of it had shed most of its leaves by now, and stood nearly naked against the lights in the windows beyond.

Enzo sat looking through rain that ran like tears down the window. He and Raffin had not had anything to say to each other since Kirsty went off to the kitchen to make tea, and he felt a weight of melancholy press down on his chest.

This apartment, in the heart of the capital, a stone's throw from the floodlit Sénat building at the top of the street, held more memories than Enzo cared to remember. All of which had been played out to the accompaniment of the clumsy pianist still practising scales somewhere in the building.

Enzo forced his eyes away from the window and glanced at Raffin. He was sitting at the far end of the table, wearing an ill-fitting mask and reading the first edition of the evening paper. It was he who had first caught Covid in the spring, bringing it home with him and infecting Kirsty and Alexis. While Kirsty had suffered only mild symptoms, and Alexis none at all, Raffin had ended up in intensive care, where it had been touch-and-go for several days as to whether or not he would be placed on a ventilator. Induced comas and ventilators were the treatment of last resort, and the prognosis was never good. Fortunately for Raffin his viral infection had peaked before that became necessary, and he had begun a long, slow recovery. But it had reduced him still further from the young man with whom Enzo had collaborated on the seven unsolved murders that the journalist had written about in his book, *Assassins Cachés*. And what was only a few years of age difference between him and Kirsty now seemed much greater.

But for her part, Kirsty appeared content with the man she had married, and although Enzo had never understood her feelings for him, he could only be happy for her.

Kirsty came in carrying a tray laden with cups and saucers and a pot of freshly made tea, a rarity for Enzo in this land of coffee. Her mask was dangling from one ear, but she looped it over the other as soon as she had laid down the tray. She was only too aware that her father had managed to avoid contracting the virus, and that at his age it was likely to be fatal if he did.

'So,' she said, as she sat down equidistantly from her husband and her father and began to pour. 'Apart from this investigation you're doing into the murder in the Lot ...'

'I'm only consulting,' Enzo interrupted.

Kirsty rolled her eyes. 'Yes, Papa. This investigation that you're *consulting* on ...' she corrected herself. 'Apart from that, what brings you to Paris?'

'To see my daughter and son-in-law, of course.'

Kirsty gave him a look. 'We all know that's just an excuse for coming to see your grandson.'

Enzo grinned. 'Can't think of a better one.'

'He won't be home for an hour or so yet.'

Enzo smiled. 'Good. That gives us time to talk.'

Kirsty shook her head fondly. 'Here we go. The real reason for the visit.'

Raffin looked up from his paper, interested for the first time, as Kirsty pushed his tea along the table towards him. He regarded it without enthusiasm. 'Maybe your papa would prefer something stronger. A whisky, perhaps?' He glanced hopefully at his father-in-law, and Enzo knew that it was Raffin who wanted the whisky.

He shook his head. 'Perhaps it's Kirsty who'll want something stronger.' And he turned his gaze towards his daughter.

She looked at him with suspicion. 'What,' she said flatly.

He hesitated only briefly. 'I want you to fly to Berlin with me tomorrow.'

Her teacup paused halfway to her lips and she stared at him across its brim. 'Are you mad?'

'I need someone to translate for me.'

'Papa, we're in the middle of a pandemic!'

'I read somewhere that public transport was one of the safest places to be because of all the disinfecting and distancing protocols they've put in place. And, anyway, you shouldn't be in any danger.'

'It's not me I'm thinking about. If you get it at your age, it'll probably kill you.'

He felt a flush of annoyance. 'I'll tell you what'll kill me.

Sitting at home in some social bubble defined by the government, counting off the days till I die of old age. I'm not an idiot, Kirsty, you know that. I learned enough about viral infection in the course of my career to be hyperconscious of the risks. Even of catching a cold. I've always carried disinfectant wipes to clean the armrests and tray tables in aeroplanes. Sophie used to call me Howard Hughes. Now everyone else is just as aware as I am, so I figure the risk of me catching anything is probably lower than it ever has been.' He paused to catch his breath and thought better of continuing. Instead he said, 'Rant over.'

She looked at him hard, and knew of old that there was little point in arguing with him. 'Why?'

'Why what?'

'Why do you want to go to Berlin?'

He released his tension in a long, slow breath, glad that the travel argument was over. 'Hans Bauer, the suspect in the Narcisse murder, lives there.'

'I thought you said he'd gone missing. You surely don't expect to find him in Berlin?'

'No. It looks like he never made it out of the locale. He might even be dead for all we know.'

'So what's the point in going to Berlin?'

'If Bauer did kill Narcisse, I need to understand why. Nicole has done a little research for me. Apparently his mother died a week or so ago, and he stands to inherit quite a bit of money. He also lived with his girlfriend in a very upmarket apartment in a chic quarter of the city. She could very well be the key to finding out what the hell went on in Carennac. Why Narcisse and Bauer were there. And what the two men talked about when they met in Paris just two days before the murder.'

Raffin was suddenly attentive. 'They met in Paris? That's new. I haven't read anything about that in the press.'

'Because not even the police know that yet.' Enzo was aware that anything fresh on the Narcisse murder would be of interest to Raffin's paper, *Libération*. He said quickly, 'But I'd rather keep that quiet for the moment. Though I can promise you, Roger, that if I manage to throw any light on this murder, you will be the first to know.' Which he knew would be enough to keep Raffin's enthusiasm in check for the moment. He turned towards Kirsty. 'Will you come with me?'

She sighed. 'Well, I'm not going to let you go on your own!'

CHAPTER SIXTEEN

PARIS, TWO DAYS BEFORE THE MURDER

Bauer gazed sightlessly from his taxi at the streets of the French capital drifting past his window, the waters of the Seine a sluggish leaden grey as it passed beneath the Pont Neuf. It was his first time in Paris, and he was surprised at how quiet it was. The pandemic, he supposed. Though the streets of Berlin were much more animated.

His driver, separated from the back seat by a perspex screen, pulled in at the Place du Carrousel, and told him over the intercom that the short drive from his boutique hotel just across the river had cost him twenty-three euros. Bauer paid by credit card on a machine in the back and felt contaminated after tapping in his code.

He stepped out into the Cour Napoléon and fished a small bottle of gel from his pocket to stand disinfecting his hands as he gazed at the glass pyramid. It was much bigger than he had expected, and clashed much less with the classical facade

240

of the palace than his lecturer in architecture at university had led him to believe.

He was trembling with excitement. Just a few minutes away from seeing her in the flesh. He had booked a time for his visit online before leaving Berlin, and hurried now across the court-yard to the main entrance, descending to the reception area to join his time-slot-specific queue. He could not stay here as long as he might have liked. His rendezvous with Narcisse was in just over an hour, the only time the art dealer could fit him in. A brief appointment. Barely time for Bauer to convince him.

He gelled his hands again from the dispenser at the door, received his map, and stood in the foyer examining it and adjusting his mask. A one-way system to minimise social con-tact among visitors had been instituted by the museum, and he traced a route with his finger that would lead him to Room 711, the Salle des Etats in the Denon wing. It took him well over ten minutes to navigate his way through long galleries, past vast canvasses; the vibrant colours of *The Wedding Feast at Cana*, David's iconic image of Marat murdered in his bath, the *Coronation of Napoleon*. In normal circumstances he would have soaked it all up, drinking in the works of artists he had only read about, witness for the first time extraordinary pieces he had seen only in reproduction. But his focus was singular and blinkered.

And then, finally, there she was. All alone, behind glass on a vast wall of midnight blue. In spite of the socially distanced crowds in the room, she saw him enter and watched as he approached. She had eyes only for him, and yet he felt himself unaccountably disappointed. She seemed small to the point of insignificance. Age had robbed her of her lustre and cracked her veneer in tiny crazed patterns. And still she stared at him, as if she knew why he was here, and slowly he felt himself falling under her spell. Even after all these centuries, she still had the power to seduce. Even if, as he suspected, she might not be what she seemed. He couldn't take his eyes off her. The room was filled with chatter, raised voices heightened by the presence of greatness. His mouth was dry. And he wanted her. So much. As so many had lusted after her before him.

But there was no time. He glanced at his watch. Narcisse awaited. An appointment with destiny.

Pewtery skies above Paris bore down on sad autumn trees prematurely stripped of life and leaves. Bauer stared blindly at them from the window of his hotel room. The pain in his clenched hand was still intense. The hole where it had torn through wallpaper and broken the plasterboard, a painful reminder of the temper which always robbed him of control. How dare Narcisse treat him like that! How dare he! It had been all he could do to restrain the urge to launch himself across the desk and punch that supercilious face until it was broken and bleeding. He had assaulted him with invective instead, a stream of abuse that carried on until he left the gallery, before cooling down just a little in the street outside.

But still his rage had burned inside him, all the way across town to his hotel, where finally he had unleashed it upon the wall, succeeding only in replacing anger with pain. Ten minutes is all that Narcisse had given him. Just time enough to explain in outline. And for Narcisse to dismiss him as a crank. Nothing could persuade him to review the evidence, or read the diary. The old bastard had simply risen to his feet and asked him to leave. His time, he had said, was far too precious to be wasted by charlatans.

Bauer stared out with simmering intensity at the light dying all across the city. Shadows gathering in the room around him. Light from the street laying oblongs across the thick-piled carpet. What now? What steps should he next take? He couldn't let it go. He couldn't! His grandfather's account of events, and his astonishing revelation, were impossible to ignore.

Finally he turned away from the window and switched on a bedside lamp. He sat on the bed and unzipped his overnight bag to take out the diaries. He needed to read again the events of that fateful day so many years before. To dispel his disappointment. To rekindle his belief.

CHAPTER SEVENTEEN

Wolff's Diary: Wednesday, September 25, 1940

Little more than a week in Paris and I am bored already. I woke to a beautiful autumn morning today, and found myself a seat under the dazzling light of the fabulous stained-glass cupola in the lounge of the Commodore. Time to think, to drink coffee and bask in coloured sunshine while I plotted my revenge.

According to inventories supplied to the Kunstschutz by the Louvre, the *Mona Lisa* has been moved again, along with all the other evacuated art. From the Abbaye de Loc-Dieu, near Villefranche-de-Rouergue in the Aveyron, to the Musée Ingres in the provincial town of Montauban in the south-west. Still in the Free French Zone, and tantalisingly out of reach. I knew I was going to have to exercise the same patience that Lange would be forced to do himself. We will, both of us, be playing a long game.

Which meant that I had time to attend to other, outstanding matters. A long overdue reckoning.

It was a little after ten when I saw Bruno Lohse cross the foyer and push through the doors into the street beyond. He was in uniform today, so must have been on his way to a meeting with the brass. Which meant he would be gone for a while. So I took my time finishing my coffee before heading upstairs.

Bruno's secretary is a pretty young thing. Lovely dark hair and the most startling blue eyes. In other circumstances, I might have been tempted to linger and chat, but although I suspected Lohse would be gone for a while, I didn't want to tempt fate. I leaned into the office, and as she looked up, I said casually, 'Bruno there?'

'He's out at a meeting.'

'Ah.' I feigned annoyance. 'I'll catch him later then.' I made to leave, but stopped suddenly and turned back as if just remembering something. 'By the way, I need the address of a French art critic here in Paris. Georges Picard. Bruno said to ask you for it.'

It is amazing the influence that the name Hermann Göring brings to bear so far from home. It opens doors and cuts through red tape. German efficiency is always to be admired, but the bureaucracy can be tiresome. To be on official business on behalf of the Reichsmarschall short-circuits all of that. As the government minister who oversaw the creation of the Gestapo, Göring is a name that evokes awe, and sometimes fear. For me it achieved almost instant results when I visited the offices of la Carlingue, in the Rue Lauriston.

Which is how I came to be standing on the first-floor landing of a very upmarket apartment building in the sixteenth arrondissement at two o'clock the following morning. Cream-painted walls, wrought-iron banisters on a marble staircase, mosaic flooring. Wealthy people lived here.

I was accompanied by two armed, uniformed officers of the occupying authority, one of whom rapped the iron knocker on the door of apartment 1B. The sound of it reverberated around the landing, up and down the stairs. Yellow lamplight threw our shadows long across the tiles as he knocked again. Louder and longer.

A door across the landing opened, and an angry young man in a nightshirt blinked in the light, demanding to know what the hell was going on. It took only a few more blinks for our little group across the hall to become apparent to him, cutting off his query mid-sentence. He hurriedly closed the door again, and we resumed our hammering on the one opposite.

Finally, an elderly man opened up, pulling on a dressing gown over patterned pyjamas. Thinning grey hair was plastered against one side of his head, and stood up on the other. Milky pale skin like parchment creased around eyes darkened by confusion. He took in the three uniformed figures on his doorstep, and confusion gave way to fear, banishing sleep.

'What do you want?'

His voice seemed very tiny in this large, echoing hallway. If I am being honest, I will confess to being surprised, and almost disappointed. It was more than twenty years since I had bloodied my knuckles on this man's face. He had been then, perhaps, the age I am now. The years, however, had reduced him to a rather frail and elderly man. But I could still conjure in my mind's eye the image of my sister as the beautiful young woman she had been, and would be forever. And my appetite for avenging her death had not diminished.

A woman wrapped in a silk dressing gown appeared in the hall behind him. 'Who is it, Georges?'

'Just an old friend,' I assured her. 'These gentlemen have come to take him to the Rue Lauriston to establish whether or not the claims against him are true. But don't worry, I will be there to ensure that justice is done.'

'What claims?' Picard was shaking his head in consternation.

'That you have been hiding your Jewish ancestry.'

'Well, that's ridiculous! I'm not Jewish.'

I smiled reassuringly. 'Of course you're not.' I paused, then. 'You don't remember me, do you?'

He looked at me with no hint of recognition in his eyes. 'Should I?'

I removed my cap and smiled again. 'We met once. Very briefly. Though I thought I might have made more of an impression on you. Perhaps the light in the bar was not so good, and I suppose it must be difficult to see with blood in your eyes. But I'm sure you'll recall my sister with much greater clarity, since you succeeded in making her pregnant.'

A flood of sudden recognition reflected itself in the fear that gripped him now. His eyes were almost black, and he knew that he was finished. No way out.

I nodded to the uniforms and they stepped forward to seize him, one on each side. They dragged him struggling and screaming across the landing to the top of the stairs in his bare feet. I remained for a moment on the doorstep and nodded to the woman who was now a shrinking shadow in the dark of her apartment and wondered if she had ever known about Erika. 'Good evening,' I said, and leaned in to pull the door shut.

I have learned a great deal in just a few days. For example, la Carlingue is what we call the French Gestapo. I had no idea that such a thing existed. It is run by French collaborators and is located in an undistinguished building at number ninety-four Rue Lauriston in the sixteenth arrondissement, not that far, in fact, from Picard's apartment. So it didn't take us long to get him there.

The torture rooms are on the top floor. When I visited yesterday they told me that they call them *kitchens*. I have no idea why. It seems an odd euphemism.

Picard was taken straight to the top floor and I left him to sweat there for a good couple of hours. Although sweat is perhaps the wrong word. Shiver, I should say. For he was stripped of his clothes, and there is no heating in the kitchens. It must have been four or five in the morning when I finally went up. Of course, I hadn't slept, but I wasn't tired. I had rarely felt so wide awake in my entire life. I don't imagine that Picard had slept either.

He was huddled on a chair when I went in. The room was otherwise empty. There was a single, naked bulb hanging from the ceiling. On an impulse I reached up and pushed it with my gloves and it swung back and forth, throwing our shadows around the room. There was an odd whimpering sound issuing from Picard's lips. Lips I had split and bloodied all those years before. Lips that had once kissed my sister, sucked on her nipples. I felt rage rise in me again like bubbles in a champagne glass, but I was determined not to lose control. Not this time. *Revenge is a dish best served cold.* I repeated the refrain to myself several times.

He hardly dared look at me. His fear was palpable. And I found so much pleasure in it that I am almost afraid now to confess it.

'I'm not Jewish,' he whispered.

'Good God, man, I know you're not. I just needed a pretext to get you here. To finish the job I began all those years ago.'

'Please. Please don't. I'll do anything.'

'Stand up.'

Picard did not move from his chair. Just stared back at me, huddled in terror.

'Stand up!' I shouted this time, and he scrambled hurriedly to his feet, embarrassed by his nakedness and doubtless feeling horribly exposed. As I reached for his chair he winced and shrunk away, anticipating the first blow. But I wasn't ready for that yet.

I turned the chair around, lay my gloves on the seat, and removed my jacket to hang on the back of it. Very slowly, very carefully, I rolled up the sleeves of my shirt. I wanted to avoid getting blood on it if at all possible.

'Did you enjoy my sister?' I asked him. 'Was she good in bed?'

'Please . . .' He backed away towards the wall. 'I loved her.'

Anger spiked through me like the blade of a bayonet, and it took every little piece of self-restraint I possessed not to grab him there and then and smash his head against the wall. 'A man does not abandon the pregnant woman he loves.' I was surprised at how calm and reasonable I sounded. 'When you have lost every one of your teeth, Georges, and I have broken every other bone in your body, I have a special treat for you. She may not be as beautiful as Erika, but I'm sure you'll enjoy her. She is so looking forward to meeting you.'

I could see confusion ripple the black surface of his fear. I stooped to pick up my gloves and pulled them on, flexing my hands to stretch the leather. This was so much more satisfying than losing control. There would be time to savour each blow and contemplate the next.

I took a single stride towards him, and I don't believe he even saw my gloved fist coming. I could feel bone break beneath my knuckles, and his head snapped to one side, throwing droplets of blood across the room. His legs folded beneath him and he dropped to the floor like a fallen sparrow, a feeble heap of bones. He started to weep, and for the first time I began to doubt my ability to see this through. In the heat of anger there is no room for empathy.

'Get up!'

He didn't move. I reached down and grabbed a scrawny arm to pull him to his feet. I wanted to tell him to take it like a man, but he was only just a shadow of the one I had almost killed twenty years earlier. He stared at me with dark, desperate eyes.

Through the blood bubbling about his lips he said, 'I know something, Monsieur Wolff. Something . . .' He appeared to be searching for a word to describe what it was he knew, but failed to find it. 'Something no one else knows.' Which even he seemed to think inadequate. 'I can share it with you if you'll let me go.'

I almost laughed. He was only succeeding in rekindling my anger.

'Information,' he said. 'In the right hands – in your hands – invaluable.'

I felt the first stirrings of interest. 'Tell me.'

'Only if you agree to let me go.'

'How can I make that judgement until you've told me.'

I could see him making the desperate calculation. Would this information he possessed be enough to persuade me to set him free? And even if it was, could I be trusted to do it? Then he whispered three words that rooted me to the spot.

'The *Mona Lisa*.'

I felt the skin on my face prickling. Myriad droplets of cold sweat. 'What about it?'

'You know who Jacques Jaujard is?'

'Of course I know who Jaujard is. He's the director of the Louvre.'

'I've known him for years. Mentored him.'

'So?'

'Jacques always knew that if France fell, the *Mona Lisa* would be the prize that the Nazis would want.'

I was aware for the first time of holding my breath.

'Evacuating her from Paris with all the other pieces from the museum was never going to be enough. We knew that the Germans couldn't just take her without arousing international fury. But we knew, too, that there would come a time when you would lose patience. And one way or another she would be gone. No doubt to hang in Hitler's super museum in Linz.'

'And?' My patience was stretching thin.

'He had a copy made.'

I frowned. Disappointed now. 'A copy?'

He sensed that he was losing me. 'Not just any old copy, Monsieur Wolff. They employed André Bernard.'

Naturally, I knew who Bernard was. He had been fooling art experts around the world for the best part of two decades. His technique and eye for detail in the forgeries he produced had convinced dealers and buyers alike to part with millions in auction houses on both sides of the Atlantic. He was wanted by almost every police force in Europe and the Americas. It was not his real name, of course. 'You know who Bernard is? Who he really is?'

Picard shook his head. 'But Jaujard does. He persuaded him out of retirement with the offer of a huge sum of money, monsieur. After all, what price could anyone place on the safety of *La Joconde*.'

I shook my head. 'A *Mona Lisa* forgery? No one would be fooled by it for one moment.'

Picard nodded vigorously. 'They would.' He paused. 'I was.'

'You've seen it?'

'Jacques showed it to me. I didn't know, you see. I didn't realise it was a forgery. And I have seen her so many times. The original, I mean. I knew her intimately. I . . . I couldn't believe it when he told me. It simply didn't seem possible. But I was holding her in my hands, and I swear to God I couldn't have told the difference.'

I lifted my jacket and turned the chair around. 'Sit down.'

He did as he was told and wiped the blood from his face with the back of his arm. I could see a little of his tension dissipate. He knew he had me now. 'Jacques was clever, you see. They sacrificed another work. A piece from the same era. The same workshop. Painted by a student of da Vinci on poplar, not canvas. It might even have been the same batch of wood on which da Vinci painted *La Joconde*. They stripped away the oils from the wood and Bernard used it for his forgery. Every scratch and dent and annotation on both sides of that piece of wood was replicated from the original. Of course the paint was too fresh, the colours too lurid. But they have very sophisticated means of ageing a painting these days. Even reproducing the typically Italian craquelure that so mars the surface of the *Mona Lisa.* Some treatment in an oven, I believe. I don't know what exactly. But I swear to God, monsieur, if I could not tell the difference, then I would defy anyone else to.'

'Where is this forgery now?'

'It was packed, identifiable only to those in the know, by a specific code on the crate. It was then inventoried with a particular batch of artworks that curators were under strict instructions not to separate. But if ever it seemed like the original was under threat, it was to be swapped for the forgery.'

I left the room then, to return a few minutes later with a glass of water and another chair. I handed him the glass, and as he drank from a trembling hand, I rolled down my sleeves and pulled on my jacket before sitting opposite him.

'Tell me about the coding on the crate. And the other works with which it has been inventoried.'

I made him go over it again, and again. And again. Paying attention to any discrepancy of detail that might lead me to disbelieve his story. But he never wavered from it. And in the end I was convinced. Against all my better judgement. For in the face of death a man does not lie. And how could Picard have had the presence of mind to invent such a tale, in such detail, in such circumstances. It was impossible not to believe him.

At length I got to my feet. 'I'll not kill you,' I told him, and saw relief surge through his body. 'But I would hate to deny you the pleasure I guaranteed you earlier.' And now his fear flooded back. 'You'll like Violette. She's quite a woman.'

'You promised!'

'I promised you nothing. But as a man of honour I will personally do you no further harm.' I crossed the room and opened the door. 'Violette!' After a moment I heard a door opening along the hall, and Violette stepped out with the light that fell from the room. I turned back towards Picard and saw the sense of betrayal in his eyes. 'I suspect,' I said, 'that she'll not be as compliant as Erika.'

His eyes then flickered away from me towards the figure which had appeared in the doorway.

Violette is a large woman. I would say that she is probably fifty, or thereabouts. She wore a white singlet stretched tightly over extravagantly large breasts, a pair of black shorts, and well-worn brown sports shoes. Flesh once toned and muscular is now white and flabby and dimpled. She wears her hair dragged back and tied in a tight knot behind her head. And as she stood in the doorway, she wore the simple smile of someone who takes great pleasure in work that has nothing to do with sex, but everything to do with pain.

I saw a judder of fearful anticipation wrack Picard's fragile frame. 'Meet Violette,' I said. 'You might know her as Violette Morris, the medal-winning athlete. Competed for France at the Women's World Games a couple of decades ago, and at the Women's Olympiad, too, I believe. Won gold medals for the discus and shot-put, isn't that right, Violette?'

She nodded.

'Her motto has always been *Ce qu'un homme fait, Violette peut le faire.*' Anything a man can do, Violette can do. 'Used to knock them down in the boxing ring, too.'

I moved aside to let Violette step into the room. She clasped her hands together in front of her and smiled at Picard. I could see that he was choking on his own fear, and not a word came to his lips.

'Good night, Monsieur Picard,' I said. 'Rest assured that as a good Catholic, Erika sends her regards from hell.'

I had reached the next landing before I heard his first scream. It actually chilled me. But not enough to distract from the extraordinary piece of good fortune I had stumbled upon by sheer chance in this early morning. Revenge and profit all in one night.

CHAPTER EIGHTEEN

He returns to the house in the early afternoon following a solitary lunch.

There were guests at two other tables in the dining room of the hotel. A travelling salesman, and an elderly couple on an out-of-season tour. But he paid them very little attention as he replayed the old lady's tale.

When he knocks and comes through from the kitchen, she is sitting exactly where he left her. The fire has been stoked. Fresh logs placed upon the embers crackle and send flames dancing against the tarry residue of the wall behind.

'Have you eaten?' he asks.

She shakes her head. 'I am not hungry, monsieur.'

'Can I get you anything? A cup of tea? A coffee?'

Again she shakes her head. 'That's kind. But no thank you.'

He is pleased not to delay the resumption of her story, for he has been absorbed by it. He settles himself comfortably in his seat. 'I'm ready when you are.'

She inclines her head a little to give him the palest of smiles and draws a long breath . . .

*

Only a handful of days had passed since the incident at the Jeu de Paume, but the frustration of her predicament was making Georgette restless to the point of distraction.

She lay propped up in her bed, pillows against the headboard, trying to concentrate on a book she had started the night before. But the words would not form images, and she found it hard to empathise with the characters.

What point had there been in returning to France only to see the war play out from the comparative safety of the hallowed halls of the Jeu de Paume? Would she ever even set eyes on the *Mona Lisa*? She had consulted a map of France to identify the exact whereabouts of the town of Montauban. It was a long way from Paris. Just north of Toulouse, which was deep in the south-west, not far from the Pyrenees and the Spanish border. It would be nearly a full day's journey by train, assuming she was ever granted permission to cross into the Free French Zone.

It didn't matter what de Gaulle wanted. He was in England, and she was here. And she wished she had never come. Surely there was more she could have done for the war effort from London than be stuck here in a gallery that had become a repository for stolen Nazi art?

It was dark out. A clear but moonless sky, and the temperature had fallen to minus seven. The heating in Rose's apartment was erratic at the best of times, and Georgette shivered, pulling the quilt around herself to keep warm. From somewhere she heard the distant ring of a telephone. Insistent and penetrating. And she realised suddenly that it was ringing in the apartment, the phone in the hall.

She heard Rose's bedroom door opening, and moments later the ringing ceased. Rose's voice was muted and indecipherable. Then silence, and Georgette assumed that she had hung up. A knock at the door startled her, and it opened to reveal Rose in hairnet and dressing gown. 'It's for you,' she said, the displeasure clear in her voice.

Georgette was startled. 'What is?'

'The phone, of course. Be quick.'

'But' – Georgette was perplexed – 'who even knows I'm here? Or your phone number?'

'These are very good questions.' Rose paused significantly. 'It's a man.' She stepped aside to let Georgette past. 'Hurry up!'

Georgette slid off the bed, pushed her feet into a pair of slippers and hurried into the hall. She lifted the receiver with great trepidation.

'Hello?'

'Georgette Pignal?' His French was lightly accented, but distinctly foreign.

'Who is this?'

'My name is Lange. Paul Lange. You might remember making a bit of an idiot of yourself on the steps of the Jeu de Paume the other day. I was the charming German officer who helped you pick up the miniatures.' Evidently he was not taking himself too seriously. But his words, nonetheless, sent a shiver of fear through her.

'What do you want?'

'You're welcome.' She could hear the smile in his sardonic drawl.

'I'm sorry, I don't understand. Why are you calling me?'

'Because I would like to take you to dinner.'

Now her breathing had stopped altogether. Her fear was marbled with embarrassment.

'I know a very nice restaurant in Montparnasse.'

No matter how nicely he was asking, it seemed to Georgette that it was more of an order than a request. How could she say no to a German officer? 'When?'

'I was thinking tomorrow evening, if that suits.'

Her mind was racing. 'Em . . . I'm not sure. I . . . I'd need to check my work schedule to see if I'm available.'

'Well, give me a call when you know. Do you have a pencil handy?'

Georgette's panicked eyes scanned the hall table and saw a pencil and notepad lying side by side. She grabbed the pencil. 'Yes.'

And he read her out his number, which she scribbled hastily on the pad. 'You can get me here most evenings.'

'Thank you,' she said, wondering why on earth she was thanking him. 'I'll do that. Goodbye.'

'Goodnight, mademoiselle.'

The line went dead and she hung up the phone.

'Well?'

She had forgotten that Rose was even there, turning to find

her still standing by the bedroom door, arms folded sternly across her chest.

'Who was that?'

Georgette hardly dared tell her. 'It was the German officer who helped me pick up the miniatures on the stairs the other day. Paul . . .'

'Lange.' Rose finished for her. 'What did he want?'

'To take me out to dinner.'

A flicker of incredulity crossed Rose's face before a deep, angry sigh issued from between clenched teeth. 'You see? This is what happens when you draw attention to yourself.' She paused. 'And, by association, to me.'

For once in her life Georgette was at a complete loss. 'What am I going to do?'

'You'll have to accept, of course. What else can you do?' She turned towards her bedroom door. 'Wherever he wants to take you, just go. And don't make a fuss.' The door slammed shut behind her and Georgette stood shivering in the cold and dark, more convinced than ever that she should have stayed in London.

Lange was waiting in a taxi outside the Jeu de Paume the following evening as Georgette finished work. In spite of herself, she had taken care to select her best dress to wear to work that day, and shortly before leaving the gallery, had spent several minutes in the lady's room applying a light make-up to her lips and eyes.

She had never ridden in a Paris taxi before, never been able to afford it. It was a big, black carriage with a canvas roof and sweeping wheel arches that belched great clouds of exhaust fumes into the cold night air. Lange stepped out and held the door open, offering a hand to help her up. She ignored it and stepped quickly into the cab, sliding herself across the seat to the far window, wanting to put as much distance between herself and the German as she could.

A tiny smile played about his lips as he settled himself in the seat beside her and gave the driver their destination. 'One hundred and two Boulevard de Montparnasse. The restaurant La Coupole.'

Georgette saw the driver looking at her in his rear-view mirror and was certain it was contempt she saw in his eyes. She wanted to curl up and die. How had it come to this? Being taken to dinner by a German army officer. 'I suppose you know all the best restaurants,' she said.

'Actually, yes.' He smiled. 'The occupying authority has been good enough to produce a guide of the best places for German soldiers to eat.' He produced a folded leaflet from the pocket of his greatcoat and flipped through the printed pages. He stopped at one headed *Wichtig für den Soldaten!* and ran his finger down a column of names. 'Here we are. La Coupole. An iconic art deco brasserie which opened in 1927.' He looked up from the page. 'Actually, I have eaten there several times. It's excellent.'

'Don't you ever wonder if they spit in your food in the kitchen?'

He laughed. 'Trust me, my dear. They wouldn't dare.' And although he made a joke of it, she understood that his subtext was deadly serious.

La Coupole was an extravagant establishment with a large terrace on the pavement, deserted now in the bitter cold of this first December of the occupation. Like the Commodore, it boasted a huge colourful cupola that dominated the interior. Elaborate hand-painted columns divided a sprawling dining area into more intimate spaces, tables and chairs set around hand-embroidered semi-circles of upholstered seating.

The maître d' greeted them at the door, an obsequious smile and an extravagant sweep of the hand to guide them to their table in the window. 'Apparently,' Lange said, 'the ground below the restaurant is riddled with catacombs. I never knew it before, but Paris is built of the stone dug out from beneath it by generations of quarriers.'

Georgette was barely listening. She felt exposed sitting here in the window, open to the gaze of any passer-by. A Frenchwoman being wined and dined by one of the hated occupiers. Her self-conscious eyes flickered across the restaurant. It was almost empty. Just a handful of tables occupied by uniformed German officers in groups of two and three. There were women at two other tables. Ladies with painted faces and loud laughter, flushed by too much wine and the anticipation of a long night ahead.

Lange was still talking. 'La Coupole has been a favourite of some very successful artists in the past. Georges Braque,

Picasso. And writers like Simone de Beauvoir and Jean-Paul Sartre.'

A waiter handed them menus, and Georgette avoided his gaze by averting her eyes to study the plats du jour. She had no idea what to order. But before she could even express her nescience, Lange lifted the menu from her hands. 'Let me order, my dear. I am better acquainted with the chef's specialities.' He handed both menus back to the waiter and ordered crevettes flambéed in whisky to start, followed by magret de canard in a blackcurrant sauce and pommes *sarladaises*. He turned to Georgette. 'I'd suggest a glass of Puligny Montrachet with the prawns and a nice Cahors with the duck.'

Georgette shrugged. It almost seemed to her as if he were trying to humiliate her. 'You're paying,' she said.

A waitress came, adjusting the cutlery to reflect their order, and placed a basket of freshly cut bread on the table. Georgette caught her surreptitious glance at Lange and then at her, and she flushed with embarrassment. She turned to gaze from the window, in the hope that the cold that pressed against it from the outside might cool her face, and that the evening might pass more quickly than it promised. After some time, she became aware of Lange staring at her. She turned her head to face him down. 'What?'

'You are very reserved.'

'Is it any wonder?' she said. 'Don't you even see how the staff look at me? Or your fellow officers and their painted women?'

'No doubt, like me, they are charmed by your radiance.'

'My embarrassment, you mean. They think I'm a prostitute.'

He raised a sceptical eyebrow. 'No, they don't.'

'Of course they do. What self-respecting Frenchwoman would be seen dead in a restaurant with an officer of the occupying force? Other than a woman who was being paid to pretend she liked him? You make me feel like a collaborator.'

He was unruffled. 'In that case, next time you shall dine with me privately in my apartment.'

'Your apartment?' She was appalled.

'Yes. I have excellent accommodation on the fourth floor of an apartment block at number thirty Rue de Rivoli.'

'A stolen apartment.'

'Certainly not. I pay rent to the owners like everyone else.'

'And its previous occupants?'

'Vacated. A Jewish family. Left the country, I believe.'

'Vacated being a euphemism for deported?'

The amusement which had hitherto crinkled his eyes vanished. He leaned towards her confidentially. 'Mademoiselle, I would keep your voice down if I were you, and be a little more judicious in your choice of words.' He paused for effect. 'Not for my sake, you understand. But they might fall on other, less tolerant, ears.'

It was both a rebuke and a warning, and neither were lost on her. She forced herself to bite back a retort about the right to express herself freely in her own country. For it was, she realised, no longer her country.

His smile returned and he sought to change the subject.

'I would be more than happy to cook for you. I have a certain reputation among my friends for fine cuisine.'

She kept her voice low. 'What makes you think that I would want to sup with the devil?'

He laughed. 'My dear, who would? But I am not the devil. I am your benefactor.'

'If you think I'm going to sleep with you, you couldn't be more wrong.'

This time his laughter turned heads from other tables and he lowered his voice. 'Mademoiselle Pignal, nothing could be further from my mind.'

And she wondered why she felt slighted.

The prawns cooked in a whisky flambé arrived, and the wine waiter poured them each a glass of white burgundy. They ate in silence for some time, and to her annoyance Georgette found that it was delicious. She said, 'I don't know what you expect from me. Or why you asked me to dinner. But it's only fair to tell you that I really don't like you.'

'But you don't know me,' he protested.

'I know that you are an officer of an occupying power, uninvited and unwanted. You have no right here, monsieur, and you should know that I detest the Nazis and everything they stand for.'

He mopped up the juices on his plate with a piece of bread. 'Well,' he said. 'I suppose if I were you, I might feel the same. This is not a war of my choosing. Or yours. And yet, here we are, on different sides of the divide. Victims of fate.'

'Are you a Party member?'

'The Nazis? Yes.'

'Hardly a victim of fate, then.'

He laid knife and fork across his empty plate and leaned towards her again. His voice was barely audible. 'I joined the Party, mademoiselle, out of a finely honed instinct for self-preservation. The Chinese have a saying: the nail that stands up gets hammered down.' He sat up again. 'You should take note of that.'

Their plates were removed by the waitress, and Georgette kept her eyes on the table as the duck arrived, and the wine waiter poured them generous glasses of a rich ruby Cahors.

It wasn't until the first two or three mouthfuls had been consumed that Lange turned towards her again. 'May I call you Georgette?'

'Would it make any difference if I said no?'

He smiled. 'You should know, Georgette, that I'm as proud to be German as you are to be French. Both of our countries have done things in the past that we each have the right to be ashamed of. I very much regret the circumstances in which we find ourselves today. I know this city perhaps better even than you. I have been here many, many times over the last twenty years, buying and selling art. Renoir, Picasso, most of the impressionists. This city is almost a second home to me.'

'I thought the Nazis considered modern art to be degenerate.'

He shrugged. 'That is a certain school of thought.'

'I wonder if your friend, Monsieur Hitler, knows about your passion for the degenerate.'

His smile now was strained. She was wearing his patience thin. 'I am sure the Führer does not count me among his friends. I have met him only twice, and never shared with him my love of modern art.' A little of the amusement returned to his eyes. 'Though I am sure my leader would share an appreciation of my choice of dining companion tonight.'

In spite of everything she smiled, and shook her head. 'It's impossible to offend you, isn't it.'

'I could only be offended by the things you say if I thought you meant them.'

'I do.'

He shook his head patiently. 'You don't. Because you don't know me. Yet. And that, I hope to remedy in the coming months. Then, and only then, will I take offence.'

Both her heart and her spirits sank. Like a fly caught in a spider's web, the more she struggled, the more entangled she became. There was no escape.

By the time they left the restaurant there were no taxis available. The curfew was already in force. From 10 p.m. until 5 a.m. daily in this first year of the occupation.

Georgette panicked. 'How will I get home without being stopped?'

Lange shrugged and steered her on to the Boulevard de Port-Royal. 'Because I will walk you there.' And for the first time Georgette was glad of his company.

An almost full moon bathed the blacked-out city in its

colourless light. Without it, their half-hour walk to the Rue de Navarre would have been well nigh impossible. There were no street lights, and apartment windows had black curtains drawn against the light within. Where they walked in shadow along narrow streets, Lange produced a torch to illuminate their passage. They were stopped three times by pairs of patrolling soldiers, and each time Lange's papers produced a clicking of heels and a stiff salute.

By the time they reached the door to Rose's apartment block Georgette was chittering with the cold. They had barely spoken during the long walk, giving Georgette all the more time to consider the gravity of her situation, and the unwanted attentions of this German army officer who, it seemed, she was going to have trouble avoiding.

They stood outside the door, breath billowing in the moonlight.

'I'm sorry,' he said.

'What for?'

'You're hardly dressed for these temperatures. I should have taken care to get us a taxi before the curfew.'

She made light of it. 'I enjoyed the walk.' Then looked at him very directly. 'Why are you here? I mean, really here. In Paris. You're not a real soldier.'

He laughed. 'No. I'm not. But these days you need a uniform to get anywhere. I deal in art, Georgette. You know that.'

She blew her contempt at him through pursed lips. 'You're not here to deal in art, you're here to steal it. Isn't that what the ERR is doing? Stealing art from Jewish collectors and storing the merchandise at the Jeu de Paume before shipping it off to Germany.'

He nodded and sighed. 'Regrettably, yes. However, I have no connection with ERR. I work for the Kunstschutz. Which translates literally as art protection. It's our job to protect art and return it to its rightful owners at the end of hostilities.' He hesitated for a long moment, then added, 'Though that's not why I'm here.'

She was surprised. 'Really? So why are you here?'

She couldn't see his eyes. He had his back to the moonlight, and his face was in shadow. But she felt the intensity of his gaze. 'The same reason you are,' he said.

For a moment it felt as if he was looking right through her, and her heart very nearly stopped. 'What do you mean?'

She heard rather than saw his smile, the separation of the tongue from the lips and the roof of the mouth as the facial muscles expressed themselves. 'I have many friends in London, Georgette. I know it almost as well as Paris. I have eyes and ears on the ground there that my superiors do not.'

A dreadful sense of foreboding wrapped itself around her, like the darkness itself.

'I know perfectly well what de Gaulle asked you to do.'

Now foreboding gave way to fear.

But he clearly had no intention of discussing it further. At least, not there, not then. 'I would like to see you again.'

She found her voice with difficulty. 'Why would I agree to that?'

'Because you and I have a very great deal to talk about, my dear.' He turned a little so that the moon lit up his smile. 'But next time I will not embarrass you by taking you to a restaurant.' He paused. 'Friday night?'

Georgette turned the key in the lock as quietly as she could, and eased the door open into the darkness of the hall. She stepped in carefully and closed it softly behind her. She stood then for several minutes, her eyes growing accustomed to what little light there was. Her own breath seemed inordinately loud, almost deafening in the quiet of the apartment.

She started taking silent steps towards her bedroom door. Rose should have gone to bed a good hour ago and would hopefully be asleep. Her fingers closed around the cold metal of the door handle as the door to Rose's bedroom flew open, and she stood silhouetted against the light behind her. She wore her habitual dressing gown and hairnet and had clearly been awaiting Georgette's return.

'Well?' Her voice barked into the darkness of the hall.

'Well what?'

'You know perfectly well what.'

Georgette drew a deep breath. 'He has asked me to go to his apartment for a meal on Friday night. He wants to cook for me.'

'Does he?'

Her next words lingered on her lips for only a second. 'He knows why I'm here,' she blurted. It had been her intention to keep this to herself, but fear made her want to share. She heard the consternation in Rose's voice.

'What do you mean?'

'He knows people in London, he said. He knows what de Gaulle asked me to do.'

The silence in the apartment seemed almost tangible, and extended itself between them for a very long time before Rose said, 'Then we have to abort your mission. And we need to get you out of Paris fast. Out of the country if possible.'

'Why?'

'Because your cover, such as it was, is in tatters. He could have you arrested at any moment.'

'I don't think so.'

'Oh, for God's sake, girl!'

'I mean it. If he was going to have me arrested, he'd have done it by now. Why hasn't he? And why hasn't he shared what he knows with anyone else? *I have eyes and ears on the ground in London that my superiors do not.* That's what he told me. So whatever he knows, he's kept it to himself. He said we had much to talk about.'

Rose breathed her exasperation. 'It wouldn't surprise me if his sole motivation was to get you into his bed.'

'I don't think so. He's not like that.'

'Hah! So you think you know him now?'

'No, I don't. But I think I should. It's the only way we're going to find out what this whole charade is about.'

Rose shook her head in exasperation. 'I knew you were trouble from the moment you arrived. All you are doing is putting at risk everything I am working to achieve at the Jeu de Paume. And if that gets shut down, I'll never forgive you. France will never forgive you!'

Georgette walked through the empty halls of the Louvre, sunlight falling through tall windows to lay itself in arches and oblongs on the floor beneath her feet and cast her shadow long across it. Her footsteps echoed back at her from naked walls.

She recalled the days and weeks she had spent here, working with teams of other students and museum staff in the race to pack everything safely into wooden crates for evacuation. It seemed a lifetime ago now. She climbed marble steps to the first floor and found the corridor she was looking for.

Jacques Jaujard's office overlooked the cobbles of the courtyard below. A small, cluttered space, half of it taken over by an enormous desk littered with the debris of his working day. He sat back in a chair that reclined a little, and dragged languidly on his cigarette. A distinctive Paris skyline was visible through the window behind him.

Jaujard had the looks of a film star. Dark, abundant hair swept back from a handsome face defined by strong eyebrows and a square jaw. He wore a double-breasted lounge suit and button-down white collar with a red tie. He waved Georgette into the seat opposite and said, 'Well, this is a fine mess.'

Georgette knew that it was Jaujard's determination and

vision, more than anything else, which had achieved the evacuation of the Louvre. History, she was certain, would recognise the role he had played in keeping the national treasures of France out of the hands of the Nazis. But right now she was stung by his words. 'Not of *my* making,' she said defiantly.

He flicked his cigarette at an overflowing ashtray on the desk and conceded, 'Yes, that's probably fair. But unfortunately, you are right in the thick of it. You've been compromised, Georgette. It's as simple as that. I can hardly send you to Montauban to watch over *La Joconde* when the purpose of your presence there would be known to the German authorities. I don't want to give them any excuse to start seizing inventory.'

'But the general specifically—'

He cut her off. 'De Gaulle is in London, we are here. And we have to deal with reality as it is on the ground.'

'If Lange is such a threat, why am I not sitting in a Gestapo interrogation room right now?'

'I have no idea. And let's face it, Georgette, we really don't want to find out, do we? At least, not in that way.'

She had no answer to this. 'So what am I going to do?'

He sighed. 'I think we have to play a waiting game. You will stay at the Jeu de Paume until it becomes clear what Lange is up to, or until he goes back to Germany and the dust settles. After all, it may be, as Rose suspects, that what he's really after is getting you into his bed.'

'So I should refuse the invitation to eat with him at his apartment?'

'Good God, no. You can't afford to offend him.'

'And if he really does just want me to sleep with him?'

He leaned forward to stub out his cigarette. 'That would be regrettable.'

Frustration gave way to anger, and anger to resignation. She was, she realised, a very small cog in a very large machine that could perfectly well function without her. But of one thing she was certain. Under no circumstances would she allow herself to be seduced into Lange's bed.

When she got back to the Jeu de Paume, Rose was keen to hear what Jaujard had said to her and steered Georgette into her office. But Georgette did not want to go into details. She said, 'He wants me to remain here in the meantime.'

Rose seemed disappointed. 'Really?'

Georgette gave vent to her discontent. 'It's like being handed a jail sentence.'

Rose bristled. 'Yes. And I'm the one who's being forced to share the cell with you.' She rounded her desk. 'But since we're stuck with each other, you might as well make yourself useful. A great deal of art has come and gone in the last few days. We need to re-inventory everything in the basement.'

Georgette stared at her angrily. 'Consigning me to the basement? That's your way of dealing with me? I'm supposed to be an assistant curator.'

'And someday you might be one for real. But I am the curator here, and your job is to assist me. And you can do that from the basement until such time as Monsieur Jaujard decides what to do with you.'

Georgette spent most of the next two days working alone in the gloom of the basement. Not only a prison sentence, she thought, but solitary confinement. The only human contact she had for hours on end were the German soldiers who arrived with frequent deliveries of new stock which they would carry downstairs. Even if she had wanted to, she could not have engaged them in conversation, since almost none of them spoke French.

The days were long, and filled her with resentment, and she found herself almost looking forward to Friday evening, and her dinner with Lange at his apartment.

He was waiting for her outside in the Tuileries when she emerged from the gallery just after seven. It was a cold, miserable evening, just five days before Christmas, though there was no sign anywhere in the city of preparation for the festivities. The temperature had hovered barely above freezing for most of the day, and a light drizzle fell now from low, brooding clouds in a black sky. His umbrella glistened in the rain, and she allowed herself to be drawn under its protection by his arm linked through hers.

She was acutely self-conscious, glancing around, certain that she would find every eye turned in their direction. But Lange was not in uniform tonight, and no one paid them the least attention.

'Thank you,' she said.

'What for?'

'Dispensing with the uniform.'

He smiled. 'Well, I was told once that no self-respecting Frenchwoman would want to be seen dead with an officer of the occupying forces.'

Which drew a reluctant smile from her, in spite of herself. 'I thought Germans were supposed to be notorious for their lack of humour.'

'It's true, George, that we don't really do jokes. But I think we have a fairly well-developed sense of irony.'

She froze. 'You called me George.'

He raised an eyebrow. 'Isn't that what your friends call you?'

Her heart pushed up into her throat, making it difficult to speak. 'How do you know that?'

His smile was almost condescending. 'By now, George, there's very little that I don't know about you.'

The walk to his apartment took little more than ten minutes and was made in silence. A confusion of thoughts tumbled one over the other in her mind. If he knew so much about her, then he must know that her position as an assistant curator at the Jeu de Paume was a sham. That she had been in London until the autumn and must have been smuggled clandestinely into France. And yet, here he was, entertaining her to dinner at his apartment as if none of it mattered.

He opened the door to number thirty Rue de Rivoli and shook his umbrella back out into the street, before leading her up an elegant curving staircase to the fourth floor. Electric bulbs had replaced the old gas lamps on wrought-iron lamp posts on each landing.

The apartment comprised umpteen huge rooms leading off a spacious entrance hall, parquet flooring reflecting harsh electric light as he flicked on light switches and led her through to a large comfortable salon. A sofa and two armchairs were gathered around a fireplace. An enormous gilded mirror set on the wall above it reflected the rest of the room, including the small table laid for two in the window alcove. Georgette could smell something delicious wafting through from the kitchen.

'I've done most of my kitchen prep already,' he said, 'which means I can devote more time to entertaining you over dinner.'

He moved about the room, switching on standard lamps before extinguishing the overhead chandelier to bathe the room in softer light.

'Here, let me take your coat.' And he removed it carefully from her shoulders. 'Have a seat at the table,' he said over his shoulder as he disappeared into the hall. When he returned he used his lighter to raise flames on two candles set in silver holders on the table. 'It's a pretty view down into the street. Unfortunately we have to keep the drapes drawn. But at least they cut down the cold from the windows.'

He poured them glasses of chilled Chablis and served a starter of sautéed plaice in a creamy butter sauce with tiny new potatoes still in their skins.

'*Santé,*' he said, raising his glass. But she raised hers only to her lips and did not return the salutation.

For a while they ate in silence, and she was impressed by the starter. Although she had no intention of telling him so.

Almost as if he had read her mind, he said, 'How's the fish?'

And she found herself unable to lie. 'Delicious.'

He nodded his satisfaction, and she glanced around the room.

'Did the apartment come furnished?' She felt ill at ease with the idea that she was enjoying the comforts of those things which had once belonged to others now stripped of their wealth and freedom.

'No. I bought it.'

She was surprised. 'Where?'

'The ERR have a warehouse across town where they keep and sell confiscated furniture. A little like one of those New York department stores. We rent unfurnished and buy our own.'

Georgette said, 'In my mother's country they have a word for that.'

'You mean Scotland?'

He really did know everything about her. But she was not going to acknowledge it. 'It's called reset.'

'Meaning?'

'In Scots criminal law, it is the possession of property dishonestly appropriated by another. For example, by theft.'

He ignored the implication. 'Your mother was a lawyer?'

One thing, at least, that he did not know about her. 'She took a law degree at Glasgow University. But never practised.'

Georgette finished her fish and laid her cutlery across her plate.

'What do you want from me, Monsieur Lange?'

'Paul,' he said. 'Please call me Paul.'

She ignored him. 'For God's sake, what do you want?'

He sat very still examining her face closely with eyes reflecting candlelight. They seemed to penetrate all her outer defences. Finally he said, 'I want to know if I can trust you.'

She frowned her consternation. 'Trust me? Trust me with what?'

He smiled. 'Well, obviously that's something I'm not going to tell you until I believe I am able to trust you with it.'

She shook her head. 'And I'm supposed to trust you? Why would I do that?'

He tipped his head in acknowledgement. 'You wouldn't. As I wouldn't if I were you. Trust has to be earned. And neither of us is going to be able to bank sufficient trust until we get to know each other better.'

He rose and lifted their empty plates from the table and disappeared into the kitchen. Georgette felt intimidated by him. Afraid of him. He was so self-possessed. So sure of himself. Leaving her each time floundering in the dark without the least idea of his motivation or his endgame. Knowledge, she knew, was power. And he had that power over her. Which made her determined to learn more about him, to share in the power, and try to find an equal footing in this disquieting relationship.

He returned with medallions of fillet steak in a cream-pepper sauce. It was cooked to perfection. Seared on the outside, pink in the middle, just a little blood marbling the cream. She said, 'People queue in the street for hours outside butchers' shops to buy cuts of meat far inferior to this. I bet you didn't have to stand in line.'

'No, I didn't.' A smile curled his lips but never quite reached his eyes. 'To the victor the spoils, eh? Enjoy.'

He poured a rich red Côte du Rhone and they ate for some minutes before she spoke again. 'Where are you from? In Germany, I mean?'

'Ah.' He smiled. 'At last, a little curiosity.' He took a sip of his wine. 'I was brought up in the Bavarian city of Augsburg. A small town by German standards. It's about fifty kilometres west of Munich. But it has a university, and is famous for being the home of the Fugger and Welser families that dominated European banking in the sixteenth century. My own family is descended from the Welsers.'

'And did you go to university there?'

'No. I went to Frankfurt to take a degree in art.' He sighed. 'It was my ambition to paint, to be an artist myself. But a simple comparison with my fellow students made it painfully clear to me that this was not my forte.' He paused, remembering Hitler's words to him at the Berghof. 'It's important to know your own limitations.'

'So what was your major?'

'The history of art.'

'And how did you become a dealer?'

'Pure chance, really. I got a job at a gallery in Berlin. The curator was a marvellous fellow called Schäfer. Took me under his wing, initially as his assistant. He brought me here to Paris for the first time. We bought and sold in the sales rooms, and it seems he thought I had an eye for it. Because it wasn't long before I was making these trips on my own. To Paris and London. And then New York. The gallery began to earn itself something of a reputation, and it wasn't long before I was being approached by private buyers anxious for me to acquire art for their collections.' He shrugged. 'On such turns of fate are careers built.'

'What happened to Herr Schäfer?'

Lange's face darkened, and for the first time he avoided her eye. 'Jewish,' he said, and clearly did not wish to elaborate.

'There are a lot of Jews in the art world.'

'Yes. And I have many friends among them.' Then he corrected himself. 'Had.' He gazed thoughtfully at the table, lost in some far-off reverie. 'In Germany, those who saw it coming fled the country. Those who didn't, were arrested.'

'In France, too.'

'Yes.'

'Look at me,' she said. And he lifted his eyes to meet hers, surprised by her strength of tone. 'These people were your friends, Paul. Your own mentor, for God's sake! And still you joined the Party that persecutes them, drives them out of their homes, puts them in prison. Murders them.'

He shook his head. 'It's an insane world, George. We do what we have to in order to survive in it.' Then a tiny sad smile lit his face. 'You called me Paul.'

'Did I?'

He nodded and pushed away his empty plate as he stood up. 'Perhaps I should take you home now.'

She sat for a moment, unaccountably disappointed, before standing up and lifting her satchel from the back of the chair where she had hung it. 'Thank you for dinner,' she said.

'It was my pleasure.' The briefest of pauses. 'Same time next Friday?'

'Do I have a choice?'

'In life, George, there is always a choice.'

Rose was sitting in the front room with a glass of red wine, fully dressed and waiting up for her. The light from the room spilled into the hall and caught Georgette as she passed through it on the way from the front door to her bedroom.

'I'm in here,' Rose called out, and reluctantly Georgette pushed open the door and stepped into the light. Rose laid down her glass and stood up. She looked at Georgette with what seemed like genuine concern in her eyes. 'Are you alright?'

Georgette was taken aback. 'Do you care?'

Rose sighed. 'Believe it or not, I do.'

Chastened now, Georgette lowered her eyes. 'I'm fine. Thank you.' Then, after a pause: 'He wants me to go again next Friday.'

Rose looked at her long and hard until Georgette couldn't bear it any longer.

'What?'

Rose said quietly, 'Did you sleep with him?'

Annoyance flared in the young woman. 'Of course I didn't.'

Rose nodded. 'Good,' she said. And after a hesitation, 'If you ever do, it will be the end of you, you know that?'

CHAPTER NINETEEN

The flight to Berlin had been half-empty, and the cabin crew rearranged the seating so that everyone aboard sat well apart. Enzo wiped down his tray table twice, watched by Kirsty who told him that she thought once was probably sufficient. She took a coffee, but Enzo refused. He had gelled his hands before entering the plane, and again as he left. And now, as they sat in their taxi, separated from the driver by Plexiglas, he was glad of the card terminal in the back that accepted contactless payment.

They stepped out into a chill wind blowing along the canal, and a brooding sky that seemed to scrape the rooftops.

Bauer's apartment stood near a bridge that led across the water to Maybachufer, and the red-roofed, six-storey, white-painted apartment blocks that lined it. A path flanked by black wrought-iron railings led to an arched doorway, past a row of mailboxes. Tall windows in the varnished wooden door revealed a long marble hallway beyond it.

Enzo stepped back and looked up at the building. 'Nicole wasn't wrong when she said there was money in his family,' he said. 'Apartments in a place like this must cost the earth.'

Bauer's name was printed beneath a third-floor buzzer on the door entry system. Enzo pressed it and they waited for a response that never came.

Then the rapid sound of heels on concrete made them turn as a young woman approached. She pulled up her mask when she saw them standing by the door, and navigated around them to punch in her entry code.

She seemed startled when Kirsty spoke to her. In German. And Enzo had no idea what she was saying. He watched the girl carefully as she and Kirsty exchanged several words, and he saw her pupils dilate and the skin around her eyes turn pale. Immediately she delved into her handbag to retrieve her mobile phone, tapping a name hurriedly into its memory before making a call.

Enzo's impatience was barely contained by his mask. He turned to Kirsty. 'What's going on?'

'She lives across the landing from Bauer. She and Bauer's girlfriend, Lise, were friends.'

'Were?'

'Apparently Lise moved out when she and Bauer split up.'

'Recently?'

'Last week,' Kirsty said. 'She hasn't seen or heard anything from Lise since. She was shocked to hear that Bauer was mixed up with a murder in France and thinks that Lise will be, too. She's calling her now.'

*

It was a good twenty minutes before Lise turned up at Katie's Blue Cat. The café stood just across the canal in Friedelstrasse, next to the orange-fronted Neuköllner Backstube bakery. It was little more than a collection of fold-up wooden tables and chairs on the uneven stone mosaic of the pavement outside a large window displaying cakes and pastries. Lise had suggested it as a meeting place.

It was cold, and Enzo and Kirsty sat huddled over their cappuccinos, lowering their masks to take sips, and looking up and down the street with impatience as they waited.

At length a young woman wearing a large pair of sunglasses appeared from Maybachufer, walking briskly around the corner, a long fawn coat unbuttoned and billowing in her wake. She wore jeans, and knee-length high-heeled leather boots, and a fawn beret that matched her coat. Black hair cut in a fringe fell over the lenses of her shades, and tumbled to her shoulders at either side. She came to a stop in front of them. 'Herr Macleod?' she asked. Unnecessarily, it seemed to Enzo, since he and Kirsty were the only ones there.

He nodded. 'Lise, I take it. Your friend said you spoke English.'

She nodded and sat down at the next table, taking out an ill-fitting mask to slip over her face before pushing a cigarette between its folds to hold in her lips through the cloth. She dipped her head to her lighter and sucked in smoke through the cotton. A circle of nicotine stained the mask, betraying this to be a regular habit. Smoke seeped out from either side of it.

'Would you like a coffee?' Enzo asked.

She shook her head. A quick, nervous dismissal. 'Hans has murdered someone?'

'We don't know that,' Enzo said, 'but he is the prime suspect of the French police.'

Her hand trembled as she took another draw on her cigarette. 'I knew it would happen someday. I knew it.'

'What makes you say that?'

'He has a fearsome temper, Herr Macleod. When he loses it, he is capable of almost anything.' She drew away her sunglasses to reveal the bruising around her eyes and cheekbones. 'I should know.'

Kirsty gasped. 'Good God, he did that to you?'

Lise nodded and slipped on her sunglasses once again to hide her shame. But not before Enzo had taken in the sadness in her dark eyes.

Enzo said, 'It would appear that this was not a murder committed in the heat of the moment, Lise. From what we can tell, it seems to have been pretty much premeditated.' He saw her frown.

'Then I doubt if it was Hans.'

'Why?'

'Because in normal circumstances he was not a violent man. And when his temper led him to lose control, he was almost crushed by contrition afterwards. He hated himself for it. I can't imagine him committing a murder in cold blood.' She paused. 'Who was killed?'

'A French art dealer from Paris. A man called Emile Narcisse.' He wished she were not wearing sunglasses so that he could see her eyes. 'Do you know that name?'

But she shook her head. 'I've never heard of him.'

'Did Hans speak to you of his plans to go to France?'

Again a shake of the head. 'No.'

'So you don't have any idea what he was doing there?'

'None.'

Enzo was disappointed. It looked like this was going to prove a wasted journey.

Kirsty said, 'How long was he abusing you? Physically.'

'As long as I've known him.'

Kirsty frowned. 'And you were with him for how long?'

'Two years.' She pre-empted Kirsty's next question. 'I know. Why did I stay with him? Everyone asks me that.' She took another nervous puff at her cigarette before throwing it away across the cobbles. 'It's hard to explain. I guess I loved him. And probably still do. He wasn't like this all the time.' She touched her face. 'He was loving and kind and generous, and he hated himself when he lost his temper.' She lowered her head and took off her sunglasses again, this time to wipe the first tears from her eyes. Then she stared them down, almost defiantly. 'He'd got kind of obsessed about it, lately.'

'About what?' Enzo said.

'Whatever it was that made him mad, that caused him to lose control and lash out. He told me once that when he was a child he had discovered pleasure in hurting a neighbour's dog, and that it frightened him so much he wouldn't go near it again, even though the animal itself seemed to bear him no ill will. I think he believed that there was some kind of malign force within him that made him do these things. Recently he'd been searching the internet for something he called the evil gene. I truly think he wanted to believe that it wasn't his fault. That it was inherited in some way, and that he really wasn't to blame.'

Enzo was intrigued. 'What did he find?'

'Oh, nothing much, I don't think. Some shit about inherited violence. When his mother died he discovered some stuff among her papers. An old birth certificate that showed his father had been the illegitimate son of a married man killed in the war. His real grandfather. There were letters that this man had written to Hans's grandmother, and diaries that he had left in her care.'

She fumbled to light another cigarette with hands that shook, and Enzo could not tell if it was the cold or emotion.

'And that became his new obsession. Finding out who his grandfather was. What kind of man he had been. There was no one else in his family that Hans knew of who had ever displayed his violent tendencies.'

Kirsty said, 'So he thought he might have inherited it from his grandfather?'

'I'm sure that's what he hoped. Anything that would relieve him of responsibility for his own behaviour. He went to the records office in Würzburg where his family are from, to see if he could find out.'

'And?' Enzo was fascinated. His sense of Bauer was becoming more three-dimensional with everything that Lise revealed about him. But he was disappointed by her response.

'I don't know. I took advantage of him being away to pack my things and leave.' She had no intention of sharing with them the ugly scene which had played out in the apartment when he returned earlier than expected.

'So you don't know what he found out?' Kirsty said.

'No, but you could ask his *Mitarbeiter*.'

'*Mitarbeiter*?' Enzo was at a loss.

'Volunteer,' Kirsty told him, though it didn't make much sense to her either. She turned to Lise. 'What kind of volunteer?'

She shrugged. 'Apparently the archive people appoint a *Mitarbeiter* to help people find their way through the records. Hans asked me to scan some documents for him and send them to her. The email address must still be in my phone.'

She dug it out from her coat pocket and began navigating through her mailer.

'How far to Würzburg from here?' Enzo said.

'Four or five hours, I think.' Lise's focus was still on her phone.

Enzo and Kirsty exchanged looks. Enzo checked the time and said, 'We could hire a car and overnight there. Then drive back first thing tomorrow to catch our flight.'

'Got it.' Lise looked up. 'Greta Jung. Do you want me to email her, or will I forward you the address?'

*

It was a long drive for a short meeting. Greta Jung had responded to their email while they were still on the road. She had lectures all day, she said, and could only spare fifteen minutes or so in the late afternoon.

They met her at the same Zweiviertel café where Bauer had bought her an extravagant breakfast in return for the information she had dug out of the archives. Enzo and Kirsty kept their masks firmly in place and made no attempt to drink the espressos they had ordered to reserve their table. Greta Jung, on the other hand, while she described her meeting with Bauer, was gulping down cake and cappuccino as if she hadn't eaten for a week. Her leggings today were red, her lips black, and she wore a scarf that alternated blocks of red, green and blue.

'Strange guy,' she said. 'Good-looking. Might even have fancied him. But he had such cold eyes.' Her English was crisp and concise.

'What were you able to tell him about his grandfather?' Enzo asked.

'Well, he already knew the name from his father's original birth certificate. I got him extracts from family records going back a couple of generations. Nothing very exciting. The most interesting stuff I found was on the internet.'

Kirsty expressed her surprise. 'There was information available about his grandfather on the internet?'

'Sure. He was a big time art dealer in the twenties and thirties. And during the war he was co-opted on to Hermann

Göring's staff to acquire – or should I say steal – art for his private collection. Göring got him a commission in the Luftwaffe and had him attached to the ERR in Paris.' She looked up from the last of her cake. 'You know what that is?'

Enzo nodded. 'What was his grandfather's name?'

The girl reached down and into a knitted orange and yellow satchel that she had hung from the back of her chair. She produced a red folder. 'It's all in here. If you're interested.' A knowing little smile animated her lips.

'How much?' Enzo said.

Greta Jung said, 'I get nothing for my work as a *Mitarbeiter*. And all I got from Herr Bauer in return for my efforts was breakfast.'

Enzo sighed and took out his wallet. He slipped a fifty-euro note across the table. 'Enough?'

Greta Jung smiled and quickly took the note before sliding the folder towards him. 'His grandfather's name was Karlheinz Wolff.'

'What happened to him?' Kirsty said.

The student just shrugged. 'No one knows. He was listed as missing in action somewhere in France in 1944.'

CHAPTER TWENTY

It was late afternoon by the time Enzo was driving east again on the Boulevard de l'Hautil at Cergy-Pontoise. The flight back to Paris from Berlin had taken under two hours, but followed a five-hour drive back from Würzburg, and Enzo was feeling the travel stress of the last two days catching up with him.

He had cleaned off Greta Jung's folder and its contents with disinfectant wipes before handling them, then spent the evening in his hotel room reading through her researches. Twice. And once again on the plane. He had been fascinated by the story of revenge recounted in a memoir by a friend of Wolff. The trip to Paris to exact retribution on the man who had made Wolff's sister pregnant. The art critic, Georges Picard. The frenzied display of violence that could so easily have led to the man's death.

Enzo could see how Bauer would have been seduced by all of this. He had followed his grandfather's footsteps into the world of art. Had that been inherited? It certainly wasn't environmental, since grandfather and grandson had never met. And artistic talent was often passed on through a family, sometimes skipping a generation. Bauer, Enzo was sure, must also have wondered if he had inherited his grandfather's temperament, a tendency towards irrational and uncontrollable violence. Wolff, his friend had written, would certainly have killed Picard had his companions not stopped him.

The sky to the west was painted red by the late autumn sunset, a few bruised and purple clouds bubbling up along the horizon. And the traffic was still light as Enzo turned into the campus of the Institute de Recherche Criminelle Gendarmerie Nationale. At the airport he had put Kirsty in a taxi, and driven straight out to Cergy-Pontoise.

A call to Magali Blanc's office on landing at Charles de Gaulle confirmed that she had, indeed, followed Enzo's suggestion of extracting DNA from the bones of the Carennac remains. Her assistant, however, was not privy to the results, and Magali was on a conference call that was likely to last most of the afternoon. Hence his drive out to the IRCGN. Enzo had grown increasingly impatient with age.

By the time he had cleared security and been taken up to her first-floor lab, darkness had fallen, and cold night air pushed against all the windows of the Human Identification wing. Her assistant was gone, and Enzo was left sitting in her office replaying everything he had learned in the last forty-eight hours. It was there, while he waited, that he made a decision that would probably haunt him for the rest of his days.

He placed a call to the Ministry of Justice and found himself talking to someone who had reason to be grateful to him for services previously rendered. A favour owed, now called in.

He hung up as Magali breezed into her office. She seemed surprised to see him. 'Two visits in one week,' she said. 'I'm flattered. What are you after?'

'I'm told you took my advice. About the DNA.'

'I did,' she said. 'Developed a complete profile.'

'And?'

'Asked the boys across the way to run it through the European database.'

'And?'

She laughed. 'You never have learned the art of patience, have you, Enzo.' Then sighed. 'I don't know. I haven't had the results back yet. Unless . . .'

She sifted through fresh piles of documents on her desk.

'Ah yes, here we are. Must have come through this afternoon.'

Enzo was annoyed to think that they had been sitting there under his nose the whole time he had been waiting. He could certainly not have resisted taking a look. He watched Magali's eyes as she scanned the paper in her hand, and saw her eyebrows push up on her forehead.

'Well, well. You were right.' She looked at him and grinned. 'As always.' Then turned back to the document. 'It seems that the search turned up a familial match in the German database. A teenager with a record for assault in Berlin. His DNA has been on file for the last seven years.'

Enzo said, 'And his name is Hans Bauer.'

Magali's head snapped up and she looked at him in astonishment. 'How can you possibly know that?'

'An educated guess,' he said. 'But since I seem to have hit the
mark, then I know more than that. I know that the remains
you have in your lab belong to a man called Karlheinz Wolff.
A Hauptmann in the Luftwaffe, employed as a procurer of art
by Reichsmarschall Hermann Göring, and listed as missing in
action somewhere in France in the summer of 1944.'

The document she was holding went limp in Magali's hand,
and if it were not hidden by her mask, Enzo was sure he would
have seen her mouth hanging open. But he wasn't finished yet.

'He is also the grandfather of the murder suspect in the
case I've been consulting on. Which bears out my instinct to
be sceptical about coincidence.'

'So that explains what Bauer was doing in Carennac,' Raffin
said. He stuffed another forkful of *chou farci* into his mouth,
quickly followed by a mouthful of Vin de Savoie rouge. Enzo
hadn't seen him this animated since his illness.

He and Kirsty, and Enzo and Alexis, were all seated around
the dinner table in the apartment in the Rue de Tournon, well
separated despite the almost negligible risk. Alexis had his
father's hair and his mother's dimples, and his latest hearing
aids were both highly efficient and almost invisible. It would
have been impossible to tell from his ease of interaction that
the boy had hearing difficulties caused by the Waardenburg
syndrome inherited from his grandfather. Ten years old now,

he was sprouting rapidly, and demonstrating that he had also inherited his grandfather's intelligence. But for the moment, he was engrossed in the stuffed cabbage.

'It might explain what led him to Carennac,' Enzo said, 'but it doesn't tell us what he was doing there. Or what passed between him and Narcisse in Paris. Or why both men were in Anny Lavigne's house the night of the murder.'

'Not yet. Though I'm sure you'll find out,' Raffin said. 'The possibilities are intriguing. All the players in this little narrative have some connection with art. Narcisse was a dealer. Bauer ran an art gallery. Karlheinz Wolff stole art for the Nazis. I mean, do you think this whole thing could have something to do with stolen Nazi art?'

Enzo didn't respond. For the moment he seemed lost in thought and forked his *chou farci* absently into his mouth. Raffin noticed that his wine glass was still full.

'Drink up, man,' he said. 'You haven't touched your wine.'

Enzo looked up to find Kirsty watching him, concerned. A daughter's instinct. 'What is it, Papa?'

Very quietly he said, 'I'm going to visit Charlotte in prison tomorrow.'

The silence around the table was broken only by the scrape of Alexis' fork on his plate. He was oblivious to the bombshell that his grandfather had just dropped into the middle of dinner.

'You have got to be joking!' Kirsty stared at him in disbelief. 'I mean, really, you're not serious? You can't be.'

'I am.' Enzo glanced at Raffin and saw that the blood had left his face. It was easy to forget that Raffin and Charlotte had once been lovers, before Enzo ever met her.

Kirsty turned to Alexis. 'Go to your room.'

His face crumpled in dismay. 'Aw, Mama, I haven't finished my dinner.'

'Take it with you. You can watch TV while you finish it.' Which broke a golden rule. Dinner was always eaten as a family, around the table. Alexis' dismay was displaced by delight. He grabbed his plate and made off with it before his mother changed her mind. When he had gone, Kirsty turned back to her father and scrutinised his face. 'You really *are* serious.'

He nodded.

'Papa, she tried to kill you. *Twice!*'

Enzo closed his eyes and the image of the dark figure who very nearly drove a knife through his heart high up in the Château des Fleures in Gaillac flashed painfully through his memory. And then Charlotte standing over him in the rain, a gun pointed at his head, ready to pull the trigger. And he knew that she would have done it if Sophie had not knocked her to the ground with a wheel brace.

Raffin found his voice, finally. 'You can't just go visiting prisoners at a moment's notice, Enzo. It takes time to set these things up.'

'Which is why I called in a favour earlier today. I'm cleared to visit her tomorrow morning.'

'But why?' Kirsty wouldn't let it go. 'Why, for God's sake?'

'Because Bauer is an enigma, Kirsty.' He laid down his knife and fork. 'Here is a man prone to reckless violence and then instant regret. He is accused of a murder that I have reason to think he might not have committed. He is the grandson of a wartime art thief, obsessed with the idea that such a thing as an evil gene might actually exist. Or, at the very least, an inherited propensity for violence. The only person I know who can give me an insight into the psyche of a man like that – a man who is still missing, by the way – is Charlotte Roux.'

'Don't do it, Papa.' Kirsty reached out to place a hand over one of his. 'There are other forensic psychologists you could consult.'

Enzo nodded. 'Yes. There are. But none of them is the mother of my son. And I haven't set eyes on her for nearly ten years.'

CHAPTER TWENTY-ONE

Enzo felt sick as he drove into the visitors' car park in front of the women's wing of the *maison d'arrêt* at Fleury-Mérogis. It was just under an hour's drive from Paris, directly south of the city and close to the edge of the Forêt de Sénart.

This was the largest penitentiary in Europe, built in the 1960s in the conventional style of French prisons. Five blocks, each with three wings, radiated from a polygonal central building. The MAF, or *maison d'arrêt pour femmes*, hosted more than 270 female prisoners in fewer than 170 cells, which meant that many of the women were forced to share.

A time-worn French flag fluttered listlessly in the autumn sunshine of this October morning. And somehow it seemed wrong for the sun to be shining, when people were locked away in tiny cells where the light of freedom was limited by small barred windows that provided only a tantalising glimpse of the world left behind. Parking slots were arranged around a scrubby patch of lawn boasting a few stunted shrubs. Enzo switched off the engine and sat holding the steering wheel for some minutes in an attempt to stop his hands from shaking.

He was aware that he was under observation from security cameras left and right and knew that he could not sit here for any length of time. He drew a deep breath and stepped out into the cold morning air.

At reception in the *tour centrale*, they checked his identity and authorisation, and handed him a bar-coded security badge to pin to his coat. A female prison officer escorted him up a large spiral staircase to the *couloir des parloirs*, a long, pale blue corridor with tall, narrow windows along one side that spilled incongruous sunlight across a polished grey floor. A row of shiny, blue-painted doors on the wall opposite opened into the *parloirs* themselves, the private visitors' rooms. Narrow floor-to-ceiling windows next to each door allowed for observation by prison officers.

The officer who led Enzo along the corridor wore a dark blue skirt and open-necked pale blue blouse with dark blue epaulettes. Her hair was dyed blond and tied back in a ponytail, and her shoes slapped softly on reflecting sunlight. She stopped at a door halfway along the corridor and opened it for Enzo to step inside. This was a narrow room with an identical door and window at the far end of it leading to the cells beyond. It was divided in half by a thick wall that stood a metre high, designed to separate prisoner from visitor. It was clad in tiny flaking mosaic tiles, and Covid precautions had seen the installation of a Plexiglas screen that extended from the wall to the ceiling.

There was a solitary chair on Enzo's side and the prisoner officer said curtly, 'Sit one metre back from the screen.'

302

It wasn't until she closed the door behind him, and the reflected sunlight vanished from the Plexiglas, that he saw Charlotte seated in a chair on the other side of it. At first he thought there had been some mistake. That they had brought him to the wrong room. Before he realised, with a shock that almost stopped his heart, that this, after all, really was Charlotte.

In his memory she had always been the woman he had fallen for all those years ago. A sardonic smile playing about full lips. Lustrous dark hair tumbling in glistening curls to her shoulders. Dark eyes which had held him in their thrall from the moment they met. He could still hear the laughter that spilled so freely from the mouth he had kissed so often, the cries of passion that accompanied their lovemaking. The vibrant young woman who had stolen his heart and his reason.

And here sat a woman he barely recognised. An old lady with grey hair cropped to an unruly shag. Dark shadows beneath dull eyes that seemed to absorb rather than reflect the light. A blue mask hid half of her ravaged face. She wore a short-sleeved smock, exposing skin stretched tightly over fleshless arms. Shrunken hands were clasped together in her lap, outsized knuckles on painfully thin fingers.

Instinctively she raised a hand to her mouth as she barked into her mask, a retching cough that left her breathless and brought tears to her eyes. The first light he had seen in them since he stepped into the room.

She blinked them away and stared up at him for several

303

long moments. 'For God's sake, sit down,' she said. 'And don't look at me like that. The shock on your face is like looking at a reflection of what I've become. One I never look at myself.' She was breathing with difficulty, and her breath rattled in her throat.

Enzo lowered himself into his chair, face stinging as if she had slapped it repeatedly. He attempted to blink away involuntary tears and saw Charlotte flinch from his reaction. Somehow it had not occurred to him that the woman he had come to visit would not be the Charlotte he remembered. He could never have imagined that the woman he had once loved might be reduced by prison and time to the shadow that sat before him now.

She said, 'Last year a fashion designer came to the prison to dress us up and make us walk the walk, parade her clothes down the red carpet. Sakina M'sa. I'd never heard of her. Of course, she chose all the young ones. The girls who still had their looks. I remember her looking at me, and how quickly her eyes moved on. Had she been casting a pantomime, she'd probably have given me the role of the wicked witch.' She forced a laugh. 'Typecasting.' Then launched into another bout of coughing that lasted a full half minute.

Enzo could only watch from his side of the screen, shocked and unable to disguise his distress.

When finally the coughing subsided, she said in a voice scraped thin, 'I caught Covid in the spring. It was rampant in the prison. They say I have recovered from it, but it has left me without any sense of taste or smell. And this damned cough.' She drew breath with difficulty. 'Damage to the lungs. They say it's permanent.'

'Jesus, Charlotte,' he said. Which seemed to amuse her.

She shook her head. 'Not often I've seen you at a loss for words, Enzo.' But the smile which briefly lit her face quickly vanished. 'How is Laurent?'

Enzo found it hard to meet her eyes. 'He's doing well.'

'Does he ever ask about me?'

'He used to. All the time.'

'And what did you tell him?'

'I made excuses. You'd gone abroad. Work meant that you couldn't come back. At least not immediately. He couldn't understand why you never wrote or phoned, and it broke my heart to lie to him.' He fixed his eyes on white-knuckled hands interlocked in his lap. 'Of course, he knew I was. He's a smart kid. In the end he decided you were dead.' He looked up to see tears brimming on the brink of her lower lids. 'And maybe that's better than the truth. Though one day, I suppose, he deserves to know.'

He saw her swallowing hard to try to control her voice. 'I don't think I'll live long enough to see out my sentence. So I'll probably not see him again before I die.' She sucked in more air. 'Then it won't be a lie any more.' She looked very directly at him. 'I didn't believe anything could ever be worse than death, until they brought me here. I wish Sophie had killed me that day.' And Enzo could still see the scar on her temple. 'I wish I was dead, Enzo.'

This time Enzo couldn't stop his tears. Hot and silent, springing from the depths of his despair and regret. He brushed them away with the backs of his hands.

'Good to see we can still cry,' she said, just a hint of the old Charlotte in her voice. 'We spilled a lot of tears together in our time, you and I.'

'We did.'

He watched her use her mask to dry hers away, and was glad he had his own mask to hide behind. She said, 'So why are you here?'

The whole Bauer enigma seemed almost irrelevant now. And for a moment he considered not even raising it. But how else to explain his visit? 'A case I'm working on,' he said. 'A murder suspect who is a complex and unusual individual. I thought your special insights might throw light into some dark places.'

An exhalation of air filled her mask. 'I might have known. You always did have an ulterior motive, Enzo. Your own priorities. Selfish, self-obsessed, regardless of others.'

And he knew that this had been a mistake. 'I'm sorry,' he said. And stood up. 'Really. I thought you might have relished the challenge. A distraction from . . .' He looked around and spread his hands out hopelessly to either side. 'This.' He sighed. 'But I can see I was wrong. I won't waste any more of your time.'

He turned towards the door, and her voice came to him like an arrow out of the darkness, piercing him so painfully he almost cried out.

'Don't leave.'

He stood for a moment, still with his back to her, before turning to see that she had risen to her feet. And he was shocked all over again at how much weight she had lost.

'Time is all I have.' He saw her struggling for control. 'Please stay. We have forty-five minutes before they throw you out.'

He sat down again, and wondered if Bauer had only been a pretext, the excuse for seeing her that he had never been able to find before. He realised now it would have been better had he stayed away, held on to those memories of her as she had been. Now, forever, he would see this wasted creature behind the Plexiglas who wanted nothing more than forty-five minutes of his time. And to die.

'Tell me.'

And so he did. Everything from the remains under the dead tree to the familial DNA tying the cadaver to Bauer. The mystery of who killed Narcisse and why. The doubt that the blood spatter had created in Enzo's mind about Bauer's guilt. The young German's temper-fuelled violence, his search for the truth about the existence of an evil gene, his obsession with his dead grandfather and the possibility that he had somehow bequeathed his grandson the curse of inherited violence.

She listened in silence, interrupting him only once with a fit of coughing. When he had finished she said, 'Quite a story.' And he could see that in her mind at least she was no longer sitting in a visitor's room at the woman's prison in Fleury-Mérogis. There was light and intelligence again in her dark eyes, a brain left to atrophy in a prison cell now actively sifting through her extensive knowledge and years of experience as a forensic psychologist. 'There is no such thing as an evil gene, Enzo. Evil itself is far too difficult a concept for a scientific enquiry. Though it hasn't prevented people from trying. A couple of researchers in San Diego managed, after twenty-one generations, to breed a fruit fly that was intensely aggressive. In its brain they found higher levels of a particular enzyme that seemed to be the cause of the aggression. And that enzyme was produced by a single gene. But an evil gene? I don't think so. And given that it would take twenty-one generations, it's hardly an experiment that could be conducted with humans.'

'What about inherited violence?'

'Oh, there's plenty of evidence for that. Several genes acting together, with the right environmental conditions, can drive people to pathological violence. Genes that are inherited and lead to a genetic predisposition for aggression. Plenty of evidence.'

'So Bauer was right to search for something in his family history that might explain his behaviour?'

'I can see why he would want to. Lets him nicely off the hook, doesn't it? After all, from what you tell me, there doesn't seem to have been anything environmentally that would have led him to violence. Except of course for a domineering mother, the absence of a male role model, and probably the need to vent his frustrations. Men often feel emasculated by a dominant woman.' She smiled, and it almost broke his heart to see how it brought a glimpse of the old Charlotte to the ruined face. 'Never had that effect on you, though, Enzo.'

And had he been able to, he would have reached out to touch her. Brush her face with the tips of his fingers.

'Those same researchers in San Diego studied a large number of males from birth to adulthood and found strong evidence of a genetic predisposition to violence. A couple of other studies showed a genetic variant in a particular enzyme called monoamine oxidase A, which had a significant impact on whether a man developed antisocial problems or not. A male with low levels of the enzyme was more likely to veer towards adult violence if someone had severely abused him as a child. High levels appeared to give protection against ending up in trouble, even if there had been earlier mistreatment.' She paused. 'It seems that only men carry this genetic variant.'

A silence fell between them, each aware of the unspoken question about what might explain Charlotte's predilection for violence. A question that neither of them was about to address.

Enzo said, 'There's nothing that I know of in Bauer's background to suggest that he had been abused as a child.'

But she just shrugged. 'It's not an exact science, Enzo. But it's true that behavioural patterns, or personality traits, or talent, often skip a generation. So it's perfectly possible that Bauer might have inherited his tendency towards violence from his grandfather, particularly if there was no history of it in the rest of his family. The fact that he is abjectly apologetic afterwards suggests that he is engaging in an internal battle where violence wins out over an otherwise empathetic personality. A combination of psychology and genetics.'

'A pity he didn't have you as a therapist.' Enzo attempted a smile which froze awkwardly on his lips.

'Maybe I could have done with a therapist myself.' That self-mocking look in her eyes that he recognised of old.

Reluctantly he said, 'Do you want to talk about that?' He had no real desire to rake over the ashes of those events that had led her to this end, but thought that maybe she would. Even if just to apologise.

To his relief she said, 'Good God, no! We've done well thus far in avoiding it. Let's not spoil things now.'

And silence descended again between them. A difficult silence, reminding them both that it was using up what little time they had left. He had no idea what to say. And in the end resorted to the prosaic. 'Do you share? A cell, I mean?'

She shook her head, resigned to the fact that the remainder of his visit would be conducted in an exchange of the banal. 'I have a single cell. They force me to exercise every day and eat their lousy food.' And then for just a moment she lit up. 'A Michelin-starred chef came once to do a cookery course with us, and we got to eat the food that he'd taught us how to prepare. What a treat after the pigswill they feed us here. All that was missing was a fine wine.' She smiled sadly. 'No doubt you could have suggested something appropriate.'

He returned an equally sad smile.

'Of course, that was before Covid. I can taste nothing now. Even if you took me to the best restaurant in Paris there would be no pleasure in it.'

More silence. The door behind him would open any moment, and Enzo found himself wishing that his visit would not end this way. That he would not have to go and leave her like this. Even though she had attempted to kill him twice, he felt no hatred for her in his heart. Only the pain of remorse, and a deep hollowing sadness that her life would end so unhappily in this miserable place.

And even though he was expecting it, he was still startled when the door actually opened. The officer who had shown him in stood in the doorway. 'Time's up,' she said.

Charlotte remained seated as he stood. He knew that she didn't want him to go.

'See you,' he said.

'Will you?' Her voice was tiny.

He said, 'I'll come again.' Though both of them knew that he wouldn't.

At the door he glanced back. She remained in her chair, hands clasped in her lap, tears running down her face.

Enzo was numb as he walked back out into the sunshine. If there was any warmth in the air, he could not feel it. Only the chill of the wind that stirred the faded French flag flying over the car park.

He slipped behind the wheel of his car and pulled the door

shut, cocooning himself in its silence. A silence in which every movement he made seemed unnaturally loud, his whole world reduced to this tiny space where only he existed. He stared sightlessly through the windscreen at the sixties world of concrete and glass that contained and constrained the woman he had once loved. And maybe still did. In a life of many lows, this was one of his lowest.

He had left his phone in the glove compartment of the car, and an alert from within reminded him now that it was there. It startled him out of his reverie, and he opened the glove box to reclaim it. The home screen revealed several missed calls and a text from Dominique. Ironic, he thought, that it was Dominique who had interrupted his thoughts of Charlotte. He tapped the text icon to bring up the message.

Sophie has been rushed to hospital with pain and bleeding. Come as soon as you can.

CHAPTER TWENTY-TWO

The old lady sits in silence. Her eyes closed. And he watches the infinitely slow rise and fall of her chest as she collects her thoughts.

Suddenly she opens her eyes again and turns her head to look at him. A sad little smile animates her face, and she continues with her story . . .

Georgette was in Paris for more than a year, monsieur. To her it felt like a lifetime of incarceration. All through that winter of 1940 into 1941, and then the next. 1941 into 1942. Spring was on the horizon. A change in the air. Gone were the February frosts, and warm air was pushing up from Africa to bring leaves prematurely to the trees of the city's boulevards.

All that time she had spent buried away in the basement of the Jeu de Paume. Cataloguing incoming art, keeping a secret log for Rose of all outgoing shipments. The Friday evening meals at Lange's apartment had become both a fixture and a bright spot in her dull routine. A routine that seemed to hold out little hope, if any, of the chance to fulfil the role with which she had been charged by de Gaulle.

From time to time Lange returned to Germany for short

periods of leave, and she found that she missed him. Missed his dry sense of humour, the way he poked gentle fun at her. Missed their lively exchanges long into the evening on subjects as diverse as art and politics, philosophy and literature. Missed his cooking, and the sound of his voice when she made him laugh. Missed the way he looked at her with fond, smiling eyes when she told him stories of childhood, of growing up in Bordeaux. His periods of absence seemed interminable, even if only for two or three weeks. Those Friday evenings at his apartment in the Rue de Rivoli were all that kept her sane during these long months spent treading water at the Jeu de Paume.

And yet in all that time, there had never once been a hint of impropriety. No accidental touching of hands, meaningful looks or nearly kisses. Nothing to suggest that he had designs on her in any sexual sense. And although, perhaps, some part of her felt disappointed that he showed no interest in her that way, she had long since stopped feeling threatened by him, or trying to discern some hidden motive for his weekly invitations to dine at his apartment. They were simply two people taking comfort in the predictability of an uncomplicated relationship in an uncertain world.

It was a beautiful early spring day, some time in mid-March, when Georgette heard a commotion from the main gallery upstairs as she was cataloguing a fresh arrival of artworks in the basement. There were raised voices, and footsteps clattering across the parquet, and she hurried up the stairs to see what was going on. Several staff were running out into the gardens, Rose among them. German soldiers who were a fixture at the museum followed curiously in their wake.

Georgette ran the length of the grand gallery, casting her shadow through the wedges of sunshine that fell from arched windows, and out into the Tuileries. She smelled woodsmoke, and the antiseptic perfume of hot turps and burning oil, and saw clouds of dark smoke billowing up into the clear blue of the Paris sky. Several tarp-covered troop carriers were pulled up side by side on the path. Soldiers inside were throwing frames and canvasses out of the trucks. A hushed crowd had gathered around the blaze. A large bonfire that crackled and burned, and threw up sparks with the smoke as soldiers on the ground piled yet more paintings on to the flames.

Georgette elbowed her way to the front of the crowd, and stopped, open-mouthed, as she saw priceless works consigned to the conflagration. Hitler's 'degenerate art'. A Picasso that she recognised. Works by Degas, and Manet, and Henri Matisse. Van Gogh. André Derain. It was unthinkable. She wanted to scream at them to stop. But knew it was pointless. Someone somewhere had ordered this vandalism. To prove what? Power? Strength? Stupidity?

To the soldiers carrying out orders, it meant nothing. The burning of refuse. Bits of wood and canvas. But Georgette could see the dismay on the faces of those German officers permanently stationed at the gallery. Mirroring the stricken look on the face of Rose Valland who stood on the far side of the flames. Georgette caught her eye through the smoke and the air that shimmered in the heat of the fire, and each shared the pain of this moment of barbarism.

Among the crowd, but a little apart from it, stood a man she recognised. He wore a black leather flying jacket and a peaked cap embellished with the insignia of the Luftwaffe. It took her a moment to remember him as the officer who had berated her on the steps of the museum during Göring's visit the day after her arrival in Paris. His face was set, his skin pale. Whether simply a winter pallor or shock at what he witnessed, she couldn't tell. His eyes flickered in her direction and he saw that she was watching him. She looked quickly away, and when next she dared to steal another glance, he was gone.

A hammering on the door echoed through Rose's apartment, and startled Georgette awake. She had been so deeply asleep that it was some moments before she could shake herself free of it and make sense of what it was that had wakened her. She turned on her bedside lamp and sat up, reaching for her watch. It was after two and there was rain pattering against the window in the darkness outside.

She heard Rose's bedroom door opening and her footsteps in the hall. Something in the small, hurried steps conveyed fear. The banging on the door had not stopped.

Georgette slipped from her bed, pushing her feet into a pair of slippers, and wrapped a towelling robe around herself. The hall light was on as she stepped out of her room, and she saw a dishevelled Rose, tying her dressing gown at the waist as she opened the door.

The landing light threw the long shadows of two men across the hall floor. They each wore three-quarter-length leather coats and wide-brimmed black hats. One of them stepped forward and barked in Rose's face. 'Georgette Pignal?'

Rose took a step back in fright and half turned towards Georgette.

Georgette hurried quickly towards the door. 'That's me,' she said.

In bad French the one who had barked at Rose said, 'You come with us.'

'Who are you?' Rose stood her ground defiantly.

'Geheime Staatspolizei.'

Words that chilled Georgette to the bone. The Gestapo.

'What do you want with her?' Rose demanded.

'None of your business!' He looked beyond her at Georgette. 'You come. Now.'

Georgette was gripped by panic, her breath coming in short bursts. 'If you give me a minute to get changed . . .' Anything to delay the moment.

'No need for that.' He took three quick steps into the hall and grasped her arm. Fingers of steel clamped around soft flesh. She almost fell as he pulled her towards the door. When they reached the landing the second Gestapo officer grabbed her other arm, and between them they half dragged her towards the stairs. Georgette was in tears by now, and threw a panicked backward glance towards Rose who stood helplessly in the doorway, all colour leached from her face.

The room was dark. There were no windows. Georgette sat in a chair at a scarred wooden table stained by blood and tears. A solitary desk lamp, its cable trailing away across the floor, cast a pool of cold harsh light on the wood. Otherwise the room was empty. The night outside was warm, a soft mist lingering on the river. In here the air was cold and fetid and Georgette shivered in her robe and slippers, hugging herself to keep warm.

Neither Gestapo officer had spoken to her on the journey through Paris to the apartment block at eight-four Avenue Foch, an address known to every citizen in the city. An address that inspired fear. An address whose visitors walked upright through the front door and left horizontally via the back. They had marched her up stairs to the sixth floor. Then left her alone, seated at this table which bore witness to all those who had passed through here before her. She faced the door and dreaded the moment it would open again. If she closed her eyes and wished long enough and hard enough it might never happen. And she would waken to find herself in her bedroom at Rose's apartment realising it had all been a bad dream. But the light on the desk burned red through her eyelids, and no matter how hard she tried, reality closed in all around her, like hands in the dark.

The sound of the door opening crashed through her

desperate attempts to wish it all away, and she opened her eyes, temporarily blinded and blinking in the light, to see the figure of a man silhouetted against the illumination of the hallway behind him. He closed the door and was consumed by darkness before stepping up to stand just beyond the circle of light around the table. He held his shiny-peaked Luftwaffe cap in his hand, and his leather jacket hung open. He placed his hat on the tabletop and turned the chair around. He sat, straddling the seat, and arranged his arms on the back of it. Then leaned into the light.

He gazed thoughtfully at her for a very long time. She stared back at him. He had such cold blue eyes, and dark hair so black she suspected it could be dyed. In other circumstances she might have thought him handsome. Ages, perhaps with Lange. And suddenly she remembered his name. Wolff. She heard Lange's voice on the steps of the Jeu de Paume as clearly as if he were in the room with them. And how ardently she wished that he was. *Lay off her, Wolff, it was an accident.* Was it a Christian or a surname? She took a gamble, based on Lange's tone, and tried to keep the tremor from her voice.

'Why am I here, Herr Wolff?'

He raised a lazy eyebrow in half surprise. 'So you know my name?'

'It's on the lips of every socialite in Paris.'

He frowned and she saw that she had disconcerted him, if only momentarily. 'No doubt Herr Lange has discussed me with you at length.'

'Actually, he's never mentioned you. Not even once.'

'So how *do* you know my name?'

'It's what he called you when you were so rude to me on the steps of the Jeu de Paume.'

He considered this for some time, pursing his lips and nodding almost imperceptibly. 'What is your relationship with Paul Lange?'

'I have no relationship with him.'

'Yet you spend every Friday evening at his apartment.'

'Not by choice.'

He canted his head sceptically. 'Really?'

'Really.'

'Do you have sex with him?'

'Of course not!'

It was clear he did not believe her. 'So what do you talk about during all those long evenings?'

'He cooks for me. And we talk about art.'

'How very cosy. You know that he is married.'

It wasn't a question. But as a statement of fact it struck her with the force of a blow to the midriff. And he saw that he had hit home. Not that Lange had ever told her he wasn't. The subject had never arisen. And why would it? They were not in a relationship, after all. Still, it felt like something of a betrayal. For more than a year, they had been spending their Friday evenings together in his apartment. Why wouldn't he have told her?

'And two children.' Wolff smirked. 'Where do you think he goes when he returns to Germany on leave?'

Georgette tried to recover herself. 'Home, of course. And why wouldn't he?'

'So he told you?'

And for some reason she found herself unable to lie about it. 'The question never came up.'

He smiled again. 'I bet it didn't.' He reached into an inside pocket of his leather jacket and drew out a folded wad of papers which he carefully smoothed out on the table in front of him. Without looking up, he said, 'Where were you between May and December 1940?'

Fear prickled all across her skin. 'I was unwell. I spent most of that time recuperating at the home of friends of my parents in the Charente.'

'Ye-es . . .' he drawled. 'So you said in your statement to the occupying authority.' Now he looked at her very directly. 'But I have obtained papers from official French records which show that you volunteered for the Armée de Terre in the autumn of 1939, and that in May of 1940 you were given compassionate leave to travel to London following the death of your mother.'

And she knew that she was finished. If Wolff had acquired official French records then she had been caught cold in a lie. It was almost a relief to no longer have to carry on the subterfuge. Still, she was not going to admit to anything. Her eyes flickered towards his cap on the table.

'You're not Gestapo,' she said.

'Good heavens, no!' As if he might have taken offence had

she suggested it. 'But I have some influence. And they have their uses.'

'So what do you want?'

'I want to know about your relationship with Lange.'

'I told you. I have no relationship with him.'

At which he leaned further into the light, an intensity burning behind the cold light of chilling eyes. 'I don't think you understand, mademoiselle, just how much trouble you are in.'

The sound of the door slamming open behind him startled Wolff out of the circle of light. He jumped to his feet and spun around. A fine plaster dust from the hole punched in the wall by the door handle billowed into the room.

Even in silhouette, Georgette could see that it was Lange. He wore his greatcoat, and army cap, and seemed enormous, framed as he was in the doorway. He reached for a light switch and a single, overhead lamp washed the room in sudden cold light. One of the Gestapo officers who had brought Georgette to Avenue Foch stood agitating at his back.

'You cannot come in here, Hauptmann.'

Lange turned slowly to cast him a withering look. 'I am here on the authority of the Führer himself. If you have a problem with that, then you had better take it up with him.'

He stepped around Wolff, who stood rooted to the spot, and took off his coat to drape over Georgette's shoulders and raise her gently to her feet. 'I'm deeply sorry for this,' he said. 'Let's get you home.'

As he guided her towards the door Wolff moved to block their way. The two men were face to face, just inches apart.

'Get out of my way, Wolff.' Lange almost spat the words in his face.

Wolff was unflinching. 'You've gone a step too far this time, Lange.'

'Have I?'

'Maybe you think a piece of paper from the office of the Führer can keep you safe forever. But you're wrong.' He pushed his face even closer. 'Sooner or later I'll deal with you.' And he turned his contempt towards Georgette. 'Both of you.'

Lange placed a hand squarely on Wolff's chest and pushed hard enough to make the other man take a backward step. 'I'm not the pushover I was twenty years ago, Wolff. If you mess with me again you'll do so at your cost.'

He steered Georgette, then, towards the door, forcing the Gestapo officer to step aside, and they passed on to the landing and the staircase beyond. Georgette's legs nearly folded beneath her in relief, and only Lange's strong arm around her shoulders kept her on her feet.

'Thank you,' she whispered. And wasn't sure whether she was thanking the man, or the God who had sent him.

A car with driver stood idling out in the Avenue Foch and took them back to Lange's apartment in the Rue de Rivoli. Lange sat close to her in the back seat, so that she felt the warmth of his body next to hers. They passed the journey without a word.

By the time he got her up the stairs to his apartment she was almost ready to collapse. She allowed him to lead her into the sitting room where the embers of a coal fire in the hearth still warmed the air. He lowered her into the settee, finally removing his coat from her shoulders and throwing it across an armchair. He sat down beside her, and quite involuntarily she threw her arms around him, burying her face in his chest, tears releasing the toxicity of fear that had built up inside her during the last hours. She felt his arms encircle her, and as she turned her face up to meet his, their lips met for the first time. It seemed like the most natural thing in the world and they each surrendered to it without reserve. With her hand on his face she felt the stubble of a day's growth, smelled the warm, earthy perfume of his body. And then it was over.

They moved apart, quite suddenly, as if shocked by what had just passed between them, and he seemed flustered, almost embarrassed. He stood up. 'I'll get you something to drink.'

He returned with a large Cognac and soda in a glass full of ice cubes. She received it in both hands to sip gratefully, feeling the healing cold of it fresh on her lips, the alcohol warming her inside. He moved his coat and sat on the edge of the chair opposite, leaning forward, elbows on his knees. There was genuine concern in his eyes.

'Will you be okay?'

She nodded and said, 'How did you know where I was?'

'When I called you that first time, I gave you my number. It must still have been by the phone. Mademoiselle Valland called me.' And Georgette realised then that she probably owed her life to Rose. Lange reached out a hand to place over hers. 'What did he do to you?'

She shook her head. 'He didn't do anything.'

'Then what did he want?'

'He wanted to know about my relationship with you.' She saw his mouth set.

'What did you tell him?'

'That we had no relationship. That I came here every Friday evening because you wanted me to, and that I didn't feel I could refuse.' Which appeared to unsettle him. He sat back a little.

'And is that how you feel? Really?'

'No, of course not.' She hesitated for a long moment. 'Wolff said you were married.' And somehow there was an accusation implicit in it. Lange stood up and turned towards the fireplace.

'Yes,' he said, his back to her so that she couldn't see his face.

'You never told me.'

He turned. 'There didn't seem any point. It's a marriage in name only. My wife was seeing someone even before the war began. But she's a Catholic. So divorce isn't an option.' Bitterness crept into his voice then. 'Adultery, it seems, is an acceptable sin. But God forbid you break the rules of the club by asking for a divorce.'

Georgette searched his face and saw only pain there. In her mind she wrestled with mixed emotions. Confusion. Disappointment. Relief. Jealousy. 'Why do *you* think Wolff had me arrested?'

Lange sighed. 'We have a history, Karlheinz and I.'

She frowned. 'What do you mean?'

'We were students together at university in Frankfurt. Both of us majoring in the history of art.' He shook his head and chuckled at the irony. 'We were actually friends then. Part of a group, you know. A bunch of us who socialised, studied together, talked art and philosophy and religion together. And there was this girl . . .' He laughed, but without humour. 'Isn't there always? Hanna. A beautiful young woman. Smart, talented. Classic Aryan looks. Blond-haired, blue-eyed. She and Wolff were a thing, right from first year. By third year they were engaged. He didn't see any point in hanging around. Was even prepared to drop out of university to marry her.'

He moved away again, towards the fire, and stooped to scoop up a small shovelful of coal to feed the embers. As he stood, he turned again to Georgette.

'Of course she cheated on him.'

And she guessed what was coming. 'With you.'

He nodded. 'I'm not proud of it. At the time it didn't really mean anything. We were at a Christmas party, and we both had too much to drink. If Karlheinz hadn't found out, it probably wouldn't have altered the course of events. But he did. And, boy, did it change things.'

He slumped into his armchair again as she leaned forward on her elbows, sipping at her Cognac and soda, watching him closely while he spoke. He was somewhere far away, in a long-distant youth, reliving mistakes, rekindling regrets.

'Karlheinz has the most foul temper, and is very much prone to bouts of anger-fuelled violence. In this case, directed at me. He sought me out in the student common room, and simply attacked me. With fists and feet and head. I never saw it coming. Had no reason to expect it. I didn't even know he'd found out about me and Hanna. I was down on the floor before I knew what was happening.'

She saw the pain of recollection in his eyes.

'I didn't have a lot of meat on my bones in those days. Didn't stand a chance. I actually think he might have killed me if the others hadn't pulled him off. I had broken ribs, a broken nose and jaw. I missed weeks of lectures.'

'What happened to Wolff?'

'Someone reported him to the hierarchy.' He added quickly, 'It wasn't me. He was summoned to a meeting with the head of the university and summarily expelled.'

'And Hanna?'

'Oh, she and Wolff were finished. She was appalled by what he had done to me. And he wouldn't have had her back anyway. He saw it as humiliation. Would never have forgiven her.' He stretched himself out in the armchair and let his head fall back, eyes closed. 'And here's the irony. It was me that ended up marrying her.' He opened his eyes and pushed himself up again, barely able to meet Georgette's eyes. 'Yes.' He nodded in response to her unspoken question. 'The same woman who cheated on me seventeen years later. Who gave me two beautiful daughters that she won't even let me see now.' The smile that curled his lips was filled with bitterness. 'You'd have thought that might have been revenge enough for Wolff.'

'And that's why he had me arrested by the Gestapo? To get back at you?'

Lange shrugged doubtfully. 'In part, maybe. But there's more to it than that.'

Georgette cradled her now empty glass between cupped hands and sat forward. 'I don't understand. What?'

Lange looked at her very directly. 'He knows you were in London. He knows about de Gaulle. We have the same friends in common there. I'm sure he thinks that by getting at you he's undermining me.'

'Just because of what happened at university?'

Lange shook his head. 'Because I know the reason he's here in Paris.'

'Which is?'

'To procure the *Mona Lisa* for Hermann Göring's private collection.'

The glass slipped from Georgette's hand and smashed on the floor.

Lange said, 'He's just biding his time.'

The first grey light had appeared in the east. Rose was sitting by the fire in her front room when Georgette took the spare key from beneath the mat and let herself into the apartment. The older woman was on her feet immediately and hurried into the hall. She took one look at her assistant curator and let out a long sigh of relief. 'Thank God,' she said, and took Georgette by the arm to lead her to the fireplace. 'Come in, child. Warm yourself at the fire.'

'What time is it?' Even to herself, Georgette's voice sounded tiny.

'It's almost seven. I couldn't sleep.'

Georgette turned towards her. 'Thank you,' she said. 'I might be dead by now if you hadn't called Lange.'

Rose examined her face and Georgette saw trepidation behind the curiosity in her eyes. 'What happened?'

And she knew that she would have to tell her. Everything.

The rain of the night before had passed, and early morning sunshine glistened on still wet cobbles in the courtyard of the Louvre. Jacques Jaujard was brisk and businesslike. He stood behind his desk in his lounge suit, smoking a cigarette, and did not ask her to sit. Georgette knew that Rose had spoken to him at length in a phone call even before it was fully light. He pushed a leather document wallet across the desk towards her.

'Your travel documents.'

'Where am I going?'

'To the Musée Ingres at Montauban, where the *Mona Lisa* resides for the moment.'

Georgette felt as if an enormous weight had just lifted from her shoulders. At last. At long last this interminable confinement in Paris was over. But then doubt immediately crept in to cloud her relief. 'But you told me there was no point, since my cover was blown.'

Jaujard shrugged. 'After what happened last night there is no way you can stay in Paris. And consider this. While Wolff and Lange know about you, equally you know about them. And of Wolff's intentions. Who better to watch over *La Joconde* than someone who knows exactly who it is that wants to steal her?'

He stubbed out his cigarette and blew smoke at the ceiling.

'No one at the Musée Ingres will know the purpose of your presence there. You will just be another assistant curator. But I have told the curator himself that I am sending you to keep a special eye on *La Joconde*. He doesn't need to know why. The fewer who do, the better. But I have complete trust in René Huygue. He was curator of the department of painting here in the Louvre for ten years before the war, so if you need someone to turn to, he is your man.' He tipped his head towards the document folder. 'Take your papers, go home and pack. You'll travel to Montauban by rail first thing tomorrow, leaving from the Gare Austerlitz.' He rounded his desk to take her arm. 'Now come walk with me.'

The Louvre was deserted. There was some activity in the basement, but the main galleries were empty. Their footsteps echoed back at them from walls once graced by priceless paintings. Sunlight laid itself down in faint yellow slabs where those windows not yet boarded up let the outside in.

Jaujard's voice was hushed as he said, 'What I'm about to tell you is known only to a handful of people. I'm trusting you with it because, frankly, there will be no one else better placed to make use of it for the protection of *La Joconde*.'

He delayed for several more paces before finally, reluctantly, letting go of his long-held secret.

'Early in 1939, with the prospect of war on the horizon, we not only began to enact the evacuation of the Louvre, we took exceptional steps to secure the *Mona Lisa* from the possibility of confiscation by the Germans.' He ran a tongue over dry lips before popping a cigarette between them and lighting it. 'You've heard of André Bernard?'

'Of course. He's probably the most notorious forger of the twentieth century.' Georgette stopped suddenly in her tracks. 'You didn't . . . He didn't . . .'

'I paid him a very great deal of money to create a reproduction of the *Mona Lisa* that would fool even the most experienced of art experts. I won't bore you with the details, but he was virtually incarcerated in a basement room here in the Louvre every night for nearly six months. Most forgers don't have the luxury of working from the original. Bernard did. We procured a piece of poplar board of the same vintage as da Vinci used to paint *La Joconde*, and he replicated the *Mona Lisa* in every possible tiny detail. On both sides of the wood. He aged and dulled the oils and, using heat and varnish, reproduced the Italian craquelure that so characterises her.' He pulled long and thoughtfully on his cigarette. 'You know, when he first showed me them side by side, I couldn't tell the original from the copy. It's a truly extraordinary piece of work.'

Georgette stared at him with incredulity before growing self-consciously aware that her mouth was gaping. She snapped it shut.

'I know that you were on the team that crated the original, so you also know that we coded all the crates with a series of one, two or three coloured dots. Yellow for very valuable pieces. Green for major works. And red for world treasures. The *Mona Lisa* was the only work to have her crate stamped with three red dots. The forgery has been identically crated, but stamped uniquely with three yellow dots. We attached it to the same inventory as the huge canvasses that we had to strip from their frames and roll around long wooden poles for transportation. You know the ones I mean?'

Georgette said, '*The Wedding Feast at Cana*, by Veronese? And presumably David's *Coronation of Napoleon*.'

'Yes, and *Napoleon on the Battlefield of Eylau*, as well as *Napoleon Visiting the Plague Victims of Jaffa*. There are others inventoried in that batch. But the instruction is that under no circumstances are works on the same inventory to be separated.'

'So wherever *The Wedding Feast at Cana* is being kept is where the other *Mona Lisa* can be found.'

'Exactly.'

'And where are they?'

'Everything is at Montauban.'

They were standing now in a shaft of sunlight and Jaujard's cigarette smoke hung blue in the still air, trapped by the warmth of the light, curling slowly around his head in gauze-like wreaths.

'Does René Huygue know?'

'He doesn't. For all practical purposes, only you and I now know of its existence. The copy is catalogued as *Sketch for the Feast*.' He paused. 'If you believe that *La Joconde* is in real danger of falling into enemy hands, then I am authorising you to switch the copy for the original.'

They stood in silence for a very long time. The burden that Georgette had earlier felt lifting from her shoulders descended again, weighing even more heavily than before. This was both a momentous and a terrifying responsibility.

'One more thing,' Jaujard said, and the light faded in eyes which had so animated his face as he talked about the *Mona Lisa* and her copy. Even his skin seemed to grey. 'The intelligence that originally came to us from Berlin, alerting us to Hitler's designs on *La Joconde*, has now come up with a name. The person he has delegated to obtain the painting for his collection.' He drew a deep breath. 'It is Paul Lange.'

She was waiting for him on the landing outside his apartment when he returned home shortly before eight. All day, it had eaten away at her like a cancer. Her sense of betrayal. The humiliation. The realisation of just what a fool she had been. She felt sick, and exhausted, and was still trembling with anger. And there was no question about it in her mind. She had to confront him.

His face lit up as he reached the landing and saw her there. He stretched out an arm to pull her into his embrace. 'George!' There was undoubted pleasure in his surprise. And so he was not expecting the slap that resounded around the fourth-floor landing and stung his face. The strength of it nearly knocked him off balance, but he saw the second one coming and grasped her arm at the wrist to stop it.

'What the hell . . . ?'

'You bastard!' She struggled to free her arm from his grip, but he held on to it.

'For God's sake, George!'

'You lying, cheating, duplicitous bastard!'

He became conscious suddenly that others in the building might hear this. It would be entirely inappropriate for a German officer to be assaulted and verbally abused by a French citizen. He fought to hold her at bay while he fumbled to get his key in the lock. And then finally they were in the entrance hall and he pushed her forcefully away. He shouted. And his voice seemed excessively loud in the confined space as he slammed the door shut at his heels. 'Stop! Stop it!'

Each stood breathing hard, and glaring at the other.

'Are you going to tell me what this is all about?'

'So Wolff is acting on instructions from Göring to seize the *Mona Lisa*. What you conveniently forgot to tell me is that Hitler asked you to do exactly the same thing.'

His eyes opened wide, and she found it hard to read the expression on his face. It might have been anger, or guilt, or both. 'For heaven's sake,' he said, and strode past her into the front room. He shrugged himself free of his coat and threw it over the settee, turning to face her as she entered behind him. 'After all this time, I might have hoped you would credit me with a little more sophistication than that.'

'You lied to me.'

'I did not.' He strode to the drinks cabinet and poured himself a large Scotch. 'Yes, Hitler asked me to procure the *Mona Lisa* for him.' He turned to face her, glass in hand. 'But I never had the least intention of doing it. For God's sake, George, art has been my life. An appreciation of the one civilising factor and saving human grace in nearly two thousand relentless years of war and destruction. The *Mona Lisa* is, perhaps, the most important artwork in the world. The epitome of everything to which Man is capable of aspiring, a quintessential icon of what it is that sets human beings above every other animal on the planet. Art *is* civilisation, and the Nazis the antithesis of everything that stands for.' He took a long, breathless draught of his Scotch. 'Did you really believe I would betray all that for a cretinous little man like Hitler?'

Georgette stared at him, face stinging as if he had slapped her, too. She wanted so much to believe him. 'And what's he going to say, or do, if you don't deliver?'

He threw a dismissive hand towards the ceiling. 'Jesus, George, do you not think he's got other things on his mind? The war is not going well on the Eastern Front. Rumours are rife of an imminent Allied invasion of North Africa. There's the constant threat of an Allied invasion of Europe. I'm quite sure he's not lying awake at night wondering why I haven't brought him the *Mona Lisa*.'

'So what were you planning to do?'

'To keep her safe. Play a long game and hope that I'll never be called to answer for it. And in the meantime do everything I can to keep her out of the hands of Karlheinz Wolff. Because make no mistake, Göring's obsession with *La Joconde* far exceeds that of Hitler. At least Hitler wants to make her available to everyone. While Göring's desire is to shut her away in the dark, a part of his private collection. For his eyes only.'

He drained his glass and stepped towards her. His words and his passion had stolen away all her anger, and all her doubt. He took her by the shoulders and looked earnestly into her eyes.

'I'm here to help, George. To be around when Wolff makes his move. As he will. A week from now, a month from now. A year. Who knows? But you can bet it will come when we least expect it. Especially if the war is going badly and all eyes are elsewhere. He won't do anything precipitous, because he won't want to alert Hitler to Göring's designs on her. But don't be in any doubt. One day he'll come for her, and we need to be there to stop him.'

CHAPTER TWENTY-THREE

The waiting room was small and overlit. Unforgivingly hard plastic chairs and an ancient coffee machine whose hum filled the silence. Distant, muffled sounds from the maternity wing seemed to come from a very long way off. The pervasive perfumes of disinfectant and floor polish hung in the air.

Enzo sat next to Dominique and could barely meet the gaze of his son-in-law. Bertrand was perched on the chair opposite, despair apparent in the eyes above his mask. From time to time he stood up and paced the length of the room, then back again to resume his seat.

Enzo's eyes stung with fear and fatigue. It had taken him a little over six hours to drive down from Paris, stopping only twice. Once for a coffee to keep his eyes from shutting as he drove. And once to call Dominique for an update. The only news had been no news, which was good news in the absence of bad.

He had arrived at the hospital a little after five and watched darkness fall through the windows of a waiting room witness to both the tears and the joy of all those who had passed through it over the years. It was now nearly midnight. A stream of coffees from the machine had kept hunger at bay but set him even more on edge.

The doctors believed that Sophie was suffering from what they called placenta praevia, in which the placenta that the baby required for nourishment had detached itself from the womb. She was several weeks premature and they were attempting to prevent her from going into labour. Both were at serious risk.

None of them had spoken for what seemed like hours.

And then swing doors pushed suddenly open and a lady doctor, still in gown and mask and shower cap, breezed into the room. Enzo and the others were on their feet immediately, fearing the worst, hoping for the best.

She said, 'We've carried out a caesarean section.' And raised a quick hand to pre-empt questions. 'Successfully. Mother and son are both doing well.'

Enzo's legs nearly buckled under him.

The recovery ward was somewhere at the far end of the corridor. Bertrand had been in with Sophie for nearly fifteen minutes. They had let him into the recovery room shortly after she came out of the anaesthetic.

At this end of the corridor, light flooded through a large window that gave on to the incubation room. Enzo and Dominique stood gazing through it at a row of six incubators. Three were occupied. Sophie and Bertrand's little boy was in the middle. A tiny, crusty newborn baby, kicking and waving his arms energetically inside the plastic bubble that fed oxygen to lungs breathing prematurely. He had a fine head of dark hair, and Enzo had every expectation that one day there would be a silver streak running through it, and that his classmates would nickname him badger or magpie, as they had done with him. He only hoped that other less pleasant symptoms would not accompany it.

Dominique hooked her arm through his and gave it a tiny squeeze. 'Just like his grandfather,' she said. 'Causing trouble already.'

Enzo's smile was pale and barely extended beyond his lips. He didn't quite trust himself to speak just yet.

'I should probably get back to the apartment to check on Laurent,' Dominique said. Nicole had driven over from Gaillac to sit with him. 'And I should make us all something to eat. Bring Bertrand with you, Enzo. We can't have him going back to an empty house on his own after all this.'

Enzo nodded distractedly and she kissed his cheek before uncoupling her arm and slipping softly away. Enzo stood staring at his grandson and knew that a little bit of Pascale lived on in him. And it broke his heart that she had not lived to see it.

He had no idea how long he'd been standing gazing past his own reflection in the glass when he became aware of Bertrand tugging gently on his arm. 'She wants to see you,' he said. 'The doctor says it's okay. Just for a few minutes.'

*

339

Her face was chalk white, brown hair lacking its usual lustre and sprayed out across the pillow. Her eyes followed him from the door to the bedside, where he sat down and took the hand that was outside the covers. There was still an intravenous cannula taped to the back of it. The thought of the surgeon's knife cutting open his baby girl almost brought tears to his eyes. Hers, by contrast, were clear and smiling, and all he could see in them was her mother. The effects of the anaesthetic were more apparent in her voice, which was faint and husky.

'Are you alright?' she asked. Which made him laugh, almost out loud.

'Me?' He held her hand in both of his and squeezed it. 'I was so scared for you, Soph, after what happened to your mum.'

Somehow she managed to free her other hand and clutched both of his with both of hers. 'I knew you would be. But Papa, I was never ever going to die on you. Never. No way I could let that happen to you twice.'

And just as he had spilled tears for Charlotte at the start of the day, he spilled them again for Sophie and her mother at the end of it.

The lights of Cahors reflected in the loop of the River Lot that contained it. A town built by the Romans two thousand years ago. Once the financial crossroads of Europe. And now a sleepy departmental capital that had been Enzo's home for nearly forty years. From where he sat now in the dark, at the top of Mont Saint-Cyr, he could see it stretching north, past the tower where the public hangings once took place, and beyond that to the rocky uplands they called the *causses*. Rocky scrubland washed by moonlight. Away to his left, he saw the lights of traffic crossing the viaduct on the RN20, and the sound of it carried faintly to him on the night.

By day this was a spectacular viewpoint that attracted crowds of tourists. By night a quiet spot for young lovers to bring their cars. But on this cold early morning in late October, Enzo was quite alone. As he had been that night thirty-five years ago when Pascale died giving birth to Sophie. The place to which he had retreated, like a wounded animal, to spill his tears and try to come to terms with his loss. From here it was possible to achieve a different perspective on the world, but he had never quite found a context in which he could place the tragedy that had marred his young life.

Raising his daughter on his own had never been easy. They'd had their moments. Quite a few of them. But he could hardly be more proud of her than he was now. Or of his new grandson. If only Pascale had lived to share in it.

He heard the tyres of a vehicle on gravel, and headlights raked the night air. He stood up. But from here, where the bench was set just below the lip of the hill, he could see nothing. A car door slammed shut and there were footsteps, crisp in the chill night air.

'Who's there?' he called, and was relieved when Dominique came into view at the railing above him. Moonlight picked her out sharply against the black of the sky behind her.

'When Bertrand came back to the apartment on his own he said he thought I might find you here.' She skirted the railing and climbed down the steps to the viewpoint below. She ran her hand gently down the side of his pale moonlit face, then put her arms around him to pull him close. 'I know what you are feeling right now, darling. And I don't want to take the moment away from you. I want to share it with you.'

He slipped his arms around her and held her tight. 'I love you,' he whispered. Then drew back and touched her face and gazed into her eyes. 'You would have liked Pascale.' A sad smile. 'And I'm quite sure she would have approved of you.'

He released her to turn and gaze out over the town below.

'It all feels so long ago now. Like other people in another life.'

'You still miss her?'

He shook his head. 'It's not that. I accepted losing her a very long time ago. But I've never stopped feeling *her* loss. Everything she's missed out on. Watching her daughter grow.' He chuckled. 'Coming to terms with her son-in-law. As I had to. Looking through the glass tonight at her grandson. And just ...' He shrugged hopelessly. 'Just ... life. The whole life that lay ahead of her. I think of her every time the trees push out fresh leaves and another year passes that she never got to see. It's so unfair, Dom.'

'I know.' She took his arm and moulded her body to his. 'Her death took away your life, too. But you have another life now. With me. And you need to live every moment of it. And know that whatever happens, I'm not going to leave you, Enzo. Ever.'

He turned his face to hers and they kissed. Then he sighed and said, 'Sadly, it's me who's going to have to leave you.' And when he saw the alarm in her face, laughed and added, 'Though not for long. But I'm going to have to go back up to Carennac tomorrow and try to bring this whole damned case to an end, once and for all.'

CHAPTER TWENTY-FOUR

SOUTH-WEST FRANCE,
THE DAY OF THE MURDER

Bauer's train arrived in Brive-la-Gaillarde from Paris shortly after midday. The conductor had explained to him that he should only exit the train on the left if he was leaving the station. Otherwise he should step out on the right and the connecting local train would be waiting on the next platform.

He found himself a seat in it, a single-carriage bullet-shaped blue train whose final destination was Aurillac, one of the coldest towns in France. But he was not going anywhere near that far.

It pulled out of the bourgeois Corrèzienne town, with its grey slate roofs and tall narrow houses, and gathered speed into the bleak October landscape of the Département du Lot. A landscape characterised by forests of oak and chestnut and lime, and rolling hills cut through by tiny meandering streams.

He was both excited and apprehensive. All of this would have been so much easier if only Narcisse had been prepared to accept his proposition. It never, for one moment, occurred to him that his train might be speeding him towards an encounter with the man himself. And ultimately with death.

He climbed down from the train at Biars-sur-Cère and waited until it pulled out again before crossing the line to exit through the station into a deserted car park. To his relief, a taxi sat outside a café opposite the station and he went in to enquire if someone could take him to Carennac.

His first impression as they turned off the Alvignac road into Carennac village was that they had just driven into a medieval fairy tale. Steeply pitched red roofs, and slated turrets, the bell in the abbey chiming the hour. Streets barely wide enough for his taxi to negotiate. It was here, he was almost certain, that his grandfather's life had been cut short. Here that a story never previously told had played out among the Carennac stone. A story whose ending, he felt, had yet to be written. Quite possibly by him.

His taxi pulled up outside the Hostellerie Fenelon, and he carried his overnight bag across the paved terrace, through glass doors and into reception. A young man confirmed his reservation, took his details and handed him a key. 'Upstairs and to the right,' he said.

Bauer was just about to head for the stairs when he caught a glimpse of a familiar figure sitting at a window table on the far side of the restaurant. And it was as though every joint in his body had suddenly seized. He couldn't move.

Narcisse's focus was on his lunch, and so he didn't see the

young German glaring at him across the tables. Beyond his initial shock, Bauer felt anger fizzing inside him, that old familiar feeling. His fists clenched at his sides. After insulting him, and feigning disbelief, Narcisse was flagrantly betraying his confidence. Evidently he did not, as he had claimed, believe Bauer's story was so far-fetched. What was it he had called the German? A crank and a charlatan? And yet here he was. Bauer was having trouble controlling his breathing now. He moved quickly out of Narcisse's line of sight and headed for the stairs, determined that the old bastard would not get away with this.

Bauer did not linger long in his room. He dropped his bag on the bed and crossed to the window to look out through a latticework of branches and dead leaves at the slow-moving water of the River Dordogne below. His thoughts were a confused jumble of uncertainty. What to do? Almost on an impulse he decided that the first thing would be to find the house. Then he could take it from there. A way of procrastinating. Avoiding the issue. And most of all, Narcisse. Since he knew that a confrontation at this point could lead him to violence. And that would ruin everything.

He drifted quietly downstairs, hesitating at the doors to the restaurant to establish that Narcisse was still lunching, before slipping unseen out into the street.

It was cold. Only the faintest warmth discernible in a sun that barely rose above the rooftops. Bauer smelled woodsmoke in the air. Medieval buildings crowded narrow streets and cut crystal-sharp outlines against the pale autumn blue above. He realised very quickly that he should have obtained a street plan. The village was far bigger than he had imagined. The village store and the post office were shut. A faded sign above a shuttered property on the edge of the tree-lined palisade read *Café Calypso*. But it didn't look like a café. The palisade itself was deserted, apart from a solitary car parked up against the wall. It was a steep drop to a footpath that ran along the bank of the river below, where wooden rowing boats were moored in twos and threes, some half submerged in brackish green water. The walls of the château rose steeply on the other side of the road. At the far end, an archway led up a narrow cobbled street to the precincts of the abbey. Beyond that, a long bridge spanned a cleft in the rock, and a road led away from the village along the riverbank.

Bauer turned left and found himself walking unwittingly in the footsteps that Enzo and Dominique would leave in the same street less than twenty-four hours later. By which time Narcisse would be dead, and Bauer missing.

He followed the street along the basin of the village, aware that it climbed higher to both left and right, tiny alleyways branching off in either direction. At a crooked, cantilevered house at the end of the street, he turned left again, climbing a steep hill past a converted barn to the fenced playground of the village primary school. It too was deserted. A turn to the right led on to the main road to Alvignac and a bus shelter where an elderly lady sat leaning forward, both hands crooked over the top of her walking stick. Arthritic knuckles on age-spattered hands.

In his schoolboy French he asked if she could direct him to the home of Anny Lavigne, and she pointed him back along the road he had come, down past the school and a handful of houses. Where the road branched, she said, there were steps leading up to a tiny park and a war monument. Anny Lavigne lived in the big house that overlooked it from the far side.

He thanked her, hoping that he had understood, and followed the road back over the hill and down to where the road divided in two. Just as she had described, steps led up past a stone cross and into a small park where four stout tilia trees flanked a monument to the dead of both world wars. Beyond them, a dead tree had fallen over, pulling its root system free of the earth that had nourished it for who knew how many decades. A slight breeze stirred in the still of the afternoon, and red and white striped tape fluttered listlessly all around the area of disturbed ground.

He stopped and realised that this, almost certainly, was the place his grandfather had lain undiscovered for more than seventy years. Shot in the head by persons unknown and buried in haste. It was chilling to feel this close to the man who, all these years later, had brought him here. But Bauer knew that he was no longer at peace in the ground which had held him for so long. Every last trace of him had been removed and taken to Paris, and to Bauer it felt like desecration. He stood staring at the disinterred grave with an inexplicable mix of sorrow and anger.

He turned and found himself looking past an old chapel

turned exhibition space, shuttered and closed for the season, towards the house that overlooked the park. Anny Lavigne's house. The house described by Wolff in his diaries.

Steps climbed back down to the street beside it, a stone staircase doubling back and leading up to a small covered terrace at the front door.

He heard the scrape of footsteps echoing off cold stone in the chill of the afternoon. The first and only sign of life he had seen in this deserted place, except for the old lady at the bus stop. The shadows of trees that lined the railings were already long as the sun dipped away to the west, and Bauer moved into the cover they provided as the stooped figure of Emile Narcisse came into view, slowly climbing up from the main street below.

He stopped at the foot of the stairs to Anny Lavigne's door and hesitated a moment, consulting a piece of paper before pushing it back into a pocket of his long winter coat. He wore leather gloves, and Bauer could see a white shirt and blue tie where the coat was open at his neck.

There was still not a soul in sight, not even the chatter of birdsong to breach the silence of the village, as Narcisse climbed the dozen or more steps to the door of the house. The sharp rap of metal on wood echoed all around the tiny square as he employed the wrought-iron knocker to announce his presence.

Bauer watched as Narcisse shuffled impatiently before knocking again. And then the door opened. But from where he stood, Bauer could not see who had opened it. Just the animated discussion that followed. Their voices were hushed, and at the same time raised, like loud whispers that filled the air. Bauer was unable to make out a word of it, but discerned at least that the other voice was that of a woman.

Then silence, and a long period of what appeared to be a stand-off, before the door opened wider and Narcisse disappeared inside. The door closed softly behind him and Bauer stepped out into the sunlight. He was shaking with anger, and it was all he could do to stop himself from running up those steps to hammer on the door and beat the life out of the treacherous bastard. He took long deep breaths, condensing now as the temperature of the air around him dropped, and he glanced behind him to see the sun slip away beyond the roof of the nearest house, throwing the whole park into shadow.

CHAPTER TWENTY-FIVE

She is more animated now in the telling of her tale than she has been at any other time, and he has the sense that perhaps it is nearing its end. But then he realises, with something of a shock, that the story cannot reach its conclusion until the summer of 1944. And that she has only reached the spring of 1942.

Georgette arrived in Montauban in late March that year, full of hope and the expectation that at last she would take full responsibility for the safety of the *Mona Lisa*. She had been unaccountably saddened to say goodbye to Lange, but he had promised to stay in touch and assured her that she would see him again before long.

The Musée Ingres is a huge brick building that stands on the east bank of the River Tarn, a stone's throw from the medieval centre of Montauban. The whole town is built from the same red-brick that characterises the nearby city of Toulouse, known as *la ville rose*. The pink city.

The museum is built on five, or six, levels, depending on whether you include the rooms in the towers that stand on each corner, and the upper basement level. Below it all there is a huge basement that fills the footprint of the building. Its four tall arches are visible from the Pont Vieux which spans the river from the museum to the west bank, and much of the evacuated art from the Louvre had been stored there.

On the day that Georgette arrived, she was shown into René Huygue's makeshift office on the first floor. Huygue was a handsome man in his late thirties. He had dark hair silvered at the temples and brushed back from a distinguished face marked by a long, aquiline nose and a neatly trimmed moustache. Georgette thought he had the air of a man of aristocratic heritage, although she knew nothing of his family history. He wore a dark green blazer over moleskin trousers and a pale green tie neatly knotted at the neck of a crisply pressed white shirt. He regarded this young woman foist upon him by Paris with deep suspicion as she handed him her letter of introduction from Jacques Jaujard.

He sat down at his desk to open it as she remained standing, like a school pupil called before the head teacher. A deep frown furrowed his brow as he read, and he looked up at Georgette with renewed interest and even deeper suspicion. 'Sole custody of *La Joconde*?' he said, hardly able to keep the incredulity from his voice. 'What credentials could you possible have for this?'

Georgette shrugged. 'You're holding them.' And something about her bravado immediately communicated to him the sense that if he chose to fight her, he would lose. She was, after all, correct. The only credentials she needed were the letter he held in his hand from Jacques Jaujard. And he knew Jaujard well enough to realise that he would not ask this of him without good reason. Still, it irked him that he was being kept out of some very private loop.

He sighed. 'Very well. There's a spare room in the north-west tower. You may sleep there. Jacques says you are to be an assistant curator. I'll expect you to fulfil that function for however long we might be at Montauban.' He laid the letter on his desk and eyed her very directly. 'The way things have worked until now is that *La Joconde* resides with me during the day.' He nodded towards the other side of the room, and Georgette turned to see the very crate she had helped pack, sitting on an armchair set into a corner by the window. Planks of rough white poplar nailed together and strapped above the stamp of the Musées Nationaux by a strip of wood bearing three large red dots. Inside, she knew, was the humidity-resistant leatherette and fireproof paper designed to protect the painting from external damage. Huygue said, 'After all this time the *Mona Lisa* and I are accustomed to each other's company. So she will remain in my office during the day, where I can keep a personal eye on her.'

Georgette nodded. 'But she will sleep with me at night. Where you will not, I can assure you, keep an eye on either of us.'

And so Georgette spent the greater part of the next year living in the museum, sharing a bedroom with the most famous painted lady in the world. In all that time she heard nothing from Lange, and often wondered what he would make of the relationship she had developed instead with *La Joconde*. More than once she had opened up the crate to peel away the leatherette and fireproof paper to gaze upon the smile that had so bewitched the world. The slight, enigmatic curl of the mouth, the dark eyes that seemed to look at only you, regardless of where you might stand in the room. The road that snaked towards her from distant rocks with the latent menace of a serpent preparing to strike.

She was not conventionally beautiful. Prominent brows shadowed hooded eyes. Her nose was, perhaps, overlong, her mouth and chin somehow too small for the rest of her face. And yet she was utterly captivating. It was little wonder that men such as Hitler and Göring had fallen under her spell.

The following August, rooms on the ground floor and in the basement of the museum flooded during a summer storm, rainwater cascading down narrow streets from the centre of town and pouring in through the entrance courtyard. A number of paintings were water-damaged, and experts brought in to repair them. Had it not been for the sleeping arrangements, *La Joconde* might very well have been among the casualties. Georgette's first act of keeping her safe.

In addition to being an important year for Georgette, this was a transitional year in the war. That summer the Germans and the collaborationist régime in Vichy stepped up their actions against the Jews. Thousands were rounded up and sent off to work camps in Eastern Europe. The Musée Ingres itself lost several Jewish guards, René Huygue unable to prevent it, although he tried everything in his power to do so.

Then in early November the Allies landed in North Africa, and in France everything changed. The German army invaded what they had always laughingly called the Free French Zone, and German troops swarmed into Montauban, strutting about the town with cameras, for all the world like tourists on holiday.

Thanks to orders from the Kunstschutz, the museum was out of bounds to German soldiers, but the artworks themselves were subject to a new and different threat.

Georgette was summoned, along with the rest of the staff, to a meeting in Huygue's office in early December. Nearly fifteen of them squeezed into his tiny bureau, along with *La Joconde*, and listened in grave silence as he told them that the museum could no longer be considered a safe haven for the evacuated art from the Louvre. Even as he spoke, Georgette could see through the window behind him the troop carriers and tanks rumbling through the town, soldiers in twos and threes posted at every corner.

'We are protected from the army by order of the Kunstschutz,' he said. 'But it's anyone's guess how long that will last. More importantly, we are now under threat of aerial bombardment. With Montauban full of German troops and munitions, we become a legitimate target for Allied bombers. One stray bomb could destroy everything we have here.'

'What can we do?' an earnest young curator asked.

Huygue sighed. 'Move.' And there was a collective exhalation of disappointment. Most of those present had already been involved in the three previous evacuations, and knew just what a transfer involved.

Georgette said, 'Couldn't we notify the Allies somehow that the artworks are here, and have this area designated out of bounds for bombing sorties?'

Huygue shook his head. 'The collaborators in Vichy have refused us permission to communicate with the Allies.' His lip curled in anger. Even the mention of the name Vichy seemed to leave a bad taste in his mouth. 'Presumably they're afraid the Germans will accuse them of collaborating with the enemy. After all, the Vichy régime is good at that.' And Georgette got more than a little sense of his hatred for the Pétain government. He drew a deep breath. 'Paris have identified a château to the north-east of here, in the Département du Lot, that can take most of what we have. The Château de Montal. It's only two to three hours away by road and far removed from any strategic bombing targets. Unfortunately, we need vehicles and fuel to make the transfer, and up until now Jacques Jaujard has been unable to persuade either Paris or Vichy to supply them. So unless anyone has the ability to conjure a convoy of trucks and the diesel to power them we're stuck here.'

During nearly nine months at Montauban, Georgette had found herself thinking about Paul Lange less and less, becoming absorbed by the work of curating and protecting the treasures of the Louvre being sheltered at the Musée Ingres.

By December he had become a distant memory, as had his nemesis, Karlheinz Wolff. The dangers she had faced in Paris faded to insignificance somehow in this provincial town so far away in the extreme south-west.

She had fallen into the habit of walking up through the cobbled streets each morning to the Place Nationale in the centre of the *vieille ville* to take coffee and croissants in what had become a favourite café beneath the arches of the perfectly preserved bastide in the old square.

It was a cold grey morning when she set off one day in mid-December to walk through the little park opposite the museum, castine crunching underfoot, and climbing up to the vast crumbling edifice of the Eglise Saint-Jacques at the top of the hill. Built in 1230, and rebuilt twice, the base of the bell tower still bore traces of the damage caused by cannonballs during the siege of Montauban in 1621. She turned into the Rue Princesse and was almost at the arch leading to the square when she became aware of footsteps falling in with hers, and a shadow at her side. She turned, startled, to find Paul Lange grinning at her from beneath the brim of his soft grey fedora.

She felt suffused by a sudden warmth, as if he somehow radiated sunshine on this dull winter morning. A feeling she would have found hard to explain to anyone, let alone herself. 'Well,' she said. 'Speak of the devil.'

'And he's sure to appear.' Lange laughed. 'An English idiom, isn't it? Which must mean you were thinking about me. Although, I thought we'd agreed that I was *not* the devil.'

She smiled. 'The jury's still out on that one. I'd almost given up on you.'

'Oh, never do that, George. Wherever Wolff might be, I'm bound to appear.'

She stopped dead. 'Wolff's in Montauban?'

'He is.'

'Doing what?'

'I have no idea. I take it you haven't seen him?'

She shook her head and all the old fears and uncertainties of her time in Paris came flooding back.

'Don't worry. I doubt if he's ready to move just yet. But something has brought him here.' They had reached the Place Nationale, and although a busy farmer's market filled the square, the stalls were only sparsely stocked with winter vegetables and meagre rations of cheese and meat. 'I thought *you* might be able to tell me why.'

'Let's have breakfast,' she said, and was grateful that he was not in uniform. But he wore a long winter greatcoat beneath his fedora, and leather boots beneath that, and he could not have looked less like a local if he had tried. The sooner they sat down at her café the less conspicuous they would be.

They found a table beneath the arches and ordered *café crèmes* and a basket of croissants. As they ate he said, 'I was recalled to Germany for nearly six months. Everyone's nervous now, following the Allied invasion of North Africa. Expectations are

358

high that there will be an invasion of Europe too. Sometime soon. Maybe even in the next year. That's when I think you can expect Wolff to make his move. Though it doesn't explain why he's here now. I arrived back in Paris last week, and only found out yesterday that he was in Montauban.'

Georgette said, 'The authorities at the Louvre are preparing to move everything again. To a château and other locations in the Département du Lot, which is a couple of hours north-east of here.'

Lange cocked an eyebrow. 'Ah. That would be a vulnerable time. When will they make the transfer?'

She shrugged. 'No one knows. We can't get any transport. Not from the Germans, or from the French. But everyone's afraid that if the Allies bomb the town, everything in the museum will be in danger.'

He nodded thoughtfully and sipped at his coffee, lifting his eyes then to meet hers over the brim of his cup. He replaced it in its saucer and reached out to touch her face with the tips of his fingers, eyes searching deep into hers. 'I've missed you, George. Missed our Friday nights in Paris. Missed the escape from the war that we always seemed to manage over dinner.' He sighed and closed his eyes. 'I hate this war. The sooner it's over, the sooner we can get on with life. We surely have a higher calling than the killing of one another.'

'Speak to your people, Paul. They started it, I think.'

He withdrew his hand, as if stung. He drained his cup, and to her disappointment stood up to throw some coins on the table.

'Don't worry about transport for the transfer,' he said. 'I'll see to that.'

He nodded curtly, and strode off through the tables to disappear among the shoppers at the market, leaving her frustrated and angry with herself. The barb had been out of her mouth before she could stop it. And now he was gone. And she realised that she had missed him much more than she had ever dared to admit.

It was a month later that Huygue announced the granting of permission to move the artworks north. A promise of vehicles from the occupying authority had been given. Privately, Huygue told Georgette that even Jaujard, who had been lobbying for this for weeks, had been taken aback by the unexpected announcement. She had allowed herself a small sense of satisfaction in the knowledge that it was almost certainly her relationship with Lange that had procured it.

On March 1st, eight hundred pounds of packing material arrived at the Musée Ingres, and after an all-night packing session the first convoy left for Château de Montal with police motorcycle outriders. Georgette watched it go, heading across the bridge, and wondered how Lange had managed it all. There had been no further sign of him, and although he had reported Wolff's presence in the town she had not seen him either. It had not stopped her taking extra precautions, though. She had made a place for the crate that held the *Mona Lisa* beneath the floorboards in her bedroom, and insisted above the objections of René Huygue that it remained there during the day also.

The major problem in the evacuation of the artworks had been in finding a vehicle long enough to transport the huge rolled canvasses, which would be accompanied by *Sketch for the Feast*, *La Joconde*'s doppelgänger, for which Georgette now felt equally responsible. The scenery trailers which had brought them here were no longer at their disposal, and it was only at the last moment that the Germans made a gazogène-powered cattle truck available. Although big enough for the job, this vehicle was fuelled by a wood gas generator which converted timber or charcoal into a gas capable of powering an internal combustion engine. It also had a reputation for spontaneously bursting into flames.

As a result, Huygue obtained a jeep, which he filled with fire extinguishers, leaving only enough space for Georgette and the *Mona Lisa* to join him in accompanying the cattle truck north. There were several other trucks in the convoy and a number of armed outriders for security.

It was a bumpy ride on narrow roads, spring barely settling across a landscape still winter-dead. Only the willows showed signs of budding this early, with the occasional splash of pink cherry blossom. In a few short weeks the whole landscape would be covered with the white blossom of apple and plum and pear trees, the yellows of forsythia and the vivid reds of flowering japonica. Rich, red soil feeding new life to the start of a new year. Spring, 1943.

Georgette recalled Lange's words expressing German fears of an Allied invasion of Europe. She fervently hoped it would come, and soon. But for the moment it seemed no more than a glimmer of hope on a very distant horizon. The fact that the Germans were still very much in control was emphasised by the number of military convoys they passed on the RN20 heading north.

On the steep, winding descent from the *causses* into the valley of the River Dordogne, Huygue explained why the rolled canvasses they were following in the gazogène cattle truck could not be housed in the Château de Montal. 'They're just too long,' he said. 'We'd never get them in. And the château's not really big enough for everything anyway. We're going to have to split things up. The bulk of it will go to Montal, the rest to other properties in the area, as well as downriver to Château La Treyne. We'll be staying at Montal with the *Mona Lisa*.'

'And the big canvasses?' Georgette was anxious to know where she would have to go to lay hands on the forgery.

'The village of Bétaille,' he said. It sits on the edge of the flood plain, about half an hour from Montal.

'What's there?'

He laughed. 'Nothing much. A small château on the hill where some of the artworks will go. But *The Wedding Feast at Cana*, the *Coronation of Napoleon* and the others will go above a garage that can accommodate their full length.' Which sounded less than secure to Georgette.

A long, straight stretch of road between towering cliffs

followed the line of the railway, leading them through the town of Vayrac and into the village of Bétaille. Most of the village itself climbed the hill to the left of them, crowned by the tiny Château la Tourette. The convoy stopped in the road outside two *maisons bourgeoises* at the entrance to the village. Both sat in sprawling grounds, and between them stood a double garage with distinctive red-chequered window jambs and door arches. Two windows above roller doors opened into an apartment above the garage. Signs beneath each of them read MUSÉES NATIONAUX. Nothing, Georgette thought, like advertising your presence.

A military-green truck with a crane mounted above eight rear wheels awaited them. Half a dozen German soldiers joined museum staff in carefully attaching each of the rolled canvasses to the crane's hoist and lifting them to the left-hand window where they were fed in, one by one, to lie on the floor along the full length of the building. The remaining pieces were carried in by hand up a staircase at the rear. Georgette watched *Sketch for the Feast* with its three yellow dots being taken up to the apartment by an assistant curator. At least she knew exactly where it was.

'There will be two armed security guards permanently posted here,' Huygue told Georgette. Then dropped his bombshell. 'I'm afraid there will be no room for you to sleep at Château de Montal. We've managed to secure a house for you in the village of Carennac just across the valley there.' And he pointed to where distant cliffs rose above the far side of the river. 'So you're going to have to give up your sleeping companion of the last year. It's quite a short cycle to and from the château. Only about forty-five minutes.'

Georgette glared at him. It was his way of attempting to wrest control of *La Joconde* back for himself. A petty revenge for being kept out of the loop. But she just shook her head. 'Then I'll sit up with her at night if I have to, and snatch some sleep at the house during the day.'

He shrugged unhappily, but knew he couldn't argue. 'Suit yourself.'

Once the large canvasses were safely installed above the double garage, the convoy set off again towards its final destination. As they passed the pumps outside a petrol station just twenty metres further on, Georgette saw a black Citroën sedan idling on the pavement. A uniformed figure wearing a leather flying jacket stood leaning against the wheel arch smoking a cigarette. And Georgette realised with a sudden stab of apprehension that it was Karlheinz Wolff. She caught her breath and instinctively her hand reached for the packing case that held *La Joconde*. And she had never been more acutely aware of just how ill-equipped she would be, when the time came, to stop a determined Wolff from seizing it.

Anny Lavigne glances towards the old grandfather clock ticking solemnly against the far wall and places a hand on each arm of her rocker.

She says, 'I think, perhaps, Monsieur Macleod, I have told you as much as I can for today. I am tired now, and a little hungry. I should eat before I go to bed.' She eases herself stiffly out of her chair. 'I'll finish my story in the morning.'

Outside it is dark now, and for the last hour her tale has been told only by the glow of the fire. She reaches for a light switch and they both blink in the sudden harsh light that casts itself across the room.

Enzo, too, eases himself out of his chair. His hands and feet have become cold without him realising it. He stamps his feet and pushes his hands into his pockets. 'Thank you, madame, for your patience. It is an extraordinary tale. I look forward to hearing how it ends tomorrow.' At lunch he had reserved a room for himself to overnight at the Fenelon and phoned Dominique to tell her he would not be home until the following day.

'It is me who should thank you, Monsieur Macleod, for being such a patient listener. I'm sure you have much better things to do with your time.'

He just smiles. 'I'll see you in the morning, madame. I'll let myself out. Sleep well.'

And she is thoughtful as she watches him go, through her kitchen and out into the cold of the night where the sky is so clear that the heavens seem just a touch away.

CHAPTER TWENTY-SIX

Enzo closed the door behind him and drank in the cold night air, almost heady after the stuffy warmth of Anny's salon where he had spent most of the day listening to her story, growing gradually colder with the dying of the fire. He stood for a moment on the terrace replaying it all in his mind. Georgette's extraordinary journey from London to the Outer Hebrides, and from Paris to Montauban, and finally here. Her relationship with Lange, her brutal encounter with Wolff at the headquarters of the Gestapo. All so long ago, and yet so vividly brought back to life in Anny's telling of it. He knew he would not sleep tonight, counting off the hours until he could return here in the morning to hear the end of her story. And somehow hoping that it might bring clarity to the killing of Narcisse and the disappearance of Bauer.

He started down the steps to the street below and into a pool of lamplight. To his left, the park from which Wolff's remains had been recovered simmered in darkness. He was about to turn right, down the narrow street that would take him back to the Fenelon, when a movement among the trees in the park caught his eye. He stood stock-still and listened, but heard nothing.

'Who's there?' he called out, as if believing that someone might actually answer. He shook his head at his own stupidity and was about to turn away again when he heard the unmistakable sound of a twig snapping underfoot. This time he took several paces towards the steps that led up into the park, peering through the darkness.

The shape of a man suddenly detached itself from the shadows to flit almost silently between the trees around the war monument. It was there, and gone again, in little more than a second. But Enzo knew now that there was definitely someone in the park.

'Who the hell are you?' he shouted again into the shadows, and in response heard the soft sound of footsteps in fallen leaves. Then the silhouette of the man he had glimpsed earlier moved through the broken light of a street lamp filtering through the trees. Alarmed by the movement he had provoked, Enzo found himself confronted by the fight or flight response. He chose flight, and hurried off down the street, covering ten or fifteen metres before realising he had gone the wrong way.

He cursed under his breath, stopping to turn back, but froze as he saw the shadow from the park hurrying down the steps to follow in his wake. The man's breath billowed rapidly in the lamplight. Enzo turned quickly to continue down the street. The buildings on either side seemed to close in around him.

It was darker here, the glow of the next street lamp hidden by the angle of the street.

He turned right at the bottom of the hill and saw that the way ahead would take him to the far end of the palisade. It was more open there. Better lit. Behind him, he heard the scrape of leather soles on asphalt, hurried footsteps turning into a run. Enzo started to panic and began running himself. It was with relief that he passed the deserted café at the end of the street and moved out on to the palisade. The lit walls of the château rose almost vertically on his right. The tree-lined parking area stretched away on his left above a sheer drop to the river below.

There he stopped in his tracks. A figure at the far end of the palisade was coming towards him. Behind him the rapid footsteps of his pursuer. He was caught between the two. Panic morphed to blind fear and rose in his throat to very nearly choke him. His only escape route was through the arch that led up a cobbled alley to the church. He suspected it could very well be a dead end, but there was nowhere else to go.

He ran through the span of the arch, past an artist's atelier and a gift shop. Both shuttered up for the season. A wide stone staircase climbed to the gaping entrance of the church, an elaborate archway supported on ten pillars that led into darkness. The ivy-covered walls of the abbey itself rose sheer into the night. He ran past the tourist office and stopped at the entrance to the cloisters, a pay-gate that would open only with a token from the Office de Tourisme. Ahead of him, as he feared, lay a dead end. He looked back down the hill and saw the figure from the palisade pass through the frame of the arch. A man walking a dog.

Enzo cursed his stupidity. He could simply have continued along the palisade, past the dog walker and the shops, arriving at the safety of the Fenelon in a matter of minutes. Instead of which, he had trapped himself here in this religious cul-de-sac.

Almost as soon as the man with the dog had passed out of view, Enzo's pursuer from the park ran into the light, a slight figure that stopped, looking either way, before turning to see Enzo at the top of the alley that climbed to the cloisters. He stood breathing heavily for several moments, as though contemplating his next move. Then turned through the sweep of the arch and started walking slowly up the slope towards Enzo.

Enzo braced himself for a confrontation as the figure approached. With the light behind him his face was in shadow. But Enzo could see that he was young.

'Bauer?' He called out the name and the man stopped at once. Enzo knew he had a reputation for violence and didn't want to provoke him. And if he had killed Narcisse, then who knew what he was capable of.

With panic robbing him of clear thought, Enzo turned into the entrance to the cloisters, and yanked hopelessly at the paygate. To his astonishment it opened. Someone had forgotten to lock it. Or maybe at this time of year they didn't bother. He chose not to dwell on it, but hurried through the door and into a courtyard bathed in moonlight. The door swung shut behind him.

He had entered on a corner of the quadrangle. Colonnaded cloisters ran off to his left, and straight ahead. Vaulted stone walkways set around a sad-looking square of lawn bordered by autumn-withered shrubs. Moonlight fell in through the colonnades to lie cold across dusty flags, and he took the option to his left. His footsteps echoed back at him off ancient stone, and as he reached the end of the walkway, he heard the door opening from the alleyway outside. He turned right, still running. Past an open chamber where stone figures stood around the prone figure of Jesus laid out on a slab. A narrow doorway at the end of the passage had been bricked up, and he turned into the third side of the quadrangle. Had his pursuer taken the other route around the square he could easily have cut Enzo off. But Enzo could hear his feet on the flagstones running along the top end of the square, following in Enzo's footsteps.

Now he saw a maroon-painted wooden door set into the far corner. It had to be the entrance to the church. He slithered to a halt and pulled on the handle. The door didn't budge. He looked back along the cloister and saw the young man who was chasing him run into moonlight at the far corner. He stopped and they looked at each other along the length of the north passage, the breath of both men rasping in the silence of the night and echoing among the vaults. In desperation, Enzo turned and put his shoulder to the door. It swung violently open, and his momentum carried him staggering in astonishment into the vast breathless nave that rose endlessly above him into darkness. The damned door wasn't locked. It just opened the other way.

Multiple columns rose up to support an unseen vaulted ceiling. Moonlight bled through stained glass to sprinkle dead light among the pews. Enzo clattered between the bench seats, the chancel and altar away to his right, and sprinted up the central passage towards the entrance. To his immense relief, the door opened on to the covered area at the top of the steps he had passed just minutes earlier. He ran from darkness into street light, and scampered down the steps and out through the arch into the open stretch of palisade.

His legs were shaking, his breath tearing at lungs that hadn't had to cope with this level of exercise in years. He just wanted to stop. To lean forward, hands on thighs, and try to regain some degree of control over his breathing. He worried that his heart rate was now reaching dangerous levels. It felt like something in his chest was trying to punch its way out through his ribs. But the sound of feet on the steps behind him robbed him of that option. He crossed the road and started running. And it was a full ten seconds or more before he realised that he was sprinting across the bridge that led west out of the village, further away from the sanctity of the Fenelon with every step.

Where was everybody? He wanted to shout for help, but there was nobody here. Full-time residents had long since shuttered up windows in thick stone walls, and were sitting watching TV or preparing dinner.

At the far side of the bridge he stopped again and clutched at the handrail. Looking back he saw his pursuer jogging steadily towards him.

'Jesus Christ!' he shouted at the night. 'What do you want?'

Which brought the chasing figure to a halt at the mid-point of the bridge, and there was a stand-off that lasted almost half a minute. Just enough time for Enzo to regain his breath and look around for some way out.

A cobbled track dropped away from his end of the bridge, past a dark house on three levels, down towards the river and the footpath that ran back below the palisade towards the village.

He set off again on legs that would barely support him, slithering and sliding on dew-wet cobbles, to stagger on to the footpath by the river. The black water of the river itself reflected shimmering moonlight. He saw clusters of narrow wooden rowing boats tethered to trees, bobbing gently on slowly eddying water. And he set off back towards the village, legs burdened by lead weights that made every step a supreme effort of will.

The palisade rose into the night above him now, and he glanced over his shoulder to see his stalker walking after him, no more than twenty metres back. He no longer felt the need to run in order to catch up with his prey.

Enzo had reached that moment in the chase when the will to run had left him. When the need simply to stop was greater than the fear of facing up to his pursuer. But a part of him was still looking for a way out, a brain that remained functioning more efficiently than his body. Just ahead of him, a rowing boat, like the ones he had already passed, was tied to a tree on the riverbank. If he could get himself into that boat and push off into the flow of the river . . .

He stooped quickly to untether the rope, and stepped into the boat. Immediately it moved away from under him, rocking dangerously, and he fell along its length, crashing through the cross boards. To his horror, he felt the whole boat disintegrating beneath him, rotten wood giving way to drop him into icy water.

The cold stole away what little breath he had left, and he was incapable even of crying out with the shock of it. The water here was not deep. No more than a metre. But the riverbed comprised a thick sludge of mud and decaying vegetation, and he found it impossible to get back to his feet. His nostrils were filled with the stench of decomposing flora, and the more he struggled, the more he felt himself being sucked into the alluvium. It was all he could do to keep his head above water. And then he felt it wash over his face and knew that he could not hold his breath for more than a few seconds. The final seconds of his life. Time enough to curse his stupidity and regret all the foolish things he had ever done in his sixty-five years on this earth.

He prepared himself for the shock of cold water filling his lungs, and felt fingers close around a hand still above the surface. Another hand joined it, and their combined strength pulled him clear of the water. They grasped him now beneath the armpits and dragged him free of the clawing sediment and up on to the footpath.

Enzo lay on his back, shivering uncontrollably with the cold. He gasped to fill his lungs with recuperative oxygen, his eyes open, staring up at stars that glistened like jewels fixed to an eternity in which, to his amazement, he still existed. A face swam into view above him. A face caught in the moonlight. A young face, full of concern. This was his pursuer, and Enzo was shocked to see that he was no more than seventeen or eighteen years old.

'Are you alright?' the teenager asked him.

When finally he found his voice, Enzo spluttered, 'No, I'm not alright! Do I look all-fucking-right?'

The young man seemed distressed. 'I'm sorry,' he whispered. And then he was up on his feet and sprinting away along the footpath, back the way they had just come.

Enzo heaved himself up on to one elbow and glared after him. 'What the hell?' he shouted. 'Come back here, you wee bastard!' But the youth was gone, quickly swallowed by the night, and Enzo lay for several minutes recovering his breath before attempting finally to get to his feet.

Just a handful of tables in the dining room were occupied when Enzo walked into reception, dripping wet and shaking violently from the cold. His ponytail had long since escaped its clasp, and his hair hung in tangled ropes over his shoulders. The young proprietor looked at him in astonishment, and heads in the dining room turned curious eyes in his direction.

'Are you alright, monsieur?' the young man asked. An echo of the question posed by the teenager who had so nearly killed him just five minutes earlier.

Enzo held out an open palm and growled, 'Key, please.'

CHAPTER TWENTY-SEVEN

It was fully daylight, although the sun had not yet risen above the cliffs behind the village. The sky was clear, and it was bitterly cold, mist drifting lazily from the surface of the Dordogne into the early morning air as Enzo stepped from the Fenelon into the village main street.

A hot meal the night before and a full eight hours' sleep had partially restored him. A copious breakfast of hot milky coffee and pain au chocolat had set him up for the day ahead. Almost. Every muscle in his body had stiffened up. Every joint ached. He walked in pain, but was determined to keep going until the circulation of his blood had restored him to at least some semblance of normal movement.

Besides, he wanted to retrace the footsteps of his chase the night before, to get to know and understand the layout of this village that had been so bewilderingly confusing to him in the dark. To place Anny's house, and the park next to it, in the greater context of the whole place. And he spent the next half hour simply wandering through the labyrinth of streets and alleys and footpaths of this medieval jumble of stone houses.

Courtyards and gardens, bridges and lanes, and crystal-clear streams that disappeared beneath narrow streets to emerge tumbling through rocky outcrops and into the river.

Finally he found himself standing on the palisade looking down on the scene of carnage which had played out in the dark the previous evening. The remains of the boat he had attempted to climb into were no longer visible. Sucked down into the glaur. Its tethering rope lay in a tangle on the footpath next to the debris he had dragged with him from the water. The ground was still wet.

A voice at his shoulder startled him. An elderly man, shrunken by age and tanned to leather by years in the sun, stood next to him, smiling behind his incongruously pale blue mask. He wore a cloth cap and a threadbare blue jacket. 'Ah, there's not many of the old boats left,' he said. 'I think they only keep them tied up along the bank for the tourists to take photographs. Most of them are full of water half the year and the wood's just rotted.' He nodded further downriver. 'They've got new ones now that actually float, though I wouldn't want to risk falling into that water myself. Centuries of sewage in it.' He chuckled. 'Find yourself just going through the motions.'

Enzo blenched.

When he got back to the hotel, he stood out in the street, where he still had a Wi-Fi signal, and called up a Google Earth image of the village on his phone, and tried to make sense of everywhere he had been in the last thirty minutes. Arriving, belatedly, at some kind of understanding of its layout.

He slipped his phone back in his pocket, and went in search of his car to drive across the river and over the flood plain towards the village of Bétaille. He glimpsed the château on the hill, dominating the disparate collection of houses below it, and the red-brick church that stood on its eastern edge. And as he headed out of the village towards Vayrac, he spotted the double garage with its chequered doors and windows that Anny had described. He marvelled at the thought that the apartment above it had once, long ago, played host to some of the most priceless canvasses in the world. And a perfect replica of the *Mona Lisa*.

In a quiet Vayrac cul-de-sac, he parked outside the single-storey gendarmerie lying in semi-anonymity behind green metal gates, and told the duty officer across the intercom that he would like to talk to Capitaine Arnaud.

When, at length, they let him in, he sat waiting in reception until the capitaine was free. Time to reflect on exactly what he would tell the investigating officer. About what he had discovered to date. About the attack which had so nearly killed him the night before. But he could barely concentrate for a middle-aged woman loudly haranguing the duty officer at the bar. She wore mud-caked gum boots and filthy blue overalls, and looked like she might just have stepped off a farm. A tangle of grey hair, like fuse wire bursting from its sheath, was held in a clasp behind her head, and her cheeks glowed red with indignation.

'Well, just how far down your list of priorities am I?' she

demanded, her mask dragged beneath her chin. 'Or are you too busy hiding round street corners to catch law-abiding folk going five kilometres an hour over the speed limit?'

The duty officer recoiled a little and pulled his mask higher up his nose. He sighed patiently. 'We're doing our best, madame, but we've got a murder under investigation, and there's been a spate of burglaries in the area. And last night there was a serious bust-up between locals and *gitanes* in a bar in town. A missing bicycle hardly qualifies as a pressing concern.'

'Of no concern at all, if you ask me. More than a week's gone by, and no one's even called by the house. That bike cost a small fortune. Money that me and my husband could ill afford. And the boy's heartbroken. It was his sixteenth birthday present, you know.' She shook her head vigorously. 'What kind of world do we live in where folk would steal a boy's *vélo* from his own door?' But she didn't wait for the gendarme's reply, and answered for herself. 'One policed by a useless bunch like you.'

She turned and marched towards the door. When she reached it, she held it open to throw one final recrimination over her shoulder.

'*Putain con!*'

Which Enzo translated for himself as a boldly vulgar epithet, and wondered at her fearlessness. In France, gendarmes were not to be taken lightly. By way of mitigation, he smiled sympathetically at the duty officer whose loss of face prompted him glower back.

The door to Capitaine Arnaud's office opened, and he gestured Enzo in, pulling up his mask as he rounded his desk and waving Enzo into a seat. 'So sorry to keep you, Monsieur Macleod. It's been a hectic few days.'

'You've made progress, then?'

'We have.' He sat back in his chair and smiled. 'I think we've pretty much worked out what happened.'

Enzo sat forward, interested. 'Oh? Tell me.'

'We conducted door-to-door interviews in the village and found an elderly lady who encountered Bauer early in the afternoon on the day of the murder. He approached her at a bus stop and asked for directions to Anny Lavigne's house. Obviously establishing in advance where she lived. Then the proprietor of the Fenelon reported that Bauer had been seen in the bar of the hotel shortly before Narcisse left that evening. Although no one actually saw Bauer himself leave, he was not in the bar very shortly afterwards.'

'So you think he followed Narcisse to the house?'

'No. I think he knew where Narcisse was going, and took a different route. Immediately opposite the hotel, monsieur, a gate leads to the garden of a house belonging to a summer resident. A path leads up through that garden to the top of the hill, where another gate leads into an alleyway behind Madame Lavigne's house. Steps lead up from there to the terrace at the side of it. Taking that route, Bauer could have got to the house before Narcisse and entered from the side terrace, since the door is never locked.'

Enzo thought about it, visualising the route from his exploration of the village that morning, and from the Google Earth image he had called up on his phone. He also remembered the gate opposite the hotel, the path up through the garden, and the night gate that Bauer would have used to access the side entrance to Anny's house. 'And what was his motive?'

'Bauer's?'

'Yes. For killing Narcisse.'

Arnaud shrugged. 'I have no idea. Is it so important to know why he killed him?'

'Not if you're Chinese and don't believe in motive. All you would need then is sufficient evidence to know that he did. But in this case you don't have that. So motive is important. To understand why he would do it is crucial to establishing whether he did or not.'

'You think he didn't?'

'I think there is sufficient doubt to make us look for another explanation.'

'What doubt?' Arnaud was genuinely puzzled. 'We know he was there. He left bloody fingerprints all over the door, and in his hotel room before he disappeared.'

'Let's come to that in a moment,' Enzo said. 'Did you know that Bauer and Narcisse had met at Narcisse's gallery in Paris two days before the murder?'

Arnaud paled, perhaps starting to suspect that his investigation might not have delved as deeply as it should. 'No, I didn't. We had someone talk to Narcisse's people in Paris, and take possession of all his computers.' He shook his head. 'But we didn't find anything useful.'

Enzo said, 'His protégé told me that his meeting with Bauer was brief and fractious. Bauer left in a temper, and an hour or so later Narcisse reserved his train tickets to Brive and a room at the Fenelon.'

'You've been to Paris?'

'And to Germany.' He saw Arnaud's jaw drop behind his mask. 'I've done quite a bit of research on Bauer. You already know, of course, that he had a conviction for assault. But that wasn't the only fight he got into. He's a young man, it seems, with a fearsome temper and a history of violence. Most recently against his girlfriend. Violence followed by shame and remorse. Which doesn't appear, however, to have stopped him from doing it again.'

'So he had some kind of grudge against Narcisse and got to the house ahead of him to lie in wait and take his revenge.' Arnaud felt back on safer ground.

'Perhaps,' Enzo said. 'But this was no temper-driven frenzied attack. It was one single deliberate slash of a knife.'

'And then he panicked and tried to get out of the house fast.'

'Slipping in the blood of his victim, and leaving messy handprints all over the door?' Enzo's scepticism was patent.

Arnaud was defensive. 'Which would be consistent with panic.'

Enzo shook his head slowly. 'Why didn't he leave the house the same way he entered it? By the door to the side terrace.

That way he would have avoided having to pass the body and slip in the blood.'

Arnaud opened his mouth to suggest some plausible explanation, but none would come.

'And why did it take several minutes before his panic set in?'

Arnaud stared at him in silence for a very long moment. 'How can you possibly know that?'

'Because the drops on the periphery of the blood spatter had partially dried before he slipped in them. That would have taken two, maybe three minutes. It makes no sense, capitaine. Premeditation is out of character for Bauer. He would have had to plan this. Be lying in wait for Narcisse and kill him in cold blood. Then, apparently, stand around for a few minutes before suddenly panicking and charging out of the house through the blood of his victim.'

Arnaud sat back. He could find no fault with Enzo's logic. 'So what do you think happened?'

Enzo sighed. 'I don't know. Yet.' He paused. 'But someone is clearly worried that I'm going to figure it out.'

Arnaud frowned. 'Who?'

'I don't know that either. But someone nearly killed me last night.'

Now Arnaud sat forward, alarmed. 'What?'

And Enzo related the whole sorry tale of the chase through the dark streets of Carennac which ended in the river. Arnaud listened with increasing incredulity. 'And this teenager tried to kill you?'

'Not exactly. In fact, he ended up saving my life.'

'So why was he chasing you?'

'I haven't the faintest idea.'

'What did he look like?'

Enzo shook his head. 'I couldn't really say. I wasn't exactly making notes at the time.' He stood up, and Arnaud rose hastily to his feet.

'Monsieur, perhaps it was a mistake to involve you in this. I would never forgive myself if anything happened to you.'

'I wouldn't be too happy about it either.' Enzo turned towards the door then stopped. 'Oh, by the way, those remains found in the park a couple of weeks ago . . .'

'What about them?'

'They belong to a Luftwaffe officer who was an art dealer in civilian life. His name was Karlheinz Wolff. Apparently he obtained looted art for Hermann Göring, who asked him to acquire the *Mona Lisa* for his private collection.'

Arnaud blinked in astonishment. He waved an arm vaguely towards the door. 'But . . . but the *Mona Lisa* was kept just a few kilometres away at Château de Montal, for most of the latter stages of the war.'

'Which explains why he was here.'

Enzo turned towards the door again, but stopped once more to give voice to an apparent afterthought. 'One other thing. Hans Bauer is Wolff's grandson.'

*

Having dropped a hand grenade into Capitaine Arnaud's day, Enzo closed the gendarme's office door behind him and crossed to the counter, where the duty officer was filling in forms. 'Excuse me,' he said.

The officer didn't bother to look up. 'Yes?'

'That woman who was in earlier.'

The man's face coloured a little as he raised his eyes towards Enzo. 'What about her?'

'She reported a bike stolen.'

'Yes.'

'When?'

'That's confidential information, monsieur.'

Enzo said, 'Well, let's ask Capitaine Arnaud, shall we? Though I imagine he won't be very pleased if we disturb him in the middle of a murder investigation.' He started towards the office of the investigating officer.

The duty officer stood up. 'That won't be necessary,' he said quickly, and glared at Enzo. 'I'll need to check.'

Enzo waited as the gendarme went to his desk and sat at the computer. Two fingers tapped at the keyboard. 'Ten days ago. It disappeared overnight.'

The Scotsman did a quick calculation. 'That was the same night as the murder in Carennac.'

The policeman thought about it for a moment. 'Yes.'

'So where do these people live?'

The duty officer returned his eyes to the screen and scrolled up. 'A farmhouse at Les Arses.'

Enzo laughed involuntarily. 'Really? A-R-S-E-S?'

The gendarme frowned. 'Yes. What about it?'

Enzo shook the thought away. 'Doesn't matter. Where is that?'

'A couple of kilometres outside Carennac off the road to Alvignac.'

The farmhouse at Les Arses was visible from the main road. A well-rutted track led through trees to a yard flanked by an open barn in front of a large, picturesque stone house with electric-blue shutters. Ducks scattered left and right as Enzo drove into the yard. The woman he had seen at the gendarmerie emerged from the barn with a bucket in her hand and a scowl on her face. Her mask was still hanging beneath her chin. As he stepped out of the car she said, 'You were at the gendarmerie.'

He was surprised she had noticed him. 'Yes.'

'You've got news about the bike?'

'I'm afraid not.'

'What do you want, then?'

'I'm consulting on the murder that took place in Carennac the night your son's bike was taken.'

She seemed taken aback. 'Is there some connection?'

Enzo shrugged. 'I don't know, but it would be helpful if you could tell me exactly what happened.'

She exhaled loudly and started throwing handfuls of feed from her bucket for the ducks. They gathered excitedly around her, making such a racket that she had to raise her voice above it. 'It was sitting here just inside the barn, propped against the upright. You'd never have imagined that it was anything but perfectly safe.'

Enzo glanced over his shoulder and realised that the bike must have been visible from the road.

'It cost an arm and a leg, monsieur. A fine, eighteen-gear racing bike. It's Enzo's passion, you see. He has the whole outfit, everything. The shoes, the helmet. Can't keep him away from the TV when the Tour is on.'

Enzo's smile was curious and laced with surprise. 'Enzo?'

'My son, yes. That's his name. Is there something wrong with that?'

Now a full smile creased his face behind the mask. 'No,' he said. 'Absolutely nothing at all.'

It was a little after ten when he got back to his room at the Fenelon and sat on the end of the bed going through the tourist maps and leaflets which were presented in a holder on the dresser below the mirror. There was a simplified large-scale map of the whole area that stretched as far as the town of Rocamadour, the second most visited tourist site in France, which was twenty kilometres away. With his finger he traced the blue line that represented the road to Alvignac as it serpentined up the hill to Les Arses. He laid it aside and sat thoughtfully replaying everything he had learned this morning, sifting idly through the other leaflets as he did. He paused at a trifold advertising a gîte for rent at Padirac. The name seemed familiar, and he returned to the map to find the village of Padirac just thirteen kilometres south of Carennac. What looked like a farm track cut cross-country from a place called Broche, just beyond Les Arses, knocking a good couple of kilometres off the journey. He opened up the trifold and saw that the holiday home was just minutes from the Gouffre de Padirac. Another consultation with the map showed him that the Gouffre was even closer. The gîte was available from Easter until the end of September. So it would be closed up for the season by now.

A *gouffre*, Enzo knew, was a chasm, or just a great big hole in the ground, but he knew nothing about the Gouffre de Padirac. Another of the leaflets from his dresser provided elucidation. It offered tickets for sale, online or by telephone, to a tour of what it described as the biggest underground attraction in the country. The hole itself was 103 metres deep, and 33 metres across. It led to an underground river and cave system, and was accessed by a lift and staircase that took tourists all the way down. Punts were available to travel along the underground river to visit the caves.

Enzo laid the leaflet aside and picked up the advertisement for the gîte again. He tapped it thoughtfully with his fingers before checking the time. Madame Lavigne would have been expecting him some time ago. He picked up his satchel, which he had left drying on the radiator overnight, and hurried down to reception. There was no one there. But he could see the room keys hanging on a board behind the counter. Number five, he knew, was the room that Bauer had occupied. He took a quick look around before slipping behind the counter to lift the key to Bauer's old room, and hastened back up the stairs.

Bauer's room was remarkably similar to his own. He knew it had not been occupied again since the murder, and he went straight to the dresser and the holder with the map and the leaflets. He flicked quickly through them with nervous fingers, searching for the trifold advertising the gîte at Padirac.

The opening of the door startled him, and he looked up guiltily to see the young proprietor standing in the doorway looking at him curiously. 'What are you doing in here?' he asked.

Enzo searched for a plausible excuse. 'Lifted the wrong key,' he said, laughing at his own stupidity. 'Only just realised it wasn't my room.'

He saw the proprietor's eyes drop to the leaflets in his hand.

'I was trying to find a trifold on a gîte at Padirac that I was looking at earlier.' He paused. 'Do you put the same tourist information in every room?'

'Each room gets exactly the same maps and leaflets. Why?'

Enzo shrugged and held the leaflets out towards him. 'The trifold on the Padirac gîte doesn't seem to be here.'

The proprietor frowned.

Anny called that he should let himself in when he knocked at the kitchen door. She was sitting in her accustomed rocking chair by the *cheminée*. The house felt warm, and he expected that she had stoked the fire early and been waiting for him.

'You're late,' she said.

'My apologies, madame. I had to go to the gendarmerie for a meeting with Capitaine Arnaud.'

'Hah!' Her exclamation was laden with derision. 'And is he any further forward with his investigation?'

Enzo shook his head. 'It would seem not. Can I make you a tea or a coffee before we start?'

'No, thank you.' She waved him towards his armchair. 'Have you heard the news?'

He looked up, filled with curiosity as he dropped into his seat. 'What news?'

'The government announced last night that they are going to reintroduce a national lockdown. Apparently Covid infections are increasing exponentially again.'

This was a shock to Enzo. He had not been following events in recent days. 'When?'

'From midnight tonight. Though it won't affect me. I have nowhere to go.'

But Enzo knew that if restrictions mirrored those imposed the previous spring he would not be permitted to travel any further than a kilometre from his home. Consulting on this murder enquiry was unpaid and would not qualify as work. So he would not be exempt from the travel ban. Which meant that if he could not conclude his investigation by midnight, he would be forced to retire from it without resolution. And he had no confidence that Arnaud would be able to bring it to a conclusion without his help.

No pressure, then, he thought.

'Circumstances beyond our control, Monsieur Macleod. But in any event, I am anxious to finish this now. The telling of my story has aroused some unhappy memories. Having a murder committed in my house has been very upsetting. And I've indulged you thus far. But I would really like to put the whole thing behind me.'

'Of course. Again, my apologies.' Enzo looked at her expectantly. 'I'm ready when you are, madame.'

CHAPTER TWENTY-EIGHT

Georgette's first year in her new home fell into a pleasant, if uneventful, routine. And for much of it, the war seemed a million miles away.

She was pleased with her house. An L-shaped stone dwelling that sat above a large cellar. A farmhouse kitchen, a bedroom, a large salon with an enormous *cheminée*, all on the one level. The attic was, as yet, undeveloped. It sat next to a small park in the middle of the village of Carennac, and a terrace at the side of the house gave directly on to the park itself.

The owner of the house had died intestate, and the estate was in the temporary stewardship of the mairie, and so volunteered as accommodation for Georgette.

She was less pleased with the cycle to and from the Château de Montal. Although the route followed the meandering path of the River Dordogne through the silt flats of the flood plain, it took nearly fifty minutes. In spring and autumn it was an easy and pleasant commute, but in the searing heat of summer she would arrive at either end of her journey dripping with perspiration. And in the winter, temperatures could dip as low as minus ten or fifteen, and the road was often obscured by a freezing fog that followed the path of the river, and therefore the road.

Early on, she had taken the decision to set up a canvas camp bed in the Grande Salle du Rez-de-chaussée, the largest room on the ground floor of the château, where the greatest number of the most important crated works were stacked, including the *Mona Lisa*. Although René Huygue still insisted on keeping *La Joconde* in his quarters in the Chambre de Nine on the first floor, Georgette wrested her from his grasp each night to sleep with her in the *grande salle*, also known as the *salle des gardes*, among the crates. This vaulted chamber with its flagstone floor, and intricately carved stone *cheminée* was cool and conducive to sleep in the summer, but like an icebox in the winter, even when a fire had been set in the hearth. And Georgette would often cycle home in the morning with leaden legs to catch some much-needed sleep and garner a little warmth from her bed during the hours of daylight.

Food seemed more plentiful in this part of south-west France, and the curators and all the guards at the château ate well. Duck and goose, lamb and limousin beef, and wonderful salads with cheese and *gésiers*, liberally sprinkled with walnuts from the trees that grew everywhere here. Neither was there any shortage of fruit. And there were several local red wines, a little unsophisticated but still quaffable.

It was easy to forget that the world was at war, and the outcome as yet far from certain. In all this time they had barely seen a single German soldier, and Georgette made frequent outings on her bike to explore a countryside rich in forest and fruit, tobacco and wheat, cliffs rising sheer from rivers and streams that in eons past had carved their way through a landscape of solid rock. There was a regular market in the nearby town of Saint-Céré. She often went shopping for essential food and clothing in the medieval Place Mercadial, where merchants traded in the shadow of the Tours Saint-Laurent, an ancient fortification on a hilltop that dominated the town and the countryside for miles around.

She was unconcerned that she had neither seen nor heard anything of Lange in all this time. Although she missed him, his absence meant that there was no imminent threat from Karlheinz Wolff. Of Wolff himself, she had seen nothing since that day at Bétaille. Both men had receded into a past that seemed much darker and more distant now, viewed from this privileged vantage point in the southern sun.

But by the spring of 1944, these months of comparative idyll were drawing to a close. Rumours of an imminent Allied invasion of Europe were circulating in the villages and marketplaces. The war was going badly for the Germans following defeat in North Africa the previous year, and there was bloody stalemate on the Eastern Front with Russia. The French Resistance, now collectively known as the Maquis, were more and more active in the area. Acts of sabotage on bridges and railway lines provoked savage reprisals from the Germans, and the mood of everyone at Montal had become febrile and tense.

It was one hot night towards the end of May that year that Georgette found herself in the *salle des gardes* unable to sleep. She lay awake on the unyielding canvas of her camp bed staring up at the vaulted ceiling. Moonlight flooded in through the windows that she had left unshuttered, laying its shadows among the silent crates. Outside, the screech of cicadas and the croaking of a thousand frogs filled the night air, a deafening cacophony in the sultry still of the small hours.

Finally she got up and slipped on her shoes to pad through the adjoining Salle Robert de Balsac, weaving her way among the stacks of crated paintings to the narrow door that led to the north turret. There they had established a small kitchen to prepare food for the staff. If she couldn't sleep, then she might as well have a coffee. She placed the kettle on a tiny gas ring and wandered off through the salon to gaze through one of the windows on to the courtyard. Moonlight shimmered on the crushed white castine gravel. The château formed a right-angle on two sides of the square. The north-east side was bordered by a line of trees and a couple of stone benches, beyond which lay the château garden, given over now to growing vegetables. Between the trees on the south-east side, a gate opened on to a drive that turned around the slope of the hill, past outbuildings that provided accommodation for the guards, and down towards a road leading to the village of Saint-Jean-Lespinasse. Georgette could see the silhouette of one of the guards sitting on the wall by the gate, his cigarette glowing red in the dark.

It was only then that she became aware of the voices that

seemed to drift in from the stairwell at the far end of the salon. The château's main staircase was a broad sweep of well-worn stone that climbed through the levels of the building at the angle between the two wings. But here, at the end of the north wing, a narrow flight of wooden servants' stairs rose all the way up to the attic. The voices were coming from one of the upper levels. Hushed male voices. By the light of the moon that fell in through every window slit, Georgette tiptoed slowly up the stairs, cringing at every creak.

On the next landing the voices were louder, amplified by stone walls and tiled floors. She slipped through shadows cast by artworks stacked ceiling high in the Chambre Régence and the Grand Salon d'honneur, to emerge into the first-floor hallway at the top of the staircase. A door led off into the Chambre Fenaille and the tower at the north-west corner. Flickering candlelight sent long shadows dancing through the open door to meet her. She recognised René Huygue's voice, and sneaked a peek into the one-time bedroom of what had probably been a lesser family member. A group of half a dozen men were grouped conspiratorially around a candle placed on the floor among the crates. They were being addressed by Huygue, but other voices raised themselves in disagreement, only to be shooshed sharply and told to keep the level down. These were rough-looking countrymen in boots and overalls, paysan jackets and cloth caps, but among them Georgette saw a face she recognised. Jean-Luc Percet, one of the château guards. A man in his forties, with a shock of unruly black hair shot through with wiry silver. A wit about the place. Always smiling, laughing, and cracking jokes.

She drew back into the hallway in case they saw her, and pressing her back against the wall, tried to follow the argument. It seemed they were discussing the blowing up of a railway junction near the town of Gramat, a few kilometres south of Montal. Georgette listened, heart pounding so loudly she was sure they would hear it echoing along the stone passages of the old château. The disagreement concerned the when, as well as the precise location. The Germans were using the line to send troops and munitions north, and the destruction of a junction south of the town would cause considerable disruption to their traffic. But it was well guarded and would be a risky venture.

Finally, agreement appeared to be reached, and Georgette prepared to retrace her footsteps quickly to hide herself among the crates in the Chambre Régence. But no one was leaving. She summoned her courage to satisfy her curiosity and stole another glance into the Chambre Fenaille. The men were all clustered around an open door at the entrance to the north-west turret, a door Georgette knew had always been kept locked. Huygue stood in its lit entrance, handing out rifles and pistols, and rucksacks of what she could only imagine must be explosives.

She caught her breath and wheeled away. Huygue was keeping arms in the château and supplying the Maquis! It was madness. If the Germans chose to make an unannounced visit to inspect the premises, they would all be sent off to the labour camps. And God only knew what would become of the art they had tried so hard to protect from the ravages of war.

It was sunlight now that lay dazzling arcs of light on the stone flags of the Château de Montal, and Georgette's voice that rose in pitch to echo among its vaults. She strode after Huygue through the Salle Robert de Balsac. 'You're an idiot!' she shouted at him.

He strode on, regardless, past the rows of crates.

'You're a member of the Maquis, aren't you?'

At which he stopped abruptly and turned on her, his voice reduced to a hiss. 'Do not repeat that, ever! Do you hear me? To anyone.'

'But you are, and you are putting everything we've all worked for here at risk.'

'I know what I'm doing.'

'I doubt that very much. You're letting your heart rule your head. It's insanity to keep weapons in the château.'

He lowered his head to breathe into her face. 'Keep your voice down!' And he glanced left and right, afraid that they might be overheard. 'Your problem, George, is that you've got your priorities all wrong. What exactly is more important to you, eh? Art or freedom?'

'Both,' she said emphatically. 'You can't sacrifice one for the other and expect either to be worth a damn.'

He gasped his frustration, and marched off into the *salle des gardes*, heels clicking with irritation on the flagstones.

Three days later, word reached them that the Maquis had blown up the main railway line south of Gramat, and Georgette held her breath for retaliation. To her relief, none came. At least, not in the immediate vicinity. But it was less than a week afterwards that René Huygue came to her in a state, his tone very different from the last time they had spoken.

She had just arrived on her bicycle from Carennac. He took her by the arm and led her upstairs and into the Chambre de Nine, closing the door behind them. It had rained the night before, and the cloud cover was low, blanketing the area in a gloomy crepuscular light. Huygue's office and living quarters were obscured by shadow, and his face seemed very pale in the poor light. She heard a tremor in his voice which was little more than a whisper. 'I just got word from Paris. The Germans are sending a detachment of troops to search the château. It's part of a clampdown on all the depots of the Louvre. Apparently they have permission from the high command to open any crate they want.'

Georgette was horrified. 'What are they looking for?'

Huygue blanched, and couldn't quite bring his eyes to meet hers. 'Weapons. But it's just any excuse to confiscate the art.'

Georgette closed her eyes, and a thousand abusive epithets flitted through her mind. But she stopped herself from giving voice to them. It would serve no purpose. She forced herself to try to think straight. 'Are the weapons still in the château?'

He nodded.

'Then we've got to get them out of here. When are the Germans coming?'

'We think sometime tomorrow morning.'

'Jesus! Where are we going to put them?'

Huygue braced himself. 'In the cellar of your house in Carennac.'

The rain of the previous day had cleared, and a blue sky was punctuated by soft white clouds rolling across the hilltops that ringed the river valley. They would soon evaporate in the heat. Sunshine lay in late spring swathes across a landscape in full leaf, blossom shed and fruit forming in the orchards that grew across the flood plain. The air was warm after a fresh start, and heating up towards midday, with the promise of a hot early summer afternoon to come.

But the tranquillity of the morning was soon disturbed by the roar of two Panzer V tanks that stationed themselves at the foot of the hill and left their engines idling. A canvas-covered troop carrier brought a detachment of crack SS soldiers up the road to the château where they jumped down and fanned out to cover the courtyard and the front entrance.

The commanding officer drove his lightweight Kübelwagen through the gate and into the courtyard. It had a round-bladed spade clamped to the wheel arch, and a spare wheel bolted to the slope of the bonnet. The canvas roof was folded down over the rear of the vehicle. SS-Standartenführer Harald Schneider swung himself out and over the door without opening it, and cast a deep shadow in the castine. He wore dusty baggy breeks tucked into brown leather boots, and a short, double-breasted reed-green jacket with a leather holster belted around the waist. His field-grey shirt was open at the neck, and an SS Panzer field cap the same colour as his jacket was pulled down over straw-coloured hair that grew abundantly beneath it. He could not have been much older than Georgette, but he had world-weary eyes which had witnessed too much, and disillusion seemed solidly settled on his square shoulders.

The entire staff of the castle, including the guards, were assembled in the heat of the sun to greet him. Somewhere around twenty people in all. Georgette was nervous, in spite of the fact that she and Huygue and Jean-Luc Percet had loaded a farm vehicle with all the weapons from the north-west tower at two o'clock that morning, and driven them the fourteen kilometres to Carennac to hide them in the cellar beneath her house.

Schneider surveyed them with an indifference that suggested that he would much rather be somewhere else. Half a dozen of his men assembled behind him, rifles held at the ready. 'Who's in charge here?' His French was perfect.

Huygue stepped forward. 'I am.'

'Your name.'

'Huygue. René Huygue.'

'Well, René Huygue. We are here to take a look at exactly what it is you have in this château.' He paused. 'And we have information that one of your guards is a leader of the local Maquis.' He drew a small, leather-bound notebook from a trouser pocket to consult. 'A man called Jean-Luc Percet.'

Georgette saw Huygue's face pale, and her eyes flickered towards Jean-Luc standing at the back of the crowd. Huygue said, 'He isn't here.'

'Well, we'll find out soon enough when we check everyone's papers.' He turned towards the group of guards and curators. 'In the meantime, you can all lie face down in the courtyard where we can keep an eye on you.'

As Schneider turned away towards his men, Huygue caught his arm to catch his attention, and the German wheeled round, eyes blazing.

'Don't touch me!'

Huygue took a step back, but maintained an external calm that Georgette was sure did not reflect how he felt inside. He said, 'With the greatest of respect, sir, there is a sign out front provided to us by your own Kunstschutz, which forbids army personnel from entering the premises.'

'Is there?' Schneider very slowly and deliberately unclipped his holster and drew out his pistol. With a ramrod-straight arm he pointed it directly at Huygue, the muzzle a matter of centimetres from his forehead. 'Well, this is my authority, and it outranks anything your precious Kunstschutz might have to say on the subject.' In a movement so fast and unexpected that it took everyone by surprise, he grasped the pistol by its barrel and clubbed Huygue across the head with the butt of it.

Huygue dropped immediately to his knees. His hand flew to his forehead, coming away with blood on the fingers. But he made no sound. Schneider reholstered his weapon and turned to the others.

'Down!' He pointed at the ground, and everyone fell to their knees to stretch themselves out on the warm castine. 'Not you!' He grabbed Georgette by the arm as she was about to do the same. 'You'll take my men round the château. Every room in the place. And you'll open any crate they ask you to.'

It took almost an hour to pass through every room in the building, stopping frequently to uncrate random works of art for inspection. Georgette was intimidated by the eyes on her. Six war-weary young men with appetites that had been denied them by conflict. There was not a smile among them, nor a single moment of human empathy. She felt their contempt for her at the same time as their animal appraisal. And she was afraid.

When finally they reached the *salle des gardes*, one of them kicked over her camp bed, tipping its sheets and blankets across the floor. 'What's this?' he said. The only one of them who had any French.

'It's where I sleep.'

She saw them exchanging glances. 'Alone?'

'There's not exactly room for two,' she said.

He lowered his face towards hers. 'Don't be so fucking

insolent.' Then he nodded towards the crate with the three red dots. 'Open it.'

Georgette began to panic. Could there be anyone in the world who would not recognise the face of the *Mona Lisa*? And who knew what would happen if they did. 'It's just a painting,' she said.

'Open it!' He bawled in her face.

But she stood firm. 'It's too delicate to be exposed to the sunlight.' And was unprepared for the rifle butt that clubbed her to the ground. Her head struck the flagstones and light exploded in her skull. Almost immediately she was being yanked back to her feet and dragged out through the entrance hall to the courtyard.

Schneider was sitting on one of the stone benches, in the shade of the trees at the far side of the square. He stood immediately, throwing his cigarette away across the gravel, sending up a shower of sparks, and strode across to the group emerging into the sunlight. One of the troops was carrying the crate that held the *Mona Lisa*, and the soldier who had struck Georgette held her arm in a vice-like grip. She could barely stand, and felt blood trickling down the side of her face.

A rapid-fire exchange that she didn't understand passed between the commanding officer and his men before he turned to Georgette. 'I'm told you obstructed the opening of this crate.'

'No,' she said. 'I advised against it because of the fragile nature of the painting inside.'

'I told you to open any crate they asked you to.'

She pulled her arm free of the soldier who held it and straightened up defiantly. 'And there are some things just too precious to be exposed to the elements. But then, I wouldn't expect a man like you to understand that.'

She had half expected it, but the open palm that he took across the side of her face still knocked her over and left her sprawling in the gravel. 'What the hell is that supposed to mean?' he shouted.

She glared up at him with hatred in her eyes. 'I think you just answered your own question.'

He turned away and barked a command at the nearest soldier, who immediately drew a long-bladed knife from his belt and began prising open the wooden crate. The sound of nails freeing themselves from the grain of the wood echoed back at them off the carved stonework of the château, and the soldier pulled away the protective leatherette and fireproof paper to expose the *Mona Lisa* to the gaze of every man and woman in the courtyard. A face that stared back at them across four centuries.

'Mein Gott,' she heard Schneider whisper.

'What the hell is going on here?' A familiar voice rang out through the still, warm air.

Schneider spun around to see a figure in field-grey army uniform and peaked cap striding across the courtyard towards them. He looked at the rank on the newcomer's epaulettes and curled his lip in a sneer. 'How dare you, Hauptmann! You are outranked here, and this is none of your business.'

Paul Lange reached into an inside pocket and drew out a folded sheet of paper which he shook open and held in front of the Standartenführer's face. 'I don't think you outrank the Führer,' he said. 'And I am here on *his* business.'

Schneider cast eyes across the sheet of paper that Lange held before him, and Georgette saw the skin tighten across his face. Lange gave him time to read, then carefully folded it away, and slipped it back into his jacket. He turned towards Georgette, holding out a hand to help her back to her feet, and looked with concern at the blood trickling from her hair. Red welts were raising themselves across her face where Schneider had struck her.

He wheeled around to smash a clenched fist squarely into the face of the SS officer, knocking him into the dust of the courtyard. And every rifle was suddenly trained upon him. He ignored them and glared at Schneider with contempt. 'What kind of barbarian are you?' He had raised his voice only a little. 'A German officer does not strike an unarmed woman.' He turned towards the open crate. 'This is the world's most famous painting, exposed to full sunlight in a dusty courtyard. It needs to be repacked immediately and taken indoors.' A flick of his head raised several curators to their feet, and they collected the crate and the packing to carry them quickly back into the château.

Schneider was on his feet again, wiping blood from his face with the back of his hand. He picked up his SS Panzer field cap and his humiliation was almost painful. But regardless of

Lange's apparent rank, the man carried a piece of paper that superseded pips and stripes, and Schneider knew better than to question it. He did his best to recover his dignity, reaching into an inside pocket to produce a folded sheaf of documents which he held out towards Lange. 'I have papers, too. Orders to search the château and arrest a guard here called Jean-Luc Percet.'

Lange ignored his papers. 'Well, you've searched the château. Check the documents of the guards, and if you find your man, arrest him and be gone.'

Fear for Jean-Luc rose again in Georgette's breast, and she quickly searched the faces of everyone in the courtyard only to realise that Jean-Luc was gone. Somehow, in all the distraction, he had seized his opportunity to slip away. Through the château, no doubt, out into the kitchen garden on the blind side and away across the fields to the safety of the woods.

Nonetheless, everybody stood tense in the midday heat, as soldiers examined the papers of every person in the courtyard. When they failed to turn up the suspected Maquis leader, Schneider spat in the castine and threw a dangerous glance at Lange with icy blue eyes. 'If we ever meet again, Hauptmann, there will be a reckoning.'

He jumped back into his Kübelwagen, and with spinning wheels throwing dust and chippings up into the fibrillating air, he accelerated out through the gate. His men ran at the double to their waiting troop carrier and scrambled on board. Within minutes the roar of its diesel engine, and the growl of the tanks that awaited it at the foot of the hill, became a distant echo.

There was an almost audible sigh of collective relief, but still nobody spoke. Most eyes turned towards Huygue, who gently touched the wound on his head. The blood had dried, coagulating quickly in the sun, but a swelling like an egg had raised itself on his temple, and the bruising all around it was already starting to show. He glanced at Lange. 'Thank you, Hauptmann,' he said.

But Lange ignored him. He turned, concerned, to Georgette, and took a handkerchief from his pocket to wipe the blood from her face. 'Do you live in the château?'

She shook her head.

'Then you should go home and get that wound dressed. Is it far?'

She shrugged. 'Thirteen, fourteen kilometres.'

He seemed surprised. 'You have a car?'

She smiled at his naivety. 'A bicycle.'

'Good God,' he said. 'You can't cycle fourteen kilometres in this state. I'll give you a lift.'

Georgette flushed self-consciously and glanced towards Huygue. 'I'll be fine.'

'I insist. You could be concussed.'

Now she felt Huygue's eyes on her and couldn't meet them. All the weapons they had removed from the château the night before were neatly stacked beneath a tarpaulin in her cellar.

*

Lange's car was parked at the foot of the hill. A brightly coloured green, open-topped sports car with extravagant front wheel arches that ran the length of its extended bonnet to running boards that stepped up to a two-seater bench seat behind the wheel. It was dusty from the drive down from Paris, its windscreen smeared with dead flies. Still, it was the kind of car Georgette had not seen since before the war.

'Where did you steal this?' she asked.

'I bought it. In Paris.'

'Do ERR have car showrooms now, as well as department stores?'

He chuckled. 'You never change, do you? I have no idea who owned it before. But it's British. An MG T-type. Drives like a dream.'

As Lange strapped her bike to the leather roof folded back above the boot, Georgette glanced up the hill towards the château. Turrets and chimneys rising from steeply pitched slated roofs above honey-yellow stone. And she knew that in the Chambre de Nine Huygue would be washing his wounds and panicking about what Lange might find when he got Georgette back to Carennac.

They drove along the tree-lined main road to where it veered off southward towards Gramat, and a huge old farm building sat up on the rocks, with views out across the valley. Lange took the turn-off to Carennac, and followed the tiny River Bave to where it would debouch eventually into the slow-moving westbound waters of the Dordogne. He glanced across at

Georgette in the passenger seat and saw her hair blown back from her forehead in undulating waves like water. 'How's the head?'

'A bit sore. But I'll live.'

He grinned. 'I never doubted it.' Then hesitated. 'Feel up to taking a little diversion? It's a beautiful day. We shouldn't let the Germans spoil it.'

She looked at him curiously, but he kept his eyes trained straight ahead of him. 'Present company excepted, presumably.'

He smiled without looking at her. 'Like everything else,' he said, 'there are good ones and bad.'

They turned off little more than a kilometre later, and wound up into the hills on a road so narrow that they would have been forced to back into a field had they met anything coming the other way. The climb grew steeper, and Georgette could hear the MG's engine straining. The road doubled back on itself through a copse of trees and over a tiny bridge, before emerging again into the early afternoon sunshine, and the whole valley of the Dordogne opened up below them.

This was not somewhere Georgette had ever come with her bike, and the view was breathtaking. Sunlight shimmered across the patchwork valley, ripening crops glowing gold in fields of wheat and barley, the river itself like shining loops of silver ribbon serpentining randomly between the cliffs that rose distantly on either side. In the shimmering heat, the red stone of the château of Castelnau glowed pink on the far bank, and from where Lange drew his MG into the opening to a hayfield, they had a view east beyond the turrets of Montal, to the towers that clustered around the hilltop above Saint-Céré.

A stone bench stood set into the hillside just below the road, and Lange helped Georgette climb down to join him, sitting on the warm stone to gaze out at the view. Nothing disturbed the silence of the land, except for the singing of the birds, the hum of myriad insects, and the far-off clang of cowbells ringing out across the hillside.

For a long time they sat, reluctant to spoil the moment. She felt the warmth of his body at her side, almost burning where they touched. Eventually she said, 'Do you think, if we had met under different circumstances, things would have been different between us?'

'In some ways, yes.'

She turned her head to look at him. 'What ways?'

He smiled. 'I'd have had to work much harder to get you to come to my apartment for dinner.' The smile turned sad. 'And you wouldn't have hated me just because I was German.'

'I never hated you because you were German.'

He turned amused eyes towards her. 'Oh? So why was it you hated me?'

'Do we have time? We could be here all afternoon.'

Now he laughed. 'That's what I love about you, George. You never take me too seriously.'

She felt a slight constriction of her throat, and an increase in her heart rate, and she wondered if there was anything else about her that he loved. She said, 'I take your friend Karlheinz Wolff very seriously.'

'He's not my friend.'

'But I take it that's why you're here. Because he is.'

He nodded.

'Where?'

'He's staying in a hotel at Gramat.'

She turned to look out once again across the valley. The bird-song seemed discordant now, the cowbells, like John Donne's bells, tolled for her. No longer did she see sunlight spinning gold across the land. Only the shadows it cast. Somehow, suddenly, it felt as if the endgame was very near. And fear chilled her in spite of the heat.

He said, 'I've been back in Germany again. She's finally agreed to a divorce.'

She was surprised. 'Lost her faith?'

He shook his head. 'It was never about faith. Just a way to get at me. But now he wants her to marry him, so being a good Catholic doesn't matter any more.'

He took her hand in his, and both fear and pleasure suffused her, nearly drowning all other senses. She felt an arm around her shoulder and half turned towards him to find his lips on hers. Warm, moist, tender, and she opened her mouth to his as his tongue sought hers. And she lost herself in a kiss that seemed to last for hours. Like drowning in him. Before they both broke apart to come up for air.

He looked at her with such searching tenderness, his

PETER MAY

fingertips on her face. 'Let's go,' he whispered, and she was uncertain whether she should be disappointed or excited. They stood up and still he held her hand as he led her back up to the road.

For the remainder of the drive to Carennac neither of them spoke, each lost in their own private thoughts. She was full of both trepidation and anticipation about their arrival at the house. About the decisions she would face. To commit or not. To give or withhold herself. It had been so long in coming, she had lost any sense of objectivity in how she should respond.

He parked his car at the foot of the steps, and followed her up to the little terrace at the front door. As they stepped into the house she wondered why she had ever worried about him uncovering the stash of weapons in the cellar. It was the last place they would be going.

And now it was she who held his hand as she took him through the kitchen and into the tiny bedroom at the back of the house. A decision that she seemed to have had no conscious part in making. They undressed quickly, silently, dropping their clothes where they stood. Sunlight angled across the bed through half-closed shutters as they fell together among the sheets and pillows. The hardness of his body pressed against the softness of hers. Somehow it all felt just so right. Why on earth had it taken them so long?

Afterwards they lay for a very long time in a tangle of sheets. The house was cool behind its thick stone walls, but the sunlight

413

where it fell across the bed burned their skin. Georgette's head-ache still lingered distantly, but banished from consciousness by pleasure, and now fear of a future that seemed impossible. She turned to lay her head on his shoulder, and idle fingers played with the tangle of hair on his chest.

'When will it end, Paul?'

'What?'

'The war.'

She felt the cloud of his uncertainty shadow the moment. 'I don't know. I really don't.'

'Do you think we'll survive it together? You and I?'

'God, I hope so.' She felt his fingers running through her hair, and they lay in silence for even longer now, neither of them wanting to bring this to an end.

Eventually, she said, 'I saw Wolff.'

He sat up immediately, staring at her. 'When?'

'A long time ago. The day we arrived, and delivered all the large rolled-up canvasses to a place across the valley there. A little village called Bétaille. He was parked up just along the street, smoking a cigarette and watching us unload our cargo.'

'What canvasses?'

'Oh, *The Wedding Feast at Cana* and others. Nothing that would interest Wolff.'

'So why was he there?'

She felt his eyes on her, but kept hers fixed on the ceiling, wondering whether she should tell him or not. She shrugged, as if that might somehow put off the moment.

'George?'

He wasn't going to let it go. She sighed. 'The rolled canvasses are accompanied by several other, smaller pieces. One of them is catalogued as *Sketch for the Feast*. Its crate is uniquely colour-coded with three yellow dots.'

'Why would Wolff be interested in that?'

And finally she let it go. 'Because that crate contains a duplicate of the *Mona Lisa*. A forgery so good, that you and I couldn't tell the difference. Painted on poplar, just like the original, by the best forger in a century.'

He was silent for so long that she was finally forced to drag her eyes away from the ceiling to look at him.

'What is it?'

'He could only have been there because he knows that.'

'That's what I thought. Though, I've no idea how. There are only a handful of people alive who know about it.' She hesitated. It was the last shred of her secret. 'I've been instructed to swap it for the original, if I think the real one is in danger of being seized.'

His blue eyes seemed to look right through her for some moments before refocusing. He touched her lips with a finger that he then ran down over her chin and breast, to graze a nipple and cause her to inhale sharply. 'You should do it now,' he said. 'Before he thinks you will. Then when he makes his move he'll have no idea you've beaten him to it. And if the forgery's as good as you say it is, he won't know that he doesn't have the real thing.'

And all Georgette could think of was that if Wolff ever managed to get his hands on the *Mona Lisa*, even if it was just the copy, he'd have had to come through her to get it.

Lange was still staring at her. And as if he could read her thoughts he said, 'I told you, George. Wherever Wolff is, I'll be there, too. So don't worry.'

He'd been gone for hours now, promising that she would see him again in the next days. And she had remained naked and tangled among the bed sheets, fretting about the future, both short- and long-term. Although the latter, she knew, would not be an issue if the former turned out badly.

Long before the sun vanished, she had drifted off into a shallow, dreamless sleep, waking only as night fell, and sitting up with a start. Her head was pounding, and though the blood had long ago dried, the head wound inflicted by the rifle butt still hurt.

She climbed out of bed and padded into the bathroom to wash. Then spent the next few minutes in front of the mirror examining the wound on her forehead. She dabbed it carefully with boiled water but still it started to bleed again. She staunched the blood with an application of petroleum jelly that she found in a jar in the cupboard.

Now she switched focus to look at herself. The upper right side of her face was badly bruised, and her left cheek still bore the evidence of the slap delivered by the German officer. Her hair was a mess. Cut short before the war, it had started to

grow itself out in uneven tufts. And in the absence of a functioning hairdresser, she had spent the last four years cutting
it herself. What in God's name did Lange see in her?

The thought made her smile. But it was a smile that quickly
faded as the decision that confronted her displaced everything
else. To switch the paintings or not. She closed her eyes and
took a deep breath, before opening them again to find herself
staring at doubt.

She went back to the bedroom to dress, then into the
kitchen to make herself a cup of tea and sit cradling it alone
at the long table. The painting was not big. Just seventy-seven
centimetres by fifty-three. She knew, too, that the poplar board
was not heavy. At the other side of the kitchen, she saw her
leather-bound art folder propped against the wall. It would
comfortably accommodate the size of the painting and some
soft felt to protect it.

She took a sip of her tea, cooled enough now not to burn
her lips, and made her decision.

It was a little after daybreak when Georgette cycled across the
flood plain the next morning, her art folder strapped across
her back. Wisps of mist rose from the river like smoke in the
first heat of the sun. A long straight road cut across the valley,
and she could see the red-brick of the church on the hill above
Bétaille glowing in the early light.

It took about fifteen minutes, and the guard on night shift at
the double garage was finishing a final cigarette as he waited

for his colleague to arrive and free him to head off to his billet and a well-earned sleep during the hours of daylight. She dismounted and leaned her bike against the gate and showed him her ID. 'You're not the usual girl,' he said.

She smiled. 'We all have different skill sets. I'm here to check on the big canvasses today.' All the works were inspected on a regular basis by assistant curators checking for signs of heat damage, or dampness, or mould, or invasions of insects.

He flicked away his cigarette end. 'You're early.'

'The girls tell me it gets pretty hot up there during the day.' She nodded towards the apartment above the garage. She grinned. 'Don't want to be getting sweaty hands all over the canvasses.'

He took her round the back and up steps to the door, unlocking it to let her in. 'I'll probably be away by the time you're finished. I'll let my colleague know you're here.'

When he'd gone, she stepped carefully over the half dozen large rolled canvasses that lay along the length of the hall and the room beyond it. The shutters were all closed, and sunlight lay in narrow strips across the floor where it squeezed in through lateral vents. To her left a small kitchen gave on to a larger room stacked floor to ceiling with other works on the inventory. Elaborately designed pre-war wallpaper had seen better days. With her copy of the inventory in her hand, she made her way down the hall, turning left towards a small toilet, and a room opening to her right where she knew the *Sketch for the Feast* was stored. Here the wallpaper was peeling from the walls, an old fireplace shuttered off, soot lying thick all around the hearth. The crated paintings were stacked against the wall opposite, and it took Georgette nearly ten minutes, moving each one with great care, to find what she was looking for. The crate with the three yellow dots.

She carried it out into the hall to prop against the wall, before swinging the art folder from her back and opening it out on the floor. From her satchel she took out a small hammer and a chisel and very gently prised open the case. Peeling back the leatherette and the fireproof paper she set eyes for the first time on the reproduction of *La Joconde*. She pushed open the toilet door to let light from a window high up on the wall above the cistern spill out into the hall, and turned back to the painting.

She knelt down and gazed at it with an overwhelming sense of déjà vu. She had seen the *Mona Lisa* so many times, touched her, bathed in the light of her presence, examined the brush strokes da Vinci had laid down with such tenderness on this poplar panel four hundred years ago. Cast critical eyes over the film of finely cracked paint and varnish that they called craquelure, damage that time had wrought to scar her beauty.

She found that she was holding her breath. It hardly seemed possible that this was not the real thing. She had not understood, until now, how Jaujard could claim to have been unable to tell it apart from the original. In the last two years, no one had been more intimate with the *Mona Lisa* than she. Like a lover she had slept with for all those months. And yet here, in the sunshine that slanted down across the hallway, she found herself doubting if this was the copy or the original. She touched it with a reverence born of incredulity. If she could not tell them apart, then neither could Wolff.

The sound of male voices drifted up from outside. The changing of the guard broke the spell. Quickly she lifted the painting from its crate and laid it on the soft felt with which she had lined her art folder the night before. She folded in the top and bottom flaps and tied it shut, then quickly reassembled the crate to restore it to its place in the stack against the wall of the front room. When it was safe to do so, she would return with the original and the switch would be complete. Only she and Lange would know it had been done and Wolff, she was sure, would suspect nothing. After all, there was no immediate or apparent threat to *La Joconde* at the Château de Montal. Why would she have swapped them?

Still, as she cycled away across the river valley, she harboured a niggling doubt about what she had done. Suppose what she had always taken for the original was really the copy. That Jaujard was somehow playing a game of double bluff, and had made her unwittingly complicit in the deception. She shook her mind free of the thought. It was, she knew, just the uncanny quality of the reproduction that had unsettled her. She was doing the right thing.

She felt the weight of it on her back. A load that far outweighed any reading which might be obtained by placing it on the scales. The weight of four hundred years of history.

She put her head down and pedalled faster, heading back to the house in Carennac where she would transfer it to the cardboard suitcase which had accompanied her on this whole extended adventure.

It was late morning by the time Georgette arrived at the château, the suitcase strapped to the back of her bike. As she wheeled it across the courtyard one of the guards quipped, 'Not leaving us for that German, are you, George?'

She forced herself to laugh as naturally as she could. 'You don't get rid of me that easy, Fred.' She patted the suitcase. 'Just a change of bed sheets for my camp bed after those brutes stamped all over them yesterday.'

She went into the *salle des gardes* and gathered up her old bed sheets where they still lay strewn across the floor next to her upturned camp bed. She righted the bed and folded the sheets and blanket neatly on top of it, before sliding her suitcase underneath. Then she ran up the vaulted stairwell, sunlight streaming in, top and bottom. The whole château seemed to glow in the light of the reprieve of yesterday's search by the Germans. At the top of the steps she turned right along the hallway and into the Chambre de Nine, where Huygue sat at a desk pushed in beneath the window. He slept in the apparent luxury of a four-poster bed set against the near wall, among yet more crates of paintings.

He turned as he heard her and quickly stood up. 'Shut the door behind you.' The bruising on his forehead was already yellowing around its outer edges, a dressing on the wound inflicted by Schneider's pistol grip. He lowered his voice. 'What the hell, George? I've been worried sick.'

'About me, or your precious stash of guns?'

He glared at her, and she crossed to where the crate with the three red dots leaned against the wall beside his desk. She crouched down to examine it. 'Is she alright?'

'Yes, thank God.' He let out a long sigh. 'What's going on between you and that German?'

She looked at him sharply. 'What do you mean?'

'You know perfectly well what I mean. He knew you.'

She stood up. 'Yes. He was a regular at the Jeu de Paume when I was in Paris. He's with the Kunstschutz. You do what these people tell you or you suffer the consequence.'

'What was he doing here?'

She shrugged. 'On some kind of unannounced tour of all the depots, apparently. So we can probably expect him back. It's just as well he chose to show up yesterday.'

She glanced down at Huygue's desk and saw that he was updating some kind of journal. *31 mai: ouverture de la caisse contenant la Vierge d'Autun.* Opening of the case containing the Virgin of Autun. Which Georgette knew to be a painting by Jan van Eyck dating from around 1435, depicting the Virgin Mary presenting baby Jesus to Chancellor Rolin in his church of Notre-Dame-du-Chastel in Autun in Burgundy. A bizarre portrait commissioned by Rolin himself showing him with mother and son in his church. A priceless work, in more ways than one.

She returned her attention to Huygue. 'You'd better move those weapons out of my cellar in case he comes back. He showed a great deal of interest in the property. It was all I could do to get rid of him.'

That night she stayed over at the château as usual, the *Mona Lisa* in her crate propped at the head of her camp bed. But Georgette was unable to sleep. She made coffee after coffee and sat in the dark through the early hours of the morning until she was certain that everyone else in the château was asleep.

She could see the guard perched on the wall beyond the gate to the courtyard, smoking as he always did to relieve his boredom through the hours of darkness. Earlier the moon had risen in a startlingly clear sky, to cast its luminance across the landscape and lay a dazzling white sheen on the castine of the courtyard, broken only by the shadows of trees around its perimeter.

She placed the suitcase on her bed, opening it up to unfold the green felt wrapped around the painting she had stowed inside, and was struck all over again by the uncannily familiar image she unveiled. Quickly she opened up the crate that held the real *Mona Lisa* and for just a moment placed the two side by side against the wall. It seemed almost supernatural. The same smile twice. The same gaze in two pairs of eyes that never left her. Then hurriedly she fitted the doppelgänger into the crate with the red dots, replacing the wrappings, and closed it up. With shaking hands, she lifted *La Joconde* to take the place of her imposter in the suitcase, carefully swaddling her in green felt.

She slid the suitcase back under the camp bed and lay down to stare up into the vaults, aware that her whole body was trembling, her breath coming in short, rapid bursts, as if she had just run a hundred metres.

The deed was done.

It was just a week later, on June 6, that news reached the château of the Allied invasion of Normandy, and it sent a buzz of fear and expectation through all of the staff stationed there. Already there were reports of German divisions heading up from the south, making their way north to join the battle to repel the invaders. Under constant attack from guerrilla groups of Maquis fighters, the Germans were exacting terrible reprisals on the civilian population as they went.

The following day Huygue took Georgette aside to tell her that several maquisards fighters would be calling by the house in Carennac in the next day or two to recover the weapons from her cellar. 'The Germans will be here in the next twenty-four to forty-eight hours,' he said.

They crossed the courtyard and passed through the gate to climb steps to the stone walkway above the garden. On the far side of the potager, wrought-iron gates stood open, leading to an avenue of trees and open country beyond. The means, Georgette imagined, by which Jean-Luc had been able to effect his escape from the château.

Huygue lowered his voice, although there was no one else in sight. 'We've received intelligence that the 2nd SS Panzer Division, Das Reich, has sent three regiments north by different routes. It looks like the second regiment is going to come through Saint-Céré. Might even pass our door. There's something like a hundred and eighty-eight tanks, sixty trucks, light vehicles and a couple of dozen motorbikes. Nearly 4000 men in total.'

'Good God,' Georgette whispered. 'It's like an invasion all of its own.'

Huygue nodded. 'And a prime target for Allied bombing.' He paused a moment to let that sink in.

Georgette was quick to realise the implications. 'If they start dropping bombs around here, they could easily hit the château.'

'Exactly. We have to get word to London giving them our precise coordinates and explain exactly why it is an area to be avoided at all costs.'

Georgette looked at him blankly. 'How can we do that?'

Huygue took her arm and led her down into the garden. 'We have a radio transmitter in the towers above Saint-Céré. It's a pretty makeshift affair, but we've been able to send and receive messages from London.' He chuckled. 'The boys call it Radio Quercy. The trouble is, none of our people have got very good English. Certainly no one nearly as good as you.'

Georgette knew now what was coming next. 'Would you be prepared to draft a concise message in English to take up to the towers tomorrow? The boys will encrypt it and send it off. The transmitter will be dismantled immediately afterwards and taken away. Because there's nothing surer than that the Germans are going to come looking for it.'

Georgette closed her eyes and nodded. There was no need even to think about it. Whatever the risks. This was her duty. She felt the same sense of obligation as when de Gaulle had asked her to look after *La Joconde*. 'Of course,' she said.

The Tours Saint-Laurent stood proud on a conical volcanic peak that threw its shadow across the town of Saint-Céré below. There were four towers, two of them taller than the others, and a two-storey dwelling comprising the remains of what had once been a fortified château. It had had an impressive lineage of ownership over the centuries and was then in the stewardship of the Countess Annie de Coheix who, Huygue assured Georgette, had given tacit approval for the installation of radio equipment in the tallest of the towers.

Georgette had only ever seen the towers from the valley that they dominated, often lost in cloud, but was still unprepared for the steepness of the climb she had to make on her bike to reach them. In the heat of the early afternoon, she cycled through the tiny village of Saint-Laurent, past the mairie, and pushed her bike up the final slope to a door set in huge wooden gates built into an arch in the fortifications. She was breathless and perspiring by the time she got there, the folded message tucked into her bra, damp from her exertions. A handle dangled on a chain almost beyond her reach. She had to stand on tiptoes to grasp it and pull hard to set a bell ringing somewhere on the other side of the gate. It seemed inordinately loud in the still of an afternoon whose heat almost vibrated with the hum of a million summer insects.

The door creaked open just a little, and a tanned leathery face peered out at her. The face of a man she recognised from the gathering of resistance fighters the night she stumbled upon Huygue handing out weapons at Montal. He opened the door a little wider, peering out to make sure they were not being observed, before waving her in and slamming it shut behind her. She left her bike inside the gate and followed him up a steep climb between high stone walls, emerging through overhanging trees and shrubs at the entrance to the residential quarters of the old castle. Red and blond sandstone, rust-coloured shutters and doors. Extensive gardens stretched off to the towers at the south side of the hill, oak trees casting dappled shade on long grass. The maquisard took her the other way, past the echoing profundity of a deep dark well, to the highest of the towers. He opened a tall door to usher her in.

'I don't need to go inside,' she said. 'Just to give you this.' And she pulled out the folded sheet of paper from beneath her blouse to hold towards him.

He shook his head. 'No, no. There might be a reply. If you translate, there'll be no misunderstandings.'

She glanced up at the square tower which soared into the blue sky above them. There were glazed windows set into the wall about six metres up, and unglazed openings cut into the stone at seemingly random intervals above that. She sighed and stepped inside, climbing narrow stone steps in the dark that led up to a floor lit by the window she had seen from the outside. Another, on the facing wall, looked out over the valley and the jumble of red-tiled roofs of Saint-Céré immediately below. She could see the Place de la République at its heart, and the four-storey lycée building on the far side of the River Bave. And away to the right, the turrets of Château de Montal shimmered in the afternoon heat.

A battered, old blue leather suitcase with rusted clasps sat open on a rough wooden table pushed against the wall below the far window. It was tightly packed with black bakelite units of interconnected electrical equipment, sliders and dials, knobs and switches. A tangle of black and red wire spewed out from one side of it to trail away across the floor into darkness. A Morse code transmitter key pivoted on a wooden block screwed to the table. A young man sitting at the table swivelled in his chair as they came up the stairs. He wore a grubby blue and white striped shirt that billowed baggily beneath his braces. His sleeves were rolled up to the elbows, and he wore a dusty cap pulled down over a shock of pure black hair. He smiled when he saw Georgette, revealing a missing tooth at one side of a crooked and discoloured row of them. He stood up immediately and pulled off his cap to grin shyly. 'Mademoiselle,' he said. 'I'm Michel. Welcome to Radio Quercy.' He waved a hand at the suitcase. 'Best-equipped radio station in all of the Lot.'

Georgette looked at it in amazement. 'Where do you get stuff like this?'

Michel said proudly, 'It's a Type A MkII suitcase radio made in Britain. Brought by an SOE agent parachuted on to the *causses* a few weeks ago.'

Even just the mention of SOE transported her back, however briefly, to that cold, wet, windy week on the Isle of Lewis.

'Can we get on with it?' The man who had let Georgette in at the gate glanced anxiously from the window.

The young radio operator held out a hand towards Georgette. 'You've got the text?'

She handed him her piece of paper and he sat down with it to open a black leather notebook filled with lines of text and numbers, and embark on the process of encoding it. He scribbled the revised text that he would actually send on to the page of an open jotter. The pencil he held in oil-stained fingers was little more than a stub, its lead point blunted by use.

Georgette said, 'What if they catch you with that notebook on you? Won't they know your code?'

Without looking up, Michel said, 'We use a poem I've selected. And that's the key. The poem's in my head.' He tapped the notebook. 'These are just transpositions. Wouldn't mean anything to the Krauts.'

When he finished his encoding, Michel flicked switches and turned knobs and Georgette saw the needle on the circular dial dance into life. And he began his transmission, two fingers placed delicately on the transmitter key to tap out sequences of long and short beeps.

His companion was becoming agitated. He whispered to Georgette, 'They know it the minute we start transmitting. And they know we're somewhere in the area. They've been looking for us for days. It's only a matter of time before they find us. This'll be our last transmission from here.'

If he heard, Michel did not react. His focus was concentrated entirely on the key beneath his fingers, until finally he sat back, and Georgette saw sweat trickling down his neck from beneath his hair. 'Done,' he said.

'How long do we have to wait?'

Michel looked at the other man. 'As long as it takes.'

'We don't have as long as it takes, Michel. We need to be out of here.'

Michel raised a steadying hand. 'Just give it a few, Jacques.'

The distant rumble of diesel motors carried to them on warm afternoon air and Jacques pressed his face to the window. 'Jesus!' Georgette heard him whisper under his breath. 'They're here.'

'Who's here?' She was alarmed.

'The Das Reich tank regiment.' His breath condensed like bullet shots on the glass. 'You can see them coming down the hill from Figeac on the far side of the town.'

Georgette crossed to the window and wiped away the grime to peer through it. And there in the distance, beyond the lycée, she saw a long column of tanks snaking slowly down through the trees on the road from Figeac. Trucks and motorbikes were already assembling beneath the plane trees in the Place de la République. She was startled by the far-off crackle of gunfire and recoiled from the window as if from an electric shock.

Jacques turned to Michel. 'We need to go now!'

Michel nodded and stood up, shutting down the transmitter, and quickly unscrewing the transmission key from the table. He crossed the room, coiling lengths of wire to stuff hastily into the suitcase and snapped it shut. He stuffed his notebook in his pocket and tore the page with the encoded text from his jotter. Together with Georgette's original text he crumpled it up and dropped it on to the floor, stooping down with a cigarette lighter in his hand to set them on fire. He stood up and watched as the paper burned, and when the writing on it was no longer legible, he stamped out the flames and grabbed his suitcase. 'Let's go.'

They hurried down the dark staircase to emerge blinking into the sunlight, momentarily blinded by it, before running for the gate. Down the narrow passage to the door that opened out through the fortifications on to the hillside beyond.

Georgette grabbed her bike and the three of them stood listening for a moment on the far side of the wall. The roar of the tanks was louder now, rumbling in the afternoon heat like summer thunder.

Michel nodded to Georgette. 'Merci, mademoiselle.' And he turned and ran off through the trees, hefting his transmitter.

Jacques said, 'You're on your own now.' And he jumped over

the wall to crash off through the undergrowth into the cover of the woods below.

Georgette mounted her bike, frightened and feeling very exposed. Her only way back to Montal was by road. She started off down the steep incline, gathering speed. At the mairie she rounded the bend and set off down the narrow road that wound its way around the hillside and down to the town below.

It was much faster on the way down than the way up. The air felt hot in her face, and she was having difficulty controlling her breathing. A long way off lay the safe haven of Château de Montal, and it seemed impossibly distant. Immediately below, the rooftops of Saint-Céré reflected afternoon sunlight off red Roman tiles.

She came fast around the final bend and on to the long straight stretch that descended to the hospital, and her heart very nearly stopped. The road at the foot of the hill was swarming with SS troopers, a truck and a couple of motorbikes. There was no way she could turn back, and nowhere for her to hide. She braked and drew to an unsteady stop as one of the soldiers stepped out into the road with his hand raised. He grabbed her bike and shouted at her to get off. Another caught her by the arm and marched her into the road. It was only then that she saw two men backed up against the wall at the foot of the hill. Civilians, beaten and bleeding, cowed and fearful. Georgette saw the fear in black eyes that met hers as half a dozen soldiers on a shouted command raised their rifles and shot them where they stood.

Georgette was shocked to her core. How easily the lives of those young men had simply been erased. All their memories, their hopes and expectations. The pain of growing up, falling in love, raising a family. The patriotism that had moved them to fight for the freedom of their country. Extinguished in the blink of an eye. Perhaps for the first time in her life, she understood the true frailty of human existence. That our time on earth is just a split second of eternity. 'Full of sound and fury, signifying nothing.' The words of the Shakespeare play they had studied at school came back to her, and she realised how easily she too could be gone in just a heartbeat. In just the next few moments. And what would any of it have meant?

The blood of the resistance fighters was already coagulating in the dust of the pavement, and she was pushed violently in the back before being made to walk among the soldiers along the road towards the centre of town.

She half turned, protesting. 'My bike!'

The one who had wrenched it from her said, 'You won't be needing that again, mademoiselle.' And the sense that her own death was imminent struck her with such force that her legs very nearly folded beneath her. Seldom in her life had she felt so utterly powerless.

As they turned into the Rue de la République, she saw yet more soldiers herding a large civilian crowd of mostly women and children into the Boulevard Gambetta. Perhaps forty of them or more. The two groups of soldiers met up and Georgette was shoved into the boulevard to join the other civilians. She saw dark frightened eyes flicker momentarily in her direction. A pall of fear that was almost palpable hung over the group, nervous soldiers prodding them with semi-automatic rifles, tension heightened by the shouted commands of their agitated Sturmbannführer. A man called Christian Tyschen.

An involuntary gasp escaped collectively from the townsfolk as shots rang out from the direction of the Pont Neuf which spanned the river at the Hôtel de la Truite. Tyschen screamed at his troops and rifles were immediately raised towards the crowd. Georgette heard children crying and several of the women called out, pleading with the Germans not to shoot.

Georgette felt sick to her stomach. So much for her brave notion that she could in any way protect the *Mona Lisa*. She couldn't even keep herself safe. So this is how it was all going to end. In a hot dusty street in a provincial town in south-west France. In a hail of bullets from a trigger-happy bunch of SS troopers. The confidence of the occupiers had been shaken as they sensed that the war was starting to slip away from them. Their desire for revenge fed by fear.

Incongruously, a woman's voice speaking German rose above the hubbub, and Georgette pushed herself up on tiptoes to see a small woman in a print dress belted at the waist addressing herself to the German commander. Short, crimped hair was parted at one side above a pretty face with an upturned nose. Tychsen was trying to ignore her, but she followed him as he strode among his troops, gesticulating with expressive hands, voice plaintive and pleading. The conversation was too fast for Georgette to follow, but the woman was persistent and fluent. Someone whispered, 'That's Berthe Nasinec. She's Czech. Married to the hairdresser.'

'What's she saying?' another asked.

'No idea.'

Whatever it was, it was bothering the German commander. Initially, to Georgette, he had appeared young for a commanding officer, but watching for his reaction he seemed older now than his years. A thin face, badly scarred around the chin and mouth, blond hair greying beneath his peaked hat. As he removed it to wipe the sweat from his brow with the back of his sleeve, Georgette saw that he had very little of it left. She saw, too, that his sweat-stained uniform was punctuated by badges for bravery. And pinned to his shirt at the neck she recognised a Knight's Cross with oak leaves. But it didn't take much courage, she thought, to turn guns on a group of unarmed women and children.

For the first time Tyschen met Berthe's eye and he shouted at her. Words that no one could understand. But she was unperturbed, and continued following in his wake, pleading, cajoling. Suddenly he turned, taking his pistol from his holster, and pointed it at her head. She stopped, but stood her ground and thrust her chin out in defiance, almost daring him to shoot. Whatever she said then either embarrassed or shamed him, for the Sturmbannführer turned away, reholstering his weapon, and started shouting fresh orders at his men. They in turn lowered their weapons and headed off at

the double along the boulevard. Very quickly the crowd began
to disperse, hurrying off through alleyways mired in shadow,
along the street in the direction of the factory, or turning the
other way towards the fire station, mothers raising children
in their arms as they fled.

Georgette felt a hand on her shoulder. She'd barely had
time to absorb that they had somehow been reprieved. Only
history would reveal just what a narrow escape it had been.
For the next day, Tyschen's soldiers would go on to hang
ninety-nine men from an avenue of trees in the nearby town
of Tulle.

Her legs were still like jelly and she turned, startled, at the
touch on her shoulder. A grim-faced Lange stood behind her.
He was in uniform, but seemed much less sure of himself than
the last time she had seen him.

'Come with me, quickly,' he said. 'They're shooting resistance people all over the place. We don't want to get caught
up in this.'

They cut through a narrow passageway to a street of terraced houses shaded by old plane trees in full leaf. At the
end of it, they turned down a lane that led towards the rugby
stadium and the cemetery, and she saw his green MG parked
there in the shade.

'Wolff's here,' he said breathlessly. 'He's chosen his moment
well. When he has brute force on his side. He can take the
painting and kill whoever he needs to in the process, and with
all this confusion no one will be any the wiser.'

They climbed into the car and he started the motor, before turning anxiously towards her.

'Did you make the switch?'

She nodded, still barely able to find her voice.

'Where's the original?'

'Still at the house in Carennac. I've hidden it.'

He seemed relieved. 'Good. We need to go now and get her to safety.'

At the junction with the road south to Gramat, they were forced to stop where soldiers had established a roadblock to allow free passage of an endless convoy of troop trucks and motorcycles and other vehicles heading north. They sat with the engine idling while half a dozen soldiers pointed their rifles into the car and a senior officer checked both sets of papers. He scrutinised them carefully, then examined Georgette with curious eyes which flickered then towards Lange. After the briefest of pauses he saluted, then shouted an order to halt the convoy and let the MG through. Lange accelerated away with relief. He said, 'A piece of paper from the Führer's office is useful, but might not always count for much in present circumstances. Nervous soldiers shoot first and ask questions later.'

The drive on the long winding road back to the house seemed endless. Glimpses through the trees of sunlight coruscating on the slow-moving waters of the Dordogne, nothing moving in the flood plain beyond. The turning of the world, it seemed, had been put on pause by the momentous events unfolding elsewhere. Georgette could not stop her hands from trembling.

When they got to Carennac the village was deserted. Shop, café, hotels all shuttered up. People locked away in their houses. No one wanted to attract attention to themselves, and only the spectres of the past walked the streets, silently inviting them to become phantoms of the future.

Lange drew in at the foot of Georgette's steps, killed the motor and stepped out on to the asphalt. He stood for several long moments, listening intently, eyes scanning the park and the streets that led off into the silent heart of the village. But there was not a sound other than the slow tick-tick of the engine as it cooled, and some somnolent birdsong among the trees in the park.

He nodded towards the door. 'Let's go in.'

He followed her up the stone stairway and into the cool of the house, passing through the kitchen and into the grand salon. There she stopped, and he walked briskly past her, casting anxious eyes around the room before turning to face her.

'Where is it?'

'Don't worry. It's safely hidden. And anyway, Wolff won't know where to find me if I'm not at the château.'

'Of course he will!' Lange snapped. 'He's been tracking you all this time. He'll know everything about you.' He paused. 'Where's the painting?'

She frowned. 'I told you, it's perfectly safe.'

Lange drew his pistol and pointed it at her. 'Tell me!'

Georgette was startled and looked at him in wide-eyed astonishment. This couldn't be happening. It *couldn't* be. 'What are you doing?'

'Jesus Christ!'

'Paul?'

He shook his head. 'Where is it?'

But for Georgette time had come to a dead stop. Her life, she knew with a greater clarity than she had felt even in the Boulevard Gambetta, was over. Only now, she *wanted* it to be over. Because how could she ever live with this betrayal. With her own blind stupidity. She felt the first warm tears track their way slowly down her cheeks. In a tiny voice she said, 'That's all you ever wanted from me, wasn't it? The *Mona Lisa*?'

'It's what Hitler asked me to get for him, and it's what I intend to deliver. Now where is it?'

'What if I won't tell you?'

'Then I'll kill you and tear the place apart until I find it.'

She stared at him for a long, long moment. In her heart, what she had taken for love morphed into hatred, and for a few fleeting moments she thought he felt it too, and saw discomfort or maybe even guilt in his eyes. 'You'd better kill me, then,' she said. 'Because I'm not going to tell you.'

She closed her eyes. Not wanting to see him as he pulled the trigger to compound his treachery. More tears spilled from between eyelids squeezed tightly shut. She had seen the lives of men extinguished in a split second less than an hour before. And now she saw her own brief life flash before her eyes. Like a film that spooled too quickly, allowing for only a handful of memories to register. The childhood tragedy of a much-loved father taken too soon, the sadness of her mother's passing. Lange as he made love to her, touching her face with tender fingers. Rose's words to her that night at the apartment in Paris. *If you ever sleep with him, it'll be the end of you, you know that?* She had been right. And now she remembered the day in the blackhouse overlooking the beach at Uig Bay, when Mairi's grandmother had seen the halo of darkness around her.

In the stillness of the house she could very nearly feel Lange squeezing the trigger, and she flinched at the sound of the gunshot when it came. Something whistled past her and embedded itself in the door. She opened her eyes, startled to see Lange gazing down in astonishment at blood bubbling through a large hole in his chest. He looked up to see Georgette staring at him, and as if shutters had come suddenly down on his life, his eyes turned up towards heaven and he toppled forward to hit the flagstones with the sickening slap of flesh and bone on unyielding stone.

As he fell she saw, standing behind him on the side terrace, the pale figure of Karlheinz Wolff, arm raised, his pistol trembling just a little in his hand as he pointed it through the open door. His leather flying jacket hung open, sweat trickling from the hairline beneath his cap. The faintest of smiles lit a troubled face. He said, 'You put your trust in the wrong man, Georgette.' He drew a deep breath. 'You know what a Mischling is?'

She had no voice to find, every sense and sensation numb with shock. She shook her head.

'It's the German word for a half-breed. The Nazis stole it specifically to describe someone of mixed Jewish and Aryan race. It's what they call me.' His voice was laden with bitter irony. 'Some grandmother I never even knew.' He ran his tongue over dry lips. 'I was never, *ever*, going to deliver the *Mona Lisa* to that condescending, Jew-hating cretin Göring. From the moment he asked me to, I knew that my whole war was going to be dedicated to keeping her safe from him. And from Hitler.' He cast his gaze down towards the man who had stolen his fiancée, blood pooling slowly around his body on the floor.

He raised his eyes again to meet hers, and his head snapped suddenly to the side as a single shot rang out. His pistol clattered away across the flagstones, an arc of blood spouting from the side of his head as his legs buckled beneath him and he fell on to the terrace just beyond the door.

Georgette heard cautious footsteps approach, and the shadows of three men darkened the doorway as they stopped to check that Wolff was dead before turning into the room. One of them held a pistol in his hand and pulled off his cap with the other. And Georgette saw that it was Jean-Luc Percet, the guard from the château. He grinned when he saw the prone figure of Lange on the floor. 'Two for the price of one, eh? Good thing René Huygue sent us to get those guns from your cellar this afternoon, or it might have been your blood on those flagstones.'

The three maquisards buried Wolff's body in a half-dug trench in the park next to the house, where the *cantonnier* had been preparing to lay a drainage pipe. They bundled Lange's body into his sports car and drove it off through the still deserted village, not a living soul daring to open a window or unlatch a shutter. The burned-out remains of the MG were found two days later at the foot of cliffs downriver, the remains of its driver burned beyond recognition.

Georgette was left alone in the house, with blood on the floor, and the world's most famous painting secreted away in her attic where no one, now, would even come looking for it.

It was almost a year later, on May 7, 1945, that the Germans surrendered and the war came to an end. In all those months, the dead place, seared into her soul by the events of that June day the previous year, had prevented Georgette from spilling so much as a single tear.

And just as it had on that fateful day almost a year before, the sun was shining the day the war ended. Instead of cycling to the château, Georgette took her bike and retraced the route Lange had taken her on their drive into the hills. She found the entrance to the hayfield where he had parked, and the stone bench set into the hillside just below the road where he had kissed her.

She climbed down to sit alone on the cool stone and gaze out across the landscape that dropped away into the valley below. The turrets of Château de Montal catching the oblique light of the sun, its honey-coloured stone glowing warm against the spring green and all the fruit trees in blossom. The towers of the Tours Saint-Laurent, from which they had transmitted her message to London in an effort to try to keep the artworks in the château safe from bombers, stood in stark silhouette against a painfully blue sky.

The same hum of insects and the same dull clunk of distant cowbells filled the air, just as it had the day she felt Lange's lips on hers and knew that they were going to make love. There were so many reasons to remember him, but only one that now brought the tears she had refused to cry in all this time. And she wept. And wept. With unrestrained grief.

A little over a month later, on June 15th, the *Mona Lisa*, along with many other artworks from Montal, made the return journey to Paris to resume her rightful place in the Louvre. Eight months later, the rolled canvasses which had been stored above the garage in Bétaille, including Veronese's *The Wedding Feast at Cana*, and *Sketch for the Feast*, also made the long trip home. When the crate containing *Sketch for the Feast* was eventually unpacked, it was found to be empty. No copy or reproduction of the *Mona Lisa* was found. And no one, least of all the authorities at the Louvre, were going to admit that it had ever existed.

CHAPTER TWENTY-NINE

Enzo blinked, almost as though waking from a dream, or with the lights coming up at the end of a movie. The completion of the story had taken most of the day, and only now did his stomach growl its displeasure at missing lunch. Outside it had grown dark, earlier since the turning back of the clocks the week before, and the fire had all but gone out. The air in the room had turned chill, and it was only now that he noticed it. Moonlight flooded in through the stained glass, and Anny sat like an apparition in her rocking chair, looking at him expectantly.

He said, 'And the one reason that Georgette had above all others for weeping over Lange . . . was you.'

Her smile was so distant it barely registered. 'I was just two months old when the war ended and she made her pilgrimage to that bench on the hill. It was a month after his death that she discovered she was pregnant. I always loved my mother with a passion, monsieur. And never knew, of course, the man who had betrayed her. The man who was my father. I would have wished to have known him. Truly. If only to find that one redeeming feature, the reason that he did what he did.'

He heard the tiniest break in her voice. 'None of us would like to believe that their father was a monster.'

'And did your mother ever find it? That one redeeming feature. In retrospect, I mean.'

'I don't believe so, monsieur. She never got over it, right up until the day she died. Although she spoke of him often, and sometimes with a fondness that I found hard to credit.'

'And the story you have told me is the story she told you.'

She smiled. 'A story I heard so many times. Over and over, from my earliest recollection. Until it seemed to me, monsieur, that I had been there myself. Felt her pain, her love, her sense of betrayal, as if it were mine.' She turned her gaze to the floor where the door opened into the hall towards the kitchen. 'If you look carefully, you can still see where the blood of my father stained the flagstones. In a way, he's always been here. My mother acquired this house from the mairie, with money inherited from her mother. I was born here, grew up here, have never known any other home.'

'Your mother married, didn't she?'

'Yes. A doctor. Albert Lavigne. The only father I ever knew. My mother gave birth to my half-sister a few years later, but Albert died before Claire even reached her teens, and my mother was alone again. And remained so for the rest of her life.'

'That's sad.' Enzo grieved for Georgette, too. After everything that had happened to her, she had surely deserved some happiness. 'But she always had you.'

The sadness now in Anny's smile was almost painful. 'She did. Although I was never quite able to shake off the feeling that somehow she saw Lange every time she looked at me. The sins of the father, and all that. Claire never carried that taint. Sadly, she passed before I did, so on my death I will leave the house to her daughter, Elodie, and it will remain within the family.'

'And the *Mona Lisa*?'

Sharp eyes flickered towards Enzo. 'Back in the Louvre where she belongs.'

Enzo scratched his chin thoughtfully. 'You know, it occurs to me that the reason both Narcisse and Bauer came here to seek you out was the belief that somehow you still possessed the *Mona Lisa* forgery. Passed on to you by your mother. After all, given its provenance, and the role it played in history, it must be worth a small fortune. Not to mention the story that goes with it. A bestseller if ever I heard one.' He paused. 'And, then, there is always the possibility that it wasn't, after all, the original that was returned to the Louvre at the end of the war.'

Anny laughed. 'You are letting your imagination run away with you, monsieur. Truth be told, there is actually no evidence whatsoever that such a forgery ever existed. It could just as easily have been a fanciful fabrication of my mother's. A story to entertain. Or confuse.'

'Confuse who?'

She shrugged and smiled. 'Anyone who heard it.'

'Well, I think that two men certainly heard it. Though not

from you. Or your mother. And it's why one of them is dead, and the other missing.'

Her smile faded, but it was clear to Enzo that she was going to say nothing further on the matter. He eased himself stiffly out of his armchair, and felt every ache and pain inflicted on him by the events of the night before. He said, 'I have a notion that I might just know where that missing man is. And if' – he caught and corrected himself – 'when I find him, perhaps finally the truth will come out.'

CHAPTER THIRTY

It was very nearly a full moon. A hunter's moon. And since it was the second one of the month, a blue moon also. Tomorrow, on a Halloween when the streets would be deserted, and children confined to their homes by the lockdown, it would reach fulfilment. But Enzo found it hard to believe that it could cast any more light than it did tonight. The *causses*, as he drove south on the narrow D20, shimmered in what seemed like daylight. Red rocky soil turned over for the coming winter, drystone walls glowing silver at the roadside, trees stripped of leaves casting deep, dark shadows. For the first time, Enzo realised why they called it a hunter's moon. It was the last full moon of autumn, when night hunters could go out to stock the larder for the lean months ahead.

But Enzo did not have the luxury of waiting for tomorrow's full moon to go in search of his man. From midnight tonight the lockdown would kick in and it would no longer be legal for him to be out and about.

Turning off at the tiny village of Miers to head cross-country, it took him another fifteen minutes to reach the junction where the road doubled back towards the Gouffre de Padirac.

The Gouffre de Padirac was a tourist construct a couple of kilometres from the village of Padirac itself. No one lived there. Bars and cafés, restaurants and hotels, bordered a long road lined by trees that led gently downhill to a sprawling white and red-brick building on the very edge of this huge black fissure in the earth. Beyond it, the Auberge du Gouffre cast long shadows in the moonlight, and a small park stretched away across the valley floor towards wooded countryside in the west. In summer, thousands of tourists would queue here for hours below long covered walkways to hand over their euros and enter the building, gaining access to the stairs and lifts that would take them deep into the bowels of the earth. But as Enzo cruised slowly down the hill, the place was utterly deserted. Shutters drawn. Not a single light in the windows of the three-storey Padirac Hotel. The ghosts of summer long gone, a bleak and desolate winter in prospect.

At the foot of the hill Enzo parked his car and stepped out into an eery silence. Street lights seemed superfluous in the phosphorescent light of the moon. He consulted a crude little map in the trifold advertising the gîte available for summer let. And followed a path along the far side of the park to where a gravel track cut away through long grass. A house sat up on the slope in the shade of several large oak trees.

He hardly needed his torch to find his way up to it, acorns and beech nuts breaking open underfoot. It was built into the side of the hill, a shallow Roman-tiled roof above a bungalow with cellar and terrace out front, a short flight of steps leading to the main door. All of its windows looked securely shuttered. A carport adjoining the left side of the house languished in deep shadow. Enzo shone his torch into the darkness and saw a racing bike leaning against the wall. And his heart began to beat just a little faster.

He made his way through the long grass to the far side of the property and climbed up to the back of it. A rear door opened on to an overgrown garden where fruit trees offered scented summer shade and escape from the sun. To the left of the door, shutters on a window stood almost imperceptibly ajar. Enzo directed the beam of his torch at them and saw splintered wood where they had been forced open.

He doused the light of the torch and tucked it into his belt before reaching up to swing them fully open. A pane of glass in the window beyond had been smashed, and as he stepped closer he heard it crunching beneath his feet. He looked around and spotted a white plastic table and two chairs beneath the nearest tree, green-streaked and discoloured by damp. He fetched one of the chairs to place beneath the window, and standing on it, pulled himself up on to the ledge. From here he could reach through the broken pane to release the clasp on the other side and push the window open. The house breathed warm air and the smell of stale cooking into his face. And something else that he couldn't quite identify. Soap. Or perfume. Or, perhaps, aftershave. Carefully he grasped the window frame at each side and dropped silently into the dark.

He crouched for a moment, letting his eyes accustom themselves to the change in light, and listened intently for the
slightest sound. But the silence was more profound than the
dark, and he slowly stood up to take the torch from his belt.

It was perfectly possible that Bauer was long gone. That he
had been here, Enzo was in no doubt. The bike in the carport
was witness to that. But there was also a chance that he was
still there. That he had heard Enzo climbing in through the
window, perhaps seen his torchlight as he approached the
house.

That torchlight now revealed him to be in a small bedroom.
The bed was neatly made and had not been slept in. Enzo wondered about calling out. But if Bauer were here, and perhaps
asleep, he didn't want to alert him to his presence. He opened
the door very gently and peered out into a narrow hallway
that transected the house, gable to gable. Glazed double doors
halfway along it gave on to a large front room. Enzo moved
cautiously over the tiled floor and into the lounge. A wood-
burning stove stood in a fireplace at one end, a dining table at
the other. A sofa and armchairs were gathered around French
windows that in summer would open on to the terrace and a
view of the park, and the red and white entrance to the *gouffre*
at the far side of it.

The table was strewn with documents and maps, and a pile
of black leather-bound notebooks, all picked out in sharp
relief by Enzo's torch. There were several mugs containing the
coagulated remains of half-drunk milky coffee. And something

about the smell of this room told him that someone had been in it very recently.

Enzo crossed to the table and flicked one-handed through the pages of one of the notebooks, training his torch on it with the other. Faded ink and what he realised was neat German script. Nothing he could read. He played the light of his torch across the tabletop until it settled on the printout of an article from what he recognised as the local newspaper of the south-west, *La Dépêche du Midi*.

He picked it up and scanned it quickly. *A dead tree brought down during a storm in the village of Carennac ... the remains of a body ... a German air force officer ... a bullet hole in the cranium.* Then Enzo froze. *The park is overlooked by the house that once belonged to Georgette Pignal, famous for being tasked by de Gaulle during WW2 with keeping the* Mona Lisa *out of German hands. The house is still lived in by her daughter Anny.*

So this is what had brought Bauer to Carennac. But more than just the belief that the remains found in the park were those of his grandfather, he must have known, somehow, about the copy of the *Mona Lisa*. Must have thought that, even if she didn't have it herself, Anny must know where it is. Enzo laid the article back on the table and found himself thinking the same thing himself. It couldn't simply have disappeared.

He caught the movement out of the corner of his eye too late. A figure took shape, materialising from the dark, to club him to the ground with a fist like iron. The force with which he hit the floor knocked all the breath from Enzo's lungs, and his torch went skidding away across the floor, casting crazily dancing shadows around the walls. Until it smashed against the stove, plunging the room into darkness.

His assailant stepped quickly over his body and ran through the hall. As he pulled himself groggily to his knees, Enzo was aware of the front door opening and he called out, 'Bauer! For God's sake, Bauer. I'm here to help you.' But he heard the man's feet clattering away down the steps and off into the night.

Wearily he staggered to his feet and raised a hand to his cheek. He felt blood, and a swelling coming up already beneath his skin. He hurried through the hall and out into the moonlight washing across the terrace, and saw the figure of Bauer running down the hill towards the park. Had there been hunters about, they could have fixed him easily in their sights.

Enzo sighed. 'I'm too fucking old for this,' he breathed at the night, and started down the steps after him.

He reached the park as Bauer got to the other side of it and ran up steps towards the entrance to the *gouffre*. Enzo stopped and bellowed across the park, 'Bauer, stop! I know you didn't kill Narcisse.'

Bauer stopped at the top of the steps and looked back, hesitating, clearly in a quandary. He could not have helped but hear what Enzo had shouted. And it was only in that moment that Enzo realised he had been calling after him in English. He started jogging across the path on shaking legs, breath tearing raggedly at his throat.

But as he reached the steps, Bauer appeared to have second thoughts, and turned, sprinting across the road and vanishing among the shadows of the building opposite. By the time Enzo had climbed the steps there was no sign of him. He walked across the road, moonlight casting his shadow in stark silhouette on the tarmac, and glanced towards the Auberge, then up the hill towards the Padirac Hotel. Nothing moved. A dozen steps took him up to the main entrance. Two doors, grilles drawn over glass for the season. Both leading into a darkened entrance hall where the *billeterie* sold tickets, and a passageway led off to the lift and the stairs.

He went around the front of the building to where an adjoining café would do brisk business during the summer, and placed his hands on the railing that separated the building from the *gouffre* itself.

The full light of the moon picked out a grey-painted metal staircase that doubled back on itself, zigzagging all the way down into deep shadow below. Right next to it, the cage of the elevator that would make return to the surface easier on the way back. Both were affixed to layers of rock that were like great slabs of petrified sediment piled one upon the other and vanishing into the darkness of this vast hole in the ground. It looked almost as if some alien deity had drilled down into the earth with a giant Archimedes screw. Trees and bushes clung stubbornly to its perimeter, metal webbing stretched across the face of the cliff opposite to prevent rock falls.

Enzo's attention was drawn by the clatter and rattle of metal rising up through the night, and to his astonishment he saw Bauer employing the webbing to climb down and drop on to the staircase below. The whole structure shook with the weight of his body as he dropped the last three metres. Enzo leaned over the railing and shouted again, 'Bauer, I'm here to help you.' He saw Bauer's upturned face caught ghostly by the moon, before he vanished into shadow.

Enzo could only think that there must be another way out of the *gouffre*, an exit that Bauer believed would provide him with a clean getaway. And there was no way that Enzo was going after him. He dug out his phone and found Arnaud's number at the gendarmerie in Vayrac. As it rang he checked the time. Just after eight o'clock. But the ringing went quickly to an answering service. Enzo cursed under his breath. There was never a gendarme around when you needed one. He started to leave a message.

'Hello, this is Enzo Macleod calling for Capitaine Arnaud. I've found Bauer. He's at the Gouffre de Padirac, and the idiot's just climbed down into the hole.'

He was interrupted by a sudden clatter of metal, and a blood-curdling scream that echoed all around the vastness of the *gouffre*.

'Shit!' he said. 'Something's happened to him.' And he hung up. Then shouted into the darkness below, 'Are you alright?'

It was a long moment before Bauer's voice came feebly back from the darkness. His English only very lightly accented. 'I think I've broken my leg. It's bleeding like hell.'

455

'Jesus Christ.' Enzo looked around as if somehow help might suddenly emerge from the shadows, but the street simmered in silent indifference, pools of light beneath the street lamps outshone by the moon. He looked at the webbing that Bauer had climbed down and wondered if he could do it, too. There had been a time, certainly, when he wouldn't have doubted it. But now . . .

He sighed and climbed over the railing to pick his way through the growth around the edge of the hole. It seemed like a horribly long way down. Seventy-five metres, he recalled from the leaflet. Nearly 250 feet. And he couldn't even see the bottom of it. He felt giddy just looking over the edge.

'Hold on,' he shouted. 'I'm coming down.' And he began his descent of the metal webbing. Hand- and footholds were easy to find, but the metal quickly cut into his palms. He tried to take most of the weight on his feet and felt his legs trembling as he moved one foot down below the other.

It was with huge relief that he finally reached the tin roof of a shelter above the stairs, and stood there, still shaking, and gasping to recover his breath and his courage. He glanced up, amazed at just how far down he had climbed. Then, without looking at the drop beyond the staircase, knelt down and lowered himself over the edge, finally letting go to fall the final few metres, as Bauer had done, clattering heavily on the grille of the nearest landing. The whole structure shuddered, and he crouched down to steady himself.

Looking up he saw the lip of the hole above cast a huge

circular shadow around the opposite arc of the wall. He shouted, 'Bauer?'

'Down here,' Bauer's voice rose faintly out of the dark. And Enzo started off down the stairs, reaching the next landing, to double back and head down to the next. Now he moved into the shadow cast by the rim of the *gouffre*, profoundly dark after the blinding dazzle of the moon. And just as he had back at the house, Bauer emerged from the gloom to smash a fist into Enzo's face.

This time as he went down, Enzo tasted blood in his mouth and thought he might have lost a tooth.

'You fuck!' Bauer bellowed at him, and Enzo could feel hot breath in his face. 'Leave me the fuck alone. We're both down here now, so you can't tell anyone where I am. And you'll never get out on your own.' Then he was off, leaping two at a time down the stairs and into the depths of the *gouffre*.

Enzo lay on the metal grille spitting blood and cursing his stupidity. But Bauer was right. Because of his own idiotic gullibility, here he was, down in the hole, and knew there was no way he could climb back out.

Slowly he sat up and ran the back of his hand over his lips, feeling blood smear wet on his skin. He fumbled for his phone, turned on his torch app, and directed its beam down into the hole below. Vaguely, in the semi-darkness, he could see stairways leading to a criss-cross of paths and covered walkways at the very bottom of the chasm. And he saw the tiny figure of Bauer sprinting away towards an opening at the far side of the hole, where more stairs vanished into obscurity.

He tried to call Arnaud again, but this far down there was no longer any signal, and he sat for several minutes feeling sorry for himself, leaning forward with his elbows on his knees, wondering if he was going to die in this damned hole. He shook his head. A stupid thought. There must be another way out.

Slowly he pulled himself upright, spat blood into the *gouffre* and started off down the stairs once more. The clatter of his feet on rattling metal reverberated all around him. He turned off the light on his phone to preserve its battery, and let his eyes accustom themselves to the gloom as he descended into the deepest part of the hole.

When finally he got to the bottom of it, he looked back up, and saw the rim of the *gouffre* sharply delineated against the starlit sky. An almost perfect circle. But there was no point in looking back. He had to go on. Turning, he stumbled along a path that ran past a strange white glowing statue, like a phantom sent to haunt him. Then down concrete steps set into the rock, to the entrance of a cave that cut deep down into the sedimentary layers. All light beyond it was extinguished by the night.

Now he needed the light of his phone again, and started off down steep flights of steps that dog-legged into darkness and took him deeper and deeper underground.

Tunnels hewn out of sandstone over millions of years by the

458

flow of underground rivers dripped condensation like rain on to his head, until eventually the stairs came to an end, and a narrow passage led off through a fissure in the rock face. After nearly sub-zero temperatures above ground it felt warm down here, but the darkness was profound, and his phone light barely penetrated it.

The walls closed in around him, this great crack in the rock vanishing into tenebrosity overhead as he walked steadily forward, playing the light from his phone on the well-worn path in front of him. He could hear the sound of running water, though he could not see it. And then suddenly the cave opened up around him, and light reflected back at him from black water.

Shiny metal rails, designed to divide tourists into lines, led through a turnstile to where half a dozen long, narrow punts bobbed in concrete docks. One of the slots was empty. Bauer must have taken a boat. Enzo baulked at the thought of setting off after him in a flimsy punt, in the dark. Who knew how deep the water was or what kind of current might rob him of control. He shone his phone around the walls of the cave in the docking area, and saw a stout cable descending from high above to a metal box fixed to the rock at the far side of the dock. He walked gingerly across slick concrete to pull open the box and shine his light on a large power switch. Of course! The caves would have to be lit for the tourists. He threw the switch, and coloured lights concealed overhead transformed the space around him, lighting the passage of the underground river ahead. Waterfalls of rock seemed to pour down from the heavens, stalactites like liquid spears frozen in time. Weird and wonderful formations, coloured green and red and blue by the lights.

Enzo stood gazing at it in wonder before his eyes fell on the long poles stacked in one corner, and he supposed that the water couldn't be too deep if these could be used to propel the punts along the river. He snatched one, and sent the nearest punt rocking crazily beneath him as he stepped on to the nearer end of it. He held the pole horizontally to regain his balance, and when the punt finally stopped dipping he moved forward to better distribute his weight before pushing off.

The vessel cut a silent swathe through the black water, walls encroaching as he steered it from one side to the other, avoiding rock that jutted into the river, bumping from time to time against it and pushing himself free with the pole. Calcium salts deposited by dripping water hung in cascading columns and the smooth swish of water against the punt now filled the air, along with the sound of myriad drips like rainfall.

He lost track of how long it took before the narrow underground river opened out into another cave, and a docking area containing just one boat. The one that Bauer had taken. When Enzo docked he stopped and listened intently. But he could hear nothing, and supposed that Bauer by this time must be long gone.

The passage leading away from the dock lay in darkness, until Enzo found another junction box on the wall and threw a switch to illuminate the way ahead. Bauer had done this entire trip in the dark, probably by the light of a phone, and somewhere up ahead, perhaps, he was now spooked by this sudden explosion of light.

For Enzo there was no alternative but to press on, and hope that there might be a way out somewhere in his future. The taste of blood was still strong in his mouth, but it had dried on his lips and crusted on the back of his hand. The pain had reduced itself to a dull ache, but his whole body hurt, and he found it increasingly difficult to put one leg in front of the other.

He stumbled on for several minutes, until this narrow passageway opened out into a vast underground cave, a lake lit turquoise from beneath its still waters and reflecting light from soaring walls that vanished into a mist of obscurity.

It was a dead end. From the far side of the lake, water flowed into another river that completely filled the path it had carved for itself through the rock. Off to the right, a metal staircase set into the stone climbed away into the crevice above, rising steeply and curving away out of sight. It had to be the way out.

Enzo trekked across a rock floor worn smooth by a million tourist feet, climbing past a series of illuminated billboards, up and up into the roof of the cave. It seemed endless. His legs were shaking, muscles burning. Then, to his dismay, he saw that the walkway ahead looped around a rock formation like giant cauliflowers, before descending again into darkness. He glanced back the way he had come and was astonished at how high he had climbed. Beyond the rail of the walkway, smooth rock fell away in a torrent, like a frozen waterfall, to the floor of the cave thirty or forty metres below. He became uncomfortably aware of just how flimsy this walkway felt. Ahead he could see other walkways spanning clefts in the rock. Like some kind of impossible Escherian staircase from which there was no escape. Calcium salts shaped by hundreds of thousands of years of erosion tumbled from the walls around him like clusters of giant coloured jellyfish.

A sound from above made him look up. In time to see the dark shadow of Bauer dropping on to him from a ledge overhead. The two men crashed against the railing, and their combined weight tipped them over to tumble on to a narrow shelf of wet rock and begin to slide towards the drop. Enzo grasped at the rail with desperate fingers and clung on. Bauer slithered past him, before coming to an abrupt halt against an outcrop of rock like a growth of malignant mushrooms overhanging the lip of the chasm.

Both men lay gasping on the edge of the precipice glaring at each other.

'What the hell do you want from me!' Bauer's voice echoed off into the darkness above them.

Enzo risked a glance down, and felt his stomach turn. It would be a long fall that could only end in death, and it seemed to him that he was only holding on by a thread. 'I'm trying to help you, for God's sake, man!'

But Bauer was unmoved. He swung himself up to grab the

rail of the walkway, and pulled himself back along the ledge to where Enzo lay helpless beneath him. He crouched down and grabbed the Scotsman by the collar. 'What's to stop me from just throwing you over the edge? No one will ever know that you didn't just fall.'

Enzo was fighting for the breath to speak. '*You'll* know. And then you'll regret it. Just like you always do. But I won't be around to forgive you, like Lise. And you'll have to live with your conscience for the rest of your life.'

Bauer frowned in confusion. 'How do you know about my Lise?'

'I know a lot about you, Hans. I know that you have a temper, and you do things when you're angry that you regret later. And I know that you're not a bad person, not really. You don't have that evil gene you've been so obsessed by. You resort quickly to violence, yes, but it's hardly your fault if you inherited that from Wolff.'

Bauer's face reflected an image of himself that he had not expected to be confronted by here, by this man, in this place. Enzo felt the German's grip on his collar relax.

'I came down here because I thought you were hurt. Is this really how you're going to reward me?' Enzo pushed his luck. 'I don't believe you have it in you to kill me. Whatever you inherited from your grandfather, it wasn't the capacity to kill. And I know you didn't kill Narcisse. Someone just wanted to make it look that way.'

Bauer slumped down to sit cross-legged on the ledge of rock.

All his anger and fear seemed to leave him. Enzo saw him go limp. 'How do you know I didn't kill him.'

'Because I used to be one of the best in the business at reading a crime scene, Hans.' And Enzo told him about the dry blood spatter, and how it would have made no sense for him to exit in panic several minutes after the event. 'If you'd had it in you to kill someone in cold blood, you wouldn't have panicked at all, and you'd have gone back out the way you came in. Through the side door.'

'How can you possibly know all this? About me, about what happened that night?'

'Because I went to Germany, Hans. I spoke to Lise. I obtained DNA from the remains found in the park in Carennac and linked them to you through familial matching. Karlheinz Wolff was your grandfather, just as you thought. Lise told me you have his diaries. Is that where you learned about the copy they'd made of the *Mona Lisa*?'

He nodded, staring vacantly down at his hands. 'I knew it would be worth a fortune, if only I could get my hands on it. But I also knew that I needed help. Which is why I went to see Narcisse in Paris.' His face reflected his remembered anger. 'He laughed at the whole idea. More or less threw me out. Then the bastard came down here to try to get it for himself.'

'So what happened that night, Hans? The night of the murder.'

Bauer looked up, fire in his eyes again. 'When I arrived at the hotel in Carennac, I realised that Narcisse had already checked in. I made sure he didn't know I was there, and I was in the park next to the house that afternoon when I saw him go to Madame Lavigne's door.'

It took Enzo a moment to realise he meant Anny.

'I watched him go in, then come out again about fifteen minutes later. I waited until he had gone and then went and banged on her door myself. I was angry, and I suppose I must have shouted at her. I told her I was Wolff's grandson, and that I knew about the *Mona Lisa* forgery because he had written about it in his diaries. And I demanded to know what Narcisse had wanted with her.' He frowned, remembering the moment. 'She was so . . . how can I describe it? Calm. There was this strange little smile on her face. She said that Narcisse had come with the same ridiculous story, and that she had sent him packing.'

'Did you believe her?'

'No. I said I wasn't leaving until she told me what had happened to the painting. She wouldn't let me in. She said she wasn't admitting to anything, but that if I came back to the house at eight o'clock that night she would reveal the truth to me then.'

'And you accepted that?'

'I didn't know what else I could do.' He drew a long breath. 'I was sitting in the bar at the Fenelon shortly before seven-thirty that night, hardly able to contain myself until eight, when I saw Narcisse heading out. And I was sure, then, that she had done some kind of a deal with him. So when he'd gone I slipped across the road and into the garden of the house oppo- site. There's a path that climbs the hill through the garden to another gate that opens on to a little alleyway behind Madame Lavigne's house. It was pitch-dark there, and from the shadows I could see along to the street at the end of the house where the steps go up to her front door. I got there just before Narcisse, and saw him pass through the light. Heard his footsteps on the stairs.'

He rubbed his face with both hands, in some distress at the recollection.

'I hung about for some minutes. I didn't know what to do. Should I go and bang on the door and confront them? Should I wait until eight? But I knew I couldn't, so I was about to go knocking on her front door, when the side door suddenly opened. I saw Madame Lavigne hurry out into the moonlight and down the steps to the alley. I thought for certain she would see me, and I froze on the spot. But I was still deep in shadow, and she went straight past me. Heading off along a path that appeared to lead back up to the main Alvignac road.'

From his eyes Enzo knew that he saw nothing now but the scene being replayed in his mind by memory.

'For several minutes I just stood there. I knew that Narcisse had not left the house, and I couldn't understand why. And where was Madame Lavigne going when she was supposed to be meeting me at eight? Finally I decided to go into the house and confront Narcisse. I went up the steps to the side terrace and into the house. It was very dark, and I couldn't find a light switch that worked. I called out, but there was no reply. I kind of felt my way through from the big room into the kitchen. There was a little light there, coming through the windows from the street. But I didn't see Narcisse on the floor until I fell over him. And yes, I panicked. There was blood everywhere, and all over me. I couldn't get out of there fast enough. And even as I ran off down the street, covered in his blood, I knew exactly how it was going to look.'

'Just as Madame Lavigne had hoped it would,' Enzo said. 'Though she could never have imagined that you'd manage to get yourself covered in the man's blood. That was a piece of luck she hadn't counted on.'

Bauer nodded, still reliving the moment. 'I got up to my room without anyone seeing me, and showered myself clean. I had one change of clothes with me, so I changed and packed and got out of there. I took a leaflet I'd been looking at earlier in the day. A house for let at the Gouffre de Padirac. I knew it would be empty, and that I could probably reach it by foot in a couple of hours. Country roads in the dark. I could do it without being seen.'

'Then you saw a bike in a barn as you got to the top of the hill.'

Bauer nodded, and looked at Enzo curiously. It seemed as if this man knew everything about him, everything that had happened that night, without having to be told. 'That made it a lot easier. The Gouffre de Padirac is deserted at this time of year. No one lives here, so it was easy to break into the gîte. The last renters had left some food in the fridge, and the owners hadn't cleared the place out for the winter yet. So I was safe there, and could survive. At least for a few days.'

Enzo shook his head. 'But why? What was the point? You were going to have to give yourself up sometime, surely?'

'Not until they'd figured out that I didn't kill Narcisse. I was sure they would have to. Because I didn't. But all the reports on the internet said they were still looking for me. Then you showed up, and I got spooked.'

Enzo gathered his strength to pull himself back to his feet, holding on to the railing for dear life, and offered a hand to help Bauer to his. 'Well, I know you didn't do it. And between us we can prove it.'

Bauer nodded and reached for Enzo's hand as he stood. But on the slick rock his feet slipped suddenly from under him and he grabbed at Enzo in desperation. Their fingers touched, but then he retracted his hand involuntarily, windmilling his arms to try to keep his balance. He glanced over his shoulder at the drop. Which was fatal. And before he fell he looked back at Enzo, eyes black with fear, projecting a hopeless appeal for help. But Enzo was powerless to respond and could only watch in dismay as the young German tipped backwards over the edge to fall in the strangest silence, broken only by the sound of his body shattering on the floor of the cave when he reached it nearly a hundred feet below. The echo of his death reverberated around this ancient underground chamber, transformed in the blink of an eye into Hans Bauer's gateway to eternity.

*

It was a long time before Enzo found the strength to clamber over the rail again and on to the walkway. It took nearly half an hour for him to make his way back through the tunnels and along the underground river, emerging finally into the moonlight streaming down from the blue moon that had risen to a point in the sky almost directly overhead. It filled the *gouffre* with light by which he was able to begin his weary climb back to the top. With only a handful of flights remaining, on legs that would barely support him, he became aware suddenly of a commotion above. He glanced up to see blue flashing lights, and dark figures leaning over the rail around the hole. And then the beams of several torches picking him out on the stairs.

A voice he knew called, 'Monsieur Macleod! In the name of God, what has happened?' It was Capitaine Arnaud.

Enzo almost collapsed with relief. With difficulty he found his voice and called back, 'It's a long story, capitaine. Just get me out of here.'

CHAPTER THIRTY-ONE

It was nearly eleven by the time Enzo found himself standing on the covered landing outside Anny's door, raising the wrought-iron knocker to rap three times. The sound of it rang out across the small square and the park, where the moon cast deep shadows over what had been intended as the last resting place of Karlheinz Wolff. Enzo glanced back down the stairs at the sound of feet shuffling in the darkness of the alley that ran back to the night gate from where Bauer had seen Anny emerge on to the terrace the night of the murder.

The door opened and the old lady stood wraithlike in the moonlight. Fully dressed, but shrunken somehow.

He said, 'I hope you weren't in bed.'

She gave him a weary smile. 'Of course not. I've been expecting you.' She turned and walked back through the kitchen towards the grand salon, and Enzo followed, shutting the door behind him.

Anny eased herself down into her habitual rocker by the dying embers of the fire and watched as he sat in the armchair from where he had listened to the story of her mother, and Paul Lange, and Wolff. And the *Mona Lisa*. She gave him a curious look. Her pupils were dilated, and her eyes seemed black.

'You've been in the wars, monsieur.' Her voice was slurred.

Enzo raised fingers to his bruised and battered face. A reflex response. He'd had time to wash and change. But his face, he knew, was still a mess. 'You should see the other guy,' he said grimly. But neither of them smiled. He took his phone from his pocket and set it to record, then reached across to place it on a side table. 'I'm going to record our conversation. Unless you have any objection?'

She shrugged, but said nothing.

'You killed him, Anny, didn't you? Narcisse.'

But still she held her peace. Fixing him with those unnaturally dark eyes.

'You made an appointment for him to come at seven-thirty. You threw the switch on the *déjoncteur* so that the house would be in darkness. You slashed his throat with a kitchen knife and left him lying on your kitchen floor. You knew that Bauer would arrive half an hour later. The door was unlocked. You figured there was a very good chance that he would come in, and in the dark stumble across Narcisse. You probably didn't imagine he would slip and fall in the blood, but that only helped to serve your narrative. The fact that he then ran just embedded police suspicions that it was he who had killed Narcisse.'

She closed her eyes and said in a small voice, 'That was very calculating of me.'

'It was.'

She opened them again, but they seemed glazed now. 'I have an alibi.'

He shook his head. 'Bauer suspected you were doing some kind of deal with Narcisse, and came up the back way from the hotel. He was in the alley outside when you emerged from the side entrance and took the path up to the main road.' He sighed. 'I don't expect your friend will hold out for very much longer. Unless, of course, she was in on it.'

Anny snorted. 'Of course not! Stupid woman. When we set off in her car, I "remembered" at the top of the road that I had left my phone in the house. I got Marie-Christine to stop by the Auberge du Vieux Quercy rather than drive the whole way round again, and took the path from there back to the house. Told her I would only be a minute. Which is all it took.'

'You could very easily have bumped into Bauer on your return to the house. He must already have been halfway up the hill by then.'

'On such slender threads do the fate of all things hang, Monsieur Macleod. Timing is everything.'

'So you killed Narcisse and went off for a nice dinner with your friend in Vayrac.'

'That makes me sound very cold.'

Enzo nodded. 'Yes, it does. A little like your father, perhaps?' She flinched, and he sat staring at her for a long moment. 'Do I have to do all the work here?'

'It's your job, isn't it?'

'It might be if someone was paying me.' He paused. 'So when you got back to the house and you and Marie-Christine "discovered" the body, you told her not to mention that you had gone back for your phone, in case the police thought you might have done it. But she must have had her doubts.'

'I pay for her daughter's education at university in Paris, monsieur. She wouldn't have wanted to lose my patronage.' She sighed then. 'But, of course, she was always the weak link.' She cast a resentful look at Enzo. 'And then there was you. Sniffing around. Relentlessly. Forensically.' The breath she drew seemed to tremble in her throat. 'I'm too old to go to prison.'

'Maybe you should have thought of that before you took a man's life.' Enzo was unable to find any sympathy for her. 'Where is she?' he said.

She looked surprised. 'Who?'

'The *Mona Lisa*. The copy.'

'There is no copy.'

'Then why did you kill Narcisse?'

She closed her eyes again, and her breathing seemed shallow. Feeble. And as if finally giving in she said, 'My mother lost the man she loved, my father, to save the *Mona Lisa*. I could never have allowed her to fall into the hands of a trader in stolen Nazi art.' Her head tipped forward, her chin settling on her breast and Enzo became suddenly alarmed. He leapt up and crossed to her chair.

'Madame, are you alright?' He knelt down and lifted her chin and her eyes flickered open for the briefest of moments.

'A healthy overdose, monsieur, of those nice pink pills the doctor prescribed to help me sleep.'

Enzo stood up and hurried to the door. From the outside landing he shouted into the dark. 'Capitaine, capitaine! Quickly.'

Arnaud and two of his men emerged from the shadows and ran up the steps to follow Enzo back into the house.

'She's taken an overdose,' Enzo said. 'We need an ambulance fast.'

Arnaud barked into his walkie-talkie and they tried to rouse her. But her eyes remained stubbornly shut, before she raised her head, and with her final breath whispered, 'Too late, monsieur. Too late. For everything.'

By four in the morning, the moon was casting the shadows of the houses opposite across the tiny square below the park. Several police vehicles lined up in front of Anny's house, casting blue flashing light on cold stone walls. When the ambulance had finally come, Anny was long dead, and they had removed her to languish in the mortuary of the hospital in Saint-Céré.

Enzo sat at the kitchen table, haunted by her tale of Georgette and the painting, and by the unfolding tragedy that had finally ended here tonight. He rubbed stinging eyes as masked gendarmes and forensics officers came and went, and turned as Arnaud came down from the upstairs bedrooms. 'We've found it,' he said. 'Do you want to see?'

Enzo nodded and stood wearily to follow Arnaud back upstairs. At the door to Anny's bedroom, a variety of Belgian Shepherd known as a Malinois was held on a short leash by his handler, a rubber ball in his mouth, the reward for success.

The bed had been moved and floorboards lifted to reveal a hiding place beneath them, a space between the rafters, around eighty centimetres by sixty. Lined by leatherette and fireproof paper, it was a perfect fit for concealing the *Mona Lisa*. But it was not a painting that the Malinois had sniffed out. Wrapped in a bin bag, it was the plastic apron Anny had worn to slash the throat of Narcisse, and the kitchen knife with which she had done it. Concealed there in haste before she hurried off to dinner with Marie-Christine in Vayrac.

Enzo was disappointed. 'No sign of the painting?'

Arnaud appeared surprised. 'Did you think there would be?'

Enzo shrugged. 'Maybe not.'

'And you still think it exists? This copy of the *Mona Lisa*?'

'Yes.'

'What makes you so sure?'

'A lot of people have died because of it, capitaine. Lange, Wolff, Narcisse, Bauer. And now Anny herself.'

'So where is it?'

'I have no idea.' He nodded towards the hiding place beneath the floorboards. 'But I think it was probably here until the day that Narcisse and Bauer came knocking.'

Arnaud sighed and scratched his head. 'And the person who chased you through the village the other night, and fished you out of the river? Are you any the wiser about who that might have been?'

Enzo lifted a framed family photograph from Anny's bedside table and regarded it grimly. 'Yes, capitaine. I think I am.'

CHAPTER THIRTY-TWO

The troughs at the cemetery gates were filled with dead flowers. Yet more still lay on the graves where they had been placed by relatives at Toussaint.

The burial had been delayed because of the need for a post-mortem, and Enzo had timed his drive up for the signing of his final statement at the Vayrac gendarmerie to coincide with Anny's funeral. It was being held that morning at the tiny Cimitière Columbarium above the village of Bétaille, and it meant he would have permission to travel, in spite of the pandemic lockdown. He wanted to be there.

It was a stunning day, a clear blue sky stretching west above the river valley, the cliffs on either side of the flood plain glowing almost pink in the late morning sunshine. And it was warm. A welcome respite after the rain and cold of October. And at the very least, from here Anny would have a privileged view of the world for eternity.

Although Covid restrictions still allowed up to thirty people at a funeral, there were only a handful of vehicles next to the hearse in the car park. Enzo pulled in beside them and got stiffly out of the car. Injuries healed more slowly with age, and he still carried the scars and bore the pain of recent encounters.

He looked up the path from the gate and saw a tiny crowd of mourners assembled around the family tomb near the top of the hill. They stood socially distanced and wearing masks, and Enzo could barely hear the mumbled eulogy of a priest who, in all likelihood, had never even known Anny Lavigne. Tombs and headstones climbed in serried rows, one above the other, over the crest of the hill. A couple of tall pine trees stood sentinel at the gates opposite, and gazing over the village below, Enzo thought he could actually see the apartment above the double garage where *Mona Lisa*'s double had spent the final years of the war.

The priest and the mourners turned to make their way down the hill after the closing of the tomb, and Enzo moved back out into the car park. A few disinterested glances were directed his way before the family group from the photograph in Anny's bedroom came through the gates.

Elodie, he thought, was in her late thirties or early forties. A handsome woman, and he wondered if there was any of Georgette in her. She had auburn hair pulled back in a sombre bun and wore a dark coat that fell below her knees. Her husband was tall and balding, and looked uncomfortable in his funeral suit. Their teenage son eyed Enzo cautiously from behind his mask.

Elodie stopped and looked at him, frowning. 'You're the man who caught my aunt.'

Enzo inclined his head. 'I'm sorry, madame.'

'So am I.'

But if he had expected to feel the heat of her wrath, he was surprised when she looked at him with nothing but sadness in her eyes.

'I can't imagine what she was thinking. To have done such a thing.'

Enzo's gaze strayed towards her son. A boy of seventeen or eighteen. Tall, like his father, with a thatch of thick black hair, cropped at either side and gelled back across the crown. He flushed and cast his eyes towards the ground.

His mother did not miss the moment. 'What?' she said, glancing from Enzo to her son and back again.

Enzo said, 'Tell him to pull down the mask.'

'Why?'

'Just tell him.'

Elodie glared uncomprehendingly at Enzo then turned to the boy. 'Do what he says.'

'Mu-um . . .' he protested.

'Just do it, Franck.'

Reluctantly Franck pulled his blue surgical mask down below his chin and stared defiantly at Enzo.

Enzo said, 'You damned near killed me!'

'I saved your life.'

Enzo was incensed. 'Only after you'd put it in danger.'

Elodie was alarmed now. 'Wait! What's all this about?' And when neither of them responded she turned to the boy. 'Franck? Tell me.'

Franck pursed petulant lips. 'It was Great-Aunt Anny's idea. It was supposed to be a joke.'

'It was no joke,' Enzo said. 'It was supposed to scare me off. To make me think you were Bauer. And it very nearly got rid of me for good.'

'I pulled you out of the river, didn't I?'

Elodie looked to her husband for help, but saw only incomprehension in his face and she turned back to Enzo. 'Will you please explain?'

But Enzo just shook his head. 'Franck will do that later, no doubt. Just be grateful I haven't shopped him to the gendarmes.' Pause. 'I'd like a word if I may, madame.' He glanced towards her husband and son. 'In private.'

Elodie sighed her frustration, hesitated for a moment, then nodded.

She and Enzo walked slowly away across the car park as the two men in her life returned to their car. 'What is it, Monsieur Macleod?'

'I understand you're going to inherit your aunt's house.'

She nodded. 'Yes.'

'And what else?'

She stopped to frown at him. 'I'm not sure what business that is of yours.'

Enzo said, 'I can make it my business if I choose to make it official.'

She exhaled theatrically. 'My aunt was quite well off, but I wouldn't describe her as wealthy.'

'I think you know I'm not talking about money.'

She held his eye briefly before hers flickered away.

'I assume you know the full story of your grandmother? How she happened to be here, how she came to acquire the house.'

'Of course. I've heard all those stories since I was knee-high. I could recite them backwards.'

'Then you know what I'm talking about.'

This time she met his gaze full on and said boldly, 'I know nothing about that painting, monsieur.'

Enzo nodded. 'Well, maybe that's just as well, then. After all, if Georgette had already made the switch and hidden the original before her confrontation with Lange, who knows which one went back to the Louvre.'

She pulled a face that reflected her scepticism. 'They would have known,' she said. Then, as a doubtful afterthought, 'Surely?'

Enzo raised a solitary eyebrow. 'You would think.' He paused. 'But, then, maybe they wouldn't have wanted the world to know that they had commissioned a forgery and somehow lost the original.'

It was clear from her face that this was the first time that such a thought had ever crossed her mind. She searched for some response, but no words came.

Enzo said, 'Well, who knows?' He smiled. 'Every tale has its time, and its place. And all stories of human endeavour, of frailty and betrayal, will pass eventually into history. Out of mind. And out of memory.' He exhaled deeply, as if shedding some invisible burden. 'I wish you a very good day, madame.'

And he turned to walk briskly back to his car.

CHAPTER THIRTY-THREE

PARIS, SPRING 2021

With the lifting, at last, of restrictions to movement around the country, Enzo, Dominique and Laurent, with Sophie and Bertrand and the baby, made the trip to Paris in a rented people carrier. The first family get-together in more than a year, and the first opportunity for Kirsty to meet her new nephew.

There was a large gathering around the table in the salon at the back of the apartment in the Rue de Tournon. The coming of spring seemed to have imbued the pianist in the building with fresh vigour, and he or she was thumping out a stuttering rendition of Schubert's Scherzo in B flat.

Raffin had opened champagne, and was in better form than Enzo had seen him for some years. He was still enthusing about Enzo's exposé of the alleged existence of a *Mona Lisa* forgery commissioned during the war by the Louvre itself. It had fed him material for a whole series of articles in the Paris daily, *Libération*.

'Dropped like a hand grenade into the world of international art,' he said gleefully, pouring himself a second glass. 'And of course the repeated denials of the Louvre have only fed all the claims and counterclaims of every would-be art critic and hack in Europe and America.'

Kirsty said, 'And those excerpts you published from Wolff's diaries last month, Roger, have just set the whole thing on fire again.'

Raffin took a long draught of champagne, bubbles breaking around his lips. 'It's the story that just keeps on giving.' He raised his glass. 'Here's to Enzo.' And everyone raised their glass.

Enzo blushed and took a small sip from his own. And then he leaned towards Kirsty and asked in a low voice, 'How long till dinner?'

'We'll eat about seven, for the kids,' she said. Then narrowed her eyes. 'Why?'

'Dominique and I have a prearranged appointment this afternoon. But seven's fine. We'll be back long before then.'

'Where are you going?'

Enzo glanced at Dominique. 'The Louvre.'

It was Dominique's first visit to the Louvre, although Enzo had been many times. There was so much she wanted to see. David's *The Death of Marat*, Arcimboldo's *Four Seasons*, the *Great Sphinx of Tanis*. And it took them nearly two hours to reach the Salle des Etats. Enzo had indulged her and hidden his impatience, but now at last they were there, in Room 711 of the Denon Wing, gazing upon the *Mona Lisa* mounted behind glass on her freshly painted wall of midnight blue.

A socially distanced crowd, still wearing masks, stood gazing at her in awe. A hubbub of whispered excitement filled the room, a hushed sense of being in the presence of greatness. But Enzo was oblivious. He only had eyes for the smile beneath the eyes that wouldn't leave his. All the hairs on his arms and the back of his neck stood up. And he felt not so much in the presence of greatness, as in the presence of history. As if it were Georgette herself who sat before him. He wanted to reach out and touch her, and tell her how sorry he was. But it was all too late for that. It had all been too long ago.

Dominique whispered, 'She looks genuine enough.' Then, 'She is, isn't she?'

Enzo had difficulty speaking without his eyes filling up. 'She is what she is,' he said eventually. 'And who among us could ever say that she was anything else?'

ACKNOWLEDGEMENTS

I would like to offer my grateful thanks to those who gave so generously of their time and expertise during my researches for *The Night Gate*. In particular I'd like to express my gratitude to Dr Steven C. Campman, M.D., Medical Examiner, San Diego, California; Mike Baxter, former Head of Forensic Science Services at the Police Forensic Science Laboratory, Dundee, Scotland; Madeleine J. Hinkes, PhD, D-ABFA (American Board of Forensic Anthropology); Charles Berberich for his insights into genealogical research in Germany; the Gouffre de Padirac for facilitating my private tour of the caves; and my wife Janice Hally for taking on the role of research assistant in delving into conditions and events in wartime France.

Many of the characters described in the book are real – Jacques Jaujard, Rose Valland, René Huygue, Sturmbannführer Christian Tyschen. And many of the events actually occurred – the evacuation of artworks from the Louvre during WW2 to various châteaux around France; the burning of paintings by the Nazis (although I took a small liberty with the timing and precise location); the shooting of Maquis fighters in Saint-Céré, and the prevention of a massacre of that town's civilians by the intervention of brave Berthe Nasinec; the installation of a radio transmitter by resistance fighters in the Tours Saint-Laurent; the extraordinary courage of Rose Valland in cataloguing stolen Nazi art and tracking it down, post-war, to return to its rightful owners; the presence of the huge, rolled canvasses from the Louvre in an apartment above a double garage in the Lotois village of Bétaille.

As for the existence of a *Mona Lisa* forgery, I leave my readers to decide if that is truth, or a fictitious construct of the author.